Educated Luck

TWISTED LUCK BOOK 3

TERNION UNIVERSE

Mel Todd

D0841721

BAD ASH PUBLISHING

Bad Ash Publishing
86 Desmond Court
Powder Springs, GA 30127
www.badashpublishing.com

Publisher's Note: This is a work of fiction. Names, characters, places, and incidents are a product of the author's imagination. Locales and public names are sometimes used for atmospheric purposes. Any resemblance to actual people, living or dead, or to businesses, companies, events, institutions, or locales is completely coincidental.

Book Layout © 2015 BookDesignTemplates.com
Cover by Ampersand Book Covers

Educated Luck/ Mel Todd -- 1st ed.
Paper ISBN 978-1-950287-11-6

Howard Lowery – you were the best beta reader I've ever had. You are missed.

CONTENTS

Education is the cornerstone of all magic. While some people are naturally talented or possess an intuitive ability to use their magic, we have found most mages find their skills increase by learning the foundations of science. Magic is based on science; you just need to understand it well enough to use magic efficiently. ~ OMO statement on higher education

CHAOS

The mix of multi-vitamins, not enough coffee, and a breakfast burrito roiled around in my stomach as I re-centered my backpack and trudged towards the brick building. That imposing edifice hosted classes in magic and the science of magic, as well as more things I'd probably regret learning.

It's just college. You can do this. Get your degree. You want to be a doctor. This way you can do it and the FBI can take a flying leap, though being a pathologist might work well for both of us. Crime and medicine.

The path to my first class seemed more arduous than it really was in the chilly January morning. The last three and a half months had disappeared like a wisp of smoke. Alixant hadn't been kidding when he said my name had gotten out to the papers, and until they captured a unicorn in Centennial Park, not one with sharp fangs thank the merlins, I remained their favorite story. What I'd done, who I was, every detail they could dredge up got plastered across the headlines, especially my double merlin status. They'd even gotten a pic of my tattoo at some point.

While I looked forward to getting this new phase of my life over, I dreaded going back to school. After earning my Associate's degree in Medical Assistance, Criminal Justice, and the paramedic course, I'd figured I'd met my goals. I could have my own life. Finding out I was a merlin who emerged when my brother died a good ten years earlier threw all my plans into disarray. Emerging again as a double merlin elevated me to celebrity status among the mage stalkers. Not to mention the story of the year.

I feel sorry for all the kids who get saddled with my name over the next few years. Corisande is a bit much for anyone.

Through much negotiation with the GA MageTech administrators, with both Steven Alixant and Indira Humbert weighing in on my side, I entered as a junior. My science classes were all upper level, but the college stuck me in all the freshman magic classes as my knowledge of my abilities consisted only of what I'd read over the last few months.

"Would you stop? I can hear you stressing," Jo said, hip bumping me as we walked. "The class isn't that big of a deal. I bet you already know most of it. At least you can read without struggling." Her voice teasing.

Josefa Guzman, my best friend in the world. Her hair had grown at least six inches since she sacrificed it and more to save a stadium full of people. The vitamins Marisol Guzman, Jo's mom, shoved down our throats helped our hair grow. The glow on Jo's face and the sway to her walk were all related to Sable. They'd made their relationship formal at Christmas. I still didn't know how I felt about that. I liked Sable, but I didn't really know her. Both of our faults, I suspected. I was too busy trying to work while avoiding the press, and Jo was too over the moon with Sable to want to share, though at least that had started changing. As a Water mage, Sable seemed to take on the aspects of water just flowing with everything. I didn't know much about her besides her dad had been in the army while her mother was Japanese and had died when she was two. I couldn't even remember what her dad's name was or where he lived.

My hair had grown too, for the first time in years, and now hung in a ponytail about halfway down my back. And I'd gained weight, luckily in all the right places. It had the side effect of giving me a bit more in the chest area, bringing with it more clothes shopping, which I regarded as a definite negative. Jo, however, approved of my new figure. Too bad I didn't like girls.

"Yes I can read, and I might know some of it. But I've had to change my phone number twice. Be nice if I could keep this one. I'm just worried and not sure why. I'd rather be working. The last place wasn't too bad." I'd spent my time working as an on-call paramedic for the various companies in the area. It wasn't consistent, but they paid well. Alixant had arranged for the FBI to keep me on retainer, not that he'd needed me, but the extra money helped. Carelian ate a lot, all high protein expensive food that the stipend barely covered.

I think he eats better than me most days.

As if thinking about him grabbed his attention, his leash tugged on my wrist. ~Slow mortals. Ready for nap,~ Carelian said in my head. His voice was still that rich masculine rumble that vibrated through my mind while my ears heard nothing.

"Am I going to get used to that someday?" Jo asked, regarding him as he walked ahead of us. His rich red fur looked like rubies in the light of the halogens on the campus. He walked slowly, giving off an air of boredom, but from his twitching ears and whiskers I knew he tracked everything that moved.

"I'll let you know when I do. So far the answer is no."

Carelian talked more lately, and he had the subversive habit of ignoring all the typical familiar expectations. Most familiars were one-mage creatures. They almost never associated with anyone else outside some married mages. My familiar was an attention whore and absolutely shameless. He spoke to me, Jo, Sable, Marisol, even Stinky if he was eating a BBQ sandwich that Carelian wanted. If you offered to scratch his ears, he'd accept and drool on you. Personally, I thought he did it to thumb his metaphorical nose at someone or something, but I didn't mention that.

"Well, I'm dropping you off here. My class is in the next building. See you at home tonight?"

"That's the plan." I gave Jo a smile as she headed out, watching her go with a vague sense of envy. She still checked every box for Latina bombshell and loved playing it up. I was average as you could get, except for the merlin tattoo with four strongs filled in. I had the sudden urge to pull my brown hair out of the ponytail and cover up the tattoo that went from above my eyebrow to the cheekbone under my right eye. Which meant there was no way to hide my status.

"Come on Carelian, let's get the learning off to an educational start."

He twitched his ears at me, his opinion of school guarded, but we entered the building. A few other students were up for this early morning class, all clutching coffee just like me. At least I didn't have my first class until nine A.M. on Mondays. It was one of the few benefits, but Tuesday and Thursday mornings a class started at eight-thirty. I was cramming courses as much as I could, wanting it done as soon as possible, which meant twenty-four credit hours and early mornings.

Oh well, at least I have good coffee to get me through.

As we passed students in the building, many of them did a double take at Carelian, then a triple take when they looked at me. Carelian was worth the second look. He'd grown fast over the last three months. Where he'd barely weighed a pound when he flew into my arms, literally, he was pushing fifteen pounds now. Though he really was still just a kitten. From the size of his paws, the front ones with opposable thumbs, he had another twenty or more pounds to go. Some books suggested he would grow to about the size of a large bobcat or lynx. But human smart, with thumbs. I avoided thinking about that whenever possible. Once he realized he could operate a can opener, the apartment would reek of tuna.

The leash and harness he wore was purely for show. He could get it off if he wanted to. Per him, it was amusing to take his mage on walks. I wasn't about to argue.

The other students' hard looks at me, specifically the side of my head, made me cringe. I'd have to learn to own my status, but for now, I missed being able to fade into the woodwork. It had made everything easier.

I pasted a smile on my face and headed for my classroom. Jo and I'd mapped out all my classes last week before school started, so I knew where I needed to go. I slipped into the stadium seating classroom with seats for about fifty. Since I didn't know how full it would be, I went all the way to the back and got an aisle chair. That way if the class met capacity, Carelian could nap in the area behind my seat and be out of the way. Till then he sprawled on a ledge behind that last row, surveying his domain.

Scoping everything out, I dug out my book, notebook, and a set of pens. Five rows of ten chairs, with a podium, media stand, whiteboard, and pull-down screen. Beige walls ran into worn red bricks with windows that looked out at the Atlanta freeway system and downtown. Not the best view, but considering our apartment had the view of another apartment, it rated higher.

One other student had been there before I walked in. He had dirty brown hair, pasty white skin, and was significantly overweight. He sat in the middle front row, with his eyes closed. Glancing at my phone I saw class would start in fifteen minutes. Ten till eight and students started trickling into the classroom.

By eight the classroom contained twenty-five students. Most stayed down closer to the podium, I didn't mind. One or two glanced at me, then Carelian, but they didn't say anything. At one minute after eight, a man in jeans and a long cable-knit sweater stalked in. Part of me imagined him with a cape billowing behind him, and I smiled a bit. He looked like he just had that sort of panache. I figured his age at mid-thirties, with dark brown hair, skin darker than Jo's nutmeg color, but very European facial structure. He didn't smile, but he didn't frown; he just gazed at us.

"This is Magic Basics 101, the first class you take. As a mage you are required to take this course at the start of your academic career. I am Professor Bernard Smythe. I will be your taskmaster, your guide, and your foe as I make sure you all understand the basics of magic." He spoke with an assured manner, his accent clipped and brisk, but with an odd

13

softness to some vowels. It reminded me of an actor from a TV drama show set in New York.

"I don't care if you show up to this class or not, but let me make it very clear, you cannot graduate if you do not pass this class and I do not give easy grades. Is that understood?" His eyes roamed across the classroom and I wanted to shrink away from his gaze. As he turned, I saw the tattoo on his temple, a Pattern mage.

Odds are if he's a teacher, he's an archmage. This should be an interesting class.

I pushed my doubts away and focused on the class. The requirement to pass it factored into my thoughts, but I also needed to know this stuff. It would give me the ability to act and maybe quit letting people die.

"Everyone has different strengths, and what you are strong in tends to be what you focus on. Raise your hand as I say the element you are strong in."

"Transform." I watched two kids raise their hands. I watched him make notes on his phone as he stood erect at the front of the class eyeing all of us.

"Psychic." I raised my hand. I was the only one.

He kept going through all of them, the last one being Time. Once again, I raised my hand just as I had for Non-organic, Earth, and Relativity.

"Thank you everyone. You in the back." He pointed at me. "Stand up."

Unsure, I stood, once again a kid trying to figure out what I'd done wrong.

"Did you misunderstand my instructions?" His voice was biting and snide, and it kicked my issue with authority into gear.

"No. Your instructions were very clear."

"Then please explain why you raised your hand for five ability sets? Which isn't possible, so you must not have understood what I asked for." Even from the top of the seats where I was, I could see his sneer.

"Because I am a double merlin and I am strong in all the branches I raised my hand for, plus I have a familiar." At my words, Carelian jumped up past me, walking on the back on the seats as if they were a smooth flat surface, not pointed edges, his tail lashing, and glaring at everyone who stared at me.

Every head in the classroom turned to look at me. Bernard froze, then his sneer deepened. "So you're the one the media is fawning over. So special that you have not only double the access to power than any other mage, but a familiar to boot. The one who saved a stadium full of people with ease and fought not only a unicorn but a gorgon back to their planes."

His voice mocked me. I wanted to give Jo the credit— she'd earned it. But every time I tried people wouldn't believe me. So I'd quit and I didn't bother now.

"I was there, yes, but I'm here to learn because I don't know how to use the magic they say I have."

And I didn't. I knew that and it drove me crazy.

"At least you have some humility. Fine, Corisande Munroe. Don't expect me to go easy on you because you're the media darling or the rare unicorn mage. I have no use for people who take the painless way out."

Anger flashed through me, but I just smiled my customer service smile. All teeth, no meaning. "I wouldn't expect you to."

Bernard turned away and I sat back in my chair, all too aware of the students staring at me. Most of them didn't turn from gawking at me until he started talking. The boy, the one who I thought was sleeping when I came in looked at me for a long time and something moved on his lap. A creature with more legs than was natural even for a spider climbed his shoulder. Its many eyes didn't move away from me the entire class.

Chapter 2

It is well known that the various ranks of mages have different power levels and the more powerful you are the smaller an offering is for the same effect. While a hedge-mage may require upwards of a hundred thousand molecules for a specific action, an archmage may only require five thousand for the same action. When you factor in merlins and familiars, the cost can drop into the hundreds. As no mage does magic exactly the same even with identical understanding of science, a definitive matrix has not been created. ~ Magic Explained.

ORDER

I met up with Jo for the next class—Magic 101 Lab. My temper still simmered as I walked into class. Jo already had a seat, and I headed towards her. I saw the student with the familiar coming in after me as I reached the top of the stairs.

"I swear if this teacher is as big of an ass as the last one, I'm quitting." I all but threw my books into the chair next to me as I dropped down into the seat.

Jo flinched at my words and then glanced at Carelian, whose lashing tail reflected my mood perfectly.

"What happened?"

"Did you have Bernard Smythe for Magic 101?" I asked as I settled into the seat. I needed to calm down, but my blood boiled under my skin, making me snappish.

"No. I think he's new this year. Why, what happened?" She looked at me, brows furrowed.

I sighed. "Tonight. I start now and I'll miss most of this class due to my annoyance."

"That good? Dang. Is it okay if Sable comes over for dinner tonight? I'm going to make enchiladas."

I snorted in amusement. "For your enchiladas I might put up with Bernard Smythe coming over and sneering at me."

Jo snickered but hushed it as Indira walked in at the front of the classroom. Indira Humbert had barreled into my life as an expert to train me on closing portals. The part that I still needed to figure out is why she had tried to seduce me. Her long ebony hair, curvy figure, intelligence, and husky voice would have made most people tumble for her. Me? It kinda creeped me out.

"Oh, we get her as a teacher?" Jo all but purred the words and sat up straighter.

"And here I thought you were committed to Sable," I teased, giving her a side-eyed look.

"I am," she protested. "That doesn't mean I can't enjoy the world around me, does it?"

"No, but I guess I find Sable prettier."

"Hey, you trying to steal my girlfriend?" Jo had a smile as she wiggled her eyebrows at me.

"Please, Sable would never stoop to me. Nah, just Sable is"—I sifted through words to find the right one—"more real. Indira? I'm never sure if I'm dealing with her or the act she's putting on at any given moment. And I really want to know who was behind her trying the whole seduction thing on me."

Jo shrugged. "Ask her?"

"I have. She just smiles and changes the subject. Oh well. As a teacher, I can deal with her."

We fell silent as Indira cleared her throat and the class quieted down. "Good morning, mages. My name is Indira Humbert and I'll be your teacher for the Magic Lab. Mostly we focus on offerings and how to make them. As you get more skilled over the years, these classes will become more specific, allowing you to use stored fat, blood, even your teeth if needed. For this, your first course, we will focus on using your magic to the best effect. How many here have already made an offering of one sort or another?"

Every hand in the classroom raised and she smiled, red lips full across white teeth. "Excellent. Then you all know that feeling, that knowledge of what it will cost. How many of you were presented with a cost that was too high to pay,"—she paused and I swore her eyes darted to Jo—"or a high price that you chose to pay?"

Only three hands raised—one was Jo. I squeezed her leg, so glad the cost of saving everyone in the stadium had only been her hair and nails, things easy to grow back. Jo ducked her head and flicked her hand at Indira. I let my emotions settle and focused on our instructor.

"I see some of you have found that some things are beyond your abilities. What I'm about to tell you may or may not surprise you. You can control both where the offering comes from and the quantity of the offering based on what you offer." Murmuring met her comment, and she laughed. "I see many of you don't believe me. I'll prove it. For those of you in the back, I'm an Entropy mage also strong in Time. My expertise is planar openings and time effects on materials." She smiled again; this time her smile held a threat. "So don't think I am a pushover." Her smile felt like a bladed weapon as she raked the classroom with it. "Now that we have that settled, let's get into what I meant about offerings having different values."

Indira moved to the cabinets in a corner and brought out a candle and a clear mug. "Fire is one of my weak branches, but it works excellently for examples in lab settings. The effects are unmistakable."

She set the items on the table at the front and filled the clear mug with water from a bottle in her bag. "As I am sure, many of you have played with your elemental abilities as they tend to be the easiest to tap into, not to mention stories, movies, and boooks love to play with them. Earthquakes and fire make for sensational effects as well as primal terror. No one likes to feel the ground give beneath their feet."

Stepping back, she waved at the two objects. "Most of you have played with lighting a candle and know how little it takes. In terms of hair, what have most of you found is the standard offering for lighting a candle?"

My fire counted as null, though from what Alixant said I should be able to use it if desperate enough. I realized the only element I could access was Earth. Was that normal or strange?

Like I have to ask. It's me. Of course it's strange.

People were raising their hands and after taking answers the group agreed it cost less than three inches of a strand of hair. But when it came to boiling water at least five or more ten-inch strands—a decent sized offering.

"Here is my question—do any of you know why there is such a difference?" Indira scanned the room and I was very glad she hadn't done more than linger on me for a second. I thought I knew the answer, but after the last class I had no desire to draw more attention to myself.

The class was silent as no one provided an answer. Indira smiled. "How many of you look at the wick of the candle and will it to ignite?"

Half the room raised their hands.

"What about making the water boil? How many just will it to boil?" This time about a third. I couldn't see facial expressions, which frustrated me.

She moved back behind the table and scanned the room. "You." Indira pointed at a woman seated near the front. "Come up here please."

The woman froze for a second, then rose and moved to the front. "I asked her up here because no matter how good your eyes are, you will not be able to see me holding up a single strand of hair, but she can." She made as if she lifted something from her head. "I am holding one strand. I want my witness to watch the end of this strand very carefully."

The student leaned forward, peering at the strand. The candle lit. The woman jerked upright and looked at Indira in surprise.

"Only about a fraction of an inch disappeared. Not even half an inch," she said, her voice carrying in the suddenly quiet classroom.

"That is what you can do if you know what you're doing. Rather than me lighting the entire visible wick, I encouraged one molecule of the wick to speed up, that brought others, and once there was a flame, the rest joined in. I didn't need to make all of them burst into flames, just one."

It clicked in my head and I knew I'd be studying a lot about molecular structures and patterns so I could think how to break them. The comment Scott Randolph had made back in Rockway made sense. He talked about the difference between H_2O and H_2O_2. If you didn't understand how the molecules went together you could create the wrong one. It also meant I would be studying all those anatomy books I'd gotten until I had everything memorized. The decision to go for pre-med by getting my biology degree and to minor in Criminal Justice as well as Psychic Magic seemed perfect now that I finally realized how to get it. Back at the stadium, I'd been guessing and hoped Jo had learned enough to pull it off. I still didn't know how much Carelian had contributed to her success. I suspected lots.

Shaking myself out of my musings, I focused back on Indira who pointed at the water. "Most of you tell it to boil. We all know, or should, that the boiling point of water is 100^0 Celsius or 212^0 Fahrenheit give or take a few degrees depending on your altitude. Now don't get me wrong, depending on the profession you go into, those few degrees might make an immense difference, but for this point I'm just going with the basic of 100^0 Celsius. And note if you get into some of the edgier science jobs, knowing how pressure works can make your life easier. But we are dealing with basic molecules of water, H2O. If I want this to boil, the easiest way is to move them faster, which agitates the other molecules of water and they move faster too. This creates the temperature change we call heat. But I don't need anywhere near as many because I'm not trying to move heat into the water, I'm making the water heat itself. Watch if you please."

Indira had grabbed three strands of hair, and her hair was at least ten inches long. The student focused on those strands of hair and they vaporized as the water came to an abrupt boil and then slowed down.

"Who can tell me the problem with doing it this way?" Indira asked dropping what remained of her strands of hair, now about half gone though still a fraction of the price most of us would have had to pay.

"It isn't boiling anymore," said someone in the front row. From what I could tell everyone in the room was absolutely focused on her. Even Carelian had his ears and whiskers flicked forward, his eyes not moving from her in the front.

"Exactly. Oh, I can make tea with it, but it hits that temperature once, and as soon as you quit providing power it stops. This is why generally building a fire and then feeding it material is much more efficient than trying to heat things yourself, though chefs with fire will find they can control temperature almost exactly, pulling heat away from food with barely an offering because it is so subtle and in some ways it provides its own offering."

It what?

I jerked straighter in my chair and a mischievous grin crossed over her face. "Which you will find out about in later classes. This is an intro lab class. We will have guest speakers and talk about the intricacies of how to cast spells, even in branches you are null in for your class. So, by the time you are done in this course everyone should be able to do spells in all four of your classes. Though some of you," her eyes darted to me for a split second, "will be able to do them in all twelve."

Before anyone could react to that, she turned to the student assistant. "Thank you. You may return to your seat." As the student returned to her seat Indira addressed us again. "What if I told you I could do the exact same thing for a fraction of the offering that I paid?" As she spoke, she dumped out the still steaming water into a thermos and dropped a tea bag in it. She then refilled it with water from her bottle.

There was a murmur, but not as much disbelief as there had been. I had zero doubt about her abilities. She'd already showed me how dangerous she could be.

"Same water, roughly the same temperature as the plastic container is hot. Previously it took me what, ten inches of three strands of hair which will take me about six months to replace? Which is why you rarely do offerings like that. But you don't get to your cosmetic offering class until you're sophomores—well some of you." Her eyes flicked up to me again and I wrinkled my nose, disliking knowing she was talking to me. "But we've always known some offerings had more power than hair or nails, which to be frank, are the weakest and easiest."

Indira bent over, getting something else from her bag, and I noted half the people in class leaning forward to get a look at her ass as she bent over.

"Really?" I muttered and Jo laughed a bit.

"She does have a nice figure."

"So?"

Jo just snickered and Indira stood up, holding something, but all I could tell was she held something.

"This is a lancet." She uncapped it and jabbed her finger. A tiny spot of red appeared. "This drop of blood, as small as it is, will do the same as my multiple strands of hair did. Watch the water." She glanced over towards it and the blood disappeared in a tiny puff and the water roiled in the container.

I watched and counted internally to myself. Where before the water had boiled for a few seconds, maybe five, this time I reached twenty before it stopped boiling.

"Living cells are the most powerful offerings we have, dead cells like hair, nails, etcetera are the weakest. Often you will have to decide how important something is to you. Blood can be replenished comparatively fast, but if you offer too much you die. People have died doing that. Sometimes knowing the cost, sometimes not thinking it through. Always think it through. Though some will give their life anyhow. It might be worth it."

Indira let that sit as she filled up her thermos with the still-simmering water and sealed it. The scent of cinnamon and chai hit my nose and I snickered a bit as she sipped her tea.

"Now, since that information has sunk in, here are the realities of what this course will entail. Mostly we will parallel what you are learning in your other magic courses. This is a lab class which is why it is only one credit hour and we only meet once a week. You will do monitored experiments here and talk about the results. A lot of this will be me showing you various ways to do the spells for the different branches. The good thing for me is there is no assigned homework."

There was a low mutter of joy at that, which I couldn't argue with since just the amount of homework from my first class worried me. Her smile chilled the little spurt of joy I had, and I heard some other students wake to that fact. "I will, however, be giving you experiments to try at home. This is because your finals, which will be an all-day class, involve you coming up here and demonstrating an example of using a branch for the least amount of offering possible. If you aren't doing the experiments, trust me, you will fail."

I leaned over to whisper to Jo. "Weren't you supposed to have taken this last semester?"

Indira's comment about matching what you're doing in your other classes made me think it was for freshmen in their first semester.

Jo tilted her head towards me, her voice just as low. "Yeah, but there was a conflict on a class that's only offered once every two years and I needed it. Since this is every semester, I grabbed that one. Not like I can't take what I've already learned and try to enhance it."

That made sense so I went back to what Indira was teaching. It proved interesting.

Chapter 3

Retired mages are a strange bunch. They habitually break down into two groups. The first group rarely uses magic again outside small daily things like cooling a drink or getting something off a tall shelf. They don't push the boundaries, they act like they've never been anything above a hedgemage. The other group experiments non-stop, creating an entire second job over seeing where the limits of our understanding of magic really is. There is an oddly high death rate—those mages and merlins tend to die the most. ~ Magic Explained.

SPIRIT

Two weeks into college and I was about ready to scream. Students everywhere cast sidelong glances at me, and I had three who asked for my autograph. My tattoos were what everyone wanted to see and if people didn't quit walking up to me and moving my hair to touch them, I might kill some-one. It had gotten so bad I started wearing my hair in a ponytail just to prevent people from touching me. That creeped me out.

What it was doing was making college social isolation hell. If it wasn't for Jo, and to a certain extent Sable, I might have given up. Not having besties in class I could handle. I had be-fore. People treating me like I carried the plague was getting to me. Even Carelian was snarling more, and I didn't know what to do.

Bernard Smythe taught the Magic 101 course, while Indira ran the Magic 101 Lab course. I figured I could handle those along with the History of Magic. My schedule for this semes-ter looked packed, but I had enough money to get me through to the summer, where I would take eight to ten credits and work, trying to catch up and make it through the next semester. I'd also set up to be on-call during all the breaks, which should help with me staying above water, financially at least. The money I made while working for the FBI had been a nice chunk and my bank account almost made me happy. But I had a long way to go.

You don't have time to worry about people. Focus on class and get through it. It will be a long two years and people need a chance to let this summer fade.

Dinner with Sable tonight. I liked her, I did, but I still felt like the odd one out. Hopefully, it would change now that we had a set schedule. Either way, a Monday full of classes had left me exhausted. Bernard Smythe hadn't warmed up over the last two weeks. If anything, I seemed to present a personal affront to him I didn't understand. At least Indira had said nothing directly to me, but I only had her on Mondays. Once a week didn't seem to matter. My chem class was interesting but full of homework, as were the law, history, and biology classes. I laughed as I lugged books around. I understood why Jo had been struggling. My assigned reading list made me shiver in dread. But the day was over. Magic Law and Ethics were the last class of the day for me, so now to home, dinner, and study.

Jo still cooked, though I'd gotten MUCH better. Amazing how well you could function when things quit going wrong around you. We'd learned whenever I was stressed, or upset, I had a habit of pulling both the Murphy's Curse and Lady Luck around me. But now we could both sense them and disperse them rapidly. It made for excellent practice for both of us.

My plan for the evening was dinner, my magic paper, the same one I'd helped Jo with last semester though I'd try to come up with fresh ideas about bio matter you could use. I had a theory I wanted to play with and see if it worked. People would regard it as gross, but if it worked, it implied some interesting options should worse come to worse in a situation where you needed magic.

~Home, tired, hungry,~ Carelian whined in my head. His head stuck out of the bag, but when I looked down, his eyes were closed.

"How can you be tired? I'm the one carrying you." He didn't answer, and I laughed. Another ten minutes I should be at the apartment. Jo took a much lighter course load than I did, with only fourteen hours, and her classes were over by one on Mondays.

My phone jangled, and I fumbled to pull it out of my backpack. A number I didn't recognize sat on the screen. It didn't say Spam or Telemarketer, but I'd had too many reporters call me. I hit deny and waited to see if they would leave a message. To my annoyance, they did. With a sigh, I put in headphones and pushed play as I walked. Almost home.

"Miss Munroe. My name is David Carlson. I am the lawyer for the estate of James Wells. I need to meet with you immediately to discuss the clause that has activated for your inheritance. You can reach me at," he said the phone number twice and then hung up.

What in the world? I never met James Wells. Why would he leave anything to me?

I touched the missed call on the phone and waited. He answered on the second ring which set off alarm bells in my skull.

"David Carlson."

"Hi, this is Cori Munroe. You called?"

"Yes. Miss Munroe. When can we meet?"

His urgent request caught me off guard and I slowed my pace. I felt Carelian moving around in his bag, but I didn't look down to check on him.

"Umm, I might have time this weekend. Why? What do you need to talk to me about?"

"That is too late. How about tonight? I'm in Atlanta."

What is going on? What could be so important?

"I'm headed home, and I have a bunch of studying to do. Can't it wait until Sunday?"

"I fear not. I have your address down as"—he provided the apartment number and complex where Jo and I lived and my alarm changed to outright fear. "I can swing by in twenty minutes."

Somehow, I didn't think I'd get to say no. Sable was coming over, so that was two archmages and a merlin. And Sable knew more than both of us put together. If the three of us couldn't handle one person...

Who am I kidding? A strong merlin, learning what I am, could kill us as soon as he saw us. Either I say no or...

"Let me call you back."

"Miss Munroe, it is imperative that I talk to you immediately." He didn't sound stressed, just insistent. Two could play that game.

"And I'll call you back. " I hung up and dialed another number in my contact list.

"Cori. To what do I owe this honor?" Alixant's voice rang in my ears and I closed my eyes for a moment. Scared or desperate, both were sucky reasons to call the man. But he'd been decent over the last few months, and while we weren't friends, I'd have agreed with amiable coworkers.

"Why is a lawyer contacting me about James Wells' estate and why does he want to meet with me?" Niceties were wasted on Alixant, so I never bothered. Silence on the other end, one that I recognized. "You know something. What?"

"Know might be too strong of a word. Suspect is more likely. When does he want to meet?"

"Now. Tonight. He already knew my address." That part bugged me more than I wanted to admit.

"Meet with him. Not sure you're going to like what he has to say. Want a friendly shoulder?" His voice was a touch too casual, and I slowed my walk even more. I didn't need this today, I had homework to do, and it was already looking like a long week.

"I thought you were back at Quantico." I stood in the icy air. January was mild this year, but still it had a nip to it. The campus bustled around me, though students gave me a wide berth. Even after so short a time, the cat and my tattoos acted as a warning to everyone.

"I was. They transferred me down here last week as my new duty post. They're concerned about the sudden spike of high-level emergences in the Atlanta area."

I couldn't help it, I laughed. "So I was right? The planar rips created a bunch of new mages?"

"While there seems to be a correlation, there is no definite causation at this time," he replied, his voice dry, but I heard a hint of humor in it.

"Just tell me nothing about the rips causing emergences made it into the papers." I dropped my voice, barely whispering. "People causing rips would be bad." The thing that had come out of the Chaos plane and took the serial killer mage still gave me nightmares occasionally. While I knew there were other things roaming around, I'd take unicorns with fangs any day of the week over that thing.

"No. We never wrote that information down. While there have been a few closed-door meetings about it, it has been made very clear that nothing will be documented about it." I relaxed, but he continued. "And I assume you are being as circumspect?"

"Did I strike you as stupid and insane? The last thing I want is any more like him."

Or me.

I didn't say that last part, just let it remain unsaid in the space between the words.

"Exactly. If you want, I can show up as a disinterested third party."

I groaned silently, tilting my head back. He was too disinterested. Subtle was not something he did well.

"How badly are you going to throw me to the wolves?" I picked up my pace, wanting to be home.

"Depends on who you're talking to." He didn't pretend not to understand, and I appreciated that. "Me not at all. My superiors, more than I'm comfortable with. I don't know for sure what he has to say, though I have a suspicion. I am on your side, Cori."

"That would be more reassuring if I knew which side that was in this situation. The one with the sharks or the one with the cannibals?"

He chuckled, and the laugh made me smile. Someday, if the stick up his butt disappeared a bit more, he might be a good friend. "Let's aim for the island you have all your friends on. Jo isn't to be discounted, nor her family. And from what I know about Sable and her dad, neither of them are pushovers either."

"Really? How deep is the surveillance on me?" Part of me wanted to spin in a circle looking for the spies, but I knew I wouldn't see them.

"Not that deep. Basic records. Why don't you suggest the coffee shop off of First?"

I knew that one. It wasn't too far from the apartment. If I picked up the pace, I could drop off stuff, tell Jo, and then get there all in about twenty minutes. I pulled the phone away and glanced at it. A few minutes before five. "Fine, I'll tell him five-forty-five, which will mean I don't have to rush."

"Sounds good. I'll head that way shortly. Besides, Siab sent something for you."

Thinking of Siab garnered a smile. The Hmong scientist had been the first person to accept me in his group and she had a personality I enjoyed. "She transferring down too?"

"We're still discussing it, but maybe. There are other things at play. Remember, you're drafted, not a slave." His voice held humor and a gentle reminder.

"Uh huh. Let's have this discussion after my service is done." I hung up and hit redial on the phone. It rang once, then Carlson answered. "Miss Munroe?"

"I'll meet you at Blue Donkey at quarter to six."

"Are you sure? This really might be better at your residence."

"Blue Donkey or nothing," I replied, my voice firm. I didn't want someone I didn't know in our place. It felt too much like an invasion.

"Very well. I'll meet you there. Thank you."

I hung up, and glanced down at Carelian, who had seemed very interested in the whole conversation. "Let's get home, get you fed, and then I guess I'll be finding out what lawyers want with me."

He flicked an ear in response. I snickered and picked up the pace. I wanted to be there early. Maybe I could get something in a corner to provide some privacy.

Chapter 4

While STEM courses are required for all mages getting degrees under the Mage Draft, many will choose minors in things like fashion design, graphic design, or other creative aspects that their personal interests lead them towards. This has benefited many of those who are magicians or wizards, as this will help them get jobs in industries that are not as heavy in the hard sciences. ~ OMO informative brochure

CHAOS

I approached the Blue Donkey, Carelian on my chest, and Jo and Sable walking behind me. No one would let me go alone, and I'd run out of time to argue with them. So instead of me and Alixant, I had a group with me. But since I'd quit arguing with them and annoyance fueled my ability to walk fast, we got there about five-thirty. The Blue Donkey had lots of funky tables and corners. There was one person seated in the back corner at a large table, a four-person booth bench against the wall and four chairs. It would be perfect.

"Ugh. I hate asking people to move, but I think we need isolation." I dug in my pocket and pulled out a twenty, hoping it would be enough. "Give me a minute."

"Sure. Want me to order you something? Dinner will be fine until we get back." Jo looked at me expectantly. Personally, I wanted to be home eating her chili. That was the nice thing about slow cookers, they could be set to warm.

"Please. I have homework to do tonight. Single origin coffee, extra sugar, large?"

Sable winked at me as the two of them headed to the counter and I went to try to convince the person to let me have the table even though they were there first.

As I approached, I realized I knew him. Well, I'd seen him. He sat in the front row of the Magic Lab and Magic 101, not that I had talked to him or even knew his name. He looked up as I approached and his familiar, because there was no other way anything with that many legs would be allowed in here otherwise, peeked out from underneath the long hair that he wore loose. I cataloged him quickly—young, in worse shape than me, pale skin, light brown hair and light brown almost amber eyes. He assessed me at the same time.

"What does the savior of the SEC want with me?" His voice flat and unaccented, nothing southern in it at all.

"Oh, please, that name is so stupid and inaccurate." I felt my face heat. Of all the things the press had called me, that one had to be the worst. "I was there. I did what I could. I'm frankly relieved the unicorn didn't eat me and that that thing from Chaos left with only the jerk."

His lips twitched, but his eyes stayed steady. "That didn't answer my question."

I swallowed and tugged on my ponytail. "This is super rude, and I'm sorry to even ask, but some lawyer wants to meet me. I don't trust him, so I chose some place pubic. My friends refused to let me come alone." I waved at Jo and Sable who were waiting for our drinks. "And I'd really like a table out of the way." I thrust the twenty at him. "I can pay for the inconvenience, and I mean you don't have to say yes, but please?"

He looked at me for a long moment. "Huh, not all pretty girls are bitches or full of themselves. Come on, Arachena." He stood and gathered his books into a pile as the familiar waved a leg at me. "Keep the money. I needed to head home anyhow. Good luck with the meeting." A quick nod and he headed to the door, leaving me standing there.

"Cool, he let us use the table? Didn't charge you?" Jo asked, nodding at the twenty still in my hand.

"No. And I think he said I was pretty." The entire conversation had left me confused.

"Cori, you might not be gorgeous like Sable is, but you are very cute and adorable. Especially when confused." Jo bopped my nose as she slid into the booth and Sable followed laughing.

Before I could respond, or even address her comments, I felt Alixant come in. He had this presence that made me aware or annoyed. I couldn't decide which, but it was interesting to watch him walk across the coffee shop and see at least half the heads in the place turn to follow him.

"Damn, too bad I gave up men," Sable muttered.

"He's not that attractive," I protested, but it came out weak as I watched the calculating look from women.

"Good choice of table. Jo. Sable. Carelian. I need a drink." He nodded at each of us, including Carelian, who I hadn't had time to let out of the bag, then spun on his heel, striding towards the counter.

"Yes, yes he is," Sable muttered then looked at me for the first time ever I felt like she really saw me. The deep down me that only Jo had seen before. "Huh. Yeah, I need to quit letting Jo distract me."

"About?" I grabbed the drink and took a swig, the caffeine centering me. Nothing made sense, and I needed to focus. Before I could figure out what to follow up on, Alixant came back and pointed imperiously at the chair in the corner.

Sable shook her head avoiding my question. "Sit over there. Means you'll have Jo on one side, me on the other. And I assume Carelian will do what he does."

"He's a cat, regardless of anything else. He usually does." I let him out of the bag so he could make sure the locate met his standards, not that I had any idea what those were.

Alixant smirked as I settled down. "He figure out how to open things yet?"

"SHUSH!" All three of us said in vehement voices. "We do NOT talk about that." We knew he had an opposable thumb, we were all rather terrified of what he might realize he could do with that thumb.

A snerk escaped from him before he managed to sit down. "Understood. Sounds like stories friends tell me about things their kids didn't need to hear about saying the walk word infront of their dogs. He'll figure it out soon." He held the coffee in front of him as a shield. I just glared.

"There is no reason to hurry the apocalypse, thank you. We are already aware of the fact that his tail can be used like an extra hand."

~I can hear you,~ his voice rumbled in my mind. ~What don't I know?~

Alixant arched a brow as Jo reached down and picked Carelian up, scratching behind his ears and under his chin at the same time. "That we think you are the smartest, prettiest cat in the universe." His eyes closed and he purred as she applied her magic fingers.

~Distraction acceptable.~

I glared at Alixant who held up his hands in surrender. Once Carelian figured out just how to use his "fingers" then we were in big trouble. As it was, neither of us ever used a can opener in front of him.

"Here, Siab asked me to give this to you." He handed me a small envelope package. I picked it up and opened it, curious as to what she would send—she had my email address.

"Oh look!" I pulled out a woven strap. It was a collar about an inch wide with Carelian's name woven into it in greens and purples. "Oh, I'll need to send her a thank you." I admired the Hmong artwork, recognizing her skill in weaving it.

"She thought you might like it. It's strong, has room for a tag with your number, but since it's silk, his claws can shred it if he needs to." Alixant watched, a half-smile on his face.

"You like?" I showed it to Carelian who'd stuck his nose up from under the table.

~Yes. Worthy,~ he declared but sank back under the table, still investigating the area.

The door to the coffee shop opened just as I checked my phone—five forty-five. "That's him." Alixant sounded absolutely sure as he watched the man walk in and pause, looking around.

"Do you know him?" Jo asked it for me, which helped because a desire to dive under the table and hide had grabbed me and I struggled to not panic.

"I'm aware of him. He handles a lot of estate law for merlins."

"But he's not a mage?" Sable seemed dubious as she glanced at him, then back at all the tattoos on our temples.

"No. He is a pure mundane. And it is one reason so many people use him. No magic."

The man must have spotted Alixant because his face went into a blank mask I envied. My emotions still showed on my face. Another skill I needed to develop. He stood up straighter. The thick black briefcase in his left hand moved in front as he came forward.

What is he shielding himself from? Us?

I looked around and wanted to snort. Two women, holding hands under the table if I had to guess, me, a cat, also under the table, and Alixant. Okay, Alixant had an imposing presence. The rest of us, not so much.

"Steven. To what do I owe your presence?" His voice sounded the same as it had on the call, smooth and flat, but lacking the urgency this time.

"Cori called. Asked me to be here." Alixant nodded at me as he spoke, and the man riveted his attention on me.

I didn't pull back, but all my alarms were going off in my mind. No matter what he said I knew down to my bones that I would not like it. Even worse, I suspected my life would get measurably more difficult.

"Miss Munroe, David Carlson at your service. I thought we would talk in private." He moved hazel eyes over my motley crew, arching a brown eyebrow as Carelian jumped up behind me and flopped on the booth ledge. I could feel his paws brushing the back of my neck. It gave me an odd sense of protection. Not that I had any idea what a ten-pound cat could do if he did attack.

"Not going to apologize. After the last few months, I don't trust anyone calling me out of the blue and wanting to meet. I'd rather have witnesses to anything you say or do." Having reporters harass me for three months had refined my ability to not trust anyone by leaps and bounds. I didn't need him, so I didn't need to try to curry his favor.

I saw his jaw clench a little, but then he smiled and nodded his head. "If I may?" He waved at the seat we'd left empty for him, putting him between Sable and Alixant. He opened the briefcase and pulled out three thick folders and pushed them to me. "These are yours. Please look through them at your leisure." He pulled out another thin folder and opened it. "I need to verify a few details."

I looked at the thick manila envelopes that looked like they were bursting at the seams. They lay there in the middle of the coffee-stained table, but I didn't touch them. Instead, I looked at the lawyer.

"Which would be?"

"You are in fact Corisande Lorelia Munroe. Twenty-one years old, born April 15, at 12:00 A.M. in Nashville, Tennessee?"

"Yes," I said warily unhappy about his knowledge, but that information had been released ages ago. Reporters pried into everything.

"The date of your suspected emergence"—his eyes flicked to my temple, then he restated—"your suspected first emergence is April 14th, the day your fraternal twin Stephanos Gregori Munroe died?"

This all felt like some weird reality that I didn't fully exist in. My head nodded without my being in control of it.

"I need you to answer verbally please."

He didn't snap, or even seem angry, just someone going through a process. That helped clear away some of the fog. "Yes."

"Excellent. Then given your registered status as a Spirit merlin and the only one who has emerged in the last decade that is female, you are officially recognized as the only heir to James Wells' estate. Sign here please." He slid the paper over to me, alone in the file.

I read it over, but it didn't say anything other than I was who I said I was. I signed and slid it back to him.

"Steven, would you sign as a witness, please?"

Alixant took the paper, scanned it, and signed.

"Excellent."

"David, what is this all about?" Alixant asked, his voice not even half as annoyed as I felt. All this, just to make me verify who I was?

"All in due time. Corisande Munore, you are officially designated as the heir to James Wells' estate. Everything he owned, all the safe deposit boxes, and his private research is yours provided—" he broke off as people began speaking.

"Merlin's balls, Cori, you're rich," Jo said, her wide eyes looking at the manila envelopes.

Alixant almost spit out his coffee and looked at the lawyer. "Was he crazy? He left it all to some unknown merlin?"

"I just follow instructions. I have no idea what Mr. Wells did or didn't think. However, there are conditions to claiming this inheritance."

What little joy had been building in me snuffed out in a split second. "Figures. Oh well, easy come, easy go."

"Cori! Let's hear what the requirements are. Maybe it's easy," Jo protested, elbowing me.

"Jo, it's me. It's going to be something crazy, like climb Everest freehand or fly under my own power."

Sable snickered but she didn't disagree with my comment.

"They are not quite at that level, though, well," he cleared his throat, and I redirected my attention to him, sensing an even bigger issue than I thought. "The bequeathment is set up in stages. The first stage gets you the house. The second, all his bank boxes, and the third grants all remaining lands and holdings. It is my understanding that his research will be yours when you meet the second requirement. Let me do them in reverse order so they don't seem so daunting. I don't believe you will have an issue with the second or third."

Which meant I'd have an issue with the first, and these were a succeed in order thing. Why did magic think I was its chew toy?

Carelian snickered in my head and I turned to look at him, but he was watching my hair and avoided my gaze. With a glare I settled back against the booth and felt Carelian bat my ponytail immediately, catching and tugging, but never hard enough to hurt. I didn't mind as it let me feel him there without having to look around for him. So far, he hadn't scratched or bitten me, but being able to say stop or him give me a warning growl in my head also accounted for that. With his gentle touch keeping me centered I waited for the lawyer to speak.

"The third condition is completing your draft term of service. It is entailed so that if you die during your draft it would follow the terms of your will." He smiled at me, and if he meant that to be reassuring it wasn't. Both Jo and Sable had gone silent. "The second condition is to start your draft service. At that time, the bank boxes will be released to you."

I shrugged, trying to push away my unease at the idea of dying while in service. I still had to get through school, probably earn my masters if not my doctorate before I even started my draft.

Great the next fifteen years or so of my life all planned for me, regardless of what I wanted.

The urge to pout or throw a tantrum strummed through me, but I pushed it away.

"That sounds easy enough. What is the first condition?"

He looked down at his paper and cleared his throat again. I was about to offer to get him something to drink. "You need to understand this was all done assuming you were of college age when you emerged and when James was dying, he set all this up figuring it would be an incentive. I also wasn't involved when it was created, so I don't know what his thought processes were." He looked down at the table but shuffled the papers in his hands, making me doubt he actually saw them.

"Whatever you think it is, it probably won't be that horrid. Just say it." I just wanted this over with and had never counted on having anything to begin with.

Alixant had an odd look on his face, and I reminded myself once again that he must know something.

"Very well. Note that if you do not meet any of the conditions, all remaining items under the will are designated to Hisahito Yamato."

A hissed intake of breath had me glancing at Alixant. "What? Do you know who that is?"

He gave me an odd smile. "When you take some of the later classes you learn who the most politically influential mages are. That is the Majyutsu-shi of the Japanese Royal Yamato family. He is a merlin by rank, and the best English equivalent would be Royal Magician though his title is Majyutsu-shi Yamato. He's a Spirit merlin, and third cousin of the emperor."

There was much that lay unsaid there, like the fact the US and Japan had been on polite but distant terms since WWII, when three US merlins had transported a nuclear weapon into the heart of their military forces. The bomb had not reacted well to the teleportation and took out a nearby town, Hiroshima, at the same time. There were no survivors. While Japan bowed out of the war at that point, their government had never forgiven us, and few Americans went to Japan as tourists.

I gave Alixant a look, suspecting that the last thing the US government wanted was anything to fall into the hands of Japan, much less the royal family.

"Great. What's the initial condition?" I asked, exasperated. Tiptoeing around the issue wouldn't tell me anything.

"Yes, well. The first condition," he said, giving a reproachful glance. I rolled my eyes in response and motioned him to get going. "You will need to have your bachelor's degree by next summer. Basically, you have eighteen months to graduate."

"Are you freaking kidding me?"

Chapter 5

Estates for mages work the same as for anyone else. But those who live to old age often spent a lot of their time in retirement tinkering with things. Heirs are often surprised at the wide variety of esoteric items, both magical and mundane, that these mages seem to have attracted over their lifetimes. But all such hoards should be regarded with suspicion. More than one heir has lost their life to odd traps left behind. And sometimes, as in the Lizzy Borden case, they take others out as well. ~ History of Magic

ORDER

The outrage and arguing went on for another twenty minutes. I just sat there, thinking. Mostly thinking about how hungry I was.

"Enough." My voice wasn't that loud, but still the few people in the coffee shop not looking at us did now.

They all looked at me, and I sighed. "No matter how much you yell, protest, or anything else, he can't change it. If I want this, I need to meet the clauses in the will. Anything else doesn't matter. Now, I have dinner waiting at home, I have homework to do, and frankly I don't want to be here anymore." I pointed at the manila envelopes. "Those are mine to keep, right?"

"Yes. They detail out the contents for each section of the bequeathment."

"Great." I stood, swept them up into my arms, shoved the collar in my pocket, and grabbed the bag slipping it on. "Carelian, you coming?"

He jumped over to the table, letting me pick him up and slide him into the bag. "Jo, Sable, I'm starving. You ready to go?"

"Sure," Jo said, shrugging as she stood.

"Cori, you need to take this seriously," said Alixant. "There are dangerous people that are invested in his research. The government figured it might be something like this, but the terms were sealed. Which means they will not be happy finding out all that could go to a Japanese national." He looked at me, his eyes dark.

I'd worked my way around the table, holding the envelopes in one arm while trying not to bump Carelian into the table. As cute and funky as the place was, the coffee smells were making me nostalgic and starving. Two things I didn't want to deal with.

"Not my problem. Thanks for coming." I glanced at David. "I guess I'll let you know if I fail or make it. Don't change your number." I knew I was being rude, and I didn't care. All these people, men, telling me how to live my life. I just wanted them out of my life.

"Don't worry. Your progress will be tracked closely. Good luck." He sounded sincere, and that sent my nerves jangling.

"Thanks," I said, forcing a smile that had no amusement in it. I headed to the door, all too aware that he sat back down and started talking to Alixant, their body language intent. I shook my head and pushed open the door, Jo and Sable following close behind me.

"Cori, what in the world was all that?" Jo asked as Sable came up on my other side, framing me. Or protecting me. Both ideas made me worry. Not about them, well not about Jo at least, but either way.

"You heard what I did. I don't know anything else."

"Are you going to do it?" Sable asked, her voice low.

I half shrugged, glancing at her. She had twisted her long black hair with its eternally perfect corkscrews into a different pattern today, while her light caramel skin and almond-shaped eyes just added to her beauty. It'd be easier if she had a big scar or was fat or something. But she, like most mages, remained trim with smooth skin.

"I need to look. I'd worked it out to get my master's in two and a half years, letting classes overlap as it didn't matter. This might change things. Might mean a full load this summer instead of a partial one." That thought made me want to growl. I hated being super tight on money, and if I couldn't work this summer it would make next year difficult.

"We'll help," Jo burst out and I looked at her, confused. She grinned and expanded on her comment. "Sable's a junior, so she can help with some classes. You can use my audio stuff, maybe listen while you walk or in between classes. Means you won't have to carry as many books. And since you've already challenged some classes, for the history stuff maybe you can challenge that too, or just write a research paper. If the government is as heavy about this as Alixant says I bet they'd help to weigh in on your being able to challenge them."

"I'm willing to help. You should be taking classes with me fall semester, so I can help get you through it," Sable offered, giving me a real smile that made her even prettier.

Warmth flooded me. "I really do have the best, best friend." I winked at Sable. "And her choice in girlfriends isn't so bad either."

Sable grinned, and we stepped up our pace to the apartment, the chilly air acting as a motivator though the folders in my arms were calling to me also.

~Out!~ Carelian demanded as we stepped in, and I let him down. He raced to the bathroom, and a minute later I heard a stream of liquid in the bowl.

"I know he's as smart as we are—" Sable started to say.

~Smarter,~ Carelian interjected and Sable snickered.

"But it still seems odd to have him use the toilet."

"Trust me after the first month of needing to clean the litter box, I was delighted when he figured out how to balance. Makes all of our lives cleaner and less smelly, which I think he agrees with the most." I kicked off my shoes and headed to the kitchen. "What do you want me to do?"

"Nothing. I want to you sit down and go through those folders. I'm dying to know what is in them, even if you aren't."

"What she said. I'm curious," Sable put in as she headed to the kitchen to help.

"That, and Jo has told you horror stories about me in the kitchen."

"Possibly?" Sable drew out the word and I laughed.

"Fine, fine, but I am getting better. I can almost make soup without burning it. Besides, you're just dishing up chili," I protested, but moved over to the couch and put the envelopes on the coffee table. We usually ate there at the couch, well futon. Sable was the only person who'd really used the futon aspects of it, but it made for a nice couch.

I looked at the three envelopes, with nice legible handwriting on each. They were labeled: First Section, Second Section, Final Section.

"Oh, let's see what I'll lose first." I didn't mutter it quietly enough, so Jo heard me.

"Stop it. I know you. You don't let anything stop you once you get going. Just matters if you want this enough or not."

"And if I can pay all the bills," I pointed out as I turned to look at her. She and Sable came into the living room, carrying mugs of chili. Each mug had a creamy white dollop of sour cream covered with cheddar cheese on it. Sable had a hot chai tea for each of us. Jo made her chili with fire; milk or beer were the best options for cooling it. None of us really liked beer, so the chai with lots of milk proved the best option.

Sable started to say something, but shook her head, dropping onto the floor as Jo sat the mugs down.

"Rewards first. Then we can see if it is worth it. Heck, it might be a two-room shack in the Appalachians. Not sure that's worth anything. And, I mean, if that is the house the research might be a ratty notebook in a bank box," Jo teased me as she sat down on the other side.

"And the 'remaining lands and holdings'?" I asked, getting into the game.

"Oh, I have that," Sable said with a soft laugh. "A few acres of land that is contaminated by old leaking underground storage tanks, and the gas station remains that used to be there."

We all giggled at the ideas and I relaxed. It would be something more along that line than anything else, which made me less stressed about opening the folders.

I got a few more spoonsful of chili in my mouth, the jalapenos and the smoky bite of habanero salsa she always added fading as I sipped my tea. Sable and I found the cinnamon and cloves of the chai made a nice counterpoint to the chili.

"Okay, first one it is." I pushed the mug to the side, did a quick check to make sure I hadn't wrapped any magic around me, and opened the one marked First Section. It was the slimmest of the envelopes and I pulled out what looked like a realtor's listing stapled to a list of items, and a typed piece of paper.

I scanned the paper, but it said the same thing, providing the date I needed to earn my bachelor's degree by. A date that seemed much too close. I opted for the list of items in the house and let out a low whistle. "Somehow I don't think the place will be a dump. This lists furnishings, paintings, collectibles. It even says it's being maintained by a caretaker right now. A Lucille Magnum." I handed over the list for Jo and Sable to look at—it was five pages long—and picked up the real estate printout. It listed the appraisal, the land, address, and had pictures of the house from the outside and all the rooms, fully furnished.

I fell in love. Head over heels in love with that house.

It had three bedrooms, a study with a small library, a kitchen that Marisol would drool over, wraparound porch, and modern bathrooms. It'd been updated, but the outside screamed Victorian with character. From the deck to the burgundy trim on a light grey paint, the stained-glass windows and a third floor that was listed as unknown. I wanted that house more than I'd wanted anything. It called to me and I wanted to sink into the leather chair in the study. I wanted to put all my books in the small library and then get more.

"Wow. Cori, that house is incredible." Sable's voice made me realize I was holding the paper tight enough that it was wrinkling. I relaxed my grip and smoothed it out, then, with fingers that didn't want to release, handed it to them.

"Cori?" Jo looked at me, not the paper. "What is it?"

"I want that house. I want that to be my house. Jo, that is my house. All the dreams I never let myself dream, they are all there in that house."

She frowned at me, then leaned over Sable's shoulder to look at the pictures. I closed my eyes and took deep breaths.

Is the house worth it? Getting your degree won't be impossible, but it means killing yourself, overloading every class and fighting to challenge anything you can.

My heart responded to that internal question with a resounding yes. I swallowed. First, I needed to look at the rest.

The second section had a list of banks, the various boxes, and cryptic notes about their contents. Notebook on Psychic abilities. Planar research notes. Jeorgaz comments and instructions.

"Who the heck is Jeorgaz?" I asked looking up. Jo and Sable just shrugged as they finished studying the brochure.

"No clue," Jo said. "Friend? Imaginary friend? How am I supposed to know? But you're right, that's your house. I just have one complaint." She pushed the paper back. I resisted grabbing it and holding it to me, as if I could keep the house to myself by protecting a picture.

"And what would that be? Besides New York?"

"Okay, two complaints. New York! It snows up there and gets cold."

"Snow is fun and pretty. Drinking hot chocolate while watching it fall is delightful," Sable responded with a wistful grin. "Dad and I did that when we lived at Fort Drum. It was nice."

"Shoveling the snow after it's done falling," Jo countered, but she smiled. "But that is a minor complaint. We're supposed to grow old together. How am I supposed to do that if you live in a that house?"

As they teased, I'd pulled open the final folder, and it was the thick one. Multiple real estate listings, copies of deeds and properties owned, listings of businesses there were significant shares in, and then bank statements.

"Jo. That might not be an issue," I said, numb at this point. I slid over the real estate listings. "If I understand this, he owned the entire street. There were only three houses. The one I loved at the end of the cul de sac, a smaller craftsman on one side, and this one on the other. Says this was the original house before they parceled out the land. The Victorian was built in 1897 and the craftsman in 1928. But this one was built in 1843 and remodeled and modernized about ten years ago for his best friend, who died a few years ago."

The house I pointed out to her was a brick and wood Tudor-style mansion. My Victorian, it was already mine in my head, had three full baths and the three bedrooms, but the Tudor was a monster. Per the listing it had six bedrooms, including a master en suite, a nursery, cold room, kitchen, two dining rooms, and a back lawn you could play golf on.

"Wow. That's a nice house," Jo muttered as she traced the images with her fingers. Even Sable seemed entranced by it.

"It has a mechanics workshop and an experimental lab to one side too," I teased with a grin. "Lots of room for all the kids you want."

If I hadn't been watching her, I wouldn't have seen the flicker of her eyes and the wince that flashed across her face, but then it disappeared and she smiled at Sable.

"So, wanna move there and have a passel of kids with me?" Her eyebrows wiggled as she spoke.

"If that's a marriage proposal, it sucks. I'm worth way more than that. But, if that's your dowry, I might not say no." She grinned back, teasing as much as Jo.

"Huh. I guess I'm going to do this," I said as I looked at everything. The houses mattered more to me than anything else, though the number of zeros in the bank accounts would mean I'd never have to work when my draft ended and still have money to keep all the houses up. I paused to grab the copy of the appraisal and winced at the tax bill. Maybe I would have to work.

"No." I looked up in surprise at Jo and she smiled at me. "We're doing this. All for one and one for all." She'd been on a kick to watch all the Tim Curry movies this summer and *The Three Musketeers* had been one of her favorites. Though I thought it was because she lusted over the actress playing Milady de Winter.

"Great, now we're musketeers? Well, obviously, I'm D'Artagnan, and you're Aramis. I think Sable must be Porthos, for your fashion sense and desire to be someone. But that leaves Athos?"

~Me. After all, I'm your guide. For all of you.~ Carelian spoke in our heads and Jo and I fell down in laughter, thinking about the young kitten being the older father figure. Sable just looked at him in astonishment.

"He spoke to me!"

Jo and I started laughing even more. I still wondered who Jeorgaz was.

Chapter 6

France has one of the three family-based familiars. The Dragon of China is the second, the Wolf of Russia is the third, and France has the Phoenix. But while the Chinese and Russian both belong to the ruling families (or previously ruling family in Russia's case, as the Romanovs are down to a single branch) France's Phoenix belongs to a small family that runs a bakery in Lyon. They are all fire mages and all of them bake like it was born into their souls. ~History of Magic

SPIRIT

I doubled down on my classes over the next week, but that weekend I poured over all the courses—what I could challenge, and what was scheduled to be taught over the next three semesters. That was all the time I had and the summer semester would have limited class options.

"I think I have it, but I need to convince them to let me challenge or do independent study in five classes. And I suspect at least two classes will be at the same time in the fall, so I'll have to split my time. But it will be close. If they decide not to hold a single class, this game plan will fall apart. And I'm limited as to what I can do for some classes." That annoyed me as I wanted those extra minors.

"You going to give up your CJ minor?" Jo asked as she finished up the fajitas.

"Maybe. I shouldn't need to since I only need like 3 classes total and at least one of them is also required for the magic minor."

There was a knock on the door, so I paused as Jo went to let Sable in. She had stress lines I recognized around the corners of her mouth but smiled as Jo pulled her into a hug and a quick kiss.

"Just dump that if you have to. There aren't any time restraints and you can always go back to school later. From what I've read, some of the draft assignments will encourage you to, if you get a second degree in something they want. Especially merlins, as you're stuck there for ten years." Jo started setting the table—fajitas were too messy to try to eat at the couch.

"Yeah, that only leaves the money problem. I mean, I don't think it'll get to ramen levels, but I like being able to go out occasionally. And I really wanted to go to DragonWorldcon next year and be able to buy stuff." We already had our tickets, but if I didn't have time to go, it would suck.

"I might have a solution to that," Sable spoke, but she didn't look at me as she talked.

"Oh?" The comment surprised me and from Jo's frown, her too.

Sable cleared her throat, staring at the ground. "So, you know Jo and I are pretty serious. Well, my roommate is becoming a pain. Apparently, me making it public that I'm dating Jo is offending her sensibilities. She feels that sexual experimentation is fine, but to link yourself to another woman prevents the continuation of magical lineage and is an anathema."

My mouth dropped open. "She's a follower of Purity, really?" That was a splinter group formed in the early 1900s that decided magical lineages were all-important, even though people from strong magical lines often had kids that were hedgies at best. And then you had me a merlin from a family no one had tracked as having any magic. Most people regarded them as crackpots. I sure did.

"Yeah. Her father is some high muckety-muck in their church. So, my dad supports me, and per how the education law works, if I move in with someone else that already has the cohabitation budget covered, I get it in cash. I checked. I get basically a monthly allowance for what they were paying for my rent." A sudden vicious smile lit up her face. "And

Daniela has to pay the other half until she gets another room-mate."

"So you want to move in here? With us?" I asked. My voice was slow, hesitant, but not because I disliked the idea. I just needed to roll it around in my mind for a bit.

"Well, yeah. I was hoping maybe you wouldn't hate the idea too much?" Sable cast a glance at Jo, and I saw she looked as surprised as I did. Which meant they hadn't talked about it before.

Jo took her seat, face serious, then a smile flashed across it. "I get to wake up with you every morning? I can handle that. But Cori, what do you want?"

I sat down too, catching the almost desperate look on Sable's face. A look I recognized from seeing it in the mirror most mornings. The bedrooms were the same size, but I barely used half of my closet. Jo on the other hand had hers bursting at the seams, but she didn't have anything besides a small chest of drawers in her room, and the rooms were spacious enough she could easily get a large dresser or armoire in it. It would give me a chance to know Sable. If she was going to be a permanent part of Jo's life, I needed to. Hopefully, she wanted the same. While I still worried about Jo leaving, they were more nightmares than active thoughts most of the time. I had finally realized nothing would chase her away from me. Which helped, but I knew if I screwed up, I could push her away.

"I don't have an issue, and the extra money might help since I will be tight between paying my bills and feeding greedy guts." Carelian had his own chair at the small table with a booster seat on it, so he could sit and watch us easily, though only occasionally wanting what we were eating. Jo made most of the food way too spicy for him. Though I thought he was growing to like it.

~Growing kittar, need nutrients,~ he responded, and I could see from the flash and grin that Sable had heard that too. I filed kittar with quean as odd words he used. He ignored any questions about life on the other side of planes. Basically, a typical cat.

"Go for it. You need to file the paperwork. And figure out where your stuff can fit. You've seen Jo's room. But I do have some closet space."

Sable had a wry smile. "Yes, I have. Someone might need to do some organizing. And cleaning out of stuff she'll never wear."

"Hey! I love my clothes." Jo's instant protest made me laugh. They settled into talking about how to juggle everything while I made myself a fajita. They could have cold fajitas, I wasn't going to.

The tortillas had fajita meat, peppers, sour cream, cheese, and salsa, and my mouth watered. As I lifted it up to take a bite, my phone rang. A familiar ringtone, the blaring of a car horn. The most obnoxious sound possible without me purchasing a ringtone.

Jo and Sable stopped their discussion and glanced at my phone. "Steven Alixant?" Jo asked starting on her own fajita.

"Yes." I sighed and got up to grab it off my backpack where I'd dropped it. "What?" I didn't bother being polite, he rarely was. And when he was, I worried.

"I need to talk to you." His sharp voice could be heard clearly through the phone's speaker.

"About?" I tossed the phone on the table and sat back down, the fajita calling to me.

"It's better to talk in person. May I come over?" I knew he'd come over whether I said yes or no, and some fights weren't worth having. Besides, cold fajitas.

"Fine. When?"

There was a knock on the door and I dropped my head back. "Really? Fine." I got up and pulled open the door, revealing Alixant and Indira. Both had pinched expressions and I looked from one to the other. Then, leaving the door open, I went back to the table and picked up my fajita. If the world was going to fall down on me, I'd bloody well eat my fajita hot.

"Um, come in?" Jo said, standing and giving me meaningful glances I ignored. She ushered them in, waving at the futon. "Sorry, not a lot of places to sit. Take the couch. So, what's up?"

"Aren't you going to talk to us, Cori?" Indira had her soothing voice out, the one half sultry, half cajoling. With a mouthful of fajita, I shot her a look and she sighed, sitting up straighter. "Swear, we are delivering the news, we didn't cause it." This time normally, without the seduction lacing it.

"Fajita, hot, eat," I mumbled around food as I chewed and swallowed. Hunger had been high lately with all the practicing I'd been doing trying to ace my classes, and this was my dinner, darn it. I shouldn't have to interrupt it because they were here—I hadn't invited them.

Alixant smiled a bit. "It does smell good. That's fine, eat. But I figured you deserved to know this as soon as possible, because we had no say so in the matter. And unfortunately, neither do you."

That made me pause, the tortilla half eaten. I sighed and set it down, wiping my mouth and picking up a glass of soda. I turned my chair and looked at them. "Fine. What is it now? Trying to get through my degree in under eighteen months isn't enough?"

"That is part of what prompted this." Alixant sat stiffly on the couch and I didn't know if I should be impressed or worried. That couch invited slouching.

"Prompted what?" Jo asked, leaning forward, giving both of them hard stares. "What does this have to do with Cori?"

Indira waved her as, as if dimissing something. "The government is very invested in gaining access to Merlin Wells' research on planar rips. Even more so after the events at the stadium. They wish to make sure you meet the terms of the will, which means passing. In order to aid you with that, they've assigned mentors."

Worry sank into me. "Mentors? To do what?"

"Assist you with schoolwork, smooth any issues you might have, provide support and research if needed." She didn't look at me as she spoke.

"You mean they want me to cheat and you to do it for me, if it looks like I won't make it," I spat out my fist clenching.

"That was implied, yes." Alixant admitted. "However, we did tell them it was unlikely you would accept or allow that. I pointed out you were perfectly capable of cutting off your magic just to piss everyone off. And that you had to agree to it for it to work."

I shrugged. I had been planning on getting my degree. I wanted that house, but they didn't need to know that.

"Who are my 'assigned' mentors?" I already knew the answer but making them squirm was enjoyable.

"We were informed we would be filling that role, or our drafts would be reactivated," Indira said, her voice as dry as Alixant's and her choice of words providing a wealth of information.

"What?" Jo and Sable said together. "I thought once you finished your draft service, you were done?" Sable went on, looking at them in confusion.

"There is fine print that says something like in times of necessity any mage can be pulled back in for further service if the situation is judged dire enough," Indira said, her voice utterly emotionless, which was even creepier than her sexy voice.

"And me not graduating qualifies as dire?" I said looking at the two of them.

"Preventing Japan from getting that research does. Apparently, he'd been working on a project for the government, but since it was unfunded and off the books, they haven't been able to gain access to research notes."

"They realize forcing me into this isn't about to endear me to them, and I'm just as likely to refuse to share them," I pointed out, poking at my now rapidly cooling dinner.

"We did mention that, but they figured they would have a decade to provide incentives to get you to release them or at least tell them if it has what they are looking for. And either way, at least Japan wouldn't have them. And by then, there would be new senators, a new president, and new dire situations."

"If I get my degree, what do you two get out of this?"

"Besides not having the draft reactivated and losing my job at the university?" Indira asked looking at me. "There are a few things. But for now, mentoring a student is relatively easy." Her smile was serene, but I remembered all too well the other people she worked for. Part of the world I hadn't been exposed to yet.

"I'll think about it. If what I read about mentorships was correct, there is a contract. Something we both have to sign? Willingly?"

They nodded in agreement.

"Well, right now the only thing I need is more classes offered when I need them and a strong summer lineup. And worst case, maybe a hand with some papers. It's been a while since I've had to write a true research paper. I'm not agreeing to anything else."

"Cori. We accepted this role for a few reasons. You know us, and I think at least tolerate if not like us. We won't treat you like a child, but there are some restrictions." I jerked up straighter and looked at him, on guard. "You're confined to campus. You need to check in weekly with both of us, and all of your professors will be informed we have full access to your grades and studies. They are to let us know if you are having problems." He said all this as if it wasn't a big deal. As if they were perfectly reasonable requests.

"No."

Chapter 7

The caste society of India fractured in the early 1900s when Britain withdrew, ceding control of the East India company to the cohort of merlins that arose from the untouchable caste, preventing British forces from entering India for three months. The system shattered, breaking into two groups, mages and non. While mages enjoy better opportunities in India, the ruling parliament of India wrote in five years of civil assistance for all mages and they are encouraged to follow Buddhist traditions which revere a life of service. ~ History of Magic.

CHAOS

"Excuse me?" Alixant said. I noted Jo and Sable had both retreated a bit.

They were smart to get out of the field of fire. Not that I'd do anything to this apartment. I liked the apartment.

"I said no. I'll deal with checking in with you weekly and maybe consider a mentorship. I'm not arrogant enough to say that having a bit of a sanity check as I try to pull this off wouldn't be nice. But no to the rest. I'm still going where I want when I want. You do not have permission to speak to my teachers."

"You don't have a choice," Indira said softly.

"Yes, I do. I can drop out." They both paled at that. "I read all the legislation on the draft. They had a few people who flat out weren't capable of college, either via reading level, intelligence, or just any desire to deal with it. You can petition to add an extra two years and go in at a lower level and higher pay as they are out no money for education or board. They try to discourage it, but it is legal. But if I drop out now, even if I decide to go back, I'll have missed the date."

One corner of Alixant's mouth quirked up, but he kept a steady eye on me.

"I am required to work for the government for a decade after I graduate with whatever degree I want. I'd prefer to get my masters, then do something that will count as PhD level research for my doctorate. But I don't care enough to put up with any more interference in my life. That is all you. Tell them to take a flying leap."

I did care, but there was no way in the world I was going to let them wrap me up in their little dramas.

"You told them she'd say that," Indira murmured. "They didn't believe you."

Alixant shrugged, never looking away from me. "They see you as an impressionable young woman, overwhelmed by all the things that have happened. Desperate for guidance from your elders."

"What? Why would they think that?" I looked at them, confused. That made no sense, but then who knew how people saw me to begin with.

Alixant and Indira exchanged looks, and she lifted one elegant shoulder.

"You two provided reports on me! Oh, good grief. Why? To whom?" I had to fight not to jump up from my chair and start pacing. I wanted to tear my hair out.

How much more ridiculous can my life get? This is crazy.

"Oh, various people. I might have downplayed your stubbornness and independence. And played up your confusion and need for guidance," Alixant said, tilting his head to one side. "And we all play to multiple masters."

"Really? Indira won't tell me who is pulling her strings. Who's pulling yours?" It sounded like a question but really I demanded. I was so tired of these layers of mystery. I didn't have time for it.

"Cori, things aren't as black and white as you think they are," her voice soft as she glanced at Jo and Sable standing in the kitchen watching all of this with fascination. "You trade favors, get caught doing things you maybe shouldn't, and you make promises. Promises to people you don't double cross."

Indira looked old for the first time, old and tired. "You'll understand when you get to the other side of your draft and the choices you have to make. The deals you make."

I wanted to blurt out that I'd never do anything wrong, that I'd never make a deal that would cause me to hurt others. But Stevie's death hung in the back of my mind—always. What wouldn't I do or promise to find out why he died? To make sure no one else ever did that. To stop the person if Stevie really had been murdered like I thought.

"I get that. But that is your problem, not mine." A teeny part of me felt guilty, and I wanted to promise to be a good girl, but I clenched my jaw. This was my life. No one would tell me how to live it. "You tell whoever thinks they get to control me what I said. I'll check in and ask for help if I need it. And I probably will, but the rest. Not a chance."

"Your call." Alixant pulled up his phone and mine beeped a minute later. "There's my personal info and Indira's. If you need help, have a question, anything. Ask. And Cori?" He waited until I looked directly at him. "People will not be happy with your answer. Expect consequences. Maybe intimidation or pressure."

I shrugged, pretending indifference I didn't feel. "And if they go too far, I'll walk. I have nothing to lose."

Indira choked. "Nothing to lose? Have you seen the value of what his estate is?"

"Yes. But it's nothing but pipe dreams until it's mine, and I won't destroy myself for pipe dreams. And I absolutely won't let anyone tell me how to live." I kept my face blank, but my hand clenched the underside of my chair so hard it hurt. I wanted that house.

"I hope you always stay so innocent Cori. I'm not sure I ever was." The bitterness in Indira's voice slapped me. She rose and nodded to everyone. "Ladies. Cori and Jo, I'll see you in class. Good evening." She headed to the door, Alixant following.

"Be careful, Cori. Welcome to the real world." Those were his closing words as they stepped out and shut the door behind them.

Jo didn't say anything until she crossed over and locked it, for all the good it would do. I had the desire to get much stronger doors now.

"Did I just stand here and watch as you got obliquely threatened by the government and at least two different special interest groups? And warned that if you didn't go along with it, you would regret it?" Jo asked as she sank back down into a chair, her eyes wide and face paler than normal.

"That's how I read it."

"Cori, I was about ready to cry and tell them I'd do what they wanted. How did you sit there so calm and face them down?" Sable was shaking as she reached out to grasp Jo's hand on the top of the table.

I forced my hand to unclench from the bottom of the chair and brought it up. My knuckles were white and the indentations close to breaking the skin. "I wasn't." My voice broke and I closed my eyes as the emotions I'd locked down ripped through me. "But if I caved on this, the people who seem to control or at least influence them would think they could control me." I swallowed and looked at Jo. "Do you remember reading that fantasy series back in high school, where everyone died except the people who had blackmail material on everyone? They lived until the people they controlled finally snapped and killed them? All with swords and magic going over generations?"

Jo nodded and Sable did too. The series had been wildly popular, with magical beings, not just magic users. Set in a time where swords and chariots were the height of technology.

I sighed, poking at the remains of my fajita. "I get the very bad feeling that might be closer to reality than I had thought. I think there are a lot of people in power who read and believed in Machiavelli's *The Prince*. And I'm starting to think we need to be reading Sun Tzu's *The Art of War*."

We sat staring at each other. College didn't seem so much as a steppingstone to our adult lives, but a minefield full of traps. I forced down the swallow and looked at Sable. "You're a junior. Have you seen any hints of this or something? Are there really people like that?" I didn't know if I was begging her to tell me it wasn't true if it was. Jo turned to look at her too.

Sable frowned and shook her head, starting to answer, then she stopped, her mouth snapping shut. Her brows drew together, and I saw Jo's mouth twitch. I couldn't blame her, Sable was the image of cute with her lips pursed and brows drawn together.

"You know, I had a meeting with a group, one of the mage societies scheduled for the Monday after the game." She didn't need to specify which game, for us it all had an immovable importance. "Obviously it was canceled, and I just never re-scheduled it." Her teeth bit into her lower lip and I elbowed Jo in the ribs as she had that look in her eyes.

"You're predictable. Quit it, this is important."

Jo laughed. "Sorry. She's just so damn cute."

Sable blushed and gave Jo a look. Jo settled back, dropping the act, but it had relieved the tensions like she'd hoped.

That woman. Whatever am I going to do with her?

~Love her and keep her close,~ Carelian suggested. Since neither Jo nor Sable reacted, I figured he had said that only to me. He was winding around my legs and I bent over and picked him up.

"Always," I murmured. He butted against my hand, purring softly. "So what about this society?"

Sable shook her head. "I didn't get approached until I had passed my Magical Applications class. That is the one where you specialize in your minor and prove you can do all spells in your strongest branches. I've heard rumbles about them. You won't hear much until you get more magic under your belt."

"So what makes you think these groups have anything to do with what Cori was talking about? I thought they were just like sororities or extracurricular clubs. You know, socialize and network."

"They are, but," Sable shook her head, looking at me hard. "Now I don't know if I'm seeing conspiracy theories everywhere, but here is what I've heard. I don't know anything as I never really talked to them." She pulled her hand away from

Jo's and started fiddling with making a fajita as she talked. "Word is, you get in with the right one and they can make your career. Get you a comfy draft assignment, make sure you live in the part of the country you want, and afterward get you in with suitable companies that will appreciate your skills and pay well for them. Some alumni, heck most of the alumni I'm aware of are rich. And I've heard one or two of the mages going for master's or doctorates mention that if you had a problem they could make it go away."

"A problem? Like what?" I asked, feeling sick to my stomach.

Sable shrugged, looking decidedly uncomfortable. "From what they'd been talking about I guessed a drug charge or maybe drunk driving."

"But it could be more. Like a felony?" Jo asked.

"I'd think so. I know their parties are supposed to be impressive and people vie to get invited. I never cared much, but other people."

"Like Daniela?" I suggested. I'd met the girl once and had no desire to meet her again. Spoiled and entitled didn't begin to cover it. Even though she was only a sophomore. Her being a member of Purity kinda felt like an excuse to me, but what did I know.

"So, it starts with small, petty things, they do favors for you, collect dirt, and then they own you when you get to be Indira and Steven's age?" Jo mused, leaning back. She looked rather like I felt, green and vaguely nauseous.

"What are you going to do Cori? You can't fight groups like that."

"Fight?" My eyes widened. "I'm not going to fight, I'm just going to ignore them. Short of them putting me in prison, they can't make me do anything. There is a very valid reason why most mages are tried instantly and for any major crime their death sentence is immediate."

They both nodded and I petted Carelian. "I will get my degree and try very hard to avoid giving anyone a reason to think I owe them anything."

"Yeah. I think I'll graduate and work on my masters without aid from any of these groups," Sable muttered, though she looked much more worried about that idea. More stuff I didn't know. Oh well. One day at a time. That was all I could handle right now.

Chapter 8

Mentoring still happens in US culture, but it is much more prevalent in European and Asian cultures. Here it is more about having a favorite uncle or aunt to ask questions of. In other countries it can be as serious as an apprenticeship or selling future favors. More than one gang or organization uses this to get mages under their influence and owing them after the draft. ~Magic Explained.

ORDER

The rest of the week, even though I walked around with a hair trigger, nothing happened. I had classes, did homework, helped Sable move her stuff in. It didn't feel any different than the first two weeks did, though I was more fluent with the schedule and not feeling lost anymore.

I'd agreed to meet Alixant and Indira for lunches on Fridays as my weekly check in. That part still annoyed me, but I had questions on some reading assignments, so I figured I'd ask them the questions. Might as well make them do me some good, besides buying me lunch.

I walked down the street with Carelian investigating the foliage as we headed to the all you could eat Korean BBQ restaurant we were meeting Indira and Alixant at. It would take me about another ten minutes, but I enjoyed the walk. GA MageTech was part of the Georgia Tech College campus, which was huge, in downtown Atlanta. It incorporated multiple blocks and included the student apartments, dorms, restaurants, stores, and everything else. While there were trees and grass around this area there were others with busy road still made me nervous about his roaming around. We'd had extensive discussions about cars and the road. I think the roadkill we found convinced him of how dangerous cars could be.

I walked and tried to think about the paper I needed to write this weekend, but I kept looking behind me. It felt like someone was watching me. No one seemed to pay any attention to me, and I kept spinning around trying to catch someone. But there was nothing.

"Carelian, do you sense anything? Is someone following me? I don't see anyone."

~No human follows. I follow squirrel,~ he replied, distracted. I rolled my eyes, walking backwards to see his long tail racing up a tree. He hadn't killed one yet that I knew of. And I preferred to keep it that way. His pet store mice were bad enough. I spun back around and slammed into someone. This time I fell to the ground with a whoosh of breath.

"I am so sorry. I wasn't look-" I broke off as I saw Bernard Smythe glowering down at me. He had a good foot of height on me, not to mention close to sixty pounds, so the fact that I went toppling didn't surprise me.

"Miss I'm So Important. Too full of yourself to look where you're going?" He sneered down at me. Still stunned from the sudden impact with the ground, I had to catch my breath before I could even think about responding. "Just for your information, Miss Munroe, I have no intention of sharing your progress, grades, or anything else with the two merlins you seem to have enraptured. Though I must give you credit for having two such powerful and diametrically opposed skill sets dancing to your tune. I can see there will be multiple clubs vying for your involvement once you prove your skill set. Even mine, unfortunately."

Carelian had come sprinting over to me and licked my face once before sitting beside me and looking up at Smythe, his tail still.

I'd noticed that with people he didn't like, Carelian tended to act more like an animal than a person. Around Jo, and Sable to some extent, he behaved more like a small kid. But with strangers or people he didn't approve of, he played up the part of obedient cat. Which really, even I knew should set off alarm bells. Cats are NEVER obedient.

"Excellent. Thank you, Professor Smythe." We weren't required to call professors that, but I'd found it made them feel better if they thought you respected them. I stood and brushed myself off, watching him from the corner of my eye. The impact had driven textbooks into my back which hurt. Why couldn't everything be eBooks? Then I'd just need a large tablet and an e-reader.

He seemed a bit less put out as I stood. "Good? Weren't you the one that asked for that?"

"Absolutely not. My grades are my business and only mine. I don't authorize anyone to share how I am doing. So thank you for that on my behalf. I will address it with the parties concerned. I am sorry about running into you, I was a bit distracted." And trying to figure out if he had been the person watching me. My ability to guess where someone was just sucked. It wasn't like I was used to people following me.

"Oh. Well, yes. If that's all? I have office hours to attend to." He brushed by, but maybe not as abruptly as he might have done before.

Honey, not vinegar.

"Professor?"

He paused and glanced back at me, his eyebrow raised. "Yes?"

"What club do you belong to, if I might ask?"

Bernard frowned and then his face cleared. "Oh yes. You came in at winter, so you didn't get an opportunity to attend their welcome brunch hosted for all incoming mages." He tapped a small pin on his messenger bag, one I hadn't even noticed as it was a dark reddish brown, almost the same color as the bag. "I belong to Builders. Their society favors Pattern branch. You'll find all the groups have different specialties. They have a listing in the clubs section of the student union. You should go check them out. I'm sure all of them," his eyes flicked to my temple and he snorted, "well most of them, would be delighted to tell you all about their benefits."

"Thank you. I'm sure I will. Afternoon, Professor."

He gave me one more nod before striding away at a quick pace. I couldn't blame him, I was pretty sure his office hours started in ten minutes and even at a decent pace it was fifteen minutes away. But now I had something else to address. I'd said no to sharing my grades and apparently that hadn't been heeded.

"Come on, Carelian. I now have a bone to pick with two merlins." He came over and I snapped the leash back on. If nothing else, between the walking and my book bag, I was getting in shape faster than I expected.

I picked up my pace, headed to the Korean BBQ place, my annoyance overriding the desire for meat. Since I'd been using my magic consciously, I'd figured out why I rarely gained weight and now that I was, I knew how to burn it off. Either way, meat I wasn't paying for sounded good. Plus, they had a special menu for familiars and Carelian wanted to try it.

They were standing outside talking as I walked up. Indira in her normal slacks and silk blouse that hugged all her curves, but Alixant surprisingly was in tight-fitting jeans and a sweater in a deep green that looked good on him. I smirked as I recognized her seduction body language and wondered if she'd get him and how exactly she wanted him.

"Was there something about 'no' that wasn't clear to either of you?"

They both froze—I guess they hadn't seen me approach—and they turned to look at me. "What?" Indira finally asked as I stood there with my hands on my hips. Carelian pulled to go investigate something, and I had to move to not fall over. He was the epitome of curiosity. Jo had ordered him a special basket for her motorcycle so he could ride up to Rockway. It should be here next week, and she'd managed to keep it a surprise from him. I couldn't wait to see his reaction.

"What part of my 'no I will not provide access to my teachers or my grades' was unclear?" I didn't soften my stance at all, chanting my inner mantra to be strong.

"None of it. Why?" Alixant asked slowly, eyeing me like I might snap and bite him. Which I'd never do. I knew how much bacteria people carried on their skin. Ick.

"Then why did I have a professor inform me he will not be providing access to any merlins, and he was well aware of who you are?" I didn't move, watching.

"Goddamn idiots," Alixant muttered and Indira rubbed her temples with both hands. "I see why you mentioned she caused you so many headaches. What is it about her that brings complications?"

"I have no idea," Indira said, her eyes closed as she rubbed.

I almost smirked, Alixant sounded so put upon, but I didn't and instead kept with giving them my best glare.

"Cori, we passed that up the food chain. Either someone didn't listen and sent out the communication or they had done it prior to us even meeting with you. Trust me, they are all having conniptions about you refusing their suggestions." Alixant shrugged.

"You mean orders. Fine. Ms. Humbert, I do not give my permission for you to discuss my standing, grades, or performance in class with anyone if I am not present or provide my permission to do so."

Indira had straightened up. "So noted," her voice dry. "Does that mean you're done with us for the day?"

"No." This time I smirked, and I swore I could hear Carelian snickering in my head. "I want lunch, Carelian wants lunch, and I had a few questions and challenges I wanted to go over with you about getting my degree this fast."

They both looked at me and I resisted the urge to bop their noses. They just looked that surprised.

"You're going to try to graduate by next June?" Her voice slow as she looked at me.

"Yes. I want this. But I'm doing it on my terms, no one else's." A bit of stress fled them, and I narrowed my eyes.

Just how much pressure are they under?

"That is good to hear. But one word of warning, anything you tell us will be passed on. We don't have a lot of choice in that." Alixant held open the door for us to enter.

I mulled that over as I followed them to our table and let Carelian out into the special familiar seating area. Basically, a booster seat with a small screen guard on the table where a flat bowl waited. I guess other types of familiars must be messier eaters. Carelian was so neat he made me look like someone who played with their food.

Once we were seated and the grill heated up, I directed my attention to them. "Whose side are you on?"

Alixant shrugged. "The government's, I guess."

"My own," replied Indira. "Though I have people I owe to the point that my preferences are not always what I act on."

Taking a shot in the dark—I'd been researching the societies—I asked, "And how much is the Nyx society having input on your actions?"

She nodded her head to me. "More than I'd like."

I started to ask a question then paused. They'd have to share whatever I asked and they said, so if I asked about if I should join a society by definition she had no choice but to answer yes, which told me more than anything else.

"Do you belong to one, Alixant?"

"Yes, but at this point my career and most of the debts I owe are all wrapped up in the government. I'm at the follow orders point. But I joined Emrys, as most merlins do. And also Builders. They are more interested in creating a fascinating structure than changing anything."

I caught the undertones to what he said and felt like I needed to dive into more conspiracy theories. "But you could quit?" I asked, not a hundred percent sure he could.

"My job? I could. But with my skill set and degrees I'm not sure what else I'd do at this point. Besides, the government gives a damn good pension. As for the societies, yes, I could." He stressed "I" indicating that he didn't have anyone with something over him.

Indira snorted delicately. "Tell her the rest. That your job could make it very unpleasant for you if you quit before you reach retirement and since you don't have people who owe you in the societies, you don't have much ability to swing things your way."

We fell silent as the server got us started and laid down warm, uncooked strips of beef for Carelian, who extended his claws and tore them into pieces before holding them up to his mouth.

"Oh dear. He has opposable thumbs," Indira whispered.

The blasted cat winked at them and continued to gorge himself on the beef.

"Yes, he does," I muttered, giving him a look. The little rascal had been waiting for a chance to show off like that. Oh well. At least I didn't have to worry about him getting into things that might hurt him. Into things we didn't want him in? That was a different matter.

Once the meat was grilling, and the server left, I looked at Alixant thinking things over. Trying to figure out how to phrase the question. Indira beat me to it.

"There are good and bad things about the societies. You just need to be smart enough to only reap the good and never give them something over you. No matter what, join the House of Emrys. It's both the most powerful from a net-working perspective and the least likely to be eager to use you. Their long-term goals usually involve not being in the limelight. And remember, most societies are global, though Asia, Africa, and Australia have a few unique to them. I think that's all that is best said about them."

I nodded and pulled out a book. "I have two courses that aren't going to be offered per the school schedule before my time limit is up and I have a question about why fire and water are actually different branches when it comes to ice."

We spent the rest of dinner talking about stuff that meant a lot to me and would have, I hoped, little value to any of the people pulling their strings.

SPIRIT

I had signed up for on-call work on the weekends, and one of the local companies had pulled me in. I worked two twelve-hour shifts Saturday and Sunday. This would probably be my lightest semester until I had my degree. I struggled to line up four classes and three independent studies over the summer, which meant my ability to work would only be on the breaks between semesters. It also meant I spent a lot of time at the library researching stuff not available online and when I returned home I, like Jo and Sable, had my head down doing homework.

Sable finished moving in while I was working. I felt guilty about that and leaving Carelian there to drive them crazy, but they had waved me off and by the time I came home Sunday, I could feel her presence there in the apartment. It fit and provided a balance to my almost obsessive neatness and Jo's more haphazardness. Something I hadn't realized before we moved in together.

Tuesday, I had history in the morning, then biology lecture, a law lecture, and biology lab. The lab didn't get out until six. Bernard had assigned the homework of using your null magic to achieve something you couldn't with any of your other branches. With me that made it a bit more difficult, as most people always had the one in their class. The only nulls I had were either Fire and Water in Chaos or everything except Earth in Order. And I didn't know if null in another branch meant anything to me. Either way, Fire would be the easiest to test, as well as the most obvious. For the magic experiments I planned on doing, it would be safer to sit out on our tiny balcony.

Carelian loathed Magic Law. All he could do was mutter about power of the mighty and that laws were for the weak. That worried me a bit and I made a note to talk to Indira about it at our weekly meeting. Then the chem lab made his nose burn and it was just easier to leave him at home. Unfortunately, the chem labs and our apartments were about a mile apart, which had me headed back well after six. The evening had fallen faster than I had expected. As I walked back the lights along the path created bright spots in the gloom.

The feeling of being watched was back, usually when I was in the wider green areas, but Carelian would never tell me he sensed anyone. I just felt like there was a target on my back and it added stress I just didn't need.

I pushed it away and concentrated on what I needed to do and what deadlines I had. Things that were real and non-negotiable.

The footstep behind me, close and loud, when I'd been lost in thought startled me. A squeak escaped my mouth as I spun to see who had made the noise, my mind already racing with my heart. Two men in bland business suits were walking up to me. They had the short haircuts the government still preferred even with mages needing longer hair for their offerings. What worried me was the military precision in their gaits as they locked eyes on me.

I started to turn around to continue my walk, trying to believe they weren't here for me.

"Miss Munroe, we'd like to speak with you."

That dashed any hopes I might have had. Tension ratcheted through me as I turned to look at them. They halted a few feet away, but that didn't give me any warm feelings.

"About?" I missed having Carelian with me, but I was just as happy he wasn't here. One less thing to worry about.

"About your refusal to work with the mentors the government has picked out for you. It is in your best interest to do all you can to get that degree."

Anger sparked along the surface of my mind. My patience level with people messing with my life was getting lower every day, and now they were eating into my time for homework.

"You need better info."

"Excuse?" They looked at me with twin puzzled expressions and I narrowed my eyes.

"I am working with them. And I am trying. I'm just doing it on my terms."

The larger one, his skin seeming a shade darker in the gloom, took one step forward and I tensed to run.

"Miss Munroe, it would be to your advantage to work with the government in this situation. Your terms are not acceptable. If you choose otherwise, we can make things very unpleasant for you, your family, and your friends."

My jaw dropped. Had he really just pulled that level of melodramatic crap? That didn't happen in real life did it? "My family?" I sounded like an idiot.

"We know where your parents are. We can make their lives very unpleasant. Everyone's life will be better if you go along with our advice."

I didn't know whether to laugh or rage. This just made no sense.

"Miss Munroe, we are very serious." I giggled until he took another step forward into my personal space. With that action, my humor vanished.

"And so am I. Last warning. Back off, leave my friends alone, leave my family alone. Or I will file charges and I'll drop out so fast the school won't know what happened."

The man in my personal space smiled, and it chilled me to the bone.

"I see you might be difficult. Let me make sure you understand just how painful we can make this." His hand reached for me and I snapped.

I didn't know any fancy martial arts, I still barely knew how to use my magic. But there were two spells I knew intimately—Murphy's Curse and Lady Luck. I grabbed the offering, so tiny after a decade I didn't even notice, and threw Murphy over him and his friend while I wrapped Lady around me. My heart beating so hard I could feel it in my throat, I stepped back as he stepped forward.

My foot stepped on a rock and I stumbled, falling backwards as he swung, putting his entire body into it. I fell back out of the way as he tumbled forward, his foot slipping on what looked like goose crap and he landed directly on his elbow. I heard a crack even as I scrambled back to my feet. His other friend raced forward, eyes dark, and a bat, the school had multiple bat houses to help control insects, flew into his face. He recoiled with a shriek and tripped over his feet landing on his friend with a thud. There was a scream of pain and the scent of blood in the air.

With a few seconds to think I reached for Earth and with a desperate pull I opened the ground they lay on. That cost me more, a good inch of my hair from the bottom up. Something told me there were better ways to do this than brute force, but right now I didn't care. Fear drove me as a rumble vibrated through the earth and a sinkhole appeared beneath them.

Screams filled the air and I started hearing others react with yelling and the sound of footsteps.

Oh, Merlin, what did I do?

Not knowing what else to do, and he was supposed to be my mentor, I pulled out my phone and called Alixant. "Steve, I need you."

I heard the moment of shock at me using his name, but he didn't remark on it. "Where are you? What happened?"

"At the campus. Two men attacked me. I defended myself." My voice broke a bit as I looked at the two men lying at the bottom of the rather large sinkhole. It had to be ten feet across and at least twelve feet deep.

"Keep saying that. If anyone asks anything, say that. Share your location with me." His voice abrupt and I could hear the sound of keys jangling. It took me a minute to figure it out on the phone, but I managed to share my location.

"I'm eight minutes away, I'll make it in six. Say you have an advocate coming and don't leave the scene. Cori, I'm serious. You need to stay."

"I know the law. I'm not leaving." I didn't think I could walk, my legs were shaking so bad. People had called 911 and I could hear the odd whoop of the campus police sirens.

"Good. It'll be okay." He hung up and I didn't care. I just put the phone back in my pocket. The last thing I needed was spooked cops.

People started to arrive three minutes later, security, students, even a pizza delivery girl. Each of them looked down at the two men, then at me. No one spoke to me. I didn't know why, but every time they looked at me, they paled and stepped back. I pulled my coat a little tighter around me and wished I'd worn a hat, but the day had been pleasant so my hair was back in a ponytail, exposing my tattoos clearly. I wasn't willing to get close enough to see how badly I'd hurt them, much less have to fight with myself to try and help them.

"Ma'am, can you tell me what happened here?" I focused on the person speaking to me, a campus cop. He had a notebook out and kept flicking his flashlight between the men in the ground, my temple, and my eyes. Each time a stab of pain hit it eroded what little control I still maintained.

"They attacked me. I defended myself." The light hit my eyes and my temple again. I closed my eyes and breathed in deep.

Stay calm. Wait for Alixant.

~What wrong?~ Carelian's thoughts filled my mind and I started looking around for him.

"Are you on something? Why do you keep closing your eyes? And looking around? Was someone else with you?"

That feeling of being watched amplified and I could barely focus on the idiot with the light. I turned and looked but saw nothing.

"Carelian, stay with Jo. Don't come." I had no idea if he could hear me or not, but the last thing I needed was him here adding to the things I needed to try to keep track of.

"Ma'am, I need to ask you to come with me." That got my attention and I narrowed my focus on the idiot. He had to be about twenty years my senior, no mage tats, and nervous as all get out.

"If you'd quit flashing that light in my eyes, I wouldn't be flinching back and closing my eyes." It came out as a snarl and I didn't bother to moderate it. "They attacked me. I defended myself. I have an advocate on the way. I will not be going anywhere."

The man swallowed and I thought he would press the issue, but the blue lights of true first responders started up the road.

"Don't move. I'll be right back."

I didn't answer as he hurried away to wave them down. I just stood there. The whispers and pointing of the students and faculty that had shown up flowed over me like a river of thorns. They cut and scratched me but didn't cause enough damage individually to make reacting worth it.

I watched two firemen and two EMTs rush up, a gurney with them. They stopped at the hole, testing the ground and looking down.

"Huh. Idiots must have pissed off an Earth mage. Edge is stable. I'd give it a few inches, but we don't need to worry about it crumbling away. They did a good job of stabilizing it when they ripped open the hole." One of the firefighters was speaking and I listened with an odd feeling of detachment.

I did that. I hurt people. And I don't feel anything. Shouldn't I feel something?

"I'll put on a harness. Get some lights. If what I see is accurate, this will be interesting getting them out." They started discussing how to get down there and get them out. I listened more out of professional curiosity than anything else. Trying to think what I'd do differently, if I hadn't been the cause, of course.

"This way, officers. She's over here. She admits what she did." I looked in the direction of the voice of the campus police and sure enough he headed my way with two cops in tow. At least neither of them was detective Stone. That meant it couldn't be that bad, right?

"Here she is. She did it." The man stood, chest puffed out, as if he had gone through great effort to catch me.

"They attacked me. I defended myself. I have an advocate on the way," I repeated, already royally tired of the phrases no matter how important they were.

"Those two men attacked you?" one of the cops asked as he wandered over to the hole and peered in. The shadows and flashing lights made everything hard to make out, but he seemed a little older than me. His partner, a woman, had to be Marisol's age, so pretty old. She stood looking at me, eyes narrowed, pale skin all but glowing in the flashing lights.

I just nodded, not wanting to say anything else.

"And why would two men dressed in business suits attack you? They don't look like typical robbers or rapists," the male cop drawled slowly. "They look like upstanding citizens."

That comment got under my skin—I hated being called out on rape calls and seeing the victims. For the first time in a very long time, I delighted in the existence my magic. It ensured I'd kill anyone before they raped me.

"I didn't realize there was a type to rapists. Seems to me they look like politicians. I've read an awful lot of news stories about politicians being found guilty of rape. Or do they need to be poor and bedraggled to rape someone? Huh, guess that means all the college girls getting raped by classmates must be mistaken?" The venom in my voice should have torn the skin off his bones.

"Attitude and mouth," the female cop said in a mild way. "A bad combination in someone at the scene of a violent crime. Though I can't say I disagree about your comments. After all, some rapists wear blue." Her look skewered the younger male cop and even under the flashing lights I could see him pale and flush.

"Ma'am, you're under arrest for—" he started as he walked back towards me, reaching for handcuffs. I felt my annoyance get chased away by fear and a slowly bubbling rage.

"Yes. I'd like to hear exactly what she is under arrest for." Alixant's voice had never sounded so sweet to my ears as he walked up dressed in jeans and a polo shirt. The fact that I was absolutely delighted to see him told me how scared I'd been. Even at the stadium I hadn't been as worried.

And what does that say about me? Monsters are less scary than humans?

"And you are?" the female cop said, squaring to face Alixant, her eyes flicking over him and hitting his temple.

"Merlin Steven Alixant. Her advocate." He used the words like stones, the impact creating waves. I admired his ability to do that.

The woman turned her eyes on me. "Do you agree to him as your advocate?"

"Yes," I answered immediately. I had no desire to figure this out on my own.

"She is under arrest for attacking those two men with magic," the younger one blustered.

Merlin, had I been that stupid? How did Samuel stand me?

"Really?" Alixant walked over to the hole where the firefighters had extricated one of the men. This was the man who'd fallen on top of his comrade, not the one who had tried to attack me. He groaned a bit, but I didn't see anything obviously wrong. Granted, I stood about eight feet away and with the constantly changing light I could be wrong. "Did that young merlin attack you?" Alixant asked him. His words had steel to them I didn't expect.

The man looked at Alixant for a long time, then glanced over at me. I couldn't tell his expression from there, but I saw his body sag a little. "No. We wanted to talk to her. We didn't think about how approaching a young woman at night in the park would look. I believe we might have made her think we meant her harm and she reacted in fear. She defended herself." Those last words had an aura of bitterness to them that you could taste.

"And will your companion back you up?"

The man turned to look into the hole and winced. "When he's conscious again, yes."

"Excellent. Officers," Alixant turned to face them. "As you can see, there was no crime here, just a young woman protecting herself. Though," he paused and turned back to the man, "I am curious exactly what you wanted to discuss with her."

The man swallowed, looking back and forth between Alixant and me. "Just concerned about some of the choices she was making. We'll let our employers know she is very sure of her course."

"That would be wise. And please remind people that neither I nor Ms. Humbert take our job of mentor lightly."

I looked at Alixant funny as he stressed that last word. The man nodded and Alixant walked back to us.

Chapter 10

We know that familiars, while always animals (reptiles and other creatures included in that category) they are never Earth animals. There is always something odd about them that makes them not quite comparable to Earth animals besides their intelligence. While it is understandable no mage will allow experiments to be done on their familiar, it is odd that no familiar body, even after the death of the mage or reported death of the familiar, has ever been found. ~ Magic Explained

CHAOS

Twenty minutes later, Alixant drove me back to my apartment. I didn't protest. Exhaustion and guilt weighed on me like a cloak of mud.

"Thanks," I muttered as he parked in front of the building.

"I'm glad you called. Stuff like that is why I agreed to be your mentor."

I stopped as I pulled up my backpack to climb out. "What exactly does being a mentor mean? I thought it was just a fiction for the government to stick their nose in."

"It is and it isn't. Technically, for us to be your true mentors you would sign a contract with us. Think of it as us agreeing to let you be our apprentice. In the old term of the word where we would teach you a trade. It still has weight, and when you get out of college you might want to look for a mentor to help you navigate the draft, get a job, and learn how to do the really fun things with your magic."

"And what, traditionally, would you get out of it?" My ability to trust had been shattered long ago and everything I was learning lately had not improved it.

"A protégé, a spouse, a son or daughter-in-law more often than you would think, another link to tug on if things go wrong, and someone to make sure what I discover is passed on." He didn't dissemble, but he also didn't look at me.

"And what are you hoping for?" I had to force the words out of my throat. None of the ideas appealed to me at a base level. Though I could see why protégé might be nice.

"Honestly? You seem to be in the epicenter of trouble every time. Right now, my goal is to get you as well trained as possible so maybe when the shit hits the fan you have the skills to deal with it."

His brutal honesty scared me more than anything else I'd ever heard. "You think there'll be more?"

"Cori, I'm pretty damn sure that by the time you die, there will have been multiple books written about your exploits. I'd just like you to die of old age and not from one of those exploits. Now git. My dinner will be stone cold by now."

I climbed out of the car and lugged my bag up the stairs, the assurance in his voice weighing on me more than the books ever could have. Between exhaustion, the fear his words created, and the books, I wanted to cry by the time I got to the door.

I hadn't managed to touch the handle before it flew open and three worried faces greeted me.

"Cor, where have you been. What happened? Get in here." All of that spilled out, I thought from Jo, but Sable was also saying things, so I wasn't sure. Jo grabbed me, pulled me in, and the door slammed shut as she hugged me.

I felt Sable pulling the backpack off as Carelian wound between my legs and cried until Jo released me and I bent to pick him up.

~Worried. Mine,~ was all I could get out of him as he purred like a train and burrowed into my arms.

"Sit, then tell us what happened," Jo ordered as Sable dragged me to the table and Jo grabbed a mug of tortilla soup, threw in a dollop of sour cream and then handed it to me. I wrapped my fingers around the mug. Carelian lay across my lap, refusing to move. He kept up the steady purr, his paws kneading my leg without claws. It felt safe and familiar, and I slumped backwards holding onto the mug for the heat and the scent of meat, cumin, and cilantro that drifted up.

"Spill Cori, you're killing me here," Jo protested as she sat on my other side, while Sable took a chair and faced me, her eyes just as worried as Jo's.

Taking a spoonful of the soup to give me the heat—I hadn't realized how cold I'd gotten standing out there answering questions—I talked. I explained the men, what they had said, and how I'd reacted. I knew my fear slipped through and I took more soup to keep my calm.

~Felt, heard you, too far. Not like being so far,~ Carelian muttered.

"I agree with him. I'm worried about you, Cori. What if they had arrested you?" Jo said, biting on her lip, brows furrowed.

I couldn't resist the laugh, bitter as it was. "Well then, either they'd be bailing me out, or they'd be making sure I failed. Which..." I trailed off staring at the wall. "Why beat me up? I mean, that's what I thought they were going to do. If I got badly hurt it'd do the same thing. Keep me from going to classes."

"Maybe just rough you up a little or make you really scared. Most people don't like pain and physical intimidation can be as effective as broken bones," Sable said, her words careful as she thought through it. "Most studies say women will do more to avoid the threat of violence than the actual pain itself. We are more likely to be wired that way. A man is the opposite. They tend to avoid the pain and lean into the threat."

Jo and I exchanged glances then looked at her and she blushed. "Psych minor, remember? While I'm getting my master's in environmental engineering, I have a psych minor to aid with it, and the magic minor in Water. You aren't the only overachiever, Cori," she teased.

"Wow, I'm starting to think I'm the slacker here," Jo said, but she frowned as she said it.

"You are dealing with dyslexia and still getting good grades. You already probably have an AA in car mechanics, so I think you're fine. I worked as a customer service rep for the phone company. I can program your phone, not much else," Sable said, making a face at her girlfriend.

I laughed and let the stress bleed off me.

"But Cori, what are you going to do?"

"Talk to Alixant and Indira. They need to deal with it." I paused. "Though I'm thinking maybe I do need to join the merlin society, if nothing else. They might provide some sort of buffer. "

"Can't hurt, but just remember, don't ask for anything. I think we all realize magic has a lot more hidden prices than they ever talk about," Jo said somberly. "I wonder why my parents never said anything about it."

"Have you asked?" I pointed out. "But also, they are only wizards. Maybe it makes a difference as to how powerful you are?"

"Point, but I'll ask this weekend. You sure you don't want to come up with us?"

"Three don't fit on your motorcycle," I pointed out. "And I'm not ready to get a car or a motorcycle. Go, enjoy. Bring me back food."

"Mami will complain she wants to see Carelian."

~Like Jo's malkin,~ Carelian commented. I frowned, unsure of the word as Jo laughed.

"And not just because she saves treats for you? I swear she saves all the sweetmeats for you. She spoils you."

~Am worth spoiling,~ he said, but his eyes were closed as he kneaded.

"Okay, next weekend. Not this, but next I'll go up. I want to talk to Laurel anyhow. We can rent a car and go up," I offered in between spoonfuls of soup.

"Deal. Now eat. I've got three chapters I need to listen to tonight. Ugh, never realized how slow people talk." She slumped backward on the couch, groaning. "It's going to take me forever."

Sable glanced at her. "Why don't you listen to it at time and a half, or double time?"

Jo jerked up straight, looked at Sable. "What? You can do that?"

I laughed, dropped off my too-thin jacket and headed to the deck with my notebook and a candle. I had experimentation to do. I had planned on leaving Carelian inside, but he gave me no choice, darting out the second I opened the door and glaring at me.

"Okay, okay. You could have just asked."

He said nothing, instead jumped up on one of the two chairs we had out there and settled into the inscrutable cat pose, tail wrapped around him.

I rolled my eyes and set down the supplies. For a minute I just sat there in the night air, letting the coldness settle into me. If this was my new life, I needed to get a handle on it. And learn to use my magic faster and more accurately. I knew I'd been wasteful with the Earth, but I hadn't had time to think of a better way. I needed to start.

Do I want to live my life always on edge, always waiting to be attacked?

I mulled that over for a long time, looking at the lights of the other apartments around us. Life and excitement, people living and laughing. I wanted that.

I guess that's the key. I want to live, and live the way I want. It's looking like the price to do that means learning how to make sure I'm safe at all times.

Something in me withered as I came to that decision, but I let it go. I'd give up a lot more to be able to live my life.

"Okay, since you have decided to be my audience, I'm going to talk." I cast a look at Carelian, who didn't even flick an ear in my direction. "Humph. Fine. Fire, a null for me. It should be very difficult to light the wick. Taking twice or more what a Fire mage would take."

I set the candle down and separated out ten strands of hair, each about twelve inches long. Way more than I should need. I focused on remembering everything we'd been learning about conservation of effort and how fire feeds itself.

Start with the smallest bit and let it grow.

I focused on the wick of the candle and pushed out, willing the molecules at the very top to speed up, to burst into flame.

A flicker of question and my assent and the wick almost exploded into a brilliant white flame, quickly settling back into yellow orange.

I yanked back, surprised at the size and quickness and then I remembered the offering and looked. Half of one strand had been taken. Less than most of those with Fire as pale.

"That shouldn't have happened," I muttered into the empty balcony.

~Powerful quean. My quean.~

I gave him a dark look. "One of these days you'll have to explain exactly what a quean is."

He flicked an ear at me, and I swear he smirked. "You, Jo, Sable. Queans. Powerful queans."

"That tells me nothing other than gender and mage," I protested, feeling more than a bit frustrated.

Instead of responding, he just started grooming his paw, as if it mattered if a single strand of fur was out of place. Leaving me with no more information than what I'd started out with.

All I have are questions. What should I do and what the heck does this all mean? And should I tell anyone about how easy a null branch is?

That question nagged at me. Could I trust anyone? I knew I could trust Jo. But she had as little information as I did. Dare I trust either Alixant or Sable? I resisted the desire to scream. I packed up and headed back in, Carelian following me back into the warmth of our apartment.

Chapter 11

R&D position available working with NASA, doctorate in Theoretical physics preferred, merlin rank bonus applied. ~ Job listing on job board.

ORDER

The next day as I walked out of the apartment headed for my nine A.M. Magic Basics class, Alixant stood at the bottom of the stairs. I paused, Carelian sticking his head out of the bag. He'd refused to let me leave without him.

"Why are you here?"

"Figured you'd like to know what Indira and I found out last night. As well as to escort you to class. We have a vested interest in keeping you healthy and hale."

"But not happy?"

"That is more up to you than us, but we can try to make sure things aren't making you unhappy."

"Merlin's sake. You make me sound like a fragile flower that can't be exposed to the harsh outdoors," I snapped as I turned and headed towards my class. I had almost an hour, but it would take me a good twenty to walk it.

"Many things I might call you. Fragile flower isn't one of them," he remarked as he walked with me.

"So, you have until I get to class, your time." I'd woken up cranky and the knowledge that I didn't know if I could trust him made me snappier than I should have been, but he didn't react.

"We called our contacts and explained to them in detail what you wanted as well as the consequences if you were harassed again. We then explained exactly what you did with the Murphy's Curse, and pointed out that if you could do so much damage with a spell most regard as a minor annoyance, did they really want you to regard them as a threat?"

"What do you mean so much damage?" I figured I'd broken his arm, but not much more. And the other guy hadn't really been injured that I'd seen. They had isolated me, so I never saw the other man.

He looked at me, and I thought I detected surprise in that look, but he had an excellent poker face. "I thought you knew."

"Knew what?"

"You mean you didn't plan on that level of injury?"

"What level of injury?" My stress was climbing. Had I killed them? That was never the plan, I just wanted them to back off, go away, not get seriously injured.

"Interesting. Per the hospital, and yes, they released the data to me because of the attack, even if you didn't report it. It is still logged as a suspected assault and as a member of the FBI I can see medical data."

I found it amusing he forestalled my HIPPA argument before it could start. "You still haven't answered my question." At this point grabbing him and shaking him until he answered sounded like an excellent idea.

He smirked at me.

Jerk.

"The man who attacked you, and he also said they scared you, broke his elbow in three places. Then when the other guy landed on him, his scapula cracked as well as three ribs. The guy who held back fractured his collar bone trying to avoid landing on the first guy. Though we didn't realize it until he jumped up to help and it separated." I cringed listening to his recitation. I hadn't wanted to hurt them badly, but I had wanted them to quit attacking.

"But the best part?" He sounded even more amused at this and I looked at him, waiting. I scratched Carelian's ears as we walked, noting he was paying as much attention to Alixant as I was. "Because they attacked you and verified that you were only protecting yourself, they, or their bosses at least, are liable for all the damage you did. It's amazing you were able to do that without ripping up any gas or water lines."

That possibility hadn't even occurred to me, and I swallowed as the idea registered. I really needed to practice more and get used to being in control of my magic.

"Thanks for telling me, I think." As we walked, I noticed more than one group of students that saw me coming—I guess Carelian was a bit obvious—moving out of our way before we could get near them. I could still hear the whispers as we walked by. "Was there anything else?"

Alixant frowned, looking at the students. "You sure you don't want protection? We can get someone to walk back and forth between classes."

"No. I'm fine. I don't need any protection. But I do need to get going." I stepped up my pace and all but ran into the building, Carelian protesting at being jostled. As this was the first class of the day in this room, my normal seat up at the back was empty and I gladly hid up there. Few people wanted to sit up that high anyhow, so it worked. I watched people come in and get seated, but the only person I really noticed was the guy from the coffee shop. His familiar, Arachena, stuck out from his hair and waved at me. I waved back, oddly grateful for the notice, but he didn't seem to notice me.

"Okay, who did their practice with their nulls?" Bernard asked after he got settled at the front of the class. Everyone raised their hands. "Excellent. Who managed to do something, anything with your null?" About half of the people dropped their hands. "Not bad. How many got the feeling they could have done something, but the offering amount was more than they were willing to risk?" Ten students raised their hands and he nodded. "That matches what we expect on breakdowns. Not everyone can use it, and even if you could, the cost might be higher than you can or want to pay. But you should play with your nulls and make sure you understand that you can use them."

With that he jumped into the lecture which today was about using science and your magic to achieve better results. In some ways it was a class to encourage you to specialize, but he had both the knowledge and the ability to make me seriously think about physics or chemistry as a major. What you could do if you really understood how atoms and ions worked together was amazing.

"Next week we'll go over the same aspects with biology. I know some of you are pre-med majors, so we'll have a doctor who's an archmage come in and talk and explain how he uses his abilities. The abilities and limitations." He rattled off homework, which I didn't worry about it as it was a few chapters on basic biology and I was well past it. I gathered up Carelian ready to head to the library and study before Chem lab at one.

"I'm headed to the library. You sure you don't want to go home before lab?" I asked Carelian in a soft voice. He only flicked an ear at me and waited for me to pick everything up. "Fine, but I'll be in the library for hours, you'll be horribly bored." The other students near me glanced my way and I saw multiple reactions out of the corner of my eye. I tried not to let the flinches or sneers affect me.

Rather than replying he just stood stood up so I could put him in the bag, groaning a bit at his weight.

I headed down the steps in the classroom, mapping out the path I needed to take in my head. There was a nearby park I could let Carelian hide in while in Chem lab.

"Miss Munroe, come here please?"

Professor Smythe's words paused me in my tracks, and I pivoted to walk over to him. "Yes?" There was probably too much wariness in my voice because he arched an eyebrow at me.

"I received notice that all prior requests to access your records have been rescinded." He didn't smirk but he somehow managed to sneer at me even as he spoke. "Which I found amusing."

I shrugged. "I never authorized it in the first place."

He gave me a long look. "Hmm. How did your test with your null area go? Which one did you choose?"

Panic locked me down for a second and I chose my words carefully. "I did some experiments with Fire as that is one of my nulls." One counted as some, right? Since that one freaked me out, I figured I'd stop there.

"Oh? And how did it work out? Were you able to achieve results?"

"I did manage to light the candle, which was what I'd wanted to do."

Bernard shrugged. "That is the obvious one. Most people choose it if they are null. The elemental magics are by far the most accessible of the branches." He paused, eyes narrowing as he looked at me. Did I scream guilty or something? It felt like people always knew when I was hiding something or un-comfortable. "How much was the offering?"

I shrugged, shifting the backpack. "Not what I expected, but not unmanageable."

"Huh. Okay. See you in the next class." He looked thought-ful and until I was ready to discuss what happened I didn't want to think about it.

I headed out before he could say anything more. I didn't know why being able to use a null bugged me so much. Okay, that was a lie. I did know. Common knowledge said that your null power was unusable, but so far Alixant told me different, the class told me different, and I'd proved it. But common knowledge kept tripping me up.

Okay, so I need to trust what I can test or verify. I need to stop thinking I know anything I haven't verified. But that means what else do I know that isn't right?

The library lay on the other side of the building that held Magic Basics, and this campus, like the rest of Atlanta, had construction going on constantly. I walked down the sidewalk near the scaffolding that had been put up. A quick glance told me they were working on repairing brickwork that the kudzu had wormed its way into.

Kudzu the consumer of everything.

I grinned as I walked by, amused by the thought. A creak and a bang had me jumping and moving before I'd even con-sciously registered what I'd heard. Years of things going wrong had created a very strong preservation reflex. With a cloud of dust and a clatter of metal and bricks that had me covering my ears, something hit the ground right about where I'd been standing. I waited for the air to clear, listening to people yell in alarm. Laying there was part of the scaffolding and a load of bricks. Even from here I could see the bolts were no longer in the holes they should have been in.

"Dang it," I muttered and scanned myself. Sure enough, there was a Murphy's Cloak draped around me. With a sigh, I dissipated it. I'd thought I'd quit doing that, but with everything going on I must have unconsciously recast it on myself. I'd done it for so long without thought that magic didn't ask for much in offerings. I wasn't sure what fueled it other than my magic, which went contrary to everything they were teaching us. Another thing to follow up on at some point.

I checked to make sure no one had been hurt, but it looked like I would have been the only person hit if I hadn't moved as fast as I did. Annoyed at myself, I glanced down at Carelian. "You okay?"

I got an ear flick as he stared up at the scaffolding. I followed his gaze, but other than upset workers I saw nothing.

"Come on, library." I continued my walk to the library, mentally working on the paper that would be due in about three weeks. Unlike Jo, I really did prefer to get things done before the deadline.

Chapter 12

While many organizations that serve the public hire mages, not all of them use them in the way you would expect. For example, NOAA (National Oceanic and Atmospheric Administration) employs Air mages to help chart and understand the way the atmosphere works. They do not, however, use them to cause weather events regardless of what conspiracy theorists suggest. ~ Magic Explained.

SPIRIT

At the library, my arms weighed down with the books I needed for the History of Magic paper, I headed to where I'd left Carelian watching a table for me. After that near miss, I'd brought him in with me for now. I slowed down as I approached, seeing another backpack and someone standing there.

I knew who it was, even without seeing the creature with too many legs perched on the table in front of Carelian. They looked for all the world like they were having a serious conversation.

"New friend?" I asked Carelian as I set my books down. "Arachena, isn't it?"

The thing, as I had no idea what it was besides a familiar, gave a weird hiss chirp and waved its two front legs. Now that I was closer, I could see it had twelve, six on each side instead of the normal six or eight legs I was used to seeing, and a body in four segments. Though I supposed the front two were something other than legs, maybe the equivalent of our arms. Either way, it was a whitish pink with blue rings around the joints. I only saw two eyes, but that didn't mean a thing. With her legs spread out she was bigger than a dinner plate, but curled up with only her two front legs waving she wasn't much bigger than a

"Arachena said it was okay for me to sit here. She said she wanted to talk to your cat." The voice spoke from beside me and I turned to see the mage from the coffee shop and classes. Brown hair, those strange amber eyes, pale skin, a bit overweight, and the evidence of bad acne as a teen still obvious on his face.

"Sure. Hi, I'm Cori," I said, sticking out my hand to him.

He gave me a long look, then shifting his own stack of books to his left arm, shook my hand. "Charles." His eyes went to my temple and I sighed.

"It isn't like I asked to be a freak. Really."

He looked back at me and grinned. The smile lit up his face and made him much more friendly and approachable. "You never do. It is a curse gifted upon those of us fated to be better or at least different."

He set his books down and I did the same, grabbing my notebook. "I could do with a bit less gifting thank you very much. Though I suppose my cat isn't too bad a benefit."

Carelian glared at me. He stood up and turned around, putting his lashing tail towards me. Arachena chittered and moved away from the tail, racing up the back of a chair so she was facing Carelian.

Charles snickered. "Nice to see you treat yours the way I do mine. Were you expecting to get one?"

"Ha. I wasn't expecting to emerge, much less all this." I waved my hand at the patchwork of colors on my temple. "While I'm not sure I'd give him up, still not sure it was or is worth it."

"I hear you. Not what I'd planned either."

With that, we both started opening history books, working in companionable silence, making notes and references.

I'd managed to outline my subject, focusing mostly on the Area 51 rips and their closure for two years as well as the change in emergence stats during that time. I'd hit up Siab to see if she could ask the OMO for any other information as they were one of the few organizations in the 1950s that had any emergence data. I thought there had to be other rips around the world—mostly stable ones—but that the governments weren't making them known. If I had to guess Siberia, Japan, and Australia.

But I'd leave that out of my paper. I had no proof and only a vague feeling or idea, and I didn't want to worry about it for now. And I wouldn't mention anything about people emerging again.

"Well, look here. Chunk has sunk to trying to get lesbians to take pity on him. I guess it's about the only people that would take someone like you," a saccharine sweet voice said. I looked up to see a girl with vibrant red hair and the pale pretty skin you read about in stories about Irish lasses. She even had the pale green eyes to go with it.

Charles had gone rigid at the words and laid down his pen very carefully. His familiar skittered over to him and up into his hair.

"Ugh, I can't believe you let that creature touch you, much less live in your hair. Who knows what it's doing in there? Shitting at least, maybe laying eggs? Gods, you'd be the next star on a reality tv show, 'Spiders Came Out of My Brain'." The mocking level in her voice took me back. I glanced at Charles who had the look of someone who contemplated how many buckets it would take to contain all her body parts.

It flickered away and instead of reacting to her, he looked at me. "Lesbian, huh?"

The glimpse of pleading supplanting the calculation on his face confused me, and it took me a second for my brain to get on track.

"Nah. I just live with them. I mean, when you live with women as awesome as those two are, who wouldn't be jealous?"

"True. I mean, at least a few guys on campus have mourned their loss from the dating pool," he replied, his inflection almost flat as he struggled to maintain the mocking, but I could tell he wasn't into it.

"I'm sorry, we haven't been introduced. I'm Cori. You are?" I turned and held my hand out to her, trying to take the attention off the poor guy who I could see retreating into himself.

She took a step back as if shit smeared my hand. "Ugh. I just can't believe Sable moved in with you. I mean, having a fling on the other side is one thing, but to actually move in with a proven lesbian and you." Her eyes glanced to my temple and she shuddered. She overacted, and the effect fell flat. I dropped my hand slowly. "You're a freak," she snarled. "No one should have that much power."

"I think Sable is much happier with us, Daniela." There wasn't anything else to say.

"I just felt so sorry for her." Her voice gave lie to the statement and a tone, discordant and harsh but oh so faint, chimed in my head. "She will never have eternal joy. She'll be thrown out of Merlin's realm after she dies because she didn't bear children."

The conversation about her came flooding back, the Purity beliefs that bloodline was everything. "Well, I guess that is stuff for us to worry about." I smiled and waited for her to leave.

"At least that's your choice," she sniffed and tossed her hair over her shoulder. "Poor Chunk here would only get a girl to sleep with him by drugging her. No one else would have him." Her sneer etched ugly lines into her face, marring her beauty.

I couldn't believe she had just said that. "Did you really just say he would have to drug and rape a girl to get sex?" I realized I was standing leaning towards her. She was only about 5'5" and svelte where I'd been putting on curves and muscle since Jo had dragged me to the gym all fall.

"Well no one would sleep with him willingly," she said, the sneer still on her face.

I turned to Charles, who had gone absolutely pale. "That qualifies as slander. If you want to go to the college board, I'll back you up. That is not something you say and, per the code of ethics we signed, can get her kicked out."

He blinked at me. "You would? You don't know me."

I gave him a hard look. "Have you ever drugged or raped anyone?"

"No!" This time I heard the gentle low tone of a crystal bell, so faint that if it wasn't for the quiet of the library I wouldn't have noticed.

~He tells the truth,~ Carelian's voice whispered in my head and I looked to see he had turned and was glaring at the girl.

I looked at her. "If I were you, I'd keep my mouth shut or I'll help him file charges."

Daniela had flushed a shade of red that made her look a bit like a tomato. "Both of you are freaks. You deserve each other," she spat then whirled, her hair whipping around her like a cloak, and stormed away.

"Dang, what's her problem?" I muttered sitting back down. Carelian came over for a pet and I granted it.

"I made the mistake in sixth grade of beating her in the spelling bee and getting honors over her all through high school. I was the valedictorian. Not her. In retrospect I should have just flunked one of the tests. She's been like this my whole life. I figured after high school I'd get away from her and be done with it. But then this happened." He pointed to his temple, his smile bitter. Then it softened as Arachena stuck her head out. "And this." He smiled as he petted her. "And to make matters worse, I emerged as an archmage, she only emerged as a wizard in a family where most of them are archmages or merlins and over fifty percent have familiars. She was the escort for my orientation. At which point she made sure everyone knew I was a fat loser with a creepy fondness for bugs." His nails on his right hand dug into the hard wooden table even as he gently petted his familiar.

"Well, that's her problem. And seeing her, I get what you said the other night at the coffeehouse. I'm sorry. If you ever want to study or something, let me know." I ripped off a piece of paper from my notebook and scribbled my number down. "Besides, Carelian likes you, which says a lot."

He gave me a shy smile and I could see the intelligence in his eyes. "Arachena says the same. Thanks."

"Fudge. I gotta go. See you around." I scooped up my notes, dumped the books on the shelving cart and called to Carelian. "Come on. Dumping you in the park." He twitched his ear at me and I shrugged. "You really want to sit in chem lab for two hours?"

A tail lash and he leapt off the table and followed me out in typical cat fashion, darting this way and that to look at things, rub his muzzle on racks, and make me wait, holding the door for him.

"You're going to make me late," I scolded. He seemed unconcerned, though I managed to get him out the door. "The park is there." I pointed at the small area with trees, benches, and rolling grass. If I knew him, he'd be up a tree sleeping in fifteen minutes. After terrorizing various squirrels and birds, of course.

With a flick of his tail, which sounded like a whip cracking, he darted across the sidewalks and streaked up a tree. I laughed at the chorus of alarmed squawks as birds went flying out of the tree.

Picking up my pace, I headed to the lab to get prepped. Class might only be two hours, but it took thirty minutes or more to get ready for the experiments. By the time I left the lab I had the principals of testing various chemical compounds firmly in my head and I reeked of acetone.

~Quean!~ Carelian's voice slammed into me as I left the building. It was the first time I'd heard anything except amusement, pride, or contempt in his mental voice. I broke into a run, blessing Jo for her torture as I carried everything and still ran to the park.

"Stupid cat. Call animal control. It scratched me. It should be put down."

"Unnatural creatures, anything not of this Earth, should be killed on sight." A female voice hissed the words, but I heard lust in them more than fear.

I heard the words before I saw Carelian, and the three students surrounding him. He perched on the back of a bench, hissing, ears laid back, and tail coiled up by his side like a whip. What disturbed me the most were the smudges of dirt on his normally pristine fur, as well as the clods of dirt laying around him.

"What by Merlin's balls is going on here?" I snarled out the words and I felt my magic wrap around me, ready to attack.

"Oh look, one freak working with another," the boy sneered. The other two students were female.

I strode forward and Carelian leaped into my arms. He shook, though I had the feeling it was from rage, not fear.

"What exactly is going on?" I repeated even as I felt my emotions longing to strike at them.

"This thing was chasing squirrels. Torturing them. I knew it had to belong to the freak. Only a freak like you would have something this sadistic with her. They should have killed you when they realized what you are. You're too dangerous to live." The young man, though he acted like a spoiled teenager, stood with his arms on his hips glaring at me.

~My quean, they think funny, wrong,~ Carelian muttered as he snuggled into my arms.

"He is a familiar and is allowed here. And the penalty for attacking one is five years in prison. And I'm curious,"—I kept my voice mild, but I stepped forward with a snarl on my face—"if you think I'm so dangerous, why are you attacking my familiar?"

This time I thought very specifically about what I wanted to do, and I pulled on Fire. This time I felt a significant offering at least a half inch of my hair all the way around as I set the bench between us on fire. It burst into flames bright and hot white before fading back to orange. The students screamed and jumped back.

"As I see it, you're attacking a mage and a familiar, so I'm expected to protect myself. With deadly force if necessary." Their pale faces almost glowed in the light of the flames and they staggered back. "Getting on my bad side is stupid."

They looked at me. "You've made a mistake messing with us. We have powerful friends. You'll see soon enough." The male student yelled it as he shielded his face from the flames. "They will get what they want. Why not just give them what they want now?"

"Which is what? What do they want?"

He just gave me a smile that reminded me of a snarling dog and whirled and ran away. The other two girls followed him, casting glares back my direction. They left me standing there holding my familiar, though I saw a trail of blood from one girl's hand.

"You sure you're okay? They didn't hurt you, did they?"

Carelian didn't respond, just burrowed deeper into my arms.

"Okay, I'll carry you. Let's go home." I didn't want to let him go.

The heat of the fire reminded me and I snuffed it out, again with a fraction of the offering it should have taken. I suspected doing that would haunt me at some point, but for now I didn't care. It was the easiest way to get them to back off, but I needed to double down on how to use magic. How to protect myself and warn off others. School really was a jungle.

Chapter 13

By 1860, more and more mages appeared, and the United States government grappled with the changing world. Acceptance of magic would not occur until the mid-1900s. In 1870, forty years after the Trail of Tears, the House of Representatives was approached by a group of American Indians. Records are sketchy as to the various tribes they represented, but notes recorded five men and three women. They obtained a sealed hearing with the current congressmen. When they left, the five reservations labeled as the American Indian Nation had been granted total autonomy from the US and a pledge that the US government would never invade their territories. The records of that hearing are sealed until the year 2200. Many have tried to open the sealed book over the remaining years, but it still refuses to open. No memoirs about that hearing have ever been shared with the public. ~ History of Magic

CHAOS

Life settled down a bit, though it seemed like my stress was putting Murphy's cloak on me every time I turned around. I got into the habit of just checking every time I went outside, and at least half the time there it was.

Carelian was growing so fast, but I consoled myself knowing that packing him around added to my stamina and growing made him better able to protect himself. It seemed like since that incident with the bench he'd been growing faster and eating more than the months previously. Where he'd started out as a half-pound kitten, he now was the size of cocker spaniel, and I knew in another week or so, I'd have to have him on a harness as I wouldn't be able to pack him around.

With Carelian, I never knew if he'd reply or not. He seemed always distracted, and most of my comments were met with flicked ears or tail. Though he had no issue letting any of the three of us know he expected some of what we were eating. While obviously a carnivore, he liked some vegetables and fruits, and was addicted to whipped cream. At least we didn't need to worry about him eating chocolate because he just turned his nose up at it.

No one had said anything about the destroyed bench, and it had been three weeks. I didn't know if that was a good or a bad thing, so I just kept quiet about it. I had more than enough to worry about with classwork.

I loved the magic classes, even if I shouldn't be able to use as many things as I could. But learning just what I could do fascinated me. The magic lab that Indira taught continued to stretch me, and I was getting better at figuring out how to use my magic and understanding how I could kill myself by being stupid.

I headed down the street to my weekly meeting with my mentors, looking forward to the food and exhausted by carrying the cat and the bag.

"I think we need to switch to the harness full time. You're getting too big to carry anymore."

~Leash?~

"Yes, leash. And harness. That way you can walk beside me, and maybe even carry some of your own supplies when you get bigger."

~No leash,~ he muttered.

"Yes, leash. We talked about this. While you are a familiar and intelligent, a leash makes people feel better and keeps them from trying to take you. You know there isn't an option. Remember, you find taking your mages on walks humorous."

He changed moods and decisions like a teenage girl somedays. For a cat from another plane of existence, he had the art of pouting down to a science. And now he was sulking.

"Don't care. I can't keep carrying you." I glanced at the walk signal and started to cross the street.

"Lady, look out!" A hand grabbed my arm and yanked me back off the street and I stumbled against the curb as a car sped by. "Shit, he almost hit you. You okay?"

A man hovered near me, his face pale, and I took a shaky breath as he steadied me. "Yeah. Did I walk in front of him?"

"No. The idiot ran a red light. You sure you're okay?"

I checked for Murphy's Curse, but nothing was there. "Yeah. People need to pay attention. Thanks."

"No problem. Be careful," he said. We waited in silence until the walk signal came up again, then, both of us checking both ways, we crossed the street. He nodded once to me and left and I headed down the street, paying way more attention to my surroundings and working on getting my heart under control from the adrenaline spike.

The restaurant we were meeting in offered Indian food, which I'd never tried, so it was something that made me pick up my steps. I approached the door and saw Indira and Alixant talking. As I neared, he bent over and kissed her lips gently. I paused to take that in.

"You're dating now? Is that because of me or pressure from your other interest groups?"

Alixant turned to look at me. "No. We're dating because she's sexy, we're both single, and for some reason she likes me. Is that an issue?"

I shrugged. "I don't care who either of you date. I was just wondering if it is something they get to influence also."

"No."

"Sometimes," said Indira.

Alixant glanced at her and she shrugged. "Not you, but..."

"Me," I said, my voice flat.

"Yes," she admitted looking at me, but there wasn't any shame. "I had no reason not to try. It didn't work and I told them so."

"Huh. I guess there is more to this than what I've heard." Before Alixant could continue, they called his name and we went into the restaurant. Like most places they had a separate area for those with service animals or familiars. Once we were seated, I let Indira order for me as I had no clue what I would or wouldn't like.

When the server left, I looked at them. "So, willing to say who asked or why you were asked to seduce me?"

She'd never been willing to tell me before now, but maybe with Alixant here she'd spill.

"It really isn't that big of a deal. Sex is a straightforward way to control people and people want to control you," she said, as if she was talking about the weather. "I owed them, so when they asked me to try, I agreed. It didn't work. If it had, well, we would have seen where it went."

"That is extremely creepy and wrong on so many levels. Why in the world should I trust you? And I thought teachers weren't allowed to date students." Somehow, I kept my tone level and not shriek like I wanted to.

"If it was a genuine relationship, I would have quit my job and another one would have been found for me."

Alixant shrugged. "Sounds about right. The government and Builders don't lean towards that level of manipulation, but I've seen it. Lots of students do stupid things with their magic when they are learning. Or do stupid things period, and the society or a mentor bails you out. You then owe them. I know of one mage who is basically a slave to his mentor because the mentor sacrificed three toes and two pinkies to save his life. I'm not sure I would have been willing to do that."

The calm, logical reaction from both of them shook me to the core and even the naan and plates of food that arrived didn't do anything to chase the chill away.

"So how or why should I trust you?" I blurted the second the waitress had left.

They glanced at each other and I started shredding a piece of naan, needing something to do with my hands.

"Maybe we should talk about stupid things first," Alixant said. "I heard you set a bench on fire. It burst into white flame and basically burned down to ash, even the metal holding it melted. But interestingly, I don't see a large amount of your hair missing. How much did you offer to get a null branch to work that spectacularly for you?" he inquired, pinning me with his stare. Indira turned to focus on me too and I gritted my teeth.

"Enough to do what I needed." I evaded the question and took a mouthful of my food. I had no idea what she'd ordered, but the flavors burst across my mouth, distracting me.

"Yes. But for that level of fire that fast, even Indira with it as a pale would have had to lose what? An inch? Two?"

Indira shrugged. "Probably only an inch across the bottom. But then I've been practicing a long time." Her eyes narrowed at me. "But you haven't. Even with a familiar..." She trailed off looking at my hair.

I didn't say a thing, but in the two weeks since I'd done it, most of what I'd offered had grown back. Not even Jo had noticed what I had offered, and I never told her about it.

"What aren't you telling us?" Indira all but demanded, and that killed any guilt I might have had.

"There are a lot of things I don't tell you. You aren't my mentors, at least not how Alixant described it, so I don't actually owe you anything. I'm willing to take your assistance to pull this off, but there is no reason to trust you, so I'm not giving you, or the people pulling your strings, any more ammo than I absolutely have to." I didn't snarl or snap, and the rumbled purr in my mind from Carelian, who was busy eating the rare lamb, helped me stay calm.

She blinked and sat back, then glanced at Alixant. "She'll do. If she keeps learning and adapting at this rate, she might even survive her draft."

"I would prefer that. Especially if James' bank vaults hold what everyone seems to think they do."

"Not to mention his house," Indira commented. "She gets out of here with a doctorate and doesn't owe anyone anything, she'll be better than most. Better than me." These last words sounded bitter, and I wondered what she'd done. Or more exactly how they had trapped her.

"Excuse me. I'm right here. What are you talking about?"

Again, those glances and Alixant reached his hand out and she took it. An oddly endearing gesture that caught me off guard.

Alixant gave me a hard look. "You're getting a lot of attention and not all of it good. Just let us know if anything else like what happened with those two guys and what I assume happened in the park occurs. We have loyalties to other groups, but at this point what they can require us to do is minimal, and so far, mostly it's been passing information they could have gotten several other ways.

Indira picked up when he paused. "We are on your side, really. If you want, we're willing to sign a dual mentorship agreement. In many ways that would protect all of us as they are legal documents and anyone asking us to break the terms in them would be challenged in court. I'd like to say trust us, we have your best interests at heart, but we all know that isn't exactly true."

Alixant nodded and finished. "So how about this—trust that we have your best interests at heart and the best long-term plan we see is to get you out of college and through the draft as a free person. Then while you might not 'owe' us, you would most likely treat any requests or favors we might ask in the future with a more generous eye, and vice versa. Consider it more a strong friendship that we hope will last multiple decades. And that goes for Carelian too."

He let go of Indira's hand, and she nodded. "Having you as a 'personal friend' would give both of us shields down the road and might make a difference in the choices I at least have."

~They are right. People who owe you are always good.~

I shot a startled look at Carelian, but he hadn't even lifted his head, still working on eating the lamb.

"What did you do that they have such a hold over you?" I asked, blunt and to the point.

Indira sighed, looking a bit green, but nodded. "If I want your trust, I suppose I need to extend it."

"Do you want me to leave? I don't need to hear this," Alixant offered, making as if to rise from the table.

"No. Stay. They mainly got me because I was scared and stupid. I don't think Cori would ever be as naive as I was back then." Indira sighed and settled back a bit against the chair, glancing around. The restaurant, done in bright reds and sunshine yellows, wasn't crowded, though the scents of curry and other spices I wasn't sure of surrounded us. There wasn't anyone sitting at the table next to us, as Alixant had asked for a corner table. Unless we started shouting no one would hear what we discussed.

"Ugh, I'm going to need a drink to get through this," Indira sighed. She waved down the waiter and a few minutes later had a very large glass of wine in front of her. She took a sip of the dark red liquid and sighed.

"I was working on my masters. Going to college in Wisconsin. Let's just say my coloring, my name, and my family all made me stand out as a foreigner among all the blond and brown-haired boys. My family was a very traditional Farsi, even for women mages. You stay pure, you don't marry outside the family, and you let your family pick your husband. It was how I'd been raised, so I wasn't even interested in dating." She took another sip of wine.

I tried to imagine Indira, who screamed sex and sensuality, ever being that obedient. I failed.

"I'd been out too late at the library, lost track of time, and all the shuttles had shut down. As I walked the two miles to the public bus stop, I was attacked and raped." The words fell like stones onto our silent table. With those words a lot of my issue with her faded and fast. Alixant made a sound that I recognized. Something deep and primal, but he didn't move.

"He'd ambushed me, so I was dazed and confused for far too long. He wasn't a mage, and apparently didn't realize I was until after he was finished and standing up. By then the concussion he'd given me had cleared enough I realized what had happened. I killed him." She smiled a bitter smile. "Amazing what an Entropy mage can do when she doesn't care what she sacrifices. I caused all his organs to rupture. His screaming brought campus security. They took me to the ER, and I went through all that unpleasant stuff. Found out he'd

111

been raping women for a while, but I was the first person to get consciousness back before he left."

Her shuddering breath made me wonder if she'd ever told the story before.

"I didn't tell anyone except my mentor, and he took care of it. No charges were pressed, and no record of it entered the system. More fool I. I didn't tell my parents, and they continued to think I was their pure, dutiful daughter. I'm sure you know what happened." The bitterness and self-loathing in the words made me want to cry for her. "I got pregnant. I'd been a virgin and never used birth control. I'd been so shaken up over it, it didn't occur to me anything was wrong until three months later. My parents lost it. Oh, the accusations. And I couldn't even prove I'd been raped because there was no record of me visiting the ER, reporting it to the police—hell, even campus security had no records. They kicked me out. Turned their backs on me."

This time Alixant did move. He reached out and touched her face. She shook his hand off. "Oh, the rest plays out like any good story does. My mentor arranged for me to have the abortion, got me a place to live, and made sure I got my choice of placements for the draft. He took care of me every step of the way."

"And then he wanted payback," I said, my voice soft.

"That he did. He, of course, had all the records, things that proved I'd murdered a man, but not that he'd raped me. Proof of an illegal abortion because I was past the first trimester, and proof of bribes he'd offered 'on my behalf' to get me the position I had. I'd trusted him, and he took full advantage of that." Indira released a shaky breath. "So he has me, or at least did. His hold over the years has slipped as I earned my own favors from people, and I've gotten some information on other things he's done. This request of his, trying to seduce you, working with you and trying to sway you in some things, were easy to do and had no long-term downsides for me." A smile flashed across her face and I saw the woman I'd been getting to know reappear. "Though it never occurred to me you would turn me down. Even straight women normally crumble when I try."

I rolled my eyes. "I'm just special, I guess."

~Quean,~ Carelian murmured, but when I looked, his paw grooming had his full attention.

"You just might be. But that's why I owe people." She shrugged. "The question really lies with how much can you trust us and how much can you afford not to trust us."

Chapter 14

Join the Elemental Society and be in your element. Together the elements can do anything, and here you will
find those that will push your creativity and provide opportunities for your skills to shine. Remember, to your
element be true. ~Elemental Society Brochure

ORDER

That question followed me. We hadn't talked anymore
about it at dinner, and I focused on school. The blasted cloak
kept reappearing. I dispelled it whenever I thought about it.
And the feeling of being watched all the time didn't fade but I
couldn't pinpoint anything. Oddly, I felt most exposed outside, but Carelian seemed less stressed outside, so I just
chalked it up to all the pressure and focused on school.

Friday came around and that mean visiting the Guzman's.
The four of us piled into a rented car, as we couldn't all fit on
Jo's motorcycle, and headed up to Rockway. We had barely
gotten on Interstate 75 when Jo cleared her throat. She drove
while Sable sat in the passenger seat and I was in the back
with Carelian. He wore his new harness and kept fiddling with
it, but he'd agreed that I couldn't keep carrying him.

"So, I got approached the other day," her voice way too
nonchalant.

"By?" My attention focused on the back of her head and I
wished I'd taken the passenger seat. At least then I'd be able
to see part of her face.

"The Nyx society. They said they thought I'd get along
with their members. That they had a need for someone like
me."

"Like you? What does that mean?"

"This is just me, but I think they wanted me to think it was all demographics—female, Hispanic, lesbian. But the speaker, male and smart, not a merlin but very self-assured, asked about my roommates and what they might need to make their lives easier. So I'm pretty sure my attractiveness has a lot to do with you."

"I got something similar," Sable said. "Though the person feeling me out wasn't anywhere near as subtle. They just pointed out that same-sex relationships can face discrimination and they would assist if we needed help. The part that I found fascinating, was—and I'm quoting this because it caught me so off guard—we also fully support and can assist with legal needs in non-traditional relationships like triads."

"A triad?" I choked and leaned back, not sure how I felt. "Why does everyone assume there has to be something sexual between us? That we can't just be friends, good friends?" And Sable was becoming a good friend. I still wanted more time, but so far I didn't have many complaints. Carelian liked her.

~Triad good.~

"WHAT?" The words burst from all three mouths and we looked at Carelian, the car swerving as we did. Jo snapped her head back around and got the car straight.

"Okay, Carelian, I've got no idea what you're talking about and I'm not a hundred percent sure I want to know."

~Family, coven, triad, strong, three queans best triad.~ He sounded affronted and pulled far enough away I couldn't reach him with the seatbelt on.

"Huh. I think he means more like Wicca stuff. Not sex, but family, partnership." Sable talked it out and I could remember things from high school, but not anything we'd covered in History of Magic yet.

"Okay, the guy from the society probably meant the sex version—but the other," I trailed off then shook my head. "No offense to either of you, but I don't know if I'm even ready to consider that, because what little I remember it would be almost a relationship, I think."

"Yeah. I mean, I'm not opposed in theory, but that is way past anything Jo and I have talked about."

Jo didn't say a word, just kept driving, the traffic lifting as we got past 285.

"So back to the guy, why would he think we are in a sexual relationship? I mean, I'm pretty sure Indira passed on the word that I wasn't a lesbian, or at least she didn't do it for me."

"Indira would do it for most people, us included. Sable and I talked about it, so her not doing it for you is a relatively big indicator you're not lesbian or at least not a looks-oriented lesbian. As to the society, because mostly it's populated by males and they all think with their dicks?" Jo asked and we snickered at the truth.

"What about you Cori, anyone ask?"

"Not yet. Indira advised I feel out Emrys at the least, but I just haven't."

"Why?" Sable asked, twisting to look at me.

"I don't know. Part of it is because if I join one, it ruins any protestation that I don't want to join a society. But also, I think it isn't worth it unless they owe me for joining."

"What?" Jo craned to look at me.

"I swear, Josefa, if you don't pay attention to the road I'm going to make you pull over," I snapped out channeling Marisol to the point Jo paled and yanked her attention back to the road.

"Yes, *mami*, I mean Cori."

Sable's snickers turned into laughing which pulled me in, while Jo flushed and paid very close attention to her driving.

"So, I've been thinking a lot about what Indira told me." I'd told them about the societies and treatment, how they would try to get members to owe them, though in Indira's case it had been the member who was a creep, but the society had approved in an oblique way. I hadn't told them the details of her story. That wasn't mine to tell. "Given that, I want it so I'm doing them a favor by joining, not the other way. I am absolutely determined not to need them. But if they can owe me it might be worth it. Even if I get this degree in the next eighteen, well sixteen months now, I still have three or more years to get my doctorate. I have time to see what they have to offer and it if it is worth it for me."

Sable snickered. "I knew you were thinking this out a lot more than we were. You aren't going to be someone they use. You want to use them."

I sighed and sank back into the seat a bit. "That sounds so cynical, but yes. I don't know why I emerged so young or why I emerged twice, but you can guarantee as soon as I get my degree everyone will want to use me or worse, study me. I hate to admit it, but right now my best bet is Alixant. He's honest about what he wants."

"And Indira?" Jo didn't look at me, but I heard the worry in her voice.

"She has more people pulling her strings, but I think she honestly wants me to not be like her. Caught in the mistakes she made. But that means they need to beg for my attention, not the other way around."

"What will we be giving up by not trying to seek admittance to their societies?" Sable asked and I looked at her, oddly warmed and worried she used the 'we' word. Maybe there was more there for our future than I thought. I couldn't even put a name to my thoughts, so I shelved them. Some things needed to be dealt with only when you reached that bridge.

"Off the top of my head? I think networking and maybe draft opportunities. Isn't your dad a mage?"

"Yes. But he emerged as a wizard and chose to get only a bachelor's, then go into the military as an officer. He did his full twenty. He's now a civilian with the DoD. So he never got into the societies. Well, he's Army, and that is its own society that few others can touch."

"True. Let's talk to your parents, Jo. Maybe they'll have an idea." Because I really didn't know how much pressure the societies would put on us. Maybe I was extrapolating too much from what happened with Indira and that was one person, not the society as a whole.

"Works, we should be there in another ten minutes, and Mami is expecting us, all of us, for lunch."

I nodded and checked on Carelian. He had his paws up on the door, watching the world go by, and I grinned. He really did love the speed of our travel. I also noticed for the first time outside the apartment I felt like I wasn't being watched. Some of the tension bled from me. But there was another person I trusted.

I sent a text to police chief Laurel Amosen. *Chief, it's Cori. Societies- did you join? Have an opinion if I should?*

I left it at that. I didn't know if she'd have time to text back, but at least I'd asked. I was about to put my phone away when I remembered Shay had responded at one time. And I now had his number. With a shrug, I texted him.

Shay, Cori - should I join a society? Are they worth it?

There—at least I would have some other inputs, and one of them from another merlin, well if he ever saw his phone and responded.

We pulled into the driveway of Jo's house, and I got out with a smile on my face. Jo grabbed Sable's hand as we walked up to the door and she walked in. "Mami, we're here," Jo called out in a clear voice as I followed behind, Carelian darting in with an odd gait as he wiggled against the harness.

"Jo, in here. Cori and Sable better be with you," Marisol called out from the living room. We turned the corner to see Carelian being petted by her. "How's my beautiful boy? You're getting so big. That harness looks so handsome on you."

I rolled my eyes as he preened at her compliments and stopped picking at it so much. She looked up at me and winked.

"Thank you, *Tia*," I said as I came over for a tight hug. To my amusement, she gave Sable the same hug, proving that at least she liked this girlfriend. Most of them Jo never brought home, much less introduced to her parents. Sable really was special.

"Just a girls' day. Henri is working at the shop with Sanchez, a special project. I figured we'd have margaritas, queso, and chips, and you tell me everything." Her voice sounded chipper, but I swear it had a hint of pleading in it.

"I'm driving, Mami, but it sounds like the perfect day. Besides, we were hoping you could give us some advice."

The smile that lit up her face told me she missed her daughter, and maybe me too, more than I could have guessed. "Well, that is what mothers are for, isn't it? To provide advice?"

Ten minutes later, we all had margaritas, Jo's just missing the tequila. Carelian had mini tamales she had made for him, and we were in the dining room around the table. They'd never changed it after Jo transformed it to petrified wood. While heavy as all get out, the table was solid and gorgeous, and I suspected Marisol would never part with it.

Once we'd settled and had some of the excellent queso she always put in chilies and chorizo, Marisol looked at all of us. "So, what is the issue you need advice about? Normally I'd think it was boys, but..." She shrugged, a movement that made us laugh.

"Yes, I don't think boys are an issue right now. Unless we're talking about Carelian," Jo said with a laugh. Carelian for his part was too busy unwrapping his tamales and eating them with great delight. I watched his manipulation of the small rolls and wondered exactly what else he'd learned to get into.

"So?" She had leaned back, sipping her margarita as she watched us.

Jo looked at me and waved a chip at me. I guess they were dumping this on me. I couldn't really complain, as I was at the center of all of it one way or another.

"Did you join a society?"

Marisol arched her eyebrows looking at me. "You mean one of the magical societies?" We nodded, watching. "Yes, my sophomore year. I still am a member of Elemental if it comes to that. Why?"

"Is it worth it? What has it cost you or gained you?"

She looked surprised for a split second, then her eyes darted to my temple and then her daughter's and Sable's. "Ah. First, remember that neither Henri nor I are at the rank you two are, and definitely not Cori's. For us? It was more a social and networking group. A few people got help with tickets or getting a job after the draft. I can remember at least twice someone asking the society for tutoring of a child or aid with some accounting via the local Elemental newsletter. Henri has people who get free oil changes for life because they helped with getting us the loan to start his shop."

Jo's eyes lit up. "Aha! I always wondered why there were some people. *Papi* never explained it, just saying 'reasons'. But they were payback for the assistance getting the loan?"

"Co-signing and being our first customers. They helped bring in others. But all of that is similar to what you'd find in an Elks lodge. What you are asking, and what you'll face is much more layered." Marisol closed her eyes, sipping her drink. We just waited, well, ate more. Filling our mouths with more queso was a wonderful way to pass the time.

"I don't know that I have an answer for you. There are good aspects to them. People who have become friends over the years and opportunities that otherwise may not have come our way, but while the 'costs', as you call them, for us were negligible and in reality nothing that we wouldn't have done even without the contract, you're going to have a lot more asked of and available to you."

"Contract?" I asked. I'd never heard anything about that before.

"Oh yes. Every society had an oath, I guess you would call it. You have to swear, and in theory you swear on your magic, that you will uphold their tenets. Now, does that mean you'll lose your magic if you break it? No. But I'd guess depending on the oath you could find it used against you." Marisol looked pensive now, and I could tell she was searching back through her memories. "The more I think about it, the riskier I guess it might be. I'm not sure I ever thought about it. It was just what you did. Everyone joined by the end of their junior year—in fact anyone that didn't was regarded as strange and even might find themselves ostracized. Huh, looking back I'm not sure anymore."

I leaned back, letting the margarita wash through me as I thought. If Marisol was no longer sure, this might be one more battle in front of me.

Chapter 15

Air is one of the most maligned of the branches, with most people dismissing it as means to stay cool in the summer. While this is true for most ranks of mages, archmages and merlins have access to more abilities. Do not misunderstand, even a hedgemage has access to lightning, one of the more powerful spells. But where a hedgemage can create static electricity, a merlin can call a lightning strike strong enough to melt steel. ~ Magic Explained

SPIRIT

Saturday had been great, though Marisol had given me much to think about. We left about the time Henri and Sanchez came back, enough for hugs and waves, then we headed back. I worked Sunday, a twelve hour fill-in shift, and it helped improve the balance in my account. Monday found me back in the flow for the next week. February sped by and March arrived with a storm that meant getting to class that Monday resulted in me and Carelian both getting soaked to the skin. I don't know who was more annoyed.

~Wet,~ he hissed in my mind and I shivered as it tickled the inside of my consciousness, causing ripples down my nerves.

"I'm aware. If you didn't notice, I'm wet also," I spat out, wringing my hair. It had poured so hard it went through the zipper of my coat and under my hood. Carelian on his leash had no protection. I dug a towel out of my bag, one of those swimmers' towels that absorbed a ton of water and dried fast. I dried him off, then my hair. My shoes and socks would just stay damp.

With a sigh we headed to Magic 101 class.

Settling in, only Charles smiled at me as he came in and Arachena waved. I snickered at how many people avoided her like she was the plague. I think Charles preferred it like that. Too bad Daniela didn't seem scared of his familiar, only contemptuous.

What is her problem? If you aren't worshiping her, you are to be demeaned?

She'd attacked me more since that day in the library, though as a sophomore, almost junior, I rarely crossed paths with her. Sable had Daniela in one of her classes and just rolled her eyes when she came up in conversation, which wasn't often.

"If everyone will take a seat. Today we have speakers from three of the societies. They will present their cases and how they work to make the magic you do even better. They will talk to interested students after class," Bernard announced the second the clock ticked to nine. He was nothing if not consistently punctual. What interested me was his attitude. He was almost fawning over one of the men.

So again, people get things for being in the society.

I pulled out my phone and looked at my texts. Both Laurel and Shay had responded that weekend, and I'd thanked them, but I still hadn't decided how to take what they said. Laurel's had been direct and to the point: "Be careful. They can be useful, but make sure you know exactly what you are getting for what you are giving. In the long run they can help, but they can also destroy. With the type of person you are, I doubt you'll provide much leverage to them for use against you."

Shay, however, had responded like Shay, confusing and circuitous. "All things are variable depending on who you are and what you put into them. Think not that they are useless, but treat them like a venomous snake, dangerous if it bites you, but very useful if you can milk it. After all, venom has many uses."

I still wasn't sure of anything he said, other than be careful. That wasn't a yes or a no, so, whatever.

The first person was in the same society as Bernard, a Builder. He was in his fifties, with light blond hair and a pleasant smile. He stood and talked to us, and Carelian just slept the entire time, telling me nothing. While he didn't make me wary, his presentation left me confused. I thought Builders built things, but most of the people in the guild were doctors or structural engineers/architects. They were mostly research based. Better alloys for construction, better medicines, better spells. It interested me to a point I hadn't expected. He spoke well and by the end of his presentation I could feel the urge to go sign up and work with other people that wanted what I wanted, to solve medical issues. Basically, they promised to get you in with labs, hospitals, and construction companies either during or after your draft.

When he was done, he promised to be available for questions for two hours after our class. He sat back down along the wall next to Bernard and they fell into quiet conversation.

The second presenter stepped up, a thin man who screamed lawyer. He talked for a solid ten minutes about the benefits of joining the Nyx, an Entropy and Time Society, the one Indira belonged to. He talked about power through law and perception, that everything people perceived needed to be what you wanted them to perceive. Laws were a matter of perception, and if the laws were altered to allow mages more power and better benefits, the perception of mages having power would become reality. He talked in circles, and Carelian growled, his nose under his tail. By the time this speaker was done I just shook my head. That would never be a group I wanted to associate with. As he walked back to take his seat where the others were, I realized there were four extra people there, not three. Bernard had said three speakers, but there were four people I didn't recognize.

The third speaker rose, this one a woman dressed in what I could only describe as a bohemia style. Her long hair flowed loosely around her, and blended with the flowing dress in blues, greens, and reds. She reminded me of a flower though she wasn't all that pretty. When she started to talk her words grabbed me and her charisma more than made up for any level of beauty she might have needed.

"My name is Elenia Trainor and I am the president of the Elemental society." Her voice rippled through the hall and she held out a hand that had water and flame dancing on it. Despite my cynicism the display impressed me.

"We are one of the largest magical societies around and offer some of the best opportunities bar none. Want to get into Hollywood and motion pictures? We know people. Want to work with cutting edge technology? How about learning more about the oceans? Or even space? Our society works in every industry and in ways you can only imagine. At the basis of all things is molecular structure, and elementalists can control it better than almost anyone. Transform mages are more than one trick ponies." She gave a grin that was cute and mischievous at the same time. But I watched as she talked and realized she had more to her than being a great speaker. As she talked, she flicked her hands and had the elements dancing at what must be her mental commands, making it look powerful and easy.

"Remember our creed, Elements together are better than elements alone," were her final words before she stepped back to her chair.

While Bernard came up to thank the speakers, I thought about it. Opportunity, friends, power. Basically, everything most people wanted. The question was: what did I want?

Pfft, easy— I want my own life, with no one controlling me.

My immediate reaction made me laugh, especially right now as everyone seemed to have a say in what I did or didn't do. The government influenced my degree selection. The teachers guided what I studied. The government would control my life for the next decade after my degree. So, the only way to make sure I had my own life was what?

The three speakers stood near the door, spaced out enough that they could talk to the students that clustered around them. I didn't see the other guy who'd been sitting at the back. All I'd been able to verify had been his white hair and slacks and a nice trench coat—the classrooms were still chilly.

I shrugged, grabbed my books, and hooked the leash back on Carelian. We'd come to an agreement that I'd let him roam in buildings or safeish places, but when we moved between classes, he'd be leashed. He muttered in the back of my head, but mostly he still came along with me just fine, sniffing things and pulling at the leash would have been too plebeian for him.

It took a minute to get through the gaggle of students with Carelian having to walk almost between my legs. For the first time I looked forward to maybe him being the size of a Labrador, then we wouldn't have to worry about that. Making it through the door I headed out. Mondays were busy and I had class with Indira next.

"Miss Munroe, I was wondering if I might walk with you?" A cultured voice came from down the hall behind me.

As I glanced back the man from class stepped up next to me, but not close enough I felt uncomfortable. He fell into pace beside me as I didn't stop. Still dressed in the same trench coat, this close I could see he had to be in his late sixties, with the hair not being white, but instead white and gray, creating a silvery color. But his eyes were what grabbed me—they were the same color as his hair, a silver mix that didn't seem wise to stare into.

"It's a free country," I responded as Carelian paced between us. I could tell he'd become very focused on the man as his tail had quit flicking around, only swaying slightly as we walked.

"Indeed, it is. And remains so often because of people like us," he responded, his voice carrying hints of an English accent.

I knew what he hinted at, but I figured I'd rather play it obtuse, see if I could get him to lose his temper. Working with Samuel while in Rockway had taught me how much people revealed when they got annoyed.

"Americans? Odd, you don't sound American."

He chuckled, but I didn't look at him, still headed out and to the next building over. I only had thirty minutes between classes and having time to go to the bathroom made my life more pleasant.

"No. I call England my home, well Wales to be exact."

"A long way from here."

"You were worth the trip. I saw your results from the second OMO scan."

That shook me. It meant either he was in the OMO or had high up friends that were. I couldn't even see my own OMO scans.

"Interesting. Were they pretty?" I tried to make light of it, but my voice had a higher pitch than normal.

"Not sure I would use that word, however the range of power you should have was most interesting."

Appealing you mean. The question is what society do you represent?

Abruptly I tired of the game. I needed to go to the bathroom, give Carelian time to go, get to my seat, and maybe say hi to Charles and Arachena.

We'd made it outside and I abruptly stopped and stepped off the path. He slowed to a halt a pace or two later and turned to face me.

"What do you want? I don't even know who you are, what you represent, and more, I don't know that I care." Looking at him full on for the first time I saw a firm chin and lips, as well his merlin tattoo on the right side of his face.

He tilted his upper body in a sort of nodding bow. "My apologies. Let me introduce myself. I am Gaylord Carstiles, the father of the House of Emrys."

It took me a minute to remember that father was how they referred to their president or head of their society.

Dang, should I be worried or not that the head is here?

I resisted the temptation to remark about his first name, mainly because I figure he expected me to, and right now the last thing I wanted to do was be predictable.

"So why is the House of Emrys so interested in me?"

"Please, Miss Munroe, I am sure you are well aware of why," he chided with a tone that just annoyed me.

"Okay, I know. Exactly why should I care?"

That seemed to set him back on his heels. "Because we feel you would be an excellent member of our House. You are a merlin, in fact the first double in history, though many of our researchers are scrambling to see if they can find evidence of it happening before. I wanted to make sure you knew exactly how interested we are in you joining our mission."

"Your mission? And what exactly would that be? And why would I have any desire to join in it?"

His calculated smirk did nothing to endear me to him as he peered down his nose at me. "Why, because of all the things we can do for you. Get the right doors opened, get you the right sort of friends, make sure you have everything you ever wanted?"

"Can you raise people from the dead?" I snapped annoyed and needing to go pee.

"What? No, of course not," he sputtered looking horrified. "We are not necromancers."

"I don't need a necromancer, I need a god. Not interested." I turned and headed towards the building, Carelian trotting alongside, a snicker of laughter teasing the edges of my mind.

"But Miss Munroe, we only accept merlins. We can be your greatest asset," he protested following after us.

"Don't care. Not interested. Now I need to go. Have a day."

I darted up the steps and into the women's bathroom leaving him standing there spluttering. Personally, I found the look on his face amusing.

Chapter 16

While Japan has their mages assigned to the Emperor and Empress, China took a unique route that is contradictory in many ways. The Chinese ruler is always merlin with the same dragon familiar and is known as Child of Heaven (note that there have been male and female rulers). The Qing dynasty is going strong, but all other mages are assigned to their civil service. While it is not quite slavery, they are housed, fed, married, and assigned jobs per the whims of the Child of Heaven. In theory they retire out after forty-five years. No one has met an old mage from China. ~ History of Magic

CHAOS

I had to give him credit. He tried for three days, walking with me between classes and almost stalking me. He didn't give up until I finally turned on him, my patience cracking as I had to get three papers done and study for a chem test.

"Look Mr. Carstiles, I get that you think I should belong to Emrys, but until you prove to me I will get more than it will cost me, right now I'm not interested. Tell you what, go back, figure out why I might need you, because I can promise you, I'm going to figure out why you need me. If you can find something valid, come back after I have my bachelor's. Maybe by then I will have figured out what you can actually offer me."

He paled a bit but nodded. "Very well, Miss Munroe. Good luck in your endeavors, but please, if you feel you need something reach out to me. No strings attached, I swear." He slipped me his card, a heavy piece of dark blue with silver font.

I nodded, slipped it into my bag and walked away, Carelian loping around me in amusement. Thursdays I had law and biology eating up my afternoons and the paper for Magic Law was missing a reference. I let Carelian loose in the park, glancing at him. "No inciting mobs this time, please?"

~No promises,~ he responded, tail curved up in a question mark.

"Oh, Jo is such a bad influence on you," I sighed as I rolled up the leash.

~Excellent quean.~

"So you've said. Still doesn't tell me much. I'll be back in an hour, then biology lecture," I reminded him, though I suspected he had my schedule as memorized as I did.

He flipped his tail at me and darted up a tree. I sighed and hurried to the library. Sixty-five minutes later I had all the references I needed, and this time I'd taken pictures of the titles and copyright pages so I could notate correctly. I picked up my pace as I knew I was running late and I wanted a few minutes to scarf the granola bar and jerky I had in my bag. The librarian did not allow eating in the library. Sitting on the bench in the little park area for a few minutes sounded good.

"Carelian where are you?" I called out as I approached the little clearing.

~Tree. Meet at bench,~ he replied.

Sometimes I swear that cat knows what I want before I do.

I headed for the bench and tripped, falling flat on my face. I heard a sharp crack and one of the bench's back slats exploded into splinters in line with where my heart had been.

FUCK!

I reacted without conscious thought. I rolled and scrambled behind a tree just as another bullet ripped into the ground where I'd been sprawled.

"CARELIAN HIDE!" I screamed as I put my hands over my head, not that I knew what good that would do. The sound of the rifle cracked through the quiet campus and people were yelling. I pulled Lady Luck around me as easily as breathing. Then I waited, not sure what else to do. I didn't have a bulletproof vest, I didn't have back up. That stopped me and I dragged my phone out of my pocket. I didn't bother with 911, though that might have been smart, or smarter. I called Alixant instead.

"Cori?" he answered warily. The few times I talked to either of them outside the weekly meetings was via text. I almost never called.

"Someone just took a shot at me."

A long tense moment of silence, then he responded slowly. "You're telling me someone just fired a gun at you?" I could hear him moving, though it sounded like he was in an office from the vague background noises.

"No, I'm telling you someone used a rifle to take shots at me. I know the difference in sounds, not that I can tell what type." Samuel had taken Jo and me out to go shooting one weekend before I started college, saying with as much trouble as found me, I needed to at least know how to handle a gun. I wasn't great, but I could shoot one, and knew the difference between a rifle, a pistol, and a revolver.

"Stay down. Have you called 911?"

"No," I admitted, annoyed that I wanted him there first. The last run-in with the cops had not left a pleasant flavor in my mouth.

"As soon as I hang up, do it, and for Merlin's sake, touch nothing," he ground out. "I'll be there in twenty."

That meant he was farther away. Not good.

"Should I call Indira?"

"No...actually yes. She's faculty and has a lot of experience using her abilities. Way more than you do. Call her. I'll push it. But then call 911." The disconnect sounded in my ear. I sat huddled at the base of the tree more terrified than I had ever been in my entire life.

"Carelian?" My voice warbled as I spoke. "Are you okay?"

~Am above. Hiding. Not see villain.~ The growl in his voice oddly made me feel better, knowing at least one of us was angry.

"Stay safe. I need you to stay safe," I pleaded. I tried to stop the shaking in my hands as I hit the contact for Indira's number.

"Indira Humbert," her elegant lilting voice purred in my ear.

"It's Cori. Someone is shooting a rifle at me." I tried not to sound like a scared ten-year-old, but all I could see in my mind's eye was Stevie laying there dead. But now it flipped between him, or Carelian, or worse, me, and Jo holding me. I squeezed my eyes shut tight and tried to curl into a smaller ball, though I hadn't heard another gun shot past the first two, or was it three?

"Where are you?" Her voice sounded strong and sure, and I fought the desire to be brave like her. I didn't want to know what her life had been like to be so strong.

"In the quad between"—I told her the two buildings I was between. "In the little park. I already called Alixant."

"I'll be there in three minutes. Call the police now!" She snapped out the order, then disconnected.

All I ever did was call the police it seemed like. Someday maybe I'd quit needing to call them. That would be nice. I held the emergency button. The familiar "911, what's your emergency," did nothing to calm my racing heart or the panic.

"Cori Munroe, at the GA MageTech campus between"— I rattled off my location and closest cross street before the operator could ask any questions. "Multiple shots fired, at me I think, and I don't know where the shooter is."

"Are you injured? Is anyone else?"

"I'm not. I don't think there was anyone else." I craned my head around but saw nothing besides a few other students huddled by stairs or trees. "I can't see anyone obviously injured."

"Police have been dispatched. Do you see the shooter?" The calm voice on the other end helped my nerves, and I looked at the destroyed bench and the disturbed dirt where I'd been. I mentally backtracked where it would have come from and zeroed in on the roof of a building I didn't know, though from the air conditioning units in the windows I fig-ured it had to be one of the dorms.

"No. But given the shots, I think he was on the roof or one of the top floors of the building behind me."

"That information has been passed along. You should be hearing sirens any moment," she replied and I heard the rapid clicking of keys in the background.

I should have done a rotation as a 911 operator. I bet I would have been good at it.

Biting my lip, my hand wrapped around the phone, I strained my ears trying to hear sirens. Looking around cau-tiously something else caught my attention.

"Holy Merlin's Ghost," I whispered, my voice cracking in shock.

"What's wrong?" the operator demanded, but I couldn't find the words to respond as I stared at Indira walking to-wards me.

In the movies archmages and merlins always did fancy stuff with flames and wind, and the special effects made it look cool. Even with the showdown I'd witnessed at the fair-ground when the Bad Ass Mages biker gang got out of control, it had been flashes of fire, lightning, and wind. Im-pressive but not jaw dropping.

This was jaw dropping.

Indira stalked across the park in my general direction, though I don't think she'd seen me yet. She'd always looked elegant and what people assured me was sexy in silks, bright colors, and heels. Today she looked dangerous and every bit what you thought of when you thought "merlin". She seemed to move as if time stood still around her—in the time it took me to blink she had moved a good five hundred yards. Fire swirled around her and I swore I saw sparking in the corona that was her hair. Her long black hair waved around her as if it lived or was live wires that harnessed her power. She held her hands out beside her and they glittered as if made of steel.

I'd never seen anything like this.

Her eyes scanned and I knew the second she saw me. Before I could lift my hand to wave at her she was kneeling in front of me.

"How?" I stuttered out, looking at her.

She ignored me. "Where is he?"

I swallowed. Her voice held something hard and direct I'd never heard before, something that scared me down to my toenails. "Up on dorms, or top. Bullets hit there," I managed, my arm shaking as I pointed to the bench, then the ground.

"Stay here," she ordered, then she was across at the entrance of the building.

"Wha? How?" I stuttered, craning my neck to see her.

That isn't possible. No one can move that fast.

~Time, she is pale there, but a strong mage.~ Carelian dropped into my lap and I almost screamed, jerking back hard enough to slam my head into the trunk of the tree.

"Warn me!" I screeched, but I pulled him close and buried my nose in his fur.

~You safe. Villain eliminated,~ he purred, snuggling in next to me.

Someone tried to kill me. They wanted to put a bullet in my head.

For the first time in a very long time I wanted to roll over and throw up, something I hadn't done since discovering my third body. I sat there trembling until I saw two police officers running in, guns drawn, but I noted both of them had tattoos on their temples. It made sense, but still I didn't know how to react.

"You the caller?" one of them barked out and I just nodded. "You hurt?" I shook my head. "Where's the suspect?" He barely looked at me, instead turning and surveying the area even as his partner did it at a different rate.

"Merlin Indira Humbert went to where I thought they were. She is not the shooter, she came to-" I broke off. Came to what? Rescue me? Save me? Protect? Or just get me into her debt. A whole slew of suspicion and worry cascaded through me and the urge to cry spiked even higher.

Before I could figure out what else to say, they had snapped up their guns and were pointing behind me. "Halt. Identify yourself." Their barked-out orders made me cringe but I turned to see Indira walking out, all the magic and power gone, as if she'd not just looked like a goddess made carnate a few minutes earlier.

"Indira Humbert, merlin. I'm a teacher here. There is a dead body up there, one I didn't kill. I saw claws and puncture wounds, but I did not enter any further, and I did not disturb your crime scene." With those words everything dissolved into chaos and I just sat there holding Carelian.

A body? Someone killed the person who'd been shooting at me? That just created more questions, but at this point I couldn't even figure out anything past why.

Cops and other people peppered me with questions, and I answered when I could, but otherwise I didn't move and didn't say anything. I focused only on Carelian and my breathing.

"How're you holding up?"

I jerked sideways and jarred my shoulder against the tree. Reflexively I checked for spells on me, but neither Luck nor Murphy were there. I reached up to rub my shoulder. "When did you get here?" There had been a haze of people, and I'd watched in numb confusion as they had marked off the area as a crime scene and people kept disappearing into the building.

"About twenty minutes ago. You were in shock but functional so we let you be. They're done for now. Ready for me to walk you home?" Alixant crouched next to me, peering at me. I looked past him and saw Indira seated across the area on another bench, a man in a suit talking to her.

The time sank in and I jerked up straight, dislodging Carelian, who tumbled off my lap with a hiss of annoyance. "Shit, I'm late for class!" I struggled to get up, but my legs had fallen asleep while I sat there, and I couldn't get past the pins and needles. I sucked in a hiss of pain and began to rub them. Being late wasn't anything I needed.

"Cori?" His voice was gentle, and I looked up at him, confused by that.

"There was a shooting. Someone or something unknown killed the shooter. They canceled all classes for the rest of the day. I'm going to walk you home, then we'll talk tomorrow. Jo and Sable have been pinging you."

I looked down at my phone, lying beside me where I'd dropped it when Indira showed up. The screen was full of missed messages and calls. "Oh. Yeah, home sounds good."

I let him pull me up, latched the leash on Carelian, and started to walk, Alixant by my side.

Chapter 17

The number of people testing for magic is rising, and the overall stats associated seem to be rising as well. Ten years ago, approximately 35% of the population was assumed to be mages. However, we estimate that at least 75% of all humans are probably hedgemages. Unless testing becomes mandatory this is only speculation. ~ OMO internal memo

ORDER

I crashed after reassuring Jo and Sable I was fine, but I felt like I'd just worked three doubles back to back. I woke up when my alarm went off, saw the notice that classes were canceled again today, and went back to sleep. I didn't really wake up until about ten in the morning. When I did, everything surged to the forefront of my mind and I jolted upright the memory of Indira striding towards me looking like something out of an action movie, then the comment about a dead body.

I scrambled out of bed and hit the kitchen at almost a run.

"I was wondering when you'd come out of that. But Steven said to let you sleep. That shock would do that, and he suspected you used a lot more personal energy than you realized," Jo remarked calmly from her position on the futon, computer on her lap, while Sable sat at the computer desk. She'd turned to look at me, a half smile on her face.

"You feeling better?" Her voice was gentle and I saw genuine worry in her eyes.

"Yeah, I mean I wasn't hurt," I mumbled, feeling stupid about the way I'd reacted.

"Someone tried to kill you and instead he was killed. I think you earned a little shock. Coffee is ready to go if you hit brew." Jo's voice held a sharpness that cut through my fog, and I turned to head for the coffee.

"Thanks," I said as I hit the brew button.

"You might want to get clothes on. I mean, don't think either Sable or I mind the view of your panty-clad butt and your naked legs and short shirt." She leered at me as she said that and I rolled my eyes. I had more on than either of them normally wore. "But I don't know if you want Steven and Indira to see you dressed in that? They should be here in about fifteen minutes."

I froze, looking at her, feeling the blood draining from my face. I turned and fled for my room to the laughter of that ungrateful wench. The slap and hiss, "Jo, you're being mean," from Sable made me feel better.

Ten minutes later, after the fastest shower on record, I came back out with my hair still dripping. I had dressed in jeans and tee, just wanting comfy clothes on, and grabbed the finished coffee. I added cream and sugar, just a bit, and took a long drink, feeling it hit my mouth with the promise of brain activity.

"So, what do you know?" I asked after I'd gotten at least half of my normal amount of coffee in my system and settled down into the other chair, an overstuffed club chair in dark brown faux leather. We still didn't know if it was coffee colored or espresso. "And where's Carelian?"

~Sleeping, shush, noisy queans,~ came a drowsy voice. I looked around but didn't see him.

Sable and Jo snickered, telling me they had heard.

"Well, if he doesn't appear he'll miss hearing what Steven and Indira have to say," Jo commented as she closed her computer. "But I think he's under your bed. He acted as zombified as you did. You sure you're okay?"

"No. I mean I'm used to trauma, even bad situations, people attacking others with magic. But I've never had anyone try to kill me before." My voice broke and I snuggled down deeper into my chair. Before I could do more than take another sip of coffee Carelian was in my chair, shoving me over a bit, and then he went right back to sleep, a rumbling snore-purr as an underscore to the atmosphere.

Sable opened her mouth, but a quick rat-tat-tat on the door made her shake her head and get up. "I'll get it."

"I hope they brought food," I mumbled, knowing it was Alixant and Indira.

Sable checked, then opened the door. The small hesitation created a lump in my throat. We'd never had to worry about it before.

Alixant and Indira walked in as soon as the door opened. He wore his normal government causal—slacks, light blue shirt, with a sports coat. Indira caught me by surprise. She wore jeans that hugged her ass and a tight yellow sweater that hugged everything just as much.

I glanced at Jo and saw she was trying not to stare.

"See something you like?" I said in a sotto voice.

She flushed red and glared at me, and I just smirked. Indira laughed and put a box on the table. "I bring food to soothe the savage breast." Alixant cast her a look I'd only heard of in books—besotted. He looked besotted.

Huh. And I thought Jo's doe eyes at Sable were bad.

Indira, either unaware of his look or basking in it, opened the box to reveal breakfast sandwiches and chocolate croissants.

"Okay, now you have my interest," I said, carefully prying myself up and grabbing a ham and egg sandwich as well as a pastry.

"Ah, see, I was trying to bribe you with sex and I should have been offering chocolate. Shame on me," Indira said lightly, no hint of the powerhouse that I'd seen yesterday, just a pretty older woman.

"Chocolate, coffee, a foot massage, or meat all work as things to tempt Cori with. You just tried the wrong approach," Jo said, grinning at me as I rolled my eyes.

"Look, when you're on your feet all day, a foot massage is never turned down," I protested, managing to take a bite of my sandwich instead of the croissant.

"Try wearing heels all day," Indira commented, settling herself into one of the chairs around the table.

"Do I look like an idiot?" My mouth spoke before my brain caught up and I flushed shoving another bite into my mouth.

Why do I always say crap?

Jo and Sable were both chuckling, and Indira's mouth twitched. "Let us agree that you have distinct skill sets and I doubt you will ever be called upon to perform seduction techniques."

Alixant cleared his throat. "Regardless, I figure you want to know what is going on and what happens next?"

I just nodded; my mouth too full to safely answer.

"The police do want to talk to you this afternoon, but mostly just to verify your reactions and check the call log on your phone. Again, you are not in trouble for anything, but they want to check the timing as there were a few other calls besides just yours."

I shrugged and took another bite. Keeping my mouth full seemed safer at this moment.

"Indira found the man that is believed to have been the one shooting at you dead on the rooftop. Per what the police have released to us, and this is not to be discussed anywhere." He gave a sharp look towards Jo and Sable who both just nodded. "The shooter was killed when his spine was severed at the back of his neck where he lay in the prone position with a rifle on a tripod aimed at the park area. There were two holes from what looked like claws or talons in the middle of his back. Also not for release is the presence of some feathers and fur. At this time, they do not know what or who killed him."

"Who is, I mean, was he?" Jo asked and I noted she'd pulled Sable onto the couch next to her.

"A low-level thug named Tommy Rackis. So far, that's all we know. Mid-twenties with a police record that goes back to his early teens."

"But why was he shooting at me?" It blurted out and I sighed, picking up the croissant and taking a bite. The rich chocolate distracted me, but I still saw the glances that Indira and Alixant gave each other.

"Right now, we don't know. But because of that we want you to quit working on the weekends and we are arranging for you to have an armed guard at all times, if not an armed mage," Alixant said in his typical this is how it shall be voice.

"Uh, no," I sputtered, spraying crumbs everywhere, looking at the two of them. I forced myself to chew and swallow as fast as I could, using coffee to rinse out my mouth. "No. No guard and I'm not quitting working. Right now, working weekends is the only thing keeping me afloat." Well, I had enough saved, but probably only for a year if I went back to ramen, and dang it, I liked eating good food.

"Cori, this isn't a suggestion," Alixant started and I cut him right off as I sat up straighter, garnering a disgruntled noise from Carelian.

"Am I under arrest?" I snapped back, anger and an odd fear burning past everything else.

"No, of course not, just," Indira started, but I cut her off just as fast.

"Then I am working, and I am not having guards." I injected my words with absolute certainty even as panic rippled inside. To be controlled and watched like that, I hadn't realized how precious my freedom was until they threatened to take it. Then add in the idea of a hulk being around me all the time—I had to fight to remain calm. To be honest, the knee jerk reaction surprised me, but they didn't need to know that.

"Cori?" Jo asked softly.

"Look, how do we know he was after me? Was my name in his pocket?" I asked sarcastically. "He might have just been someone looking to kill people and me with my luck was in his sights."

"No, he didn't have your name, he had your picture." Alixant pulled something out of his pocket and slid it over to me. It was obviously photocopied, being on plain printer paper, but it was me. The sandwich and chocolate roiled together into a mess and threatened to come up.

I inhaled sharply through my nose and stared at it. "This is me in a black dress. This has to be from where? The security cameras at the stadium?" I didn't know if that made it worse or better.

"Yeah, one of the stills the press got a hold of, which I guess makes it a little better. You kept a low profile after that, so it is one of the few they widely circulated."

"So again, why me? What do they want?"

They exchanged another look between the two of them and I wanted to scream, but I bit my tongue.

"There is reason to believe that there may be a link between that attempt on your life and Japan," Indira said as if each word was being dragged out of her.

I choked. "No, no, no. This is ridiculous. You're trying to tell me the country of Japan has put out a hit on me?"

"We didn't say that," Alixant replied. "Just there seems to be a link. I very much doubt anyone in the upper reaches of government would sanction that. But I suspect that there may be other parties that would very much like to see what James owned end up in Japanese hands."

I just stared at them. This entire situation was insane.

"No. No protection, and I'm still working." I didn't even bother to try and finish the croissant, scared if I reached for it they would see my hands shaking.

"Cori, don't be ridiculous," Alixant started, but Indira laid her hand on his arm and he broke off.

She looked directly at me and smiled a teeny smile. "This seems overwhelming and scary and I get that you don't want to lose your freedom. At this point, we can't force you to accept protection, but you need to be careful. We'd also like to offer you the option to make the mentorship formal. It provides a smidge more protection."

That made me pause and I looked at her, trying to sort through everything. Jo and Sable were both pale, and that made my throat squeeze even tighter.

~Cori will be safe. Protected. My quean.~ Carelian's rumble didn't help. What could a twenty-five-pound cat do? Even if he'd end up in the fifties before he quit growing, he still was a small animal. Animals couldn't keep me safe.

"Them trying to scare me off didn't work. I'll be extra careful. But I'm not quitting, I won't let them make me quit. Because at that point they will have won. I need to think about the mentorship. If you get me a contract, I'll consider it." Even admitting that much chafed at me. You were supposed to be independent as an adult. When would I be free from other people needing things?

"Good. Be careful, Cori. Neither of us want to see you hurt. I'll work on something you might like for the contract and send it to you." Indira's voice was soothing, but I got the impression she understood my reluctance to agree to all of this.

Jo and Sable asked a few questions, but after that, there wasn't much more to say.

Chapter 18

Work for Itel today! Looking to hire mages of wizard rank or higher for Data Analyst positions. Must be at least pale in Pattern. Starting pay in the low six figures. Non-mages require a masters in computer science to apply. ~ Job listing on job board.

SPIRIT

Classes started back on Thursday as there didn't seem to be an existing threat, but my life changed. I mapped out five different routes to my classes and I randomly chose which one to take each morning. The big thing today was meeting with the police, and Alixant promised to be there. Indira had said she'd see me at our weekly meeting, but it might be wiser to hold it at the apartment. She promised to bring enough food for everyone.

Much to Carelian's annoyance I left him home as I headed to the police station at seven in the morning. I let the professor know I'd miss the lecture today, but of all my classes the History of Magic class was the easiest to keep up with by just reading and I'd almost finished my semester research paper. I took the bus, figuring it'd be hard to try anything on public transportation. With Lady Luck wrapped around me, and a hat covering my tattoos, no one even looked at me as I headed down to what had become my least favorite place in the city. Honestly, I preferred the morgue.

Once there it didn't take long before I was in a conference room waiting for people, and wishing I'd brought more coffee. I'd smelled their coffee as I walked through, and I wouldn't touch it no matter how desperate I became.

The door opened and Alixant walked in with the man I recognized from my other encounters, Captain Jessup. More importantly, Alixant held an extra cup of coffee.

"For me?"

He grinned as he slid it over to me. "I figured I'd better try to get on your good side from the beginning."

"Smart man." I took a sip and sighed with joy. Raspberry mocha. Yum.

"Miss Munroe, I'm sorry to be meeting you again under these circumstances. Agent Alixant here tells me you have declined protection? You do realize you are entitled to it as a draftee if foreign powers are actively trying to prevent you from serving."

That made me blink. "No, I was unaware of that. Why?"

"Look up the treaty of Draft Interference. All OMO participants must sign it. It should prove interesting reading, it's something you don't normally get to until your senior year. But as it is, I have your statements and the police reports. What I wanted to know is if you've sensed or had anything else weird happen to you in the last few months. Or since you started school."

I shook my head then froze, thinking. "Maybe?"

"What do you mean, maybe?" Alixant demanded, his body snapping into rigid attention focused on me.

"Look," I muttered, feeling attacked. "It's probably nothing. But I've felt like someone's been watching me for ages. I never see anyone. It's worse when I'm outside, but even in some of the classrooms it feels that way. Then last week when I was on the way to meet you and Indira?"

Alixant nodded, and I fiddled with the coffee cup for something to do.

"I was crossing the street on the walk sign and some car almost hit me and Carelian. A guy grabbed me and pulled me back before the car struck. The car never even slowed down, which I found odd, but not a huge deal. And then..." I swallowed, everything snapping into a focus that I didn't like. "The other day, scaffolding collapsed and dropped a load of bricks right where I'd been standing. If I hadn't reacted as fast as I had, it would have hit me." My voice dropped to a whisper. "Killed me."

"And you didn't think to mention this?" Alixant ground out, staring daggers at me.

"No, I didn't. Why would I? Things like that have always happened to me and there wasn't anything specific." I shrugged. "Not like people don't almost get run down by drivers in general. So there wasn't anything to tell you."

He growled low under his breath and the captain shot him a sideways glance, but Alixant just shook his head and sat back.

"This feeling of having someone watch you has changed?" the captain asked, making notes on a piece of paper.

I shrugged, not sure how to answer that. "It isn't something I'm aware of all the time, but I do notice it, then I'll get busy on other things and won't. I'm not sure how to answer that."

"I see. Well, Miss Munroe, please remember you are entitled if you want it. It would be best for you to remain out of sight or as inconspicuous as possible until we have some more time to run this down."

"I've set up routes to and from the places I need to go, but those don't really change. Even if I go in other doors, I'm still going to the same place. And I have a large red cat that goes almost everywhere with me. It's a bit hard to be inconspicuous."

Alixant snorted. "She has a point. Carelian does many things but blending into the scenery isn't one of them."

"I see. All I can do is advise you to take caution, Miss Munroe. As you are refusing protection, it limits my options. If you feel or see anything, let Agent Alixant know." Captain Jessup nodded at me and rose, the meeting clearly over.

Alixant walked me out of the station and he stopped outside. "I'll give you a ride back. And I've got the contract for you from Indira."

"Does it cover both of you?" I asked as I walked with him. I'd thought about refusing the ride, but it made everything easier, so I headed to his car.

"Yes. And I have a pamphlet for you to read."

I gave him a quizzical glance as he opened the door for me, but I didn't say anything as I got in and buckled up. I waited until he got back in before focusing on him, expectation clear in my gaze. He reached in back and handed me what really did look like a home printed pamphlet, made up of copy paper folded in half and stapled. Then he pulled a manila envelope off the dash and handed it to me also.

"The contract is in there, read it and see what you like or don't like. We are willing to negotiate some aspects. To be honest, it's a very generous contract. Just for your information, Indira included the contract she signed when she was a freshman. Granted, it was much more common to have mentors then than it is now. But things are more equal now, especially for women." He lifted one shoulder. "She didn't feel like she had a choice then. I had a mentor too, but mine was more of an advisor than anything and our contract reflected that. You'll need to decide, but read up on the legal advantages mentors give you."

"I will," I said, but I was more interested in the pamphlet. The title, in Times New Roman, struck me as odd. *Techniques to use as a Mage*. "What is this?"

He started the car and pulled out of the parking lot before he answered my question. "The military realized a long time ago that mages were important and deadly. And that pamphlet, by the way, isn't supposed to exist, but it does." He had a crooked smile on his face. "The military likes to make instructions for everything. That book talks about how to use any level of magic abilities from hedge to merlin to kill people. I'm sure you're intelligent enough to figure out how to not kill people with that and just make it so they stop trying to hurt you."

I regarded the booklet with a mix of horror and fascination. I could tell what I'd spend today doing. Well, after classes.

"Thanks. Can you drop me off at the lab building? I've got lab in about thirty minutes."

"Sure. We'll see you tomorrow? Your place, and you can ask all the questions you want."

I still didn't enjoy having them come over, but I figured going out yet again might push my luck. And this way I had Jo and Sable to help buffer the interaction.

"I guess, but be aware the others in the house are expecting a suitable offering of food for this imposition." I tried to keep my voice light and teasing, but my frustration and resentment must have slipped out in my voice.

"Cori, I hate to say this, but this is part of the price of being a mage. You rarely get to have your own life. And I have an idea of how hard you've tried, but until you are in your late fifties and think you have enough to retire on, you might never be your own person. People will always have control over part of your life. Some controls are good, others aren't."

"How are any controls good?" I demanded fighting the desire to throw a tantrum. Magic sucked.

"Jo. She has strings and controls on you. I suspect Sable is getting there too. Carelian. All of these are positive effects on your life. If you try, the draft will be a positive effect too. It can help you get into the career you want and many people, like me, stay in that career all their lives building friends and relationships. For many of us the draft guaranteed us a job we'd like."

"Paul Goins hated his," I pointed out, remembering how many people died because of one insane mages' selfishness.

"Yes, but what we didn't cover was he had turned down or torpedoed at least three other jobs, all of which would have been much better fits for him. The flame jumper job they ordered him to take or be considered obstructionary to the draft and sent to the military. A lot of things might have been different if he had been less of a pain." Alixant had a touch of bitter in his voice and guilt slammed into me.

I'm being whiney and a bitch and I need to stop it.

"Okay. I'll try to suck it up, deal, and look on the positive side of all of this. I'll be careful and if I see anything that I think is odd, I'll let you know."

"I really wish you'd accept a guard. It would make all of us feel better."

"No." My response was instant. "I'm not doing that. Most of the students right now regard me as a freak. I start walking around with a guard and I'll be a stuck-up freak. I need these students. You just told me about how you can make friends. I have at least three years to get ready for my med degree and start my internship. I need to be able to work with these people."

"True. Indira is bringing BBQ and all the fixings. There should be plenty of leftovers. And they have a familiar carnivore side that she's bringing for Carelian."

"That should make everyone happy." We were pulling up to the biology lab building. "Thanks for the ride," I said. I slid out, taking a long few seconds to scope out the area.

"Cori?" Something in his voice worried me as I turned. I arched an eyebrow, looking at him. "Don't count on that med degree, okay? I think you may need to be open to a few other things."

"Wait, what?" I stammered out, glaring at him. "It's STEM, that's what you told me it had to be."

"It is, just be aware there is pressure for you to go another direction and this isn't pressure you will be able to ignore as easily as that from the societies. Just think about it. We'll see you tomorrow."

With that bombshell he pulled away, leaving me staring after him, throttling the desire to scream once again.

Chapter 19

While not commented on often, mage deaths world-wide are higher than any other similar group. While there is a significant increase for young males between the ages of 25-35, after that the distribution remains relatively even. Roughly 31% of all mages never make it to age sixty, but there is no consensus as to why. Causes of death are varied and no conclusions have been formed from the evidence. ~ OMO Report

CHAOS

I mulled over his statement all day, trying to figure out what else I wanted. But I didn't know. How do you decide your entire future knowing if you don't do what some nameless organization wants, they'll force you to do something else? While I respected the people who served in the military, it didn't hold any interest for me. I enjoyed my privacy way too much to want to share with dozens of other women.

Carelian pounced on me as I walked through the door, leaping into my arms, forcing me to catch him.

~No more leaving me. I come with.~ His tone had an absolute imperative, and I petted him.

"I'm sorry. Today it would have been too hard to bring you. Plus labs. You hate the lab courses."

~Bring catnip, I'll sniff instead.~ I blinked at that, then shrugged. While earth cats got the equivalent of high off of it, Carelian had an allergic reaction that had his nose stuffed up and unable to smell anything. It drove him crazy. I had to fight not to sob at his selflessness. ~Then I get live mouse.~

That cured my desire to cry, and I started laughing. He rarely hunted wild animals, but as far as he was concerned pet stores were supermarkets just for him.

"One a week. And you have to eat it there. I'm not carrying it home then letting you eat it."

He narrowed his eyes at me. ~Let loose in the park, then I eat.~

I narrowed my eyes back. The nearest park was three blocks from the pet store. "You carry it in the bag."

~Acceptable.~

I laughed and hugged him. The apartment was still empty as Jo and Sable both had late classes on Thursdays. That worked for me. I pulled out something Jo had prepared ahead of time and threw it in our electronic pressure cooker. It'd finish cooking before they got home. That gave me time to sit down and pull out both the contract and the pamphlet. I chose the pamphlet first and flipped it open. The more I read, the more stunned and horrified I became. But nothing in it wasn't obvious—if you were a psychopath and wanted to kill people.

They broke it down into twelve sections, one for each branch of magic, and it listed ways even people with hedge-mage level of magic could kill or disable opponents. The first few chapters focused on the elements as those were still the most common of all the classes.

Water and the evaporate spell have excellent applications. It can range from creating a killer hangover to having them drop dead. Most people don't realize how sensitive our organs are to moisture levels. Having the water in the brain evaporate (or actually move into the bloodstream) will kill anyone almost instantly.

I fought to swallow past bile and randomly flipped to another chapter.

If you do not need your opponent alive, Entropy can break all the water molecules into hydrogen and O2 which will kill anyone. If your available offering or skill level isn't enough to do that through the body, focus on doing it only in the eyes. This will cause ex-cruciating pain and they will be permanently blind.

The cold obvious logic made me realize how much I'd been viewing magic itself with rose-colored glasses. They never talked about this stuff in the books or even classes, but if you could pull the moisture out of an orange you could pull it out of a human.

The area for Soul grabbed me, and I read it. Most branches had pages and pages of ways to use the known spells. Soul only had a single page.

Other than the possibility of projecting devastating emotions into your opponent, Soul has little to rec-ommend it as an offense branch. However, its use in counter espionage, investigation, and human intelli-gence can not be overlooked.

Great, so my strengths are all about how to find out things from people. I don't really want to become a spy.

I closed the booklet and buried it deep in my backpack. This was something I really didn't feel like explaining to Jo. And if Stinky got a hold of it? Her brother would see way too many possibilities in it. I frowned, thinking. It was so obvious. Why hadn't other people figured this out? The answer sat in front of me; they had. This book provided proof. But it wasn't anything that the general population knew about, and I'd never seen it in any of the books or stories I'd read.

It took a second, but I pulled out my phone, ignoring the five percent battery warning. I'd plug it in after this. I sent Alixant a text message. *Is there censorship about magical abilities?* The answer had to be no; I mean, freedom of speech was one of the things that America prided itself on.

Yes

The one-word answer glowed on my screen and I sank back into the chair, staring blankly at the walls. Unable to process that and wondering just how blind I and everyone else was to the realities of magic, I pulled out the contract. It was two sheets of typed paper with room on the second sheet for signatures. I stopped, moved over to my computer, and searched for standard mentorship contracts and mentorship, just curious to see what it would tell me. Most of them were full of the duties of the apprentice or mentoree, and only rarely mentioned the duties of the mentor other than to support and guide. Though older ones often included monetary compensation, but after the 1950s that clause seemed to have disappeared. The OMO mentioned that mentors were falling out of fashion and the draft had built-in training and career support, just like any job.

I pulled out the copy of Indira's agreement and read it, my blood going cold. On the surface it seemed benign but as I read, I saw he had locked her in, forcing her to do whatever he wanted, all in smooth legalese. I read what Indira and Alixant offered again and compared the two. Their contract, in comparison, was legitimate and more than fair. It made me feel better and worse.

So why tie myself to someone? I'm avoiding the societies for this reason, not sure that I'd gain anything by signing a contract with anyone.

I still needed to research exactly what Emrys could give me, but the dude they'd sent to sway me had done the exact opposite. He'd pushed me even farther away from joining. Maybe after I had my masters or something when there was less chance they'd be able to trap me into owing them, I might try. I still needed to figure out my long-term plans since Alixant had implied they might block what I wanted.

My anger at that had faded a bit, but not the frustration level. I'd wait until they provided their suggestions. Right now, I shifted my attention to the papers laying on the manila envelope.

We, Indira Amira Humbert and Steven Weyland Alixant, agree to take Cori Munroe as our mentee during her pursuit of her education for a period not to exceed five years or earning a doctorate, whichever comes first. It is understood this relationship will be superseded by the start of draft service.

We will provide support both financially and for her education. We will act as liaisons between the school, government, or any other organization as might be required. We will provide advice and lawyers if needed for legal action. We will act as wardens of moral behavior to the societies, the government, and the Office of Magical Oversight.

In exchange, Cori will pursue her degree to the best of her abilities, will seek the advice of her mentors, and upon completing her draft service will provide two years of research assistance to Indira and Steven combined.

If she wants for any necessity, we agree to provide it at our own costs and will ensure she is protected and educated to the best of our ability.

There were lines for signatures and dates, but nothing else.

I just sat there and looked at the simplistic contract. I'd be an idiot to pass it up. They were both big names and had clout not only in their fields, but they knew people and would be good resources as I got closer to my draft assignment. People like Daniela would have given anything to be offered something as low risk as what I held. Heck, it even said they'd pay my bills if I needed it.

Carelian jumped into my lap—he'd been busy grooming—startling me, and I pulled him close, petting his fur in the way he preferred.

~My quean is protected.~

"And what does that mean?" I asked looking at him. Being a cat, he didn't answer, just demanded more pets. "So? Do you think I need a bodyguard?"

He glanced up at me and huffed, then rolled over so I could rub his sternum.

"I see. That doesn't help me much. Life was much easier when I was a nobody and just had terrible parents," I muttered, trying to not to give in to moping.

~Silly quean. Will see.~

"Thanks, I think. You know, you're getting too big to do this. You get much bigger and you won't fit on my lap anymore."

He flicked an ear and tail at me. I laughed and obeyed his demands for better scratches. Then I put the contract away on my desk. I had other homework to do and I could discuss it with them tomorrow. It gave me a night to sleep on it and think it over tomorrow. By then I'd have figured out what to do.

I finished getting dinner ready, my skills having improved to the point that I could at least do that. While I waited for them to get home, I worked on my homework. With biology to study, a chem test coming up, and two more papers in Magic History and Magic Law respectively, I didn't have time to waste. There were two classes that I hoped I could do as independent study over the summer, but I had to get A's in both magic classes to even have a chance.

"Oh, I'm so glad you're here. You're ignoring your phone again," Jo gasped out as she burst through the door, followed closely by Sable.

"Huh?" I reached down and picked it up. It was dead. "Sorry, it was low and I forgot to charge it." At least I thought that was what had happened. I checked for Murphy, but I was clean. I put it on the charger and turned to look at them as they locked the door behind them. "What's up?"

"Indira was attacked!" Sable burst out, then clamped her hands over her mouth, though they still shook.

"WHAT?" I looked at them, completely lost. "Indira? Our Indira? What happened?"

"I don't know very many Indira's," Jo said as she dumped stuff on her desk. "All I know is that someone jumped her after her last class, I think about two? A mage. And she cleaned the ground with him. Some student got about half of it on vid." She held out her phone to me. "Watch."

I grabbed her phone and hit play on the video. It started about halfway in, but I saw a gout of flame burst up around the man attacking her, focusing on his hair. That made sense. You got rid of the easiest offering and you cut their strength. Then his clothes fell apart around him. He froze for a second, and that was all she needed. That weird effect I'd seen before and one moment she was five feet away, the next she was in his personal space bubble swinging a wicked strike at his throat. The video cut off there and I jerked my head up to look at Jo and Sable. "What happened?"

Jo shrugged. "Don't know about the vid, but she laid the guy out cold. Cops and OMO showed up. I figured you'd know more."

I checked my phone—it had charged enough to turn on. There was one message from Alixant.

We'll discuss what happened with Indira tomorrow.

I showed it to Jo and Sable. "Sorry ladies, your need for more will have to wait until tomorrow."

"Figures. We have an in, and you know nothing. Useless you are," Jo pouted as she released the pressure on the pot. "But at least you got dinner going so I'm not complaining."

I didn't mention the contract or the pamphlet, just let us have a normal evening, even as I wondered who would try to attack Indira and why. I had a horrible feeling it was a way to hamstring me.

Chapter 20

The American Indian Nation encompasses 23,000 square miles. It is in five sections. Umatilla in Washington is 4,000 square miles. Black Hills, sectioned between South Dakota and Nebraska, is 5,000 square miles. Iroquois, between New York and Canada, encompasses 2,000 square miles. Hopi is 3,000 square miles and is surrounded by Utah, Colorado, Arizona, and New Mexico. The Five Tribes AIN, located between Texas and Oklahoma, is the largest at 9,000 square miles. ~ History of Magic

ORDER

Carelian and I went one of the alternative routes to class that morning, and I only had a brief feeling of being watched, but it faded as I turned to check behind me. Carelian flitted in and out of the shadows. We'd had a long talk, or more accurately I'd talked to him, and we'd agreed that while I traveled he'd leave the harness on, but I'd leave off the leash so he had plenty of ability to move without being obviously next to me.

It had the odd effect of me being hyper-aware of my surroundings, always trying to spot him. Today I'd chosen a particularly winding way to class. This meant lots of pine trees, hedges with pokey leaves, and the hint of spring in the almost visible buds on what deciduous trees there were. I'd never paid much attention to plants, so for me everything was a pine or a deciduous. Anything else didn't register to me.

Carelian, on the other hand, thought they all smelled great as he investigated and slunk around everything. But he always showed up if we needed to cross a street. I paid hyper attention to everyone and everything every time we crossed a street, leaving me exhausted on the other side. GA Mage-Tech was huge, and we had to cross at least three four-lane streets to get to class. At least with this route. My more direct route cut it down to two. This did have the advantage of passing by at least two different coffee shops that I hadn't tried yet.

I walked towards my first Friday class. Students fell silent as I approached and I could feel the weight of their eyes on me. I resisted the urge to ask what and instead made myself stand up straighter and walk with a confident pace.

"What's the matter, freak? Already get your familiar killed? Or did he realize what a loser you are and dump you? I mean people trying to kill you, what do you expect. I wouldn't be around you either."

I didn't have to turn to know it was Daniela speaking, but I paused and pivoted slightly so I could see her. As I expected, her pretty face twisted up in a sneer.

"Then why exactly are you risking your life talking to me? You know I don't understand the lot of you. I'm apparently super powerful and people are trying to kill me. Shouldn't you be bending over backwards to make me like you? To make sure I don't accidentally lose control of my magic and hurt you? Huh? Guess it proves that people are sheep and don't know how to think." As I spoke the last words Carelian came bounding up next to me, brushing by some of the students who'd been staring at me.

Their jumps and shrieks amused me as I turned and continued my way in, letting Carelian walk with me as he wanted.

Rules be damned. They can all go take a flying leap.

The thought didn't help much, but it still felt good.

"You shouldn't push her too much. She has a powerful family." Charles spoke from a shadowed alcove inside the doors. I think there used to be a landline telephone there, now it was just an awkward space out of sight of most people.

"Right now, I don't care. I will not let them stop me," I almost hissed out that last part, just frustrated and feeling oddly impotent with all of it.

"Stop you from?" He had a funny look on his face and Arachena poked her head out and waved at me.

I sighed. "Sorry, long story. Doesn't matter. Thanks," I muttered.

"For?" he asked, still giving me a funny look.

"Not being like them." I jerked my head back at the milling students who now seemed too scared to follow me into the building. Whatever.

"I hope I'm never like them. I won't say having a familiar makes you a better person, but I suspect the one you get amplifies certain personality traits. At least it seems that way. You have a cat. Are you more independent and stubborn?"

I looked at him, then at Carelian, who stared intently at Arachena. I gave up and shrugged. "Maybe. But to be honest I always was. What about you? What do you think Arachena amplifies in you?" Curiosity had raised its head, and I now wanted answers. Though I resisted the urge to research it, I didn't have time.

"More calculating, less emotional. But then I never was all that touchy feely. So who knows." He shrugged and turned. "Ready for class?"

"As much as I'll ever be, I guess." We headed towards class and I hoped today would be interesting enough to keep me from thinking about people trying to kill me, classes, and the rest. The one bright spot—Daniela wasn't in any of our classes as she was a sophomore. Small blessings.

They were focusing on how the spells in Chaos worked starting with Entropy. Today though, I thought beyond what he said. One of the common aspects of Chaos was Decay for non-organic. All the applications he talked about were laboratory- or research-based. The entire attitude was that for the average mage there wasn't much use in it outside of that setting. But my mind took it and went down the path. Why couldn't you cause scaffolding to rust out and break, a tube on a brake line to crack, a pacemaker to corrode? The more I thought about it, the more nauseous I grew. You could kill people without effort, and without a Pattern or Time mage investigating, they'd never know it was anything besides an accident.

Carelian purred in my mind, but it was more like he was complimenting what I'd figured out rather than reassuring me. I wanted to ask him a question, but here in public wasn't the right way. I hadn't figured out if he could read my thoughts as he only responded to spoken words, so that aspect was still up in the air. And if asked, he pretended not to hear the question.

I headed out, not talking to anyone, but all too aware of the gap that appeared around me as I moved.

Look on the bright side, it makes getting out of classes easier.

The thought didn't help much. A sudden need for sugar and caffeine gripped me. "Come on, Carelian, I have the need for a fix."

A nearby snicker made me roll my eyes. Whatever. They could think I was doing drugs on top of it all. Not like my reputation could get any worse at this point. And what did it matter? The draft didn't care about your grades, only your proven skills.

I started out, headed towards one of the coffee shops I liked. It was a bit of a hike, but I had time and I wanted to use the walk to clear my head. I still hadn't a hundred percent decided about the mentorship. I needed to figure out my feelings for sure by tonight. Coffee and sugar sounded like a splendid way to do that.

Carelian appeared by my side at the crosswalk of the one main road on this route. Once across, the coffee shop was on the next block. The light changed, I checked both ways, still paranoid, then crossed. Four steps in, my shoe stuck, and I looked down, trying to figure out what I had stepped in. It took me way too long to figure out what I saw. The asphalt had melted and my foot had sunk into it.

"What in the world?" I muttered and looked around for a mage, but other than some guy giving me a funny look, I didn't see anyone. The flashing walk man changed to a red hand, and I started trying to tug my foot out. An explosive bang followed by a crash of metal jerked my attention ahead of me. I felt my heart skitter beat. Streets in downtown Atlanta were almost always busy, and everyone used the lanes near the sidewalks for loading and unloading large trucks for the businesses in those blocks. Seeing a lineup of semis or box trucks on the lane closest to the sidewalk was normal.

The trailer that had just disconnected and started rolling directly towards me did not qualify as normal.

"Shit!"

Already I could hear people screaming and I tried harder to get my foot loose, but the other one had now sunk into the strangely warm asphalt. I could feel the heat of it even through my boots.

~CORI! My quean!~ Carelian's cry ripped through my head leaving physical pain in its wake. I whimpered, tears springing to my eyes as that pain lanced through.

"Lady, get out of there!"

More yelling and screaming as the trailer tore through the beginning of the intersection, still on a course that would hit and kill me. There wasn't anything to stop it, and even if I could cut my feet off, I couldn't get out of the way at this point.

I'm going to die.

My heart pounded, but I couldn't inhale, I couldn't even scream. Terror beat at me, mine and Carelian's, and I saw him dashing towards me, his fur standing on end, hissing as he raced on the outside of the crossing markings.

NO!

I reached for my magic, any of it, all of it, I didn't care what the price was, I didn't care what it did, but I wouldn't let anything happen to Carelian. Magic shoved into my hands and I accepted the cost before I could figure out what it was. It didn't matter.

The ground shook and rippled. I heard the impact, felt it, even as I smelled gas, sewer, and water hitting the air. Car horns started blasting and people screamed, but none of it registered as anything other than background noise as

Carelian jumped into my arms, purring, his claws poking through my sweater and drawing blood.

I didn't care as I squeezed him tight and stood there shaking. It wasn't until someone tapped my shoulder that I bothered to look up from where I'd buried my face in his fur.

"Ma'am? Can you move?" The speaker was a cop, of course, but he looked at me with wide eyes and a face that seemed more than a touch gray. I looked beyond him and vertigo hit me as I took in what I'd done. And I knew I'd done it.

The intersection, boxed on all sides by crosswalks, had been normal boring black asphalt. Now it was a gaping hole with the semi trailer embedded in the side closest to me. Less than two feet away. I pulled earth so deep that underground mains and wires had been severed. The sewer and gas fumes were mixed together creating a noxious and unhealthy taste in the air.

"Ma'am, can you move?" the man repeated. I looked down at my feet, but they still stuck to the asphalt.

"I think," I murmured, my voice barely loud enough for me to hear it. I swallowed and tried to speak louder. "I think if I can balance, I can unzip my boots and pull my feet out."

The cop nodded wordlessly and just offered his elbow. I let Carelian down with a pang of loss, but I fought it down. I held onto the cop's elbow, reached down, and unzipped my boot. After a bit of wiggling, I pulled my foot out of the boot. A minute later I had the other one done. Standing there in my sock-clad feet on the street, I realized the asphalt was barely warm, not almost hot as it had felt through my boots.

I knew I should care, but I fought not to shake with the adrenaline dumping in my body and the chill settling in as sweat dried on my skin.

"Ma'am, if you'll come with me. We need to talk to you."

I focused on the man and realized he was being extremely polite, but I could see everyone staring at me and then back to the hole in the street.

"Yeah, of course. May I call someone?"

"We'd like to talk to you first," he said, his voice still very deferential.

Defeated, I sighed and moved to where they had cleared out the inside of a Subway on the corner. They ushered me to a back booth and settled me in it.

"The Captain should be here in a minute, ma'am." The officer backed away, but not far, and I saw other cops, who from the bright splashes of color on their temples would be mages. I could see more lights flashing, and more vehicles arriving through the windows. Power, sewer, Department of Transportation. I just watched, a sinking feeling in my stomach.

I really hope I don't have to pay for this.

Chapter 21

Studies indicate most hedgemages rarely share they are mages, and often even their closest friends are unaware. There is disturbing evidence that their mage abilities are rarely used. Add in the predominance of male pattern baldness and even wizards and magicians avoid magic due to the offerings needed. This must be addressed immediately as an entire segment of society is abandoning the gift they were given.
~ House of Emrys newsletter article

SPIRIT

"Dammit Cori! We told you to be careful!" Alixant had been yelling at me for ten minutes and I didn't even have the energy to be angry. He chewed me out for reckless use of magic, endangering civilians, and putting myself in needless danger. He was almost foaming at the mouth.

The door opened and Indira came striding in. The cop stopped her at the door, but whatever she said convinced him to let her enter. Alixant had just shown his badge to get in.

The captain, who must be getting sick of seeing me at this point, just asked me to stay put for a while until he had some more information.

"You need protection, this isn't—"

"Steven. Enough." Indira's soothing voice cut through everything and the man sagged. It creeped me out to watch him almost shrink.

"She doesn't understand," he rasped out. "She needs to understand."

"Did you at her age? Did you really understand?" She patted him on the back and turned to look at me. "Are you okay?"

"I need shoes. I liked those boots." It was a nonsensical statement, I knew it, but I didn't know what else to say.

Indira looked at my feet, and my bright pink socks, and arched an eyebrow. "So I see. They still haven't managed to get your shoes out of the asphalt. Whoever did that meant for you to not move."

"They succeeded," I muttered, feeling my face flush. I pushed it away and tried to be strong. "Am I responsible for the damage out there? I mean I know I caused it. But am I liable?"

They glanced at each other and sighed. "Let's talk about this back at the apartment. I think all three of you need to hear this," Alixant finally said. He spun on one heel, a trick that when I tried to copy usually made me fall over, and headed towards the captain.

Indira slid onto the bench across from me. "You're not hurt?"

"Physically? No." I shook my head, though I hadn't quit petting Carelian the entire time I'd been in here. And I'd missed class. That added to my upset and frustration. At this rate I'd fail because of the classes I was missing.

"Good. I'll let Steven get you out of here. I'll dash over to the CVS and get you at least a pair of slippers to wear home. I'll be back in a few minutes."

Before I could respond she had slipped back out and Alixant and the captain were headed my way.

"Miss Munroe, I'm sure you understand we have some questions," Captain Jessup said, his voice as neutral as I'd ever heard.

"Yes. Please, I'll answer everything I can."

The captain started questioning me with a detective by his side taking notes. I told them everything, but there wasn't much to tell them in reality.

Alixant kept quiet until we got to the magic and me ripping open a hole in the ground. "What was it?"

Pulled out of my rote answers, I looked at him, not following his question. "What was what?"

"Your offering, what did it cost?"

"Oh. Umm," I closed my eyes and tried to figure it out. I still wasn't used to accepting costs after all this time because I'd done it unconsciously for so long. I had to pull the ask and my response from my memory. I reached up to touch my hair and while it wasn't a huge difference it was shorter. "About an inch of hair," I said, letting my hand drop.

Both men froze and looked at me. "That was the entire offering, an inch of hair?" Alixant asked this quietly as his eyes grew distant and I could tell he was thinking about something. "Nothing else? No blood?"

"Umm, no. Just the hair."

"Where was Carelian?"

"In my arms."

They exchanged glances again. Then the questioning picked back up and I explained that I just pulled, desperate. There wasn't much more asked after that.

By the time they finished, Indira had come back with some slippers, and I gratefully pulled them on. Exhaustion hit me like a wave and all I wanted to do was sleep.

"I'll take you home, Cori," Alixant said, standing.

I knew I should follow up on what happened, but the weight of weariness overcame the desire to ask. "You'll explain things tonight?"

"Yes," said Indira. "Go home. Nap. I'll be by about six with food and we can talk then." Her voice was soft and I couldn't figure out anything from her voice other than vague worry.

I followed Alixant out and we walked to his car parked a torturous block away. I climbed into it ready to pass out. I'd been getting more in shape but walking that one block I thought might kill me. Carelian never strayed from my side and we got more than a few looks, but it didn't matter.

I slumped in the seat, closing my eyes seconds after I managed to buckle in. Carelian wrapped himself around my feet. I could feel his purr through my skin and in my mind. I must have fallen asleep or maybe just been that unaware because I didn't register anything besides his purrs until Alixant shook my shoulder.

"Come on, Cori. I'll get you into your apartment."

I nodded and let him carry my bag. The thought of even lifting the book-filled bag up to my shoulder brought tears to my eyes. Fifteen minutes later, with the door locked, I fell onto my bed and the world went away.

"Cori! What happened?!" Jo shook my shoulder hard, pulling me to consciousness. I pried my eyes open to stare at her and Sable. Memory returned, and I blinked at the surge of adrenaline.

"Oh, yeah."

"It's all over the news. You're the only person I know with a large red feline familiar. They got a pic of you on the news camera too."

I groaned and pulled the cover over my head.

"No. Up, talk."

I sighed and sat up, giving them the overview of what happened. By the time I finished we were in the living room and I almost felt like I could handle all this. Carelian was still sleeping.

"But there are questions I need answers to. They said they'd be here around six." It was ten till. Sure enough, by the time I had finished sending a few emails to teachers, there was a knock on the door.

Jo sprang up and pulled it open, letting in Indira and Alixant and the scent of barbecued meat. The sweet spicy odor flowed into my nose. Hunger flared in me like ravening fire and I wanted the food now.

Okay, down girl. Food in a few minutes.

Indira must have seen something in my face because she didn't bother with small talk, just put the dishes on the table. There was general chatter and clanking as we dished things up. In five minutes, I had a plate loaded with smoked pork, cornbread, green beans, and coleslaw. We let them take the chairs near the table, I curled up in the club chair while Jo and Sable sat on the couch. We all ate, and even Carelian deigned to wake up to come eat before sliding under the club chair and going back to sleep. His snoring was a dead giveaway.

"Cori, I believe there are a few issues that need to be discussed today, correct?" Indira's voice forced me to resist the urge to shove another cornbread muffin into my mouth. I nodded warily at her. "If I'm correct we need to discuss mentorship, the attacks on your life, and the ramifications of what you did to the intersection."

The image of torn pipes, crumpled metal and jagged asphalt appeared crystal clear in my mind, and I wished I hadn't eaten so much.

"Yeah. Can we start with the intersection?" I asked. I saw Jo and Sable glance at each other, and the fierce gladness I felt at having them here surprised me. Jo had always been my rock, but Sable fit as if she'd always been here and was meant to be.

That thought resonated in me, but Indira spoke, distracting me. "Very well. But I need to step back and talk about societies." I frowned at her but didn't say anything. "There are dues as a member, and they are hefty, but some of that goes to lawyers. That, in part, deals with situations like this."

"I've never heard of something like this happening before," blurted Jo. She blushed but held her chin up defiantly.

"Oh, you have," Alixant drawled, and that just sounded weird with his northern accent. "But it's only a story for a day or so. Then the news is encouraged to find something else to report. You'll see that by tomorrow there will have just been an incident downtown, and by Monday no one will remember it. The only reason the stadium stayed active so long is there was no harm in showing the 'awesome' things we did, because most of it was focused on the monsters who took care of the bad mage. No one is ever encouraged to do stories about the damage mages can do, in fact, they're actively discouraged from it. We don't want people getting ideas. Too many do as it is."

"The censorship!" I jerked up, looking at him, remembering the text I'd sent.

"Yes. I'll let you in on a dirty little secret. Most of the 'rogue' mages the US or OMO hunt down are not those that refused the draft. They are mages that realized how deadly they were and started using their magic in ways that would be considered unethical at best. The first year of the draft is spent with both the OMO and government beating into you exactly what the consequences are of using your magic in such ways. And how easy it is for them to kill a mage that doesn't toe the line. Note that I said the OMO. This is global. And outside a few tightly locked down countries such as North Korea or some African dictatorships, all governments understand that magic use like that will not be tolerated." His voice had no humor and threat weighed down every word.

I couldn't stop my swallow and sank further back into my chair. The pale faces of Jo and Sable under their darker skins didn't make me feel any better.

"Why didn't our parents ever tell us this?" Jo asked, her voice smaller than I'd ever heard it.

"They did. Remember the stories reminding you to be an obedient girl? Of the disdain of anyone that uses their magic to hurt? How many books and movies have you seen where the mage dies a horrible death because they use their magic to hurt? Granted, the smart ones never get caught. From friends over in ATF I know there are a few major drug manufacturers that are mages. But they stay low and no one knows who they are. They don't do anything regular drug dealers don't do. And we are damn sure there are a few professional assassins that are mages. The moral of the story boils down to don't use magic to hurt. The OMO comes down hard and their hit squads don't follow the orders of any government."

His harsh words broke what few illusions I had and for a desperate moment I wanted to never have emerged. To be a normal person and never deal with any of this.

~But then I would be without my quean.~

I didn't see him, but his words filled my head, and I swallowed.

"What Steven isn't pointing out though is for most mages to do what you did Cori would have eaten up most of their offering for months." Indira's voice was calm. "That is why merlins serve a decade compared to the four Jo and Sable will serve. To understand how serious this is, let me give you some numbers. Of all the merlins that go into the draft, only forty-three percent make it out the other end."

"It's that dangerous?" Sable squeaked, her hand and Jo's tightly clenched together.

Indira just looked at her and after a moment she paled even further.

"Oh. That many aren't allowed to leave alive because they are that dangerous?"

"Or they never prove they can be trusted to use their power wisely." Indira shifted her gaze back to me. "Which brings us to you. You are insanely powerful and your little stunt proved just how powerful you are. One of the benefits of societies is they use your dues to protect you in legal cases, and they help you get good rates on insurance for inadvertent uses of power. It is why I suggested Emrys. They have decent rates and it lets you protect yourself. Nothing is free and societies expect a lot from mages, including smarter use of their abilities." Her voice went dry at that.

"However," Alixant interrupted, "it is acknowledged, or will be, that you are young, still untrained, and at fear for your life. It will come out of a special account for mages in training to cover. However, the pressure to get you under control is increasing."

"Oh," I muttered. The meaning was clear. My options were running out. Through no fault of my own.

"Which means you are most likely only to be tasked during your draft to do a few 'favors' for the city of Atlanta. An easy price to pay."

"Favors?" I didn't like the sound of that.

"Yes. Most likely construction. Dig out a trench, or do emergency repairs, things like that. You'll be asked to help regularly until the cost of repairing the damage you did is regarded as recouped. Most cities just put it in their ledger. There is nothing sinister, they will ask for help and if you're available, you show up and help—gratefully." She stressed that last word and I ducked my head, feeling like an idiot.

"So, at this point I need to ask. Do you want us as your mentors?" There wasn't any pressure in her voice, but I could feel Alixant's intent stare.

I heaved a sigh. "I was going to say no. Say I'd rather just be friends. But I get the feeling that really isn't an option. I seem to have fewer options than what I thought. So, the answer is yes." I watched some of the stress bleed out of them and wondered what else I didn't know. And if I really wanted to know it. "But—" I stressed the word and watched them stiffen. "I want to change the contract."

Indira started to look at Alixant, but she stopped herself and shrugged. "To say what?"

I reached in and pulled out the paper I'd shoved in my bag. I smoothed it out wanting to make sure I remembered it.

"This, what does two years of research assistance mean?"

They frowned at me. "Exactly what it says. Most merlins usually have some research project going on, and you'd be excellent at assisting. I have my studies into planar rips and Alixant has forensic projects that he does for the government."

"Do I get paid? Why not just hire me? What if you want to research something I find objectionable?"

"Cori, this isn't you being Igor and us being mad scientists." Indira huffed out an exasperated sigh. "Yes, you'll come in as if we hired you off the street and just work with us. For me, it would be as a teaching assistant and your job would be to help me do my job and my research. While Alixant would probably have you come in as a junior agent and perform field work. That part is all very legitimate and often used to get people you really want into your teams and then hope they like it there."

That made me feel much better. The wording had made me think it was under the table or something. "Can it be reworded to say one year with each of you?" I didn't demand, but it was clear it mattered.

"Of course. Anything else?"

"What does 'wardens of moral behavior' mean."

"We are saying we will put our reputations and if necessary our assets behind you to ensure you don't, for lack of a better word, be an idiot." Alixant smirked at me as he answered, and I wanted to throw something at him.

"Who wants this in here? I doubt it's you."

"No. Both the government draft liaison and the OMO suggested that clause. They are anxious about you, Cori."

"What happens if I don't sign it?"

He shrugged. "I'd wager daily visits or the presence of an OMO officer or draft board officer in your vicinity. Worse case," Indira cleared her throat but Alixant gave a sharp shake of his head and continued, "you'll be killed as an uncontrollable threat."

I froze and looked at them, the reality of all of this sinking in. "What you're saying is you're putting yourselves up as scapegoats if I go rogue."

"In essence, yes."

We went back and forth for an hour, Jo and Sable watching with wide eyes. But finally, I signed it—I didn't really have a choice.

"What about Emrys, do I still need to do that? I really don't want to owe them. I had planned on making them beg me to join." I felt silly admitting it. This whole thing felt like I kept thinking I knew everything, only to find out it was just the tip of the iceberg. And the blasted iceberg kept being bigger than I expected.

"You really need to join one. They offer group insurance policies, networking, legal advice, and yes, sometimes you will owe them favors. But most of the merlins that make it out of the draft alive are very scrupulous about sticking to the straight and narrow. They know the consequences of not."

"Ugh. I just," I broke off. Whining served no purpose. "Will they try to assign me a mentor?"

"Eh. Probably not. Especially as you have one, though..." she trailed off and shook her head. "Have they approached you?"

"Yeah some guy saying he was the head. Tried too hard to impress me. Left a bad taste in my mouth."

"Hmm, let me make a call. I have a friend who is one of their outreach people. Let me get her to contact you if that's okay?"

I shrugged. I didn't have anything to lose at this point.

"We done?"

This time they did look at each other.

"Ugh, would you two stop doing that!" I snapped. My patience was at an end and exhaustion was creeping back up on me. All I wanted to do was go back to bed. I was glad I'd decided not to work this weekend. If I had a shift tomorrow, that might have been too much.

"How much did Carelian help with the offering?" Alixant asked. "I couldn't have done that. I don't have enough unless I was willing to bleed and you didn't have time to remove blood from your veins. I don't know of any merlin that could have pull that off for an inch of hair, no matter how much hair you have."

"I don't know. I didn't have time to think."

They sighed and stood. "Ladies, it's been a stressful day. I'll get someone to contact you soon, but be careful. People hired to kill you don't quit because it gets harder, they just become more determined."

Before I could say much else, they were gone, leaving me feeling like I'd been run over by a train.

Chapter 22

Magical inheritances are things of story and mystery. Not that you can inherit magical abilities, but having things left to you by a powerful mage. While most mages make excellent money and have solid careers, merlins can have things from other realms and often seem to have done things not possible according to what we know about magic. Some governments claim estates of merlins at the time of death. The US does not currently, but more than one resolution has narrowly failed to do the same. ~ History of Magic

CHAOS

My paranoia kept me jumping at shadows all week. I think it also affected Carelian. He'd barely leave my side. I spent every minute that I wasn't doing homework looking at the pamphlet Alixant had provided. I had asked him why people kept using "mundane" means to kill me. Why not just stop my heart or cause an aneurysm? Either way I'd be dead.

His response didn't make me feel better. *Part legal ramifications. If a mage kills you and it was at the order of the Emperor of Japan there would be hell to pay and the OMO would enforce it. Also, the people very good at assassinations aren't going to knock off a budding merlin because of an inheritance. But otherwise, you should already be dead. A few people are surprised you aren't.*

After that text message the entire class of Magic Basics retreated to a distant blur. As I struggled to focus on anything, I wondered if this was what a panic attack felt like.

~Quean,~ rippled into my mind and Carelian licked my wrist. That brought my attention to the two pinpoints of color on the inside of my wrist. I stared at it for a long time, then leaned back in my chair, letting Bernard's lecturing wash over me.

Is that why I'm not dead? Or is it something else? This makes no sense. But they can all take a flying leap. I'm going to do this, I'm going to own the damn world if I have to, but I'm done being the patsy.

I stewed on that for the rest of class. Thinking about how to create shields with my magic. If you could wrap luck around you, why not air, or something that would prevent things from hitting you? Like bullets. But how would I fuel it to keep it up all the time? There had to be stuff about personal protection. Which meant research. By the time I left, nodding at Charles who still was the only person even semi friendly, I'd built up a head of steam. First the library and a game plan. I still needed to challenge courses this summer and make sure the classes I needed to take were offered. But now I needed the resources the library offered.

"Excuse me. Are you Cori Munroe?"

I stumbled as I came to a stop, the unexpected hail throwing me off of my burn-down-the-world plan. A woman at least decade older than me, but not as old as Marisol, stood to one side. Dressed in nice jeans and a blouse, with long blond hair pulled up in a ponytail, the only thing that stood out was the merlin tattoo on her face. A pattern merlin.

"You are?" All the incidents lately had severely whittled away my ability to trust.

Her smile was warm, and it didn't make her pretty, but softened her from being stern to friendly. "Joanna Snowden. Indira asked if I'd come by and talk to you? I heard that Gaylord didn't go over well."

"You could say that. But why should what you say be any different from what he said?" I moved over to the side, out of people's way. Even so, more than a few students gazed at me as they walked by.

"In essence, it won't be. Look, I know Indira, I know most of the merlins. There are only forty in Georgia. I'm the liaison for the Southeast. So I manage all the chapters for Georgia, Florida, Alabama, and South Carolina. I don't normally come out and chase after mages. Usually people just apply about their junior year. You seem to be an unusual case though."

"Yeah. Everything about me lately is unusual." My voice held more than a fair amount of bitter and she glanced at me eyebrows raised.

"Am I missing something?"

"Yeah. Not your problem. Why should I join Emrys? Heck, why should I join any of the societies? So far all I've really heard is the unpleasant aspects."

"Ah. You have a class to go to? Can I buy you a coffee?"

The reminder of how Carelian had almost been killed the other day because of coffee had me flinching. "How about we talk at the library? It's quiet there and if we get one of the small study rooms, we can talk with something approaching privacy."

"That works." She didn't say another word as we reached the library and checked in. When we were settled, she spoke again. "I will give you the standard spiel then you can ask any questions. The House of Emrys"—her voice dropped into a tone I recognized from saying the same thing over and over again. I dubbed it the customer service voice—"is a society of and for merlins. We provide a safe space to discuss theories, foster friendships, and create networks of like-minded individuals. We have a pooled plan for health insurance, legal representation, and retirement. We do require dues, but we place no onus on how merlins live their lives." She cleared her throat then continued with her spiel.

"We have houses in Berlin, London, New York, Seattle, Rio, Paris, and Sydney. If you're traveling, they are always available for a meal, drinks, shower, and a simple room if needed. Our library, one of the best in the world, is located in London and access is available upon request. Access to our resorts around the world is provided at a discounted rate. Help with loans, business set up, and other situations can be found among our members via the monthly newsletter." When she finished, she smiled at me, again something warm and welcoming. "Any questions?"

"That sounds too good to be true. What about people expecting favors if they help you?" I challenged her, expecting something.

"Last time I checked, that is the way of the world. Very few people do things just to do them. If you help someone move, you expect them to help you. I've never seen the society be much different." She shrugged, a half-bewildered look on her face. "Bottom line, don't need a favor to get yourself out of a situation that can be used against you. You work to build friendships, not acquaintances."

I blinked and then slumped. Indira's story was the exception, not the rule, and as long as I didn't do things that encouraged people to break the law then there wasn't any reason to not join. And the library and club houses around the world sounded cool. It would give me reasons to travel.

"Are you allowed to bring friends? I mean to eat and if we needed a room."

"Yes, up to four other people, not including family members. While only merlins are allowed to join very few of us end up marrying another merlin or having children that are. It doesn't seem to run in families consistently." She provided this answer immediately, without hesitation, like all of her responses.

"You know, if the other guy had been this nice, I wouldn't have had as much of an issue."

"He regards being eligible to belong to Emrys as an honor rather than something forced upon you without you having any say so in the matter."

That surprised me, and I stared at her. "You're one of the few I've talked to in a while that doesn't babble on about how great magic is."

She shrugged. "All of us have dreams. Reality doesn't always allow them to come true. I take it this means you're interested?"

"I've had it pointed out by multiple people that having access to the legal aspects, given what is going on in my life right now, would be very advisable." I paused, thinking. Right now between the gym membership and what money I had in savings I should be okay through getting my degree, but if the dues were too much, I couldn't afford it. Maybe up to twenty-five a month.

"How much are the dues?"

"Thirty-five thousand a year," she said calmly.

I choked and started coughing. "Are you insane?"

"Well, that's only after you finish your draft service," she started, and I gaped at her.

"That is more than I've ever made. Ever. I can't afford that." I still was trying to breathe at the idea of paying more for dues than what I'd expect to put out for a new car.

"We know that. The membership is extended basically on credit until you start the draft. You get the membership—and most of the perks—but until your draft is finished, your yearly rate is one tenth of that, so thirty-five hundred a year while serving. And I've never seen a merlin not working in a draft service that doesn't pay upwards of one-twenty-five a year. The thirty-five hundred is cheap and gives you access to everything, though your service covers health insurance. While you are still going to school full time there is no cost, though there is a contract committing to staying a member once service is over for a decade without penalties. To be honest, I've only seen one merlin ever quit the house before their decade was up."

"Sato O'Shaughnessy," I said.

"Why, yes." For the first time Joanna looked shocked. "How did you know?"

"I know Shay, and that sounds like something he'd do. He's a weird one."

"That he is. Look, Cori. There is no pressure. Most students don't join until they are working on their masters or doctorate. And you can get legal coverage without joining, though it would be much more expensive. I'll leave you our information and our charter. And let you think it over."

"Thanks," I muttered, glancing at my phone. "Because I need to get to class. I'll let you know."

"Please do. My number is on my card with the information. Good luck, Cori."

I headed to class but spent the rest of the day pondering the offer and the information. I chomped a bit at not having as much time to research as I wanted. I still thought the idea of air as a shield would work. Just one problem—I was null in Air. Earth was the only element I registered in. But that hadn't stopped me from using fire. So, maybe?

I twisted what I'd learned about my strong areas, but none of them jumped out as being very helpful, especially if you didn't know you were about to be attacked.

Jo called as I got out of my last class. "Hey, I need to get groceries. I forgot this weekend since you kicked me and Sable up to Rockway to see my parents. Want to meet me at the store? There is just going to be too much to carry by myself and Sable has a test she needs to study for."

"Which means she could really use you out of the apartment because you're distracting?"

"That too," Jo admitted, and I could hear the smile in her voice.

"Sure, I'll meet you there." I hung up and glanced at Carelian. "I need to get some exercise in and we need to change up, so run to the store?" The Publix we shopped at was only two blocks from our apartment, and it wasn't a way I normally went. So me running and headed that way should help confuse anyone watching us. At least that was the theory.

~Run,~ Carelian agreed and took off, his bright red fur blending into the shadows better than anything that bright had the right to. I laughed and started out at a steady jog. Luckily, students were always late or exercising, so no one even looked as I headed out. For a moment as I left the shadow of the buildings, I thought I felt something, or maybe heard it, like a flap of wings. But when I looked behind me, I saw nothing. Shaking my head, I focused on running and not hitting anyone.

We got to the store in record time and Carelian lay in front of the windows panting. "You okay?"

~Water?~

I crouched, pulled my sports bottle out of its pocket and grabbed a collapsible bowl I kept with me. It was silicone so super lightweight, and didn't make noise, which had become the bane of my existence. Things clanging.

I poured water into the bowl and he sat up to eagerly drink. "Remember to tell me if you need water, silly," I admonished him. I put the water bottle away and dug for the leash. The store would allow him in, but only if he was on a leash. Odds were he'd curl up under the cart and snooze as we shopped.

"Yo, Cori," I heard Jo call as she walked up.

"Hey." I waved to her, trying to figure out what else we needed from the store. Study snacks, absolutely, and Carelian needed some more food.

"Hey Fuzzy," she said dipping to scratch his ears, then standing back up. "Ready to go?" She stood looking into the store behind me a bit.

"Yep, let me snap on his leash," I said, bending down and snapping it on his harness. I stood back up. "Oops, wait need to grab this." I darted back down to grab the bowl. The crack of a high-powered rifle sounded and all the hair on my body stood up.

"Uhh," Jo choked out. I spun to see blood spreading across her shirt.

Assassins are not unknown, though nowhere near as widespread as popular fiction would have you believe. Usually a bit of money to a local gang or thug is more common, and it makes the death much more deniable. However, both countries and individuals occasionally hire experts to eliminate threats or competition. This is different from the Rogue Mage squads governments and the OMO employ. ~ Magic Explained.

ORDER

"Jo!" I screamed. Carelian snarled, and I took all the ideas I'd had and pulled on Earth. There is dust everywhere outside, we breathe it, see it dance in the sun, and all of it answers to the pull of Earth. I yanked, the cost an inch of hair and I didn't care. I felt Carelian with me adding to the magic. I snapped it into a hard shell surrounding both of us. I felt like I looked through the windshield of an off-roading truck, but I could see figures and shapes around us. The shield arced from beside JO to other side of me, with nothing above.

There was another crack and I felt and saw the bullet impact the shield I had created. I pulled on more dust, only half an inch this time, and caused the impact where the bullet hit in a bullseye spider web. Another sharp retort, but this time I saw the trail of the bullet through the dust in the air and I followed it back with my Soul branch. My magic reached out towards the other person and with the magic, rage followed. I reached for the essence of the person trying to kill me. Then I yanked out the shooter's soul. Or life. Or magic. I don't know how to describe it. All I knew was that I reached in and everything that made him who or what he was, I pulled out, shredded, dissolved into motes of nothingness.

The cost was one drop of my blood. It came from my mouth, my teeth splitting the inside of my cheek with no hesitation.

~Yes, kill them my quean. Kill those that would hurt my queans. They are mine,~ Carelian's voice sounded like a buzz saw of vengeance in my head.

It was done. I knew I had just killed someone, even if the body hadn't realized it was dead yet. I felt once more like someone watched me, but I turned and grabbed the first aid kit out of my bag and caught Jo as she crumpled to the ground. Everything, the magic, the second attack, my response had not even taken ten seconds.

"Someone shot me?" she asked, her voice quavering, and it was everything I could do not to snarl my rage. No one hurt my Jo, no one.

"They were trying to shoot me. They missed." I had her shirt ripped open and was checking the damage. My heart slowed a bit. They'd been aiming for my head, but Jo is taller than me by about 4 inches. The shot had been at a downwards angle from where the shooter was, and it had slammed into her right shoulder. It just nicked where the cup of her bra ended.

"This is going to hurt, I need to pull you up for a minute."

"Kay," she muttered, face paling. The dark spread of blood meant she was still bleeding. I ignored her whimpers and pulled her forward onto my chest. Sure enough, blood spread across the back of her too. A clean through and through. That made my life easier. I took a spilt second to glance up and saw the glint of metal mixed with red on the wall where she'd been standing. I stared at the bullet for a heartbeat, then turned by attention back to Jo.

People were rushing out towards us as I laid her back down. "Sorry Jo, looks like you're going to get naked in front of strangers," I said as I ripped off the rest of her shirt.

"Damn, and no one has any singles," she choked out in between gasps of pain. Carelian curled up next to her head, purring, his head laying on hers.

"Oh shit, she's been shot!" someone exclaimed and somehow I resisted the urge to respond with pure snark.

"Call 911. Female injured, gunshot to the upper right chest," I snapped as I put pressure on the wound, strapped her arm down, and did everything I could to slow the bleeding. I didn't want to try to heal, I didn't know enough. Indira had made that very clear in class that until you had that medical degree and had practiced on a lot of cadavers, trying to use magic to heal might just kill you both. Instead, I stuck to what I knew. My training.

"If I die, tell Sable I love her. And my parents," Jo whispered, pain in every word.

"Oh, don't think you're getting out of exams that easy," I responded. "It's a flesh wound. You'll get a sexy scar, Sable can baby you, but you will still have to do your homework." I could hear the sirens and looked up, surprised by the number of people surrounding us.

Not good, someone else could have tried to kill us just now.

"Is she going to live?" asked one of the bystanders.

"Assuming the paramedics get here, yes. Can you wave them in so they get here quickly?"

The man, wearing a Publix's vest, nodded and raced over to where the vehicles were pulling into the parking lot, followed by the cops.

"Why me?" I muttered and felt Jo squeeze my hand.

"'Cause you scare them. And you're awesome. Call parents, Sable." Her voice was weak and I was worried about how pale she was. I didn't think it had nicked a major artery, but nobody was the same and I hadn't inspected the bullet to see if it had splintered.

The medics raced up and I rattled everything off. I'd been keeping track of her heartbeat with my hand on her wrist as we had waited.

Carelian didn't protest as they got her on a gurney, but he crouched near me, ears back every time someone got too close, his puffed fur and tail making him look cute and fluffy if you completely ignored the ready to kill look in his eyes.

They were taking Jo to Ruby, and I nodded. I itched to pick up the phone and call people, but I knew the police needed to talk to me first.

"You again," an officer spat and I just looked at him blankly.

"I'm sorry?"

"You found the dead body. The girl in the park. What are you, a magnet for trouble?" It was the young officer, the one who had tossed his cookies when he saw her. I'd just gotten to Atlanta and my luck caused me to stumble across a body that started this whole weird spiral of connections with Alixant and Indira.

I stood and forced a smile I didn't feel, my heart in the ambulance with Jo.

"You could say that." I turned and a small petty part of my mind grinned as he saw my tattoos and paled.

"What the hell are you?" The way he said the words hurt, but I just looked at him. "You need to stay. Until officers get here."

"Fine. But I need to make some phone calls." I didn't ask permission, I just moved over to an out-of-the-way area with Carelian at my heels and dialed Alixant.

"Cori?"

"Someone just tried to kill me. They hit Jo. I need you." I didn't stop the bleakness in my voice, all I could do was think about the next two calls I needed to make. And I had no idea in the world how to say the words.

"Where are you?" No condemnation, no exasperation, just asking where I was. I told him, then hung up, already trying to steel myself for the calls. I'd do the easier one first.

I dialed the number and held my breath, trying to formulate the words in my head.

"Heya, Cori. What's up? Need me to check the fridge?" Her voice bright, but distracted, and I could almost see her curled up reviewing her meticulous notes.

"Sable," my voice cracked and I had to clear it, but I could hear the sudden stillness on the other end of the line. "Jo was shot. They're taking her to Ruby."

What else do I say? Do I tell her it is my fault? Will they let her in?

Only the knowledge that barring complications Jo should recover from that wound kept me from having a full breakdown.

"Okay. Were you hurt?" Her voice shook and I heard her moving and keys being grabbed.

"No. I'm fine. It's my fault." The words slipped through and created a crack in the dam I had my emotions behind.

"Yeah, like you put a bullet in her. You aren't to blame. They chose this, not you. But now they've created a lot more enemies." Her voice had an odd distant tone to it. "Cori. Do what you need to. I'm headed to the hospital. Are you calling the Guzmans?"

"Yes. Calling them next," I said, my voice quavering, but I fought it down. I didn't have time to be weak or passive.

"Good. Tell them I'm headed there. I'll see you there later, right Cori?" Her voice hard as I heard the apartment door close.

"Yes. Bye." I hung up looking at all the police staring at me. I ignored them. Until ranking officers showed up or Alixant, I had nothing to say. I stared at my phone, call the house—they still had a landline—or the shop? I didn't have either Marisol or Henri's personal numbers.

Shop. Henri will go get Marisol. He'll take it better. I hope.

I backed further into the corner, shopping carts on one side and the crowd of people and cops on the other. Carelian at my feet. I wanted to hide, but I forced myself to stand there looking as if I was perfectly fine. Not the girl who was panicking over her best friend being badly hurt.

Why didn't it register for me? They told me, but I never thought Jo would really be at risk.

Because even after everything, I didn't think they were really trying to kill me. Maybe I was an idiot. I hit the button for the Guzman's shop and waited. Marco answered.

"Guzman's Auto Repair, what can we help with?"

"Marco, it's Cori. Can you get Henri for me, please?" I thought I sounded horrible, but maybe I could act better than I thought, because he didn't seem to notice.

"Sure, Cori. One minute." A click and staticky hold tunes piped through. They really needed better hold music.

Click. "Cori, what's up?"

I credited the cheer in his voice that I rarely called with bad news. I'd do anything to make sure this wasn't a habit I was forming. But I couldn't think of any way to lead into this kindly. Maybe being a doctor wasn't smart if I couldn't tell someone this in a way that didn't feel like swinging a sledge-hammer.

"Henri, Jo was shot. She should be fine. They are taking her to Ruby right now." My throat was so tight as I said that. This made the second child in a year to be seriously hurt. Sanchez had gotten lucky, and at least that one I was sure I had nothing to do with. Though it was possible Lady Luck had helped save him. That was one more unknown question to deal with later.

"*Merde*. She'll be fine? What happened?" His voice shook, and I wanted to die that second right then to prevent him from ever speaking in that tone of voice again.

"It looked like a flesh wound. So yes. She'll be fine." I put every ounce of assurance into that and prayed to anything listening that it was true. My life without her wouldn't be a life. I heard him yelling and responses from inside the shop. "Thank you, Cori. I'll go get Marisol. You haven't called her, have you?"

"No. I figured it would be better to come from you."

"She's in class, I'll head there now. Are you okay?"

Why did everyone keep asking me that? I didn't know, and I didn't know what to do. "I'm fine. I'm talking to the police now. Go. You have my number."

"*Si, gracias* Cori. *Tien cuidado.*" The phone clicked and I wanted to sag to the ground, scream, cry, rage, but I put it away and glanced down at Carelian, who hadn't moved away from me since they took Jo.

"You okay?" I wasn't sure what I was asking, but I was. I still didn't understand this strange creature that had attached itself to me, but I had no doubt he cared about the three of us. Though I still didn't know exactly what that meant.

~They hurt one of my queans. Tried to kill my Quean.~ I could hear the capitalization in his words and it tickled inside my head.

"She'll be okay. She has to be."

He growled and lashed his tail across my calf, which hurt more than I expected it to.

A black car pulled into the parking lot, light flashing on top, followed by another police car. I knew that would be Alixant and the Captain. Being honored with important people needing to talk to me was getting old.

Chapter 24

Mages in the government are usually well treated, not because of risk of retaliation (few mages are that stupid) but more that they are indispensable when things go very wrong. Always assume any mage you see in the police force is a valued employee and one that will uphold the highest level of ethics or will make sure you never live to refute that. ~ House of Emrys internal memo

SPIRIT

Police officers formed a little cordon to keep the onlookers away as they strung up police tape. The Captain, Alixant, and a woman I didn't recognize, wearing a colorful teal suit, walked up. At least it wasn't Detective Stone, so I'd take it.

"Cori, you okay?" Those were the first words out of Alixant's mouth, and I just nodded. Why did people keep asking that? "You sure? You're covered in blood." He gave me a funny look, and I glanced down.

My shirt and hands were covered in blood, there was blood on my phone and trickles of it had run down to drip on my pants and legs. I hadn't even noticed. How could I not have remembered to pull on gloves?

Cause it was Jo.

"Jo's blood. I'm fine. Three shots, none of them hit me."

"The shooter?" Captain Jessup asked, looking around warily.

I took a deep shuddering breath and faced what I'd been avoiding thinking about since I'd done it. "Dead." I kept my voice flat, under control. Carelian pressed against me harder, purring so deeply it felt like he vibrated against my leg.

"Excuse me, can we start at the beginning?" the woman I didn't know asked, a notebook in hand. I glanced at her bright amber eyes in a face crowned by layers of braids woven with yellow and red in her black hair, matching the yellow and cheerful red of her tattoo and telling me she was an Entropy mage. At least there was a possibility she wouldn't hate me on sight like Stone had.

"Yes, that might be wise. Cori this is Detective Olivia Jonas. I've asked her to take over all cases involving you."

I gave the captain a look and he just shrugged. "You seem to be a magnet for things going on and it would be easier to have a central person involved. Obviously, you and Detective Stone don't work well, I'm hoping you and Jonas here will."

The detective flashed me a fast smile, the signs of heavy tobacco usage clear on her teeth. But I didn't smell any cigarettes anywhere. That struck me as odd.

"Can you start at the beginning, Miss Munroe, and tell us exactly what happened?"

I took a deep breath, focusing on the calm and interested question, not accusing just interested. This I could deal with. I started with the call and me running, taking a different path, then the shot and me creating the shield.

"Wait, you did what?" Alixant burst out, looking at me, his face pale.

I stuttered trying to figure out what he wanted me to explain. I took a deep breath and tried to explain my logic. "I don't have any element but Earth," I started and saw all of them glance at my temple. I wanted to sigh but kept talking. "I'd been trying to figure out a way to create shields or something." I didn't miss the start from Alixant but ignored it. "Air would be better but I don't have it. When the shot went off all I could do was think about protecting us, but I only had Earth. But there is Earth everywhere so I took the idea I'd been playing with and I created a shield from the dirt."

Alixant dropped his glance to the line where everything had collapsed when I dropped it. "Is that what this is?"

"Yeah, everything I pulled and let drop." I looked at the line, about two inches thick and half an inch tall. Not much when you realized it had stopped two bullets.

"You said the perp was dead?" Olivia asked.

"Yeah, I killed him, I think." I didn't think—I knew. But his body might still be breathing.

"How?" If he had fired the word from a gun it couldn't have come out any sharper.

"Ummm," I stuttered, trying to figure how to explain what I'd done all on instinct and desperation. "I caused the dust in the air to condense so the bullet created a path that I could backtrack to its source."

They all looked at me and I wanted to shrink back, but I was already against the wall. "It created a ripple in the dust that I backtracked, so I reached out with Soul and pulled his out. I think."

"You what?" All three of their voices merged as they looked at me. Captain Jessup and Detective Jonas looked shocked, but Alixant looked horrified.

"Well, I think I did. I pulled out his life or what was his life. I felt him die as it shredded, or I shredded it." I really didn't know which one it was.

Alixant turned on the Captain, his voice hard and cold. "Sir, we need to stop now. We can't have this recorded. Detective, the only thing that needs to go into your notes is she killed in self-defense. This cannot go into the record, do you understand?" He had a tone of voice that I'd never heard before, even at the stadium. "This goes under OMO sanction now."

The detective swallowed and nodded. "I hadn't really taken any notes, but the official record will only be that she killed to protect herself."

"Good. Cori, you never ever mention this to anyone if I am not there. Do you understand? Either of them. The shield or the killing. You just say you protected yourself, nothing else." He had leaned in, was so close I could feel his breath on my skin. Carelian growled and stepped between us. Alixant glanced down, then stepped back. "I'm deadly serious. You do not mention it."

"Got it." I wanted to ask why, what I was missing, but I didn't. He kept looking around glaring at anyone that might be close enough to overhear anything from us.

"Miss Munroe," the detective started.

"Please call me Cori. I don't feel like a Miss Munroe."

She arched an eyebrow at me. "I can do that. Can you tell us where the building is that your assailant was on?"

I pivoted and pointed directly at a building across the street and about five stories tall. "Roof, I couldn't see him, but I could feel him."

"Cori," Alixant warned and I shrugged.

"What do you want me to do? Lie? Not say anything?" I glared at him. Right at that moment all I wanted to do was go to the hospital, verify Jo was okay, and make sure the Guzmans didn't hate me.

"Just don't admit to anything outside the normal spells," he growled out, and I looked at him surprised.

"We've only started going over the first set in one branch. Spirit isn't until next year as the number of people with it is smaller. I've only had time to read a bit on the basic spells." I paused and looked at him, a cold twisty feeling in my stomach even as Carelian twined around my leg. "Are you telling me I did something new? Something no one has done?"

"Dammit Cori, shut up." He turned and looked at the two cops. The Detective looked pale even under her French Roast complexion. The captain just looked worried and confused.

Jessup look at the three of us and shook his head. "I get the feeling I'm missing something. And in a rare turn of events I'm finding I don't want to know. Jonas, can I trust you with the department's integrity and to not get us on the wrong side of the OMO, or get anyone killed just because?"

"Yes, sir. I'll take care of it," she responded instantly.

"Alixant, don't make me regret this. I'm not a merlin, but I'll have your career in ashes if you screw me over on this." The captain glared at Alixant as hard as Alixant usually glared at me.

"I won't. She's young and should never have figured out what they are forcing her to figure out. I'll work on it."

"Good." He nodded at me and headed away, shouting at people to get to the top of the building I'd identified. I turned back to look at Alixant, who seemed to have aged five years.

"What?"

"Did you notify the Guzmans and Sable about Jo?" he asked, rubbing his face in a manner that made me feel guilty and I didn't know what I felt guilty for.

"Yes. Sable should be there or almost, and Henri had to pick up Marisol from school. She doesn't get off until 4." I looked at my phone, was it really only three-thirty?

"Good. Go there and keep your mouth shut. Cori, I mean it. I don't want to have to execute you."

The words slapped me with a physical force and I staggered. Carelian leaned against me snarling, his ears back, and tail perfectly still.

"Don't Carelian. You don't understand. Neither of you do. Cori, go. Just tell the truth, but no details, don't tell them any details. Got it?" He seemed unbearably exhausted and at the end of his rope.

Mutely, I nodded. I snapped the leash on Carelian and pivoted, walking away from all of them as fast as I could get my legs to move. No one called after me and it took everything I had not to run. Fear rippled up and down my spine as I tried to process what had just happened. A man I respected, almost liked, just implied he had the authority to execute me.

Getting yourself sick from stress does nothing. He hasn't killed you yet. Go see Jo, then worry about possible execution tonight.

I stopped my rushed walk and pulled an extra shirt out of my bag, used the ruined one to wipe up most of the blood, then changed. I ignored the odd looks as I stood there in my bra scrubbing blood off me as best as I could. Once the clean shirt was on, I called a rideshare wanting to be out of sight, protected at least by the walls of a car. Carelian said nothing, curled in my arms the entire ride. I sprang out and texted Sable. *I'm here. Where are you?*

3rd floor, she should be out of surgery soon. Meet you at elevators.

I didn't respond, just headed into the elevators, my insides clenching at the thought of Jo being in surgery. I needed to know more, study more. I would have sacrificed every hair on my head to have healed her on the spot.

The elevator took an eternity and I felt magic gathering around me in waves. I took a deep breath and made sure I hadn't wrapped anything around me, then stepped out looking for Sable.

"Cori." I spun at the sound of her voice and saw her waving me into a small waiting room. Once I got there, I wrapped her in a hug that she returned just as tightly. "She's okay. Are you? You have blood on you." She touched my neck and arms where Jo's blood had dried and I hadn't gotten it all off.

"No, it's all Jo's. Surgery?"

"Minor. They wanted to close up the wound, clean and irrigate it. She should be getting out shortly. Did you call her parents?" Sable pulled me down into a seat.

"Yeah. I think they should be here soon." I hoped. If they were still talking to me after that would be the real question.

We sat in the waiting room, hands clenched together, Carelian on a seat across from us staring at everything. But he wasn't snarling at anyone so I figured that was better.

The door flew open and Marisol rushed in. "Where is she? Is she okay?" Sable and I both stood up as Marisol looked at us. Then she pulled us both into her arms. "My girls. Are you okay? Cori, why are you bloody?"

Henri stepped in and pulled the door shut, looking at both of us. "Tell us what happened." He asked, but it wasn't a question, it was an order and one that terrified me. He pulled Marisol onto a seat and then they looked at me, waiting for answers.

Tell the truth, but don't give any details.

Alixant's words rang in my mind and I fought to swallow. "The blood is from Jo." I forced the words out but didn't stop even at Marisol's gasp. "Someone or ones is trying to kill me and when they took a shot at me today, they hit Jo instead."

Their hands were white where they were clutching each other. They didn't look at each other, but you could almost hear the conversation between them.

"Cori," Henri said in slow, heavy tones, "why is someone trying to kill you?"

"And why are we just now hearing of this?" Marisol's voice demanded an answer, but she fell silent as Henri's left hand patted her arm.

My wall broke and the words came out, tumbling over each other as I tried to explain. "There's this big inheritance thing and if I graduate, I get it. Some Spirit merlin left it to me. But if I don't graduate by June, Japan gets it. As far as I can tell they figure if I die then it's theirs. But I don't know. But they are trying to kill me. I ducked and they shot Jo instead. We didn't want to worry you. I'm so sorry. I'll leave." Forcing the words out and seeing the look of despair on their faces made my knees buckle but I didn't let myself crumple.

"Come on, Carelian." I turned to the door.

"Corisande, where do you think you are going?" Marisol snapped out.

"Um, leaving?" I quavered.

"Get back in here. While I am furious you didn't see fit to tell us someone was trying to kill you, this is not your fault. Now sit down and explain everything, slowly." Marisol pointed at the chair I'd been in, her face unrelenting.

I turned and moved back to the chair, sinking into it. Carelian hadn't moved, just flicking his ear at me. His entire attitude one of "you're an idiot".

I sat there rigid, with my hands fisted together between my legs, and started to talk, explaining everything. Well, just why people wanted me dead or to at least drop out. I didn't talk about the magic I'd used or the offerings. And they never asked.

When I was done, they just looked at me and I got ready for the attack.

"Oh, Cori. This must have been so scary and so much pressure. Why didn't you tell us?" Marisol looked at me and I just stared back confused.

"I didn't want to stress you. Didn't want you to get caught up in this mess," I muttered as I stared at the floor.

"Cori, that is what family does. We worry and get in-volved. Never fear to tell us something." Marisol took a deep breath. "But you're sure Jo will be okay?"

My headed bobbed up and down like a stupid doll. But before I could say anything, the door opened and a woman in surgical scrubs stepped in. "Josefa Guzman?" All of us sprang to our feet. I felt my world stop as I dreaded the next words.

"She's just fine. She's in recovery now and you should be able to see her in a few minutes."

The world restarted and I sagged back down into the chair. I'd do whatever they wanted, I never wanted to put any of them at risk again.

Either I give up or I accept protection. And I don't want to give up.

Chapter 25

Mages are not miracle workers or demigods, the doctor that operates on you is just as likely to be a magic-free human as a mage. Remember that next time you look down on those without magic—we are everywhere.
~Freedom From Magic

CHAOS

It took two days, but the wound had been a clear through and through. Jo got home, and Marisol only stayed through Sunday before she went home. Before she left, she read all of us the riot act and told us to let her know whatever happened, no excuses. She also told Sable she needed to inform her dad immediately.

Her absence both hurt and let us fit back into our routines, though this time Sable ushered Jo to every class and I never went outside with either of them. Even Carelian wasn't allowed to walk beside me. He skulked in the shadows and underbrush until we got into classrooms, though he made his displeasure clear. Alixant had ordered me to stay under the radar until they could come talk to me, but that wouldn't be until Wednesday night.

I spent my time fighting panic attacks and trying to concentrate on classes and making sure I stayed far away from everyone. Wednesday night I almost looked forward to Alixant's edicts.

"Ladies. How you feeling, Jo?" Alixant asked as they walked in Wednesday, both of them carrying bags with the name of a local sushi restaurant on them.

"Not too bad. I start therapy next week. Which is good, cause I'm tired of this sling," Jo replied, curled up on the couch. She'd made it through classes each day, but it wore her out. "But I think the more important thing is what's the plan to keep Cori alive to graduate?" Her words took the warmth out of the air. Alixant glanced at Indira and she shrugged.

"The government is very concerned and very interested. They have assigned me a special duty to protect you until our ambassador has finished discussing this with Japan." Alixant didn't look at me as he talked but pulled out boxes of food for us.

While I would not argue about free sushi, the information he relayed left me stunned. "I'm an international incident?" I needed to get my voice under control. Indira never sounded this shocked.

"And then some. The problem is so far Japan is disclaiming any knowledge of these attempts and pointing out that what unaffiliated groups do is not their problem. But the money offered for the hit is being held in escrow accounts. Chris is working on backtracking it. It will probably take another month or so, but as long as we can keep you alive, an agreement should be worked out and the danger should pass."

I didn't know what to say. Carelian whispered in my mind. ~Powerful, dangerous quean.~ That didn't help my mental state at all.

"What does that mean?"

"It means Indira and I will be with you when you leave this apartment. Don't sit out on the balcony and try to keep windows and blinds closed until we can get the bounty on you rescinded." He looked exhausted and I couldn't blame him. But it still didn't mean I liked any of this. "We are hoping to have it done before summer, but right now you just need to stay alive until then."

My life, how bad do I want this?

The problem was, it wasn't that I wanted the house that badly. Oh, I wanted it, but this badly? Probably not. But I couldn't give in to people threatening me, trying to control me via fear. I just couldn't. Jo and her family, even Sable were more important. But if they could get me to do things by threatening me, where would it end? I'd been worried about the societies and owing them, but this was just as bad. If I gave in on this anyone could decide threats would make me cave. And that I couldn't afford.

"Will you explain now what the issue was at the store? And why you threatened to kill me?"

Both Jo and Sable's heads snapped up as they stared at him and then me. I didn't move, just looked at him. This I needed an answer to.

"Cori, I swear you stumble into things." His voice wasn't quite a mutter, but he looked like I'd dropped another weight on his shoulders. "Yes, I'll explain. Everyone fill your plates, this will take a bit."

Even though my stomach roiled, I knew I needed the food, so I got my plate and helped Sable get a plate for Jo before we settled down. As usual, Indira and Alixant sat at the table while we curled up on the futon and chair. This had become so common we'd reorganized the room a bit to make it so the table and our living room furniture created a bit of a circle, if a rather lopsided one.

I poked at my shrimp and California roll. I knew I needed to eat, but my stomach was in such knots that all I could do was move it around on my plate. Carelian on the other hand had no such nerves. He was gleefully eating the raw pieces of fish from the pile they had pulled out for him. The sushi restaurants did a brisk side business in all the pieces of fish that weren't considered suitable for humans to eat, but carnivore familiars had no issues consuming. It was a win win for both groups. His favorite were eel and octopus. He'd mentioned once they were delicacies in the other planes, as most creatures of that type were bigger than elephants.

He never explained how he knew so much when he came here as a kitten and I got the feeling some things would always be a mystery. In the scope of things, his odd knowledge was the least of my concerns.

"Most mages aren't forced to use their magic to protect themselves, Cori. Those that are tend to be very well trained. These incidents have a large part of the magical community, and the societies specifically, in an uproar. You don't target young mages. Part of it is ethics, but the other part is what you are doing now." His voice sounded as exhausted as he looked, and I swore he'd added some grey to his temples since this summer.

"Which is what?" I asked, exasperated. I couldn't figure out what he was talking about and that worried me.

"Using your magic outside the proscribed spells." Indira's voice had a wealth of emotions to it I didn't know how to untangle, so I just looked at both of them, all too aware of Jo and Sable watching with wide eyes.

"A huge part of college is to train you in how to use your magic. We present it in boring scientific terms, measure everything out, and beat into you the spells in each branch. Generally, by the time you graduate you'll argue to the death that this is the only way to use magic, with everything quantified. And that is how most of the governments in the world want it. They want you following the rules. By the time you realize it isn't the only way you tend to be old enough to keep your mouth shut because you see the possibilities of what could happen if people realized that it is damn near unlimited if you're creative."

"I don't understand. I thought that we'd tried other ways to use magic and either the cost was too high or people died," Sable said, watching all of this with confusion on her face.

"Exactly. That is what you and everyone else are supposed to believe. And if you don't get convinced of that during your draft, or act as if you are, you'll not survive the draft. That's why this is so serious. Not because you get injured or hurt during your service, but because you get arrogant and prove you can't be trusted out in the world. You're eliminated quickly and quietly." Alixant's voice sounded like lead weights hitting the floor.

"Really? The government kills mages?" Jo all but squeaked the words and her chopsticks slipped from her fingers, hitting her plate with a dull thud.

"No, the government kills mages that are a risk to the population at large because they are too reckless with their magic. You, Cori, are finding out that magic can be used in many ways outside of the very narrow branches we teach. Most people find it rather boring, because of how we teach it, and never do much more than what they have to." He shifted his attention to Jo. "Jo, how often do you see your parents use magic? Your father shaved his head, how much does he use the magic available to him?"

Jo blinked and shrugged. "Not very often. I mean Mami will control the heat sometimes or do little things with fire. But I don't remember them using it that much." Her words were slow, and I thought back at the same time. For all that Shay, Laurel, Marisol, and Henri were mages, I didn't remember ever seeing them actually do magic.

"That is how most are. They have it. We pound into you, keep it in reserve just in case. You might need it and not having it then would be awful. But most mages below archmages almost forget how to use it outside work unless it is a true emergency. And that is how most governments and the OMO want it. Using magic makes hurting others way too easy, but most other things aren't all that improved by it." Alixant turned his attention to me. "You are very dangerous and very much at risk. You're a merlin with more power than they've ever recorded. You have a familiar. You can do things for almost nothing that most archmages can't do at all. The geeks at OMO still can't figure out how Jo managed to break all those nicotine bonds. And we've just pointed at Carelian because nothing else makes sense."

Jo focused intently on her food, not looking at any of us. Sable squeezed her hand, but they didn't say anything.

"Bottom line, we need to keep you safe, and you need to learn to follow the rules, or you won't live long enough to worry about doing anything after your draft. Much less enjoy the inheritance you are fighting so hard to earn."

I flinched back from every word. None of this sounded good. Carelian growled softly and came to jump onto the chair and lean into me, purring. ~My quean. Powerful is good.~

No one else reacted so I figured those words were just for me. They didn't help. While powerful might be good in his world, in this world it might get me killed.

"So you're telling me bow my head, be a good little girl, or I'm going to end up dead either one way or the other."

"Yes," he said, eyes locked on me.

Indira touched my arm lightly. "Cori, this is one of the reasons that we urged you to join the House of Emrys at least. You don't normally go after members of your own house and you've proved you're powerful enough that it might tempt some of the other higher level people to take you out, just to prove they can. Emrys has a habit of slapping down anyone that does that. It is more implied than actual. But yes, you need to lower your profile."

I wanted to scream, to rage, to tell them to fuck off, but the pale look on Jo's face and Sable's white knuckles made me take a deep breath and reel it in.

Time to grow up. If I shut up and be the good little girl for what, the next fifteen years, after that maybe I'll be mostly free. But only if I live.

"Very well. What next?"

Some of the tension bled out of Indira and Alixant. Indira perked up a bit, and until that moment I hadn't realized how stressed she'd looked.

"You'll join Emrys?" she asked, watching me.

"Yes. I'll contact Joanne tomorrow. I'd like to hold off on the others. But I'll join. And," I paused and looked at Steven, even thinking his name caused a ripple of pain, "I'll deal with the bodyguards."

"Thank Merlin," he muttered, rubbing the bridge of his nose.

"So, like I said. What next?"

"You get your degree. You'll get a bullet-proof vest to wear and Indira or I will be with you while you're moving between classes. We are going to get some protections, both normal and magical put on your apartment and you will hate every minute. I'm hoping we can lift it by summer, but Cori, we aren't doing this to punish you."

"No. Just to control me. Congratulations." But I wasn't bitter, just tired. Eating seemed like too much effort. But I did want to know a few things.

"So how will you protect me? I mean you said I couldn't talk about what I did. So how will you do that?"

"Air branch, Move spell. What you did with dirt, most can do with Air. Create a shield around you that will deflect or stop most things. Again, if they really want to kill you with magical means they can, but in some ways the fact that you are so high profile is protecting you from that. The ambassador is pushing, so we'll see what happens."

I nodded and forced myself to eat a piece of sashimi. It went into my stomach like a lump of mud. Dealing with reality ruined even the treat of sushi.

"What about—" I wanted to ask about what I'd done with the Soul magic but banging on the door startled me.

"I got it." Sable jumped up before anyone else could move, before anyone could protest, and pulled open the door. A huge man, at least six-foot-three, stood there, hair in long braids down his back, dark angry eyes, and muscles everywhere under skin that looked ebony in the yellow hall light. He glowered down at Sable and I felt my magic spike ready to respond, even as I scrambled to my feet. I focused on the green and white tattoo that proclaimed him a Transform mage.

Clashes between the OMO and the military are legend-ary and usually revolve around hair and nails. While merlins can perform easier with less offering, most oth-ers need the genetic material to use their magic effectively. The military has stood by their insistence on short hair and nails while in service. While women find it easier, being able to put their hair up, it requires a mem-ber of the military to fight to keep their long hair and nails. While it is illegal to force them to remove it, pressure to do so can be intense if the service member doesn't under-stand the laws that protect them. ~ Magic Explained.

ORDER

"Dad!" Sable threw herself into his arms, and the mage standing in the hall wrapped her tight.

"Baby girl," he murmured as he held her tight.

I felt my magic subside and my knees went weak as I sank back into the chair. If this was how I was going to react to everything, ready to attack, I really wasn't safe around either Sable or Jo. Maybe I should get a place by myself, a hotel or something, for a while.

Sable released the death grip she had around him and stepped back. "Come on in. I need to introduce you." He fol-lowed her in, and I saw the military in his every movement. His eyes scanned the room, lingering on the merlin tattoos of Indira and Alixant, then his eyes somehow got darker as they landed on me.

She made introductions and lingered on Jo. "And Dad, this is Jo. Everyone this is my dad, Colonel John Lancet."

John smiled, but I noted that it didn't reach his eyes. That was probably my fault. "Just John. I retired last year. I work up in Aberdeen for the DoD." He shifted his attention to Sable. "I believe you sent me a note that someone had tried to kill your girlfriend's best friend?" He looked pointedly at Jo who still had the sling on and needed at least two more weeks to finish giving the wound time to heal.

"Hi," she said weakly. "Nice to meet you." I could see the panic in her gaze. Meeting parents had never been her strong suit.

"You must be the friend people are trying to kill," he said looking directly at me.

"Um, yeah. Sorry?" I didn't know for sure why I was apologizing, but I wasn't sure what else to say.

He shifted his intimidating stare to Indira and Alixant and while they didn't flinch or pull back, I saw them react to his gaze. "Mentors? Or government flunkies."

"Both in my case," Alixant said, rising to stand between John and Indira. "Why do you ask?"

"My daughter has never been one to back down from a fight which means she won't go anyplace safe, and I can't imagine the government not being involved when there are hits out on a merlin student. So, what are you doing to keep them safe?" He crossed his impressive arms and stared down Alixant.

This guy might become my new hero. Can I trade him for Alixant?

Alixant sighed. "Take a seat." He waved at the other chair and the three adults started to talk. Or it felt like that, the adults talking and the kids waiting for orders from on high. The three of them deciding my life, without including me in it. But for now, I just sat and listened. What else could I do?

I picked at my food as they went over plans, but other than John casting a sharp eye at me and stating, "She needs to get in better shape," I wasn't part of the conversation. I curled up more and more wanting to yell and shout, but I didn't dare do any of that. Maybe this stupid house wasn't worth it. I listened to them talk, making plans as to what I was going to do, what needed to be done. I felt like an object, the precious grail they needed to protect, not myself.

"Enough. Everyone out." Jo's voice snapped out and the three people at the table turned to look at her, surprise and shock on their faces. Mine probably looked the same as I stared at her. "What? Was I not clear? Everyone who doesn't live here, out." She struggled to her feet, the greyness under her skin tone telling me how exhausted she was, and I surged to my feet, guilt adding fresh pain to my misery.

"What are you talking about? We're figuring out the best way to keep Cori safe, to keep all of you safe," Alixant said, dismissing Jo with a wave of his hand and turning back to John. Indira narrowed her eyes as she watched us. She hadn't said much in the last twenty minutes or so.

"No," said Jo. "You're trying to run our lives. And we're done. We are not twelve, we're not your responsibility. I'm exhausted, need to take pain meds, and pass out. Cori is on the verge of tears and Carelian is ready to shred all of you for making his mage miserable."

Until she said those words, I hadn't registered how agitated Carelian was. Like me, he wanted to do something—escape, attack, defend. But there wasn't anyone to attack. His rumble wasn't a purr but a low steady growl as his tail twitched and claws extended and retracted.

"Now look. Cori's agreed she needs protection, but it isn't that simple," Alixant started and John matched his expression, his gaze locked on his daughter.

"Yes, it is." Jo cut them all off. "Get out and when you show up tomorrow to escort Cori to class, you can then explain to her how you will work with her to stay safe and not treat her like some mindless piece of fluff you need to work around."

"We haven't—" he started, and Jo just stared at him, her face getting grayer.

"Yes, we have. And she's right." Indira rose and nodded to Jo and then to me. "We are forgetting this is your life too and you need to be actively involved if we want you to succeed much less thrive. Ladies, thank you for your hospitality.

Steven will be here in the morning, while I'll see you in class and probably walk you between classes. Time bubbles are perfect for protection and I'll see about training you on how to create and use them." Indira walked to the door then turned, lifting an eyebrow. "Gentlemen? This is what is known as a subtle hint. We've overstayed our welcome."

Alixant growled under his breath but stood looking at me, then his face softening a bit as he looked at Jo. "I'll be here in the morning, Cori. Don't you dare leave without me. And we'll talk more as we walk. You do need to be a part of this." He sighed and shook his head as he headed out the door. They closed the door behind them leaving John looking at his daughter.

"I did it again, didn't I?" he asked, hunching his shoulders and sinking into himself a bit. For a man who must top six feet, he suddenly looked like a little boy about to be put in the corner for a timeout.

"If you mean coming in and taking over with no care as to what I want or need, only what you think is best—yes." Sable sighed and walked over to her dad. "I love you. But we aren't kids and Cori might be the most powerful mage on the face of the Earth right now. People really need to quit treating her like this or they may lose her. And you, Dad, aren't helping."

He sighed and rubbed his head. "Why don't you go put your girlfriend to bed, she looks like she's about to fall over. Then come out and talk to me. Tell me what's been going on. Please?"

"Give us a few." She grabbed Jo and I jumped up to support her other side. Together we ushered Jo to bed as she really was about to fall over. We got pain pills in her and tucked her in. I think she was asleep before we walked out of the room.

"My dad's a good guy. Just a bit too gung-ho sometimes. Talk to him, see if he has any input. If nothing else, having another point of view can't hurt, right?"

Her tone had too much pleading in it, and I nodded. There wasn't anything to lose and right now my stomach churned too much to even think about going to bed, no matter what time class was in the morning.

"Dad, Cori's going to tell you everything about what is going on, then maybe you can give her some ideas?"

"Anything, baby girl. And I am sorry Miss Cori. I see a problem I dive in and fix it, even if no one wants me to be the one fixing it. Sable here never managed to beat that out of me, though she at least got me to listen if she told me she just wanted to vent. Otherwise I tended to jump a bit fast. Bad habit in an Army officer." His tone had mellowed, and I sat down, feeling silly. Carelian rubbed on my legs as he passed by, but he didn't seem to pay much attention now that Indira and Alixant were gone.

"I'll try, but I need to go back a bit to explain everything." I glanced at Sable one more time and she nodded encouragingly as she made us hot chocolate in the kitchen. Just the scent helped steady me, so I started to talk.

And talk.

And talk.

We'd started at around six-thirty, Alixant and Indira had left at quarter to nine when Jo kicked them out. But something about her dad and the fact that Sable just let me talk, likely hearing aspects of the story that were new to her, kept me going. By the time I finished spilling everything it was ten-fifteen and exhaustion lay on me like a layer of concrete, cracking here and there.

"You've been through a lot in the past year and it doesn't look like it'll get any more boring." He gave a sidelong look to his daughter. "You sure you want to stay around all this?" The smirk and relaxed stance of his body told me he was joking, but I still tensed a bit. After all, who wanted to stay around my brand of luck?

"No place else I'd rather be. Besides, who doesn't want the most powerful merlin on the planet as a friend." She winked at me as she said that and Carelian purred in my head.

~Silly queans.~

We both snickered though her dad just looked at us with a slight frown. "Inside joke?"

"Something like that. Any thoughts after listening to my tale of woe?" I spoke lightly, but I couldn't help but pull the cup closer to me, wanting more of the hot sweet liquid.

"You need the bodyguards, but I get not wanting to give up your life. If this was going to be a long-term problem my advice would be different, but now?" He leaned back looking at me and then his daughter. "They're that important to you?"

"Yes." Her answer had nothing but assurance, and I wanted to melt. I knew Jo was that important, but me? That still seemed farfetched.

"Very well." He shifted his attention to me, and I wanted to squirm. "You won't like what I have to say, but for now, like any other recruit in the military, you're going to have to suck it up and deal. You don't have the skill sets right now to keep yourself and those you care about safe. You might have the power but that brings down a world of hurt, as you're quickly learning. You can handle a year and a half. Eighteen months is nothing."

"I'd kinda already figured that. Doesn't mean I'm happy about it." I didn't mutter, not quite, but still, who liked to be told they didn't really have a choice in the matter.

"Welcome to the wonderful world of adulting. It's never as great as you thought it would be. As to the next part." He paused looking at his daughter who gave him a teeny nod. "Since Sable has been gushing about Jo's cooking and the fact that while the mage draft covers your tuition, you, unlike most students don't have a family or another support system to help cover you, I'm sending an extra three hundred a month for your little household." I started to protest but he stopped me with a single finger. Marisol had nothing on him for commanding an audience. "Keep my baby girl safe and shove your degree down those bastards' throats and I'll consider it well worth it. You don't need the extra stress of trying to pay for food on top of everything else. Keep what you've got saved and use it as needed. You're a smart girl. The money will get you through this."

I didn't want to accept the money. I really really didn't—but he was right. Trying to not get killed, studying, taking care of Carelian, worrying about Jo and Sable and the Guzmans was pushing me to my limit already.

"Thank you," I said slowly each word being pulled from me.

"Don't. I've had people try to kill me. Often the only thing that got me through was knowing my friends had my back. My daughter and Jo have firmly placed themselves at your back. Don't squander that. It's more priceless than anything you can imagine."

The next fifteen minutes were Sable and her dad talking as I cleaned up and got things ready for the next morning. Old habits died hard and I still didn't trust that things wouldn't go sideways and make me late. I had enough teachers miffed with me for the classes I had missed. John left about the time I headed to bed and I paused to glance at Sable.

"I like your dad."

"He's pretty great. Having me leave was hard on him—it's been the two of us since I was a baby. But that right there is why I left. He means well but he's trained to solve problems by any means necessary. Makes him a great commander," she snickered, "and a frustrating father. I needed to do college by myself." She cast a glance at the closed bedroom door where I could just hear Jo snoring. "I just never expected to find someone like her or you." Sable looked at me and smiled. "I get that the two of you are a matched pair and the more I'm around you the more right it feels. Don't worry, I'm not going anywhere, and Jo wouldn't leave you on the threat of death."

"And that's what worries me. No one should get killed because of me." I couldn't look at her. It still ate at me that Jo almost died because of me.

"No one should be killed because some dead guy left them something in his will." I felt her hand under my chin and she lifted it to look me in the eye. "Cori, you've never been allowed to have anything that is yours and under your power most of your life. I understand why you want this so badly and it's okay. We're a team. We got your back."

She pulled me into an unexpected hug and I almost started crying. Sable held me for the longest minute, her black ringlets a curtain around me. I finally managed to pull back and smile at her. "Deal. But all of us are going to get through this. No one else gets hurt."

"Then we'd all better study and learn. I know I'm a junior, but we'll need to learn everything we can to make sure these jerks can't hurt you."

The lump in my throat grew larger, but I forced a smile. "Study machine I will be."

Sable laughed at me. "Go. Morning comes early and when you're vibrating with coffee you don't process as well."

I snickered and headed towards my own bed. A few minutes later Carelian sprang onto the bed and took his usual place, a pillow near my head. He'd tried my feet at first but after getting kicked a few times in the middle of the night, up near my head on the corner of the bed with his own pillow worked much better.

~Queans will be trained. Magic is power and my queans will learn how to use that power as magic should be wielded.~

"If only," I whispered softly petting him. "Magic is a tool like anything else and they are determined to get us to use it the way they want. Being a pawn sucks. But maybe someday after the draft and everything, if I can get that house..." The words trailed off in a whisper of hope, too risky to even say aloud.

Chapter 27

Everyone knows that the realms are not survivable by humans. There have been people that walked into them the few times rips have been found low enough to be accessible. No one has ever returned. All machines sent into them have quit transmitting as soon as they cross the border. But even still, rumors and legends of people visiting over there abound, proving a deadly siren call to the foolish. ~History of Magic

SPIRIT

My dreams were filled with visions of me chained to various monoliths and being chased by men in black at every step. I woke exhausted, cranky, and needing massive amounts of caffeine. By the time I stumbled out the door, having showered, checked on Jo, said morning to Sable, and made Stinky's Mexican coffee, I had almost achieved human.

Almost.

Having Alixant standing there waiting for me with an annoyed expression didn't help with my mood. Carelian, who hadn't said a thing to me all morning, though I had gotten a leg twine, brushed by and headed out, disappearing almost instantly.

I swear some days I think he uses magic to be invisible.

Alixant pushed himself off the wall as I walked by with a grunt. Even on supposed guard duty, he still looked like an agent. Suit, tie, fancy shoes—in other words completely out of place.

"Are you trying to scream government agent?" I didn't look at him, just kept moving, sipping the coffee as if it was a lifeline.

"Yes." I shot a look at him and he shrugged. "We want the people trying to kill you to know the government is involved and I'm going to be very obvious. But first things first. Ready for your shield?" We hadn't left the shelter of the apartment hallways and he slowed, his gaze an anchoring weight.

"I guess." While I didn't care about the shield so much, I was interested in knowing how it was created.

"Warn Carelian. Until we get inside and I drop it, he won't be able to get near you."

"You just did. He can hear you, remember?" I turned and gave Alixant an unamused look.

He shrugged. "Familiars are strange. Okay." He frowned and I felt something brush against me, then it was gone. I reached out my hand but felt nothing.

"Okay? I don't feel a difference. Why is most of this magic people assure me happens all but invisible?" I knew I sounded like a raging bitch, but outside of Indira being so absolutely incredible and me ripping open holes in the earth, I was tempted to believe it was all a big con.

Alixant just smirked at me and I narrowed my eyes at him. He reached down and picked up a small pinecone and threw it at me. I lifted my hand to block it, but when it got about three inches from me it veered off and slammed into the ground hard. I pulled back in surprise then looked up at Alixant.

"It takes a bit to learn to cast so the object being deflected goes straight down and not to the side or up. And putting it on someone else took more offering than I thought. At this rate my hair might be short again if we can't get this resolved before too long."

Guilt hit me and it blew away most of my resentment. He'd had a tussle with a Fire mage before I met him, and he, Niall, and Chris all had their hair burned almost to crew cuts before they were assigned to Atlanta. Even now, and I suspected he took as many prenatal vitamins as I did, his hair just reached to the top of his shoulders.

"How much?" I asked, my voice meek. Depriving another mage of their offerings was both a valid strategy and rude as all get out.

He smirked. "About half an inch off eight strands." I rolled my eyes and turned away, my guilt evaporating. "Hey, I'm a merlin. Maybe not with a familiar, but I can do impressive magic too. It will add up after a while. Wait until you get to the cosmetic offering classes. They treat it as an elective but trust me, you want to take that one."

"Yeah, Jo mentioned it for next semester and Sable says she took it last semester. Taught her a lot."

We emerged onto the path to the buildings I needed and I felt eyes on me. I turned but couldn't see anyone. I couldn't even see where Carelian might be.

"Something up?" he asked, watching me as if I might attack him.

"Just feels like someone is watching me."

"Hmmm," he murmured and came to a sudden halt frowning. But then he relaxed. "I can't sense anyone but the few people we see and some animals. Though I can't sense Carelian either."

"Okay. So far, I'm not worried about animals."

"You do remember what killed the guy that took shots at you at school, right? Where Indira showed up?" He was giving me a funny look and I just blinked at him.

"Umm? No? I mean, I think Indira said he was dead. That was all kinda fuzzy in my brain. I know they found the weapon. I thought she killed him." I had blocked that out of my thoughts and I now I castigated myself over it.

How could I be so stupid? I knew people were trying to kill me. Why wasn't I asking about what interfered? I am such a moron.

"We don't know. They have it categorized as 'magic-probably'. But it was big, efficient, and got in and out without Indira being able to catch it. Though from your calls and the timeline there was almost ten minutes where it could have happened with no one the wiser."

"Oh." I took that in and frowned as we walked. "So what now?"

Alixant lifted his hand in a dismissive manner. "Now? I teach you more about shields and convince you that if you use magic in a way that you weren't trained for, or isn't in that book I gave you, you never tell anyone. Blame luck, or an existing magic. I'd rather you claim you used a branch you were null in and just cite being a double merlin and having a familiar and always, I can't stress this enough, always inflate the cost. Make the costs be significant even if you have to lie. Or better yet, learn to lie without lying."

"What does 'learn to lie without lying' mean? And why do I need to learn that?" I demanded. Lies never worked out for me and I usually just avoided answering. Made life much simpler.

"Remember Francine? She can hear lies when you say them. So don't lie. Example - when I asked you what you did to the guy that tried to kill you a few days ago, rather than replying with what you did, don't tell anyone what you did," he ground out again. I rolled my eyes at him.

"Yes, I got that."

He gave me a sidelong look but continued. "You would just say you used your magic to find him and stop him. No details, but no lie. Lying is dangerous but in your case the truth might get you executed." Alixant glanced at me again. "Note the difference in the words. Murder is what those guys are trying to do. Execute is what I would do."

Hot coffee couldn't disperse the cold that shot through my body, but that didn't stop me from taking a large gulp. It didn't help.

"And the difference?"

He didn't respond, just kept walking. I knew the difference. They were trying to kill me for money or a reward. He'd be ordered to put down a dangerous mage. A ronin.

We didn't talk the rest of the walk to class, though he was on high alert and Carelian kept pinging me with purrs to let me know he lurked nearby, but I didn't see him until we walked up the stairs to my first class, when he whipped through the doors and to my side, but a good foot away. Carelian glared at Alixant. The man sighed and something fell away from me, though I couldn't have said what.

"She's safe now, cat. Which is what we're trying to keep her," Alixant groused at Carelian. Carelian ignored him and twined around my legs.

"Thanks. I'm going to get to class. I'll see you after?"

"No, Indira will pick you up and show you time shields that you should be able to replicate. They are actually a side effect, not what you try to do." He gave me a smile. "Really Cori, we just want you to live long enough to..." he broke off and shrugged. "I don't know. Be something amazing. I'll see you after classes."

I nodded expecting him to walk away, but he just looked at the door and nodded at me. I rolled my eyes and headed into class. History was my first class that morning, and the teacher assigned the mid-term paper I'd expected. Nothing too worrisome—ten pages on the origin of the draft in another country. Given my current issues, I selected Japan, thinking any insight into all this mess could only be a good thing.

All through class I waited, expecting something. I'd never been attacked in class and today didn't change that. Outside a few odd looks and no one sitting by me, nothing happened. I waited until most of the class had left before heading to the door. Indira stood there and I had the awful feeling of being a kid escorted from class to class because they couldn't be trusted.

"Morning, Cori. Biology lab next?"

I nodded. There wasn't a huge amount of time between classes and getting to lab early gave you time to get equipment and set up.

"Carelian, are you going to go to class with her, or wait in the park?" Indira asked, looking at Carelian as he wound around my legs like a desperate eel.

He froze. I watched his tail flick then slump and he turned and headed out the door, disappearing before I could say anything.

"I guess that answers the question. You ready? This will feel a bit funny and you'll have to move in tandem with me. It's harder than it looks."

I felt a little panicked as I looked at her. "No?"

Indira just smiled, making her a stunning beauty for a minute, then the world stopped. Or it slowed so much it looked like it stopped. "Step with me in unison," she said, her voice coaxing.

Maybe I looked as freaked out as I felt, but I watched her feet and moved, left, right, left with her. She wasn't that much shorter than me, so by the time we got out of the hall and down the steps we had hit a pattern.

"How does this work?" I asked when I thought I could keep the steps constant without watching her feet.

"Time magic can go one of two ways, speed up or slow down. Technically it can go in reverse, but you rarely want to do that with humans in the bubble, things go wrong." She shuddered a bit at that. "Time isn't linear regardless of what history wants us to think. But this?" Indira waved around us as we walked. "This is me moving us a few seconds forward in time. Anyone trying to attack or hit you will hit where you were a few seconds ago, not where you are now. If they did a gas attack or a wide scale attack like a missile then it might get you, but I can also jump us forward further with a thought. Watch."

Around us the world stutter stepped and then seemed to resume its even slower motion.

"Isn't this expensive?" I asked, eyeing her long hair and nails, wondering what sort of debt I was incurring.

"Yes and no. The spell itself barely costs a thousand molecules. But we both pay the price," she admitted.

"What price?" I wanted to stop and stare at her, but the idea of falling out of a time bubble terrified me.

"You'll see. It isn't that big of a cost, but it is part of dealing with time. Beside we're almost there." She pointed at the lab building we were rapidly approaching. "We will stop right inside the doors, it should be relatively safe."

I bit my tongue and waited. We stepped inside and Indira smiled. "Take a breath and let it out." I did and something rippled through me, making my breath ripple and shudder, and I felt odd. Like my lungs had stuttered, then everything, the world, the people, even the surrounding sounds were back to normal. "Labs."

"What was that?" I demanded, feeling even more freaked out. When she had walked back to me looking like an avenging goddess when the guys was shooting at me, the cost for being that imposing hadn't been on my mind.

"There is always a cost for time. In this case, you aged the fifteen seconds I had us out of sync with reality. Time can't be cheated and you will always pay the amount of time you step out of time. It is unavoidable." She didn't seem worried, just stating a fact, and I accepted the information but didn't process it. This would take some thought to process. Could you step so far out of sync that the coming back would age you to death?

"Thanks. You're picking me up after class?"

"Pretty much daily until we can get this taken care of." I couldn't hear resentment in her tone, but I assumed it was there anyhow. I'd be resentful if I had to ferry a student around from place to place.

"Thanks," I said with reluctance and then headed into Biology. Whatever time we saved moving in the bubble outside of time had been lost by standing there talking. I needed to get ready for my lab.

The rest of the day went like that and by the time I got home I didn't know if I'd make it through tomorrow, not to mention the next eighteen months. I'd kill someone or they'd kill me.

As far as I could figure, I needed to get so I could protect myself and Carelian. Maybe I should move out and get my own place to protect Jo and Sable? I shook my head as Alixant stayed until I shut the door behind me. Jo and Sable were already home. I smiled at them but didn't talk, just headed to my room, Carelian on my heels.

Flopping on the bed and staring at the ceiling provided no answers. Groaning I sat back up. I had a paper to write, chapters to read, and a chem test tomorrow to study for. Self-pity did me no good.

Changing clothes, I grabbed my phone to check for missed messages before I headed back out. I'd been leaving it on silent except for my favorites, which were Jo and the Guzman's.

I should probably add Sable to that.

A message waited for me. I hit play with a touch of apprehension as there wasn't a name associated with the number. "Cori Munroe, this is Joanna Snowden. Indira told me you want to join Emrys. If it's convenient tonight I could meet you and let you sign the membership forms and take the oath. Let me know. I'm available until nine. Do be aware I leave to head back to Savannah next week. Thanks." Her number showed up on the screen.

I wandered out into the kitchen dragging my books and holding my phone. Jo had a simple stew simmering for dinner. Something she'd created in the morning and none of us needed to touch while the crockpot did its magic.

"Either of you care if the Emrys rep comes by and gets me signed up?"

Sable set a bowl of stew in front of me. "Not as long as you eat. You look exhausted. I'll get Carelian's dinner out."

Most of the time I ate in front of the computer, but today that sounded like too much effort so I sat at the table while Carelian sprang into the chair next to me, looking at the table with interest.

"Okay," I said and took a mouthful of food. It helped. I tried to remember if I'd eaten. Just a protein bar at lunch, Thursdays were busy. All of my days except Wednesdays were busy. I dialed the number.

"Joanna Snowden."

"Joanna, this is Cori. Yeah, if you can come over, that would be great. Need my address?"

"Yep, Indira doesn't share anything." I gave it to her. "Wonderful. That isn't too far from my hotel. Give me thirty minutes." She hung up, and I stared at the phone.

"Would you two think I was insane if I said I thought this might be a trap? And wonder if we should be ready if we're attacked?"

Jo turned and looked at me, then she looked at Sable. "No, I don't think you're insane. We should get ready. And I'm worried that I'm starting to see enemies everywhere."

Chapter 28

To have a familiar is every child's dream, and it is a standard trope in fantasy novels for the mage to emerge and have a wondrous familiar there to help them with their quest or defeat the monsters. The truth is only a small percentage of mages ever get familiars, and of those that do, the majority are merlins. But since there are three known hedgemages with familiars nothing is impossible. ~ Magic Explained

CHAOS

Twenty minutes later when there was a knock at the door, we all looked at each other. Jo had spent the time trying frantically to duplicate Alixant's air shield. We thought we had a poor version figured out. It would stop soft or slower things, but not a bullet. That was why Sable was ready with her fire and water. She'd had another two years of study and had proven to us she could create a shield of ice around someone, holding them immobile for a minute or two. It was why we'd boiled a bunch of water to get more moisture in the air, even with as humid as a Georgia spring was—more water in this case was better.

Carelian hadn't said much, but he crouched under the chairs around the table, something he wouldn't be able to do easily if he got much bigger, lying in wait. At least he hadn't told us we were idiots for thinking this. I just felt like everyone had a reason to attack me. It made no sense to set myself up for a straightforward attack.

I checked with Jo and Sable, each on opposite sides of the room, then headed to answer the door. After checking the peephole and seeing it was Joanna, I pulled it open. "Hey, come on in."

Joanna smiled at me, her long hair in a neat French braid that hit the middle of her back. Dressed in a causal dress suit, she looked professional.

"Evening, Cori. I'm honored you decided to join the House." Her voice was friendly as we headed to the table. Jo and Sable remained in different parts of the room acting as if they were doing something else, anything else than waiting to attack or defend. We weren't certain which it would be.

"So here is the paperwork, the commitment to pay the fees during your draft and after, and here are your probationary benefits, here is the paper copy of the oath, and a copy of the rules of the House of Emrys." She talked as she pulled pieces of paper out of her bag. "You won't get your card until about a week from now, and I need to take your pic to get it made."

Her entire attitude was matter of fact and I pushed the benefits and the rules to one side, focusing on the oath and the commitment. The commitment was exactly what she had explained before, with the promise to pay the membership dues either monthly or yearly, and the clause that they wouldn't come due until I started my draft. There wasn't anything there I hadn't expected. I glanced at her, but she just sat there friendly and waiting.

"Do you have questions?"

"Not yet. I mean, I see nothing in the contract that you didn't explain. Give me a minute to look at the oath."

"Sure. It isn't super specific. I know some other houses have a lot more buried in them, but we try to keep it simple at Emrys. Making it complicated usually backfires—badly." Her tone had a wryness to it that spoke of experience and I wanted to ask what prompted that. But since I still didn't think I could trust her, I didn't.

Stupid adulting. How sad is it that having my own place with parents that ignored my existence is looking idyllic?

I focused on the oath, but still watched her out of the corner of my eye. The spilt attention was rapidly giving me a headache.

I (state name here) agree to not take action against the House of Emrys or other members without presenting my case to the council. I agree to publicly uphold the rules and regulations of the OMO. I swear that I will take no action to harm another member of the house without sanction. I agree to abide by the decisions of the ruling council regarding any public actions. I agree to follow the directions of any house manager while staying at an Emrys house or I will leave. Above all, I swear to not disclose in a public venue any discussions brought before the council. I (state name here) swear to uphold all these to the best of my ability on (state date here) so help me magic.

The words both made sense and didn't. I read it three times, with intent, before I looked her in the eyes. "I don't understand. Why the stress on public actions and what is this about the council and sanctions?"

Joanna quirked a side of her mouth but remained relaxed. Was that a good sign or a bad? I so wasn't cut out for this cloak and dagger stuff.

"We are well aware that there are other ways to use magic outside the official spells. We require our members to not be public about them. It scares people and then government has a tendency to step in and eliminate everything that might fuel the return of anything similar to the Salem Witch trials."

That surprised me. While magic hadn't existed back then, or at least not at the widespread level it was in the mid-1800s, history suspected at least one or two of the witches were actual mages. The trials and riots and general hysteria had resulted in the deaths of over three hundred people as the fear spread through the colonies. How many had been mages and how many had been average people swept up in it was anyone's guess.

"Basically, don't go public with anything not on the official list, or make damn sure you can explain it away as a merlin-level use of the official spells. As to the council, people are people and when merlins get nasty the level of devastation can be extreme. We provide a nonbiased council to provide feedback and settle disputes. We also discuss new magic that is discovered and when it might be appropriate to disclose it to the OMO and the public. As to the house manager, that means don't be an ass. Some people think they can trash the place because they are merlins. Most of the house managers are as well. So either do what they say or leave. That one just helps keep some of the younger merlins from being ass-holes."

Her blunt tone made me snicker and I read it again. After everything Alixant said block at going public made sense, but I thought only a few people knew about the stuff that wasn't on the list. "What is this sanction thing? And action against another member?"

"Sometimes there isn't anything that can be settled. As an example, one merlin rapes another. There isn't anything to settle there and it isn't like going to the police will stop it from happening again. We ask the merlin that was wronged to present evidence to the council—and the accused can if they wish. If they agree it is rape, the wronged mage has the right to take ultimate justice, just not publicly. In other words, if we agree you were raped you have the right to kill your rapist as long as it isn't in a splashy way."

"You condone murder?" I blurted, staring at her, feeling like I'd fallen into a rabbit hole. Again.

"Condone? No. We just won't take any action against you if it is sanctioned by the council." Her calm tone didn't make me feel any better. "And remember, according to the courts the penalty for a magical rapist is death ."

"How often does this happen? Not the rape, but people coming up and petitioning?" And what in the world would I do if someone did that to me?

"Not as often anymore. The newer merlins regard it with the same level of horror you do. The older ones, well either they've already removed all their obstacles or don't care anymore. But merlins have bigger egos than most and it is best to deal with it before an impartial panel than out in public."

"What happens if they do? I mean this just says I agree not to. What if I killed someone with," I almost stumbled and said soul magic, but managed to change it, "with Time or Psychic?"

She didn't respond but reached over and pushed the rules towards me. I glanced at her and started to read. Most of this was what I expected and boiled down to don't be a dick, don't break the law on our property, and pay on time. The last page is what she wanted me to see. This one I read four times, wanting to make sure I understood it completely.

"This says if I break the rules, the least punishment is I will be banned from the House of Emrys and ten years of dues will be withdrawn from my accounts. If I break the magic prohibitions and the government or OMO steps in, they will provide all information possible on me, declare me *persona non grata*, and order none within the house to give me assistance, or as they call it succor."

"Yes."

"And you're okay with this?" The words came out as a squeaked protest and I got up to get water, needing to move. To think.

"Cori—in the last two decades, this has happened three times. Once for a serial killer that no one knew existed until he killed the child of a merlin, and twice more for people that committed major crimes in public. I believe you have heard of the Time Bomber?"

I had. He'd devised a way to create mini bubbles of time and would walk in and randomly launch them, then speed the time up. People would have their hand wither before them, aged to over a hundred in a few seconds. He would cause issues with hospitals by doing it on their equipment. He was taken down and what? I frowned trying to remember. "I know they caught him, but I don't remember what happened. I don't recall a trial."

"There wasn't one. The current head of Emrys executed him. He'd broken the oath and the OMO declared him Ronin." I swallowed, taken aback by word usage again—executed. It sounded so finite and simple. "Everything was smoothed over." She sighed and leaned forward. "Cori, unless you are planning on taking up a life of crime, killing children, or becoming a terrorist, this is not anything you need to worry about. The possible risks are outweighed by the benefits. Legal, financial, and job assistance. No one that is a member of this house or of Nyx can accept a contract to kill or hurt you without breaking the oath. There will be people to talk to who get what it is like to be powerful."

"Hey, I don't think I'm special because I'm, well whatever I am," I protested looking guiltily at Jo. She rolled her eyes at me and winked. "And what do you mean 'and Nyx'?"

"You are special. And Indira knows it. Having good friends is something priceless and I hope by the all the planes it never changes. But many people can't handle the power difference and it eats at them. While I don't know if you even have a match in power, you'll find people to talk about the challenges. More merlins than mages have familiars and talking about them can help too."

~My queans. All mine.~ The plural and the possessive growl made me want to stick my head under the table and look at him. I managed not to.

"As to Nyx. We have a reciprocation agreement. We will not attack any of theirs and they will not attack any of ours. It helped calm some issues a decade or so ago."

"Okay." I stared at the paper. Doubt, fear, worry, and a strong desire to just go pull all the covers over my head waged a war in me. But I needed the support and removing any member of these societies from trying to kill me would also help.

How did I end up here? Why?

There weren't any answers. "Can I leave? I mean, if I decide to leave the society?" I blurted out the words.

Joanna nodded. "Yes. There are penalties if you leave before your decade is up, as you committed to that. But if you want to walk away, it is however many years you have left of dues plus two years. At that point everything is dissolved along with any responsibilities you have to us."

The amount of money that represented made me sick. "You're sure I'll get a job that will let me pay that sort of money?"

This time she laughed looking at me. "Cori, with your magic levels along with the R&D places that will be begging you to work for them, you'll make that much money in a month. If you change your mind before you start your draft, there are no fines. We understand that college is a time of change and experimentation and we want to make sure the people in Emrys want to be in Emrys."

I read everything again, waiting for her to attack or something. Even Jo and Sable had sat down and were trying to keep busy. "Okay. I'll sign."

"Great. I hope you enjoy it as much as I have over the years." I signed where she pointed and then stood and said the oath. At the last, I felt a flush of heat wash over me, then gone.

"It's done. All the contact information is in there as well as the chat groups and website information. You'll be prompted to create a login. Give me at least 48 hours to get all your information into the system," she said as she snapped a pic of me for my ID and recorded my OMO number. "Call me if you have questions, and good luck. I'll get the news of your joining spread as far as I can. It might help to get people to step back."

"Thanks," I said and rose with her, tensing, ready for the attack.

"Night, ladies." She gave all of us a grin and left, the soft click of her shoes the last sound I heard as I closed the door.

"Well that was anticlimactic," Sable said. We all looked at each other and collapsed into exhausted laughter. If an assassin didn't kill me, the jumping at shadows just might.

Chapter 29

Magic Explained has a new ongoing blog series. All information presented on this blog has been thoroughly researched and vetted by OMO officials. Check in weekly to see how magic affects the world and how it works. The newest section will deal with Air magic and using it in various industries. ~Magic Explained Online

ORDER

The next few weeks seemed the same endless torture. I went to class every day with Alixant acting like a silent shadow. Half the time he barely grunted at me but would yell if I lagged or walked too fast. He surrounded me with wind and more than once a student stumbled into me, only to get shoved violently to the ground, much to their surprise. Indira at least could keep me out of sync, but even she was getting shorter and shorter with me. And the feeling of being watched every time I was outside was about to drive me crazy. If I looked, there were always people watching me, though usually with curiosity or suspicion. And Carelian would just respond he didn't see any person paying special attention to me.

In most of my classes the only thing resembling a friend was Charles. While I sat with Jo in Magic 101 lab, I began to sit with Charles in History on Tuesdays and Thursdays. He didn't say much, but he'd smile, Arachena would chitter and Carelian would do something. Commune? Talk? Stare? I couldn't figure it out, but occasionally she'd jump off Charles' shoulder and walk up and down on Carelian's back, her legs pumping up and down, while Carelian purred so loud students would glare at us.

I just smiled back at them and hated that I took pleasure in their flinching back.

Neither Alixant nor Indira would tell me anything about what was going on, and I just wanted to be left alone. Even in the apartment at night I felt under scrutiny and it was driving me crazy. All I did was study. I even had to let Sable and Jo take Carelian out to play because I couldn't be seen in such an open area and stationary for so long. No one, including Carelian, seemed worried about him being taken or hurt.

Which left me sitting in my apartment when I wasn't in class. On the upside, my grades were looking good, but my mood was foul. Bad enough that I knew I had to change something before my roommates killed me.

"Spring break is next week. Why don't you two go up and see your parents for a few days? Then go up to Chattanooga and explore. Go downtown and enjoy some you time," I said the Monday before spring break. GA MageTech's breaks made little sense to me. This year it was the first week in April and the semester ended the last week of May. But Jo's grades were up, so I knew she could get out and go have fun, not be part of my prison camp.

"Mami will ask where you are," Jo protested, but I knew she liked the idea. Loving me was one thing, not getting any alone time with your lover was something else. Sable had gone out with her dad for the evening. I liked him, but I understood why he was so worried about his daughter being around me. I would be.

"Tell her the truth. I'm basically under house arrest until this thing with Japan settles down. I'm still hoping that joining Emrys will help. But it gives me some time to veg out, and you two can get away." I kept my voice upbeat. The last thing I could do would be reveal how much I wanted to go get a hug from Marisol and have her tell me it would all be okay.

Jo still looked at me doubtfully. "I know you were originally planning on working this week."

"Yeah, well. That isn't happening. It's fine. I still have enough to do to keep busy and a night or two of pizza and watching movies sounds kinda nice." It didn't, not really.

Going out and having pizza and going to the movies sounded awesome. Staying home, not so much.

"You sure?"

"Yes, get. Get through this week and take off Friday." I waved my hand, grinning at her. If I wasn't careful, people trying to kill me would chase her away or kill her instead. And I'd burn down the world before I let her get hurt again. Only the anger in her voice when I offered to walk away kept me here. But she couldn't get hurt again. Just couldn't.

The smile that lit up her face told me everything I wanted to know. They left by three on Friday. I got a text message as they pulled out. With a sigh, I texted that I wished them well and headed to my last class. Law. It was never boring. Odd and scary sometimes, but never boring. When the class ended, I grabbed my stuff, Carelian trailing behind me, and went down to meet Alixant, bracing myself for a fight.

"I need to go to the library," I said, looking at him. I felt exhausted, and I knew he'd make it something I had to argue for. Which just set my teeth on edge another few degrees.

"No. I've got other stuff to do tonight."

"Look, just because you have a date with Indira,"—the flush on his face told me I'd hit a tender spot and my eyes narrowed, now even more annoyed—"I still need to get some materials to finish papers and lay out my magical experiments for my other class. Unless, of course, she'll just give me an A without needing to do the work." I didn't think she'd do that, and I knew I'd never accept it. But the taunt made him stiffen.

"In and out. You get what you need, then back to your secured apartment."

I'd never asked what they'd done to secure my apartment—the extent they would tell us is we needed to invite the person in. Otherwise they couldn't get in. That was all I wanted to know at this point.

"I'll take the time I need. I have to find the material, then get it, then make sure I don't need to go back this weekend. I'm having pizza and watching movies. I won't leave this weekend and I'll ask Indira to take me on a shopping trip next week."

"Fine," he growled out and we headed to the library. Well, he stalked beside me, the wind shield keeping me oddly surrounded by silence. He dropped the shield when we reached the library, but he followed me up and down every aisle until I had the four books I needed. While the internet was great to find out the basis of the stories and experiments I needed, it wasn't enough to write papers or figure out expected results from.

On the way back, not glancing my way at all, he spoke. "I know this has to be rough. I swear people are trying to get this squashed, but as far as we can tell there are still hits out on you. Give us more time." We entered the park as he spoke. On the Friday of spring break the area felt like a ghost town, and just as empty.

Maybe if he'd been conciliatory or even apologetic, I might have let it slide; but I missed having a life. I hated this and hated that the people I spent the most time with were the ones I barely liked.

"Rough? I have strangers in every aspect of my life. I can't go see the people I love like family. Hell, I can't even take my familiar to the park. I've tried very hard to not be rude or difficult, but if this continues, I'll tell everyone to go take a flying leap and I'll quit. Not like I'm not used to not having anything or being hated." I spat the words, and he stiffened, whirling on me.

"Now look here. I get this wasn't your idea—"

"My idea? It was bad enough you got me tested when I had no idea I was a mage, and frankly if I had never found out I would never have used it anyhow." I felt a bit of guilt about that statement, I mean, I had been planning on getting tested. "And then the second damn test? Making me the freak that everyone stares at? Yes, you've made my life so pleasant." Maybe that wasn't a hundred percent accurate, but I just wanted him to go away.

He tried to protest again, maybe something softened in his face. I didn't care.

"Let's not even mention the cop Jonas checking in on me every few days and cautioning me not to leave the area without letting them know." He stiffened at that and stared at me.

"She's what?"

"You heard me. I'm basically being told I can't go anywhere because they don't want to risk people getting hurt. Please tell me exactly how this is anything I asked for?" I wanted something else to throw in his face, but as fast as the anger came, it was fading. I just wanted to go home.

"Cori, you're being—" He broke off and looked towards the trees at the same time something hit the shield and slammed into the ground at my feet, distracting me. I stared at the throwing star laying there.

"Throwing stars? Really? My life is not a movie!" Bullets I expected, it was America after all, but who in the world used throwing stars?

"Cori down!" Alixant gestured and my feet were swept out from underneath me. I landed hard. The books in my backpack left indents on my back and I could feel bruises forming. "Don't move."

"I wasn't moving, I was standing there." I couldn't get up, I couldn't do anything but watch. And I watched Steven Alixant perform magic.

Outside of Indira and the maniac Paul Goins, I'd never really seen magic. Not big movie magic. The little stuff, sure. But something to make me stare? No. I knew Alixant was a Pattern merlin with pale Earth and Air, and strong in Water. But outside of Chris's little example back when we were still trying to find Goins, I'd never seen Pattern used as a skill. Just about every mage stayed under the radar and never did anything flashy.

Today I saw what I'd only seen in movies.

The ground shook as Alixant turned and wind whipped around him like a hurricane, but it was directed out towards the trees. A man, yelling and trying to turn to face Alixant, rose high in the air. Another man stepped out from behind a tree and sprinted towards Alixant's back.

"Alixant, look out!" I yelled, but my words were whipped away before the sound cleared my bubble of air. A torrent of fire came from the man, headed right towards Alixant, but it hit wind and spun down. Alixant turned and looked at the man, who snarled, the fire dying even as the ground at Alixant's feet began to smoke.

Alixant glanced down and sneered. "Really? You're, what, a magician? Not even a wizard? You think that trick will stop me?" Water pooled at Alixant's feet, creating steam as he walked forward. The man's clothes began to unravel and he snarled and spun, fire streaking towards a bright red furry figure motionless under a bench.

"CARELIAN RUN!" I screamed the words so hard my throat hurt. The red figure moved, streaking towards me. The guy attacking us turning to follow his path as fireballs shot forward.

I shredded the shield around me with magic as I reached for Carelian. I grabbed the earth in the lawn creating a barrier and blocking the fire streaking towards my familiar. The man turned to look at me and snarled, two more fireballs coming towards me. I panicked and pulled on Time. A bubble formed around me and I stood and ran, moving towards Carelian, who had stopped, fur puffed out and eyes wild in the shelter of an earthen wall I'd ripped from the ground.

With an effort, though it felt like dropping Murphy's Curse or Alixant's shield around me, I dismissed time. I felt the few seconds hit me, even as the fireballs impacted where I'd been. I scooped up Carelian in my arms as the man Alixant had thrown into the air stepped forward and grinned. He was closer than I expected, and I could see his tattoo. Spirit mage. His smile had nothing but cruelty in it as he smiled at me, then Alixant.

"Oh, fuck me," I heard Alixant say behind me.

The enemy mage threw his head back and lashed forward. I felt pain splinter my mind, and Carelian cry out in my head. I heard a screech, long, deep, and more terrifying than anything else I'd ever heard. The last sound that followed me into darkness was sound of screaming.

Chapter 30

Spirit Merlins are more mysterious than most. At the time of this writing there are only 2000 Spirit merlins alive and registered with the OMO. This is out of the thirty-four thousand active merlins. No one knows why the numbers are so low for this category and most countries hoard them, refusing to let them assist other countries. Oddly, Australia has the most at two-hundred-fifty, and of those ninety are Aborigines. The OMO has made no comment about the disparity. ~ Magic Explained

SPIRIT

The pounding in my head pulled me to consciousness. I lay there, eyes closed as I tried to breathe through the pain. The familiar rumble curled up at my side allowed some fear and stress to fade, though it did nothing for the headache.

~I apologize for the headache, it is a side effect of the twisted way your opponent used his magic,~ a strange voice said in my head.

I jerked upright intending to look around to see who had spoken, but the splitting headache forced a cry from between my lips and I curled over my knees sobbing in pain.

~Here. Water will help.~ Something bumped against my hand at the words.

I cracked open my eyes, even the dim light sending daggers into my skull. A bottle of water, condensation gathering on the outside, floated in front of me. At this point, poisoning me would be overkill. I could barely process thoughts, why bother to kill me? Moving slowly, even thinking hurt, I took the water, cracked it open and drained it. The icy liquid coating my throat did help. The sensations were psychosomatic, but still I could feel the blinding pain fade as I drank. My eyes closed to protect what brain cells I had left.

Maybe that KO spell siphons water from your brain or something.

An idle thought, but I poked at it as I let the water work into me. Magic hurt more than I had expected it to.

As I sat there, Carelian rumbling by my side, I reached out to pet him.

~My quean well?~

"Getting better," I rasped. The air smelled clean, fresh, as if we were in the mountains far away from the city and I felt my heart squeeze tight. I managed to open my eyes and take in my surroundings. The bed I sat on was made of blankets and feathers, wonderfully soft, and nothing I'd ever seen. Simple walls of wood and a roof that looked like it was made of palm fronds or some other grassy leaf rose above me. The only sounds were of leaves, Carelian, and the song of birds in the distance.

Oh shit, shit, shit.

I swallowed hard as I heard a sound I couldn't place. It sounded like scale and feathers and a rumble that wasn't a purr or a laugh, but I had the image of a chuffing tiger in my head. I turned to look where the sound had come from and froze.

Seeing the unicorn, the thing from Chaos, and even the Gorgon Tirsane had created a level of shock and awe. But I'd seen them from a distance first, had time to accept their existence before I saw them up close. It also helped immensely that they had not paid attention to me until the end, and by that time I'd gotten myself under control. This time the creature sitting not ten feet away from me paid no attention to anyone or anything else, great yellow green eyes locked on mine.

Griffin!

That word spiraled in my head in various levels of intensity and the griffin winced. The clear light displayed everything the typical description of one always had. White feathered head with a raptor's yellow beak, a lion's tawny body with wings at the shoulders, front lion claws, and a tail with a tuft of feathers. But all the descriptions didn't begin to touch on what he actually looked like. The tawny fur shimmered in the light like liquid gold, the feathers started at dark purple at his shoulders and lightened to the palest lavender at the ends. His eyes glowed with power and I wanted to cringe away from his gaze. Then there were his paws. They were bigger than my head and I could only imagine how long and deadly the claws would be.

Water splashed on my hand and I looked down to realize I was shaking so hard the condensation on the bottle was scattering on me like rain.

~Girl, what are you so afraid of?~ The voice, now that I could concentrate on it and not the splitting pain in my head, the voice called to mind wind and leaves and the purr of a lion, and was wholly masculine.

"That, tha—" I stuttered and licked suddenly dry lips. I forced myself to breathe in and continue. "That you're going to kill me and eat me," I said, my voice still squeaking.

The griffon, or was it gryphon, looked at me then down at Carelian who still leaned against me purring. Then it started to shake, a weird snorting noise coming out of his beak.

"Ummm?"

~Cori,~ Carelian said, laughter coating his words. ~If Baneyarl planned on eating you, why would he bring you here and serve you water? Why would I be here and not trying to kill anyone that dared to touch my quean?~

It was the most I'd ever heard Carelian say at once. Meanwhile, the magnificent animal kept snickering and I felt my face flush. When he put it that way my question seemed really stupid. I looked around more closely. The place reminded me of a treehouse with a large porch on one side and more rooms down a hallway out of my sight.

"So, you aren't planning on killing me. Why am I here? Where is here? And..." I trailed off looking around, dread supplanting the fear. "Where is Alixant?"

The laughter died a bit at a time, though I suspected Carelian still laughed at me. The griffin shook itself and I had to resist the urge to reach out and pet him, even if I thought he might eat me. Instead I sank my hands into Carelian's fur, it seemed a much safer option.

~The one that fought for you?~ I nodded at the question, still watching, half expecting him to pounce. ~Ah, he is alive, though I will keep him slumbering until we leave. You are in my home in what you term the Spirit plane, though that is not at all accurate.~ A note of disapproval at the inaccurate term infused his words and just hearing that so clearly made it truly register this was all via telepathy or something like it.

"Not that I'm complaining, but why am I here? Why do you care?" I knew I should probably go check on Alixant, but even if he was dead what was I going to do about it? Besides, familiars were supposed to be trustworthy and Carelian didn't seem upset.

~I believe your companion is better suited to answer that question.~

My companion?

I turned to look at Carelian, who found his tail of very great interest. "Carelian?"

He didn't look at me, just flicked his ears backwards.

~Carelian, this was your request, you are responsible for telling her.~ The rumble of Baneyarl's voice in my head caused goosebumps to ride up and down my spine, but I didn't look away from the cat who was trying very hard to ignore both of us.

~Carelian Tail-lash Xeonise, tell her!~ The snap of command made me flinch, and Carelian lifted his head to hiss, but then rose and stretched, walking, I noticed, away from me.

~You are my powerful quean. Very powerful. You needed training. Your humans and their twisted understanding cannot provide. I asked for a teacher. Baneyarl said yes.~ He paused to sharpen his claws on the post of the room.

"A teacher? I don't understand."

~You are quean, you need to understand magic. The rigid rules they put around it are right but wrong. Magic not so structured.~ He hissed in my mind and I shivered, it felt funny. ~You explain. This is not my area.~ While I heard the words, I knew they weren't directed at me and I shifted my attention to the griffin.

~Your focus is much given to avoidance and obfuscation, but it is not his area of expertise, that is true. But first.~ He rose to his full height and a wave of atavistic fear lashed at me again. His head almost brushed the top of the room we were in. He easily had to be the size of a Clydesdale and probably weighed about the same. I wanted to scoot back, away from his predator state, but I stayed frozen watching.

With his wings half mantled, he dipped his head. ~I am Baneyarl ni Keriseo. Carelian asked me to teach you if I found you suitable. I have watched you for many cycles of the sun and I believe you will do well to with the information I have to impart. It has been many seasons since I last had an apprentice.~

He turned and picked up a book and as he did so I realized his paws weren't paws like a normal cat, but more like Carelian's with long fingers and an opposable thumb that retracted into a fist-like shape to walk on. The closest I could think of was how apes walked with their hands in fists, but this seemed more flexible and less boney. I'd have to investigate Carelian's paws again.

~You are skilled in Spirit, but also blessed with access to the other realms of magic. I would teach you what my teachers passed down to me in how to use the magic of Spirit, of all magics, instead of just the forms.~ I knew he meant Spirit as he talked, but he used another word that sounded different but meant what I thought of as Spirit, yet wasn't.

"You want to teach me? As an apprentice?" That word worried me a lot. It seemed like more owing. "What would be involved in that? I still have to go to school and learn. I can't just bail."

Or if I could, why the hell have I been bothering with all of this crap over the last few months?

Griffin faces aren't really made for smiling, but I swear he grinned at me. ~Carelian did say you were a wise and cautious mage. I am bored and you may prove interesting.~ He seemed to shrug, but I caught something else in his tone that while not a lie wasn't all of it. ~An oath not to use what I teach you against me unless in defense of your life. Basically, if I decide to lose what capability for reason I possess and attack you, feel free to defend your life and honor, otherwise you will not attack me with your magic.~

I frowned, things popping off in my brain. "That doesn't really say much. I mean I could still kill you with a gun or use magic around you without using it on you. So why bother? Either I wouldn't betray you or I would, the oath won't prevent that."

His head tilted, a very birdlike move, then pivoted to look to where Carelian was prowling on his rafters. I really wanted more time to look and explore this place, but now wasn't the time.

~You are correct. She is smart.~

~My powerful quean,~ Carelian murmured, pride in his voice.

I rolled my eyes. "Don't act so smug. Not like you had anything to do with me being smart." The griffin moved or his wings did and something about it made me think of a shrugging gesture. "Did he?"

~She is powerful and curious, she seeks and probes. She will be a difficult student. A challenging one.~

~I chose queans well. I have three. They are all powerful. She would be an asset to your reputation.~ Carelian hadn't come back over to us, and I glared at both of them. This was starting to feel like a conversation with Indira and Alixant.

~True, but much trouble. Very well, I will educate her in the truths of magic. But you know they will notice.~ Baneyarl had settled back down, preening his feathers. One advantage to telepathy—you could do things with your mouth at the same time as you talked, but the idea of using my mouth to groom myself made me wrinkle my nose.

~They should notice. She is powerful. A True Quean.~ There was something about how Carelian said it that time as opposed to all the other times. I could hear the capitals in the words. My frayed nerves shredded.

"What are you two talking about? What is a quean? And who is they?"

Baneyarl looked up and through me. For a minute I thought he was peering into my soul. Maybe into my future. ~Do you want me to train you? I will teach you the truths of magic. That it is a living thing you have connected with. That all things cost, but a focus lowers the cost. A triad lowers it more. You can do brilliant things.~

"Why? Why do you want to do this? Why me?" I wanted to cry or scream. All I had wanted was a good job and my own place. To do the small things without counting pennies. And here I sat, a griffin offering me something I knew most mages would sell their limbs for.

~Reasons. Do you want to learn? You would be able to protect yourself and no longer need others to be your shield.~

That idea sounded so good. But still I hesitated. Everyone wanted me lately and I didn't understand why. I hated not understanding motivations.

"And the cost?"

Baneyarl tilted his head one way, then the other. ~Three things, I think. One is your promise not to attack me with any means.~ Again that feeling he was smiling at me. ~Unless I attack you first. Second, you will not tell other mages that you are learning from me. They would not take it well, I believe. Third, at some point in your life you will make a decision that much will ride on. I ask you to hear me out if I come to discuss your decision. Note that I am not requesting you agree with me. I am requesting that you listen to my arguments about that decision.~

"Decision, what decision?"

~I don't know. It may be the name of your first child? It may be you deciding whether to kill someone or yourself. I ask that you listen to me and let me try to sway you with my argument.~

I leaned back, licking my lips as I thought. "Could I get another bottle of water?"

One floated out of the room beyond and into my hands, icy cold again.

~Portable light containers are of great utility, too bad there is no clean way to return them to their original elements.~

"What do you mean?" I asked mainly because I wanted time to think and to figure out any pitfalls. What harm could there be in listening to one side of an argument?

~Fire melts it into a lump, it ignores water, it does not feed insects or plants. All you can do is break it back down into its original elements and then dispose of those properly.~

Oh yeah, plastic the bane of recycling everywhere. Wait, break it down?

Ideas slammed into me and I wanted to groan, then I snickered. That would give me information for some classes Sable said were coming up. Sounded like a great research paper if I could get the costs down to something that would be feasible for the mages, and a solution to a great many energy problems. I closed my eyes to process all this.

Why isn't this already being done?

Worry and suspicion about all the things in the background made me sigh. I couldn't solve all the problems in the world. All I could do was deal with what I could and try to be a person I could live with.

Refocusing on the world around me I caught sight of Baneyarl and Carelian seemed to be having a discussion that I couldn't hear. I watched them as I tried to think through the echoes of the headache.

"I have a few conditions," I said into the soft noise of birds and leaves. Both Carelian and Baneyarl turned to look at me.

Chapter 31

While the OMO is global and has a much more far-reaching effect than even the UN, there are still some nations that refuse to participate. They are few in number, as the OMO is the only agency that can consistently test for magic and maintains a global database on mages. If your country does not participate, you miss out on both the benefits and protections inherent in the OMO. ~ History of Magic

CHAOS

~And what would those conditions be?~ Baneyarl asked. I had half expected amusement, dragon to the silly girl—instead there was wariness and a hint of worry.

"First that your argument not delay or waste my time listening to you if there is a time limit. That you say what you feel must be said without causing me to be too late to decide." Magic law had been discussing some filibustering cases so the idea of Baneyarl talking to me for days made me wary.

~Very well, I agree.~ He didn't sound excited about that, but also didn't sound upset, so win there.

"Second, I get to tell Jo and Sable about you, and you agree to train them also."

This time the pause was longer and his predatory head, which looked like he could eat Carelian with two snaps, turned to look at the cat.

~The other two queans. Powerful. Smart. Damaged.~

Baneyarl stared at him for a long time, eyes narrowed, as did I. "What do you mean damaged? They aren't damaged. Jo isn't damaged," I protested, stung on her, on their behalf.

Carelian didn't answer but stalked a floating object that looked like a cross between a butterfly and a dandelion spore.

~Very well, I will train the three of you. But they must agree to the same terms as you did. Are there other conditions?~

I almost sagged in relief at that. I might have been able to keep a secret from Sable, but Jo? She'd have figured it out.

"You tell me the actual reason you're agreeing to do this." I had to know. This made no sense. I had no idea how magical he was, but the odds were he had more magic than Jo, Sable, and me put together.

~Ha, you will be an excellent student. I will tell you. But not now.~

"When?" I needed these answers, dammit. What he said might make it easier for me to trust him.

~When you understand enough magic to understand why. I see that you need something concrete. Very well. Prior to your graduation from your school with what you call a bachelor's, I will answer your question.~

"How did you know that?" I blurted out. Why in the world would a magical creature from another realm know anything about human degrees?

~I have been watching you for a while. Ever since Carelian asked for this favor. A favor I will collect on,~ he flicked a wingtip at Carelian, who didn't even move, just let the wing ruffle his fur as he sat like an Egyptian statue on the other side of the room.

"Wait? You've been watching me?" I turned to Carelian. "You said ... no, you said no human was watching me. You KNEW!"

~Not a threat. Bane teaches better when curious. You made him curious. I said you learn and be great. You will.~ Not even his whiskers moved as he sat watching both of us with his emerald green eyes shining out of his ruby red fur.

The desire to strangle him wrestled with the need to hug him. He'd found someone to teach me and keep me safe. And about freaked me out with the feeling someone was watching.

"Nothing else. I'll swear." At this point I didn't have anything to lose.

~Then we should go. It is not wise to keep the human male unconscious much longer. Besides, people will notice the time bubble soon enough.~ He rose and shook himself, and I fought the desire to cringe. My lizard brain that normally hid and made stupid suggestions was shrieking with the need to hide and cower. My snark took over and shoved the lizard back into his cave.

"That's it? No magic oath?"

~Either you will abide by your word or you won't. Why use magic to judge character when actions will prove it easily enough?~

I laughed to myself and rose. I turned and my bag with my library books was behind me on a low shelf at the back of the bed or nest. I grabbed them and stepped out of it.

"Lead the way." I figured quoting Shakespeare would be a waste of time, but for all I knew they'd known him. I'd have to ask someday.

Alixant's body floated into the room, hanging limp in the air, but he looked much the same as my last sight of him. Hair disarrayed and clothing mussed, but not bleeding and he seemed to be breathing. Though he'd probably have a headache like mine. I'd need a story, one that would be the truth. Well, he'd wanted me to learn to lie by not lying. I guessed this would be as good a time as any.

"Can I get a bottle of water?" I asked as Baneyarl started to open a portal to home. I could feel the familiar spike. "He'll probably have a headache like mine."

A bottle floated to me and I held onto it. Baneyarl pointed. ~There is where you were. Two hours have passed while I had you here, the time bubble keeping anyone from reaching in and touching you. When you step back in it will snap and you will catch up with normal time. I will see you on your Monday.~

"Jo and Sable won't be there. It is a holiday week for us," I told him, and I wanted time to explain to them what in the heck was going on.

Not to mention time to figure out how to deal with what had just happened.

~As you request. I shall be at your domicile at your seventh hour in the evening on the Sunday following this coming one. This shall be an interesting adventure, Corisande.~

Before I could ask anything else, the rip between worlds opened beneath me and I fell down to earth. It was only a few inches, but I hadn't expected it and stumbled. Carelian leaped down with catlike grace, while Alixant floated to the ground.

~I shall look forward to our next meeting.~ Baneyarl said, his voice in my head somewhere between ominous and amused. Then the rip sealed with him on the other side. A shudder washed through me as my body adjusted to the bubble of time and it collapsed leaving me standing there with an unconscious Alixant, the bodies of two attackers spread out around us, cops, and an incandescently mad Indira striding towards us.

"Oh shit, maybe I should have just stayed in the other realm," I muttered.

"Where. Have. You. Been!" She didn't shout the words but each of them slashed into me with the force of a dagger. Right then facing the throwing stars from the other idiot sounded more preferable than dealing with Indira.

"Spirit realm, I think."

Remember obfuscate, misdirect, don't tell her. You promised.

This was going to be a trial by fire. One I wasn't looking forward to.

"What happened?" She asked, waving a cop over as she knelt by Alixant's head. "What's wrong with him?"

"One of the attackers threw a KO spell at us. Knocked us out. He hasn't come to yet. I woke with a killer headache, so he probably will too."

"KO's usually do that. Who killed the attackers? Alixant?"

I paused. I didn't know. "I assume so. He was fighting when I was hit, I think. I don't know for sure if the same KO spell took him out or not. I blacked out before I saw. One was a Fire mage, the other a Spirit mage."

A groan prevented me from saying any more and I stepped back, though I remained well aware of all the cops watching me with wary eyes and Detective Olivia Jonas headed my way. Exhaustion swamped me and I sank to the grass away from any of the torn-up soil or the milling cops. If people wanted to talk to me, they could do it here.

I'd been nice and left the bottle of water with Alixant and regretted it now. Thirst, hunger, and exhaustion all hit me. A mixture of my body having lived twice the amount of time as everyone else and the adrenaline crash. I had a reason to be starving. As I sat cross-legged on the grass, my bag acting as an uncomfortable backrest, Carelian curled up in the space my legs left, purring.

~You are smart. He is worth the subterfuge.~

I gave him a side eyed glare but said nothing. Too many people would have asked questions.

Alixant was sitting up holding his head while Indira and Olivia talked to him. I just waited and tried to figure out how to not lie.

It didn't take long before the three of them headed over to me. Alixant glared at me as he approached, Indira matching him.

"What happened?" he growled out and my temper spiked.

I was so tired of being yelled at. Screw it. I knew how to create the time bubble shield. I could create a dirt shield and I could damn well figure out how to scan for people lurking around me. Hell, the first thing I might ask for training in was invisibility if it was something I could learn to do.

"Am I under arrest?" I challenged Olivia Jonas, who had taken a step back from the two furious mages.

"Not at this time. I have questions, but as far as I can tell you didn't do much of the attacking. We have a pattern mage on the way to rebuild the events."

"I can do that," snarled Alixant. "And why the hell are you asking if you're under arrest? You're going to tell us everything that happened. Where we were, who cast the time bubble. Everything!"

Anger and annoyance rippled through me. Why had I even bothered to care about him? I didn't have the patience or energy to deal with any more tonight. And I and a certain four-legged creature needed to have a long discussion.

As if he could hear my thoughts Carelian's purr stopped and he stiffened. I gave him a sharp look and he huffed out a sigh and groomed his paw, ignoring all of us.

"Detective Jonas. Am I under arrest?" I repeated.

"No," she admitted slowly as she took a cautious step back.

"Are there any legal reasons either of these two have the right to order me about?"

"Not that I know of," though she didn't sound sure and I swear she pulled up a shield.

"Excellent. Then I am leaving." I tried to sound chipper and happy, but it came out as an annoyed snarl. I stood up, pulled on my backpack, and picked Carelian up. Wisely, he didn't struggle or complain.

"Cori, sit your ass down and answer my questions." Alixant growled out the words, moving closer, looming over me.

I looked up at him and smiled, all teeth, no humor. "No. I'm not under arrest and since I'm not, I'm going home." Before he could say anything else, I snapped a time bubble around me and headed at a quick walk to my house. At the rate I was spending time I'd be older than I wanted but right now I was going home and they could all hang.

Moving out of time, or in time depending on how you looked at it, got me home without issue as no one could technically be in the same time as me, though that sounded wrong, but right now I didn't care. It kept me safe, and I dropped it right outside my door, after checking carefully that there was no one waiting for me. I shivered as time caught up with me, but I hadn't been that out of sync with it. Only about a minute. I got inside and shut the door. I still couldn't figure out what they had done to safeguard my apartment, but since I hadn't been killed here, I would treat it as a safe space.

Carelian squirmed, and I let him down. He headed straight for water. ~Hungry,~ he murmured in my head.

"Yeah, me too. Give me a minute, but don't think you're getting out of that conversation," I said as I headed to the kitchen. First, I filled an enormous glass with icy water and drained half of it, finally feeling almost human. I opened up a can of salmon for him and put it on a plate. As he tore into that I pulled out pre-made burritos from the freezer.

"Damn, I love that woman," I whispered as I put the burritos Jo, and probably Sable, had made for me in the microwave. There was enough in the freezer to cover the entire week. If I knew Jo, they probably varied between ingredients. She knew her mom would load them up for their few days in the mountains.

I took the reheated burrito and the refilled water and sat down on the couch. Carelian had finished eating and was grooming his face.

"We need to talk."

Chapter 32

Familiars have a mind of their own and have even acted against the wishes of their chosen mage. And yes, they can kill. The most famous incident known is what caused the fire in San Francisco in the early 1900s. A mage was assaulted who had a familiar that looked like a large red dog. She was caught coming from a reputable female bathhouse and was knocked out from behind. Her familiar found her as she came back to consciousness in the local med ward. It left with her pleading for it not to leave. Her attackers were later killed in a fire that then swept through thirty percent of the city. The female mage was never found for questioning. ~ History of Magic

ORDER

He didn't look up at me, but his ears laid back and he licked his paw, washing his face over and over again.

"Yeah, not buying it. You don't need your mouth to talk. So, spill. What is going on? How do you know all this? Are you a mage too?" That question had been haunting the back of my mind.

Carelian stopped washing his face and jumped up on one of the kitchen chairs that faced me. He curled up in typical cat loaf pose, his twitching red tail the only thing that gave away any emotions.

~Life in realms doesn't work like life does here. Here is odd and strange and overly logical as magic is small and weak.~

Small and weak? The idea of what some people could do even if beings from other realms regarded our magic as weak made me shiver and I rubbed my arms. Tea may have been a better choice than icy water.

"Okay, but what does that have to do with Baneyarl and me? Why is it so important to teach me?"

~You are quean. So are others. But you are first human in many lives to be a true quean. To use all of magic, not the broken shallow version that exists here. Your world would never survive full magic, but you need to.~

"I swear to Merlin, if you tell me there is a prophecy about me, I will quit right now and go find a desert island to live on. I'm no hero." I said the words with an unfeigned fervor. I had no desire to be the hero of any story. I just wanted to help people, figure out what happened to Stevie, and have a life. My life as weird as it might be.

Amusement rolled through my mind as his ears flicked. ~No. There is no such thing as prophecy. Even foresight is rarely accurate. Magic and free will not easily predicted. You too powerful not to be trained. There is fear that if you not fully understand your capabilities you might irreparably damage realms.~

That didn't sound good. Maybe a hero might be better. Because it sounded like I was the villain in this scenario.

"How do you know all this? I thought you came here as a kitten. And wait, people are talking about me?" The idea that I was a subject of conversations among creatures elsewhere made me nauseous.

~Kittar true. But still have family, friends of family, and friends I make like Arachena. We talk about our humans.~ He buried his face in his paws for a minute. ~I often go home. To see family and parents. To hear news and take lessons.~

I felt slapped. "You go back?"

~Home? When you sleep. I talk to parents and littermates when needed. Other familiars need to be within sight to talk to. But blood family is like, well, using your phone.~

"Across realms?" I squeaked out the words. I knew with absolute certainty I could not tell anyone this. The OMO and the government would have a field day with this information, and they would round up familiars. No government was good about ignoring possible exploitations for profit.

~Would you be willing to leave your home and never be able to speak to Jo again?~ His voice was acerbic, and I flushed.

"Point. But that means you can open planar rips?" The image of Elsba, a flying serpent that was the familiar of a mage I'd met in my hometown of Rockway, flying in the air and that rip jumped into my mind. "Wait, all familiars can?"

~To their home realms, yes. My magic is still young, it will be decades until reach my full power. But I make tiny rips that I slip through. Small enough that you don't notice.~

I just sat there shell-shocked. "I need to learn to shield. My mind, I mean. If anyone learned this."

~A few know. But you correct, this is not good to share.~

Leaning back against the chair, I thought. The quiet of the night seemed ominous, and I needed more food. I kept expecting there to be pounding on the door from Alixant and or Indira, but it didn't happen. I got up and headed towards the kitchen—there had to be something with sugar somewhere.

"So what? You go home and go to school?" I'd come back with some ice cream, needing the sugar rush.

~Not exactly. We are not human; we learn differently.~ He just curled up tighter and I got the feeling this wasn't a subject to push him on.

"Why Baneyarl?"

Carelian sighed in my mind. ~Reasons. He slipped out when you were at place of games. Found this world interesting and since he got here, he could go back and forth.~

"Wait, what?" The constant unexpected information was about to drive me crazy.

~Cori, you can't know everything at once. There are lifetimes of information you need learn. For now, if we come through a rip to your reality, we can then move between this realm and our realm. But if we never get here, we are blocked.~

Remembering the monsters that I'd seen lurking in Chaos and the teeth on Salistra, that made me feel marginally better. "Tirsane can come and go as she wishes?"

Carelian laughed, his whiskers twitching at me. ~She is what your mythology calls a god. She always able to go anywhere she wishes. I not supposed to understand what drives or controls her.~

"That doesn't really make me feel much better." He didn't respond and I ate more sea salt caramel ice cream. "Can I trust him? Baneyarl?"

~He has no reason to hurt you and many reasons to see you succeed. But all beings have their price. Even Jo.~

That hurt in a way I couldn't explain, and I shied away from it. "True." I played with the ice cream container, thinking. "Look, I don't control you. I know this. But can you tell me next time if someone is watching me? Or warn me? Thinking you are hiding things from me makes it hard to trust."

Carelian shifted, focusing on a spot on his tail with great intensity. ~That was ... unkind of me. I not want to tell you because you act different, or worse, attack. He needed to see real you to be interested. But swear I not lie. But am Cath, Cori. Misdirect, yes. Put you in danger, no.~ There was a strange sigh and he straightened and came over, curling up next to me half draped over my lap. He would soon be too big for even that. ~You need to know what we are. I not know any living mage that understands complexities of this relationship. Unless Jo or Sable gain a familiar, you never tell them. You must agree to this.~

Not tell Jo. Sable I could understand, but the never telling Jo? "I want to know. I mean, who wouldn't, but why do I need to know and they don't. Does this have to do with why Baneyarl called you a focus?"

~Yes.~ He sounded reluctant and I suspected that Baneyarl had let something slip. ~Humans know familiars make lower offerings needed for magic. But they not know why, or at least no one I know has come back and said their human realized. We, familiars, act as direct connections to magic. Rather than forcing your body to connect and appease the cost, we already connect and magic likes us. It comes easy and fast. From science classes we are both magnifiers and connections into magic. Different familiars have different strengths. I am more chaotic in my nature, most felines are, so anything from Chaos will cost you almost nothing, while for Spirit and Order I help, but not to the scale you would see with Chaos.~

I'd never heard so much from him, and I could hear it chafed him to release so much information. "So you're why fire was so easy?" That made me sit up straighter, and he grumbled as he rearranged himself.

~Part of it. Part is your experts don't know as much as they think. If you have one branch, as you call it, you have them all. And you are very strong. A quean.~ His eyes were closed, and he rumbled gently on my lap. I let myself stroke his red fur and thought.

If I learned everything he talked about, took classes from Baneyarl, it would make me a much bigger target. But one that would be well armed and in ways they would not expect.

"What did you mean Jo and Sable are broken?" I asked.

He stayed silent so long that I almost shook him to wake him up. ~They should be, not as powerful as you, but more than they are. They should be merlins in their elements. Jo, her brain is broken, you know this. I not know the wrongness she has, but maybe Baneyarl can help. Sable something wrong with her blood. It is too sweet. It smells wrong.~

Merlins in their own elements? Sweet blood? What is he talking about...

My thought stuttered to a stop. "Are you saying Sable is diabetic?"

~Maybe? I do not know what that means for what I smell. She is not off balance yet but is getting there.~ He huffed and rolled over so I could pet the other side. ~They should be queans and they are not. It hurts for what they should have been.~

I'd have to tell Sable to get checked immediately. African Americans were at risk for diabetes, but she was young and in shape, so it didn't make sense. But maybe it meant something else? Either way, telling her immediately was important. The ever-elusive quean word. I didn't know what it meant and even if I asked, he'd just reply with quean. It reminded me of trying to explain colors to a blind person. If they'd never seen pink, trying to describe it without using any other color was almost impossible. Maybe for him quean was like that.

"Why me?"

He flicked ears at me but didn't respond.

"I mean, why did you choose me? Why do I get a familiar and so many mages don't? Will Jo and Sable?"

~Is complicated.~ He sighed in my mind. ~Maybe. If there is something young and curious and they are looking for adventure. But I don't know. It is a random complex thing. We don't really understand it ourselves. Maybe it is magic creating the link and setting us together.~

"That doesn't explain why I'm a double merlin. Or why everything is collapsing down on me."

He didn't respond, but then what could he say. At the end of the day, as smart as he was, I didn't think he knew much more than I did. We'd just have to learn together. I sighed and picked him up. "Let's go to bed. I'm exhausted, and it'll be a long week without those two around."

Chapter 33

Familiars die or can be killed. The mage doesn't always survive, but there have been three recorded instances of familiars sacrificing themselves to take out others. All three were during World War II and are part of the reason mages with familiars are respected so highly. What was witnessed could not have been accomplished by any mage outside a total sacrifice. ~ History of Magic

SPIRIT

Much to my surprise, the first I heard from Alixant or Indira was Sunday afternoon. And where I'd been expecting the wrath of Alixant, there was a soft rap at the door. Peering out, I saw them standing there. Bowing to the inevitable, I opened and let them in. None of us said anything, though I didn't protest when she put down a bag on the table and started to pull out salad and steaks from a local restaurant.

Alixant stood up straighter and looked at me as Indira finished. I just stepped back and looked at both of them, the standoff obvious. Not that I would refuse the food. Carelian had already jumped up on his normal chair and watched her with predatory eyes. A huff of impatience pulled my attention back to Alixant, who looked like he was reporting for an unpleasant duty or something.

"Cori, we always seem to get off on the worst possible foot. My attitude the other day was counterproductive. I need to remember you aren't my employee and I don't have the right to order you around. I really need to know what happened and figure out what we need to do." He never said sorry, but it was probably as close as he'd get. That didn't mean I'd forgiven or forgotten his attitude.

"If you treat your employees like that, you're lucky you have any. And frankly, if you treated me like that and I did work for you, I'd have you up on charges or I'd be at HR complaining of a hostile work environment with a bully."

He flinched a little. "True. I need to quit treating you like a disobedient child."

"You think? I'm not yours and frankly I've been on my own for a long time. You want me to work with you, fine. But I'm tired of having this conversation. Either treat me as an equal or get out." I kept my voice hard, and I held his eyes with mine. I didn't want to do this again. I understood I needed to share information, heck I had a vested interest in sharing it. Staying alive was very important to me.

He cleared his throat but didn't look away. "Understood, Miss Munroe."

I turned and looked at Indira. "That goes for you too. I'm not a mark, a pawn, or a tool for anyone. And if they don't figure it out, they will lose any chance they have to work with me. I don't know who you report to but make it crystal clear to them that if they try to manipulate me, I'll salt the earth before I work with them. Honesty is always the best policy with me."

She dipped her head. "I will pass that along." A note of respect in her voice. That I could live with.

"Now, yay food." I helped myself and gave Carelian his due before sitting at the table and looking at them. I didn't know if they had discussed this beforehand or in the time I was getting myself food they had done their look-at-each-other-and-have-a-conversation thing, but either way, they smiled and started in. Though not until after they had served themselves.

"I remember the men attacking us. Then you yelling about Carelian, and then what happened? I don't know what was you versus them." He stayed conversational and not confrontational, which was a pleasant change.

"I pulled up earth to block them until Carelian got to me, and since I'd figured out how to do a time bubble shield, I grabbed him and threw one up. Then," I swallowed a flash of remembered fear as I saw the attacking mage getting ready to cast. "I think they hit us with a KO."

Alixant nodded. "I thought so but wasn't sure. Was relatively surprised we woke up alive. So, you were awakened when you reappeared in the time bubble. What happened?"

I chewed slowly before I answered. "Yes. It took us to another place, in another realm, I think. You didn't regain consciousness until after we got back."

"Got back? You mean someone took us?"

And here is where I lied without lying. I knew he had the ability to tell the truth if he focused, not like Francine who did it without thought, but he could make offerings to tell if I was being truthful. And I knew he would right now. I could do this.

"A creature, actually. I'm not sure why it cared. It said it had dealt with the people attacking me and brought us back."

Alixant leaned back and stared at me. "How long were you there?"

I shrugged. "I don't know. I don't think we talked that long. Maybe five to ten minutes? I didn't even think to look at my phone."

"What was it?" Indira asked.

"A spirit realm creature, I think. It implied that, but I can't swear that was true. Heck, I'm not positive if it really was in another realm or maybe something else."

"Else, what else could it be?" Alixant asked, leaning forward.

"How in the heck should I know? I don't know everything out there."

"What else?" he snapped. I gave him a warning look and he subsided. "Was there anything else?"

"Like what?"

He sighed and leaned back. "What did you talk about?"

"What do you think? Where am I? Where were you? Questions like that."

"Did you get a name?"

I panicked for a minute, but then I realized I could easily answer that all the way. I didn't remember the full name he'd given me. "Kinda, I mean I was told it, but I really don't remember what it was. That headache was enough to make me ask to die."

"Oh, I'll agree with that. That was a killer headache. The death wounds on the men attacking us are similar to the ones found on the sniper earlier. Did the being that talked to you match?"

"How would I know? I didn't see any of the wounds. And besides, I have no clue what that being could do if it wanted. I mean Carelian can have three-inch claws appear if he wants." I was exaggerating a little. At most they were only two inches long, but they were still sharp as blades.

"You're telling me a creature, for reasons we don't know and in a manner we don't know, rescued us? What? We're at the mercy of the other realms?"

I shrugged. "I was told I was amusing and that I'd been watched for a while. And it was mentioned that access to our realm was gained when the rips were open during the SEC game."

Alixant groaned. "That damned Goins. He's dead or worse, and his actions are still creating drama. That unicorn wounded three men until someone found a virgin to come talk it down."

"You can't lay that at my feet," I protested.

"I'm not. Just." He rubbed his temples. "I swear I think the Murphy's Curse and Lady Luck soaked into the cells of your body. No one else can attract this much drama just by existing."

Something about his words warned me, though I couldn't say why.

"Indira and I spent about three hours in the Capitol yesterday in a teleconference with the Ambassador for Japan, the head of the OMO, and Civil Deputy in charge of the US Mage Draft."

The food no longer tasted good, and I pushed it away. Needing to clear my throat, I got up and pulled out a coke. Maybe the sugar and carbonation would help buffer what he was about to say. At least it gave me something to do with my hands.

"Tensions are high. Japan is demanding that the estate is theirs because no one emerges at that age, so you can't meet the requirements of the will. But the estate manager insists that you do meet all the criteria. So, right now everyone is up in arms. But the government desperately doesn't want his estate to fall into Japanese hands. Tensions are still high, but no one wants to create an international incident."

"But killing one student doesn't qualify?" I asked, not snarky, more just frustrated. After all this, I'd earned that damn house.

"Not if we can't tie the attempts back to them. And right now, no one can prove Japan is behind the attacks. It is all suspicion." Alixant sighed. I liked him better when he was exhausted and not being all demandy. Made working with him easier.

"If there was proof, would it make it so they would step back? And what research could he have that the government wants so bad?" Given what Carelian told me, there was a lot of research that if he had I might not turn over. It was too risky. There were days where me being able to talk to Carelian without sound would have been nice. This was one of them.

"I don't know. Something about planes and what lives on the other side and travel to them." Alixant shrugged.

"Did James Wells have a familiar?" I asked, wondering, because that could be risky. I was rapidly starting to think mages that got familiars were those that automatically didn't trust authority.

"I don't know. He was awfully private. Didn't leave his house often. As to them backing off, if there is proof, probably," Indira said picking at her salad. "Believe it or not, the fact that you joined Emrys has raised the pressure for people to leave you alone. It also had the effect of spreading knowledge of your existence around. Have you created your logins yet?"

I looked at the pile of mail on the table. I'd piled everything I hadn't had energy or time to deal with there. "No. It's on the to do list."

"Well, it will get you into private social media groups and they can help make it harder to sweep anything that happens to you under the table. But there is one more change." She seemed to sigh and brace herself, which made me tense up. These guys made my life more difficult half the time. "Japan wants to meet you, to conduct their own tests to see if you are really the heir."

"No. Next." My voice was flat. I didn't owe them anything.

Alixant nodded. "I told them that would probably be your answer. They are also asking to increase the people guarding you." He would have talked more, but I interrupted.

"Why? I can use the time bubble as a shield. Carelian and I'll work on scanning more, and I can create an earthen shield." I didn't admit that would be the first things I'd get Baneyarl to teach me. I needed to be safe.

"They won't be happy," Alixant pointed out.

"And? Am I required to keep them, whoever they are, happy? I don't care about Japan, it isn't my problem. They can petition the OMO if they want to see my test scores. Are there long-term consequences if I don't give in to their demands?" This was what worried me, besides the risk to Jo and Sable. Yet another reason I needed them to learn to protect themselves.

This time they did look at each other, but they didn't seem to come to any decision. I just waited. I didn't know anymore what to do. If I had to guess, I think they wanted what was best for me, but they were being shoehorned into this and they didn't know any more than I did. Which meant this was my choice and my life. I'd figure it out and ask questions as I could.

"I don't know," Alixant admitted. "You've got people amused at how determined you are to be independent, and just as many annoyed as all get out you don't need them to rush in and save the day. So, you're both winning admirers and creating people predisposed to dislike you."

Indira nodded but didn't add anything to his comment.

"So I should continue to be me and ignore everyone else?" I asked and Indira snorted softly.

"I'm not sure you could do anything else. You might be the most intractable young person I've ever met, but in this situation it will serve you well." She pushed the remains of her food away. "Just remember we are here to help. You might as well get something out of it."

"Right now, just try to find out why or who is pushing for me to get killed. That would be an enormous help. All I have for the rest of this semester is school and a few basic papers that I plan on getting done this week. And I'll be careful," I said, forestalling any protestations or comments from either of them.

Alixant gave me a long hard look, then nodded. "Yes, I suppose you will. If you need something, let us know. Really."

With that, they left, and I had the apartment to myself for the next week.

Chapter 34

Have you met a ronin? If you see someone doing high level magic without tattoos or have knowledge of someone who deserted from their draft assignment, report them. The reward for citizens reporting verified ronin is $10,000. The penalties for sworn officials not reporting them is prison. ~ OMO PSA

CHAOS

I spent the week just like I said I would. I wrote my papers, studied for tests, ate almost everything Jo had left for me, and ate way too much pizza. My bank account cringed a bit at the pizza bill but I pushed it away. I'd gotten a lot done that week. But either way, I was excited and ready for Jo and Sable to come back. The place was way too quiet without them.

Sunday afternoon the door opened, and they flew in, smiling with tanned and wind burned faces if I wasn't mistaken.

"Cori, you missed it. We had so much fun. We rented sailboats and spent most of the week on Lake Lanier. It was wonderful," Jo gushed as they piled stuff into the apartment. I settled back and let them babble. It felt good, and I was very glad they had a marvelous time. My twinge of envy didn't last long. Letting them talk about everything they did made me see how much they had needed this time together. They almost glowed with happiness.

When they had unpacked, and we warmed up leftover pizza, they shifted their attention to me. "So? Quiet week?" Jo asked as she grabbed a slice. Even two-day-old Fellini's was good pizza.

"Not so much. So, what would you two think about having specialized training that you can't tell anyone about? Not your parents, no one."

"Umm, Cori, what are you talking about?" Jo had paused with the piece of pizza halfway to her mouth.

While I'd practiced my evasions for Alixant, I hadn't really for Jo and Sable, and I didn't want to. "Remember me complaining that it felt like someone was watching me all the time?" They both nodded and started eating again, but they watched me carefully. "It turns out I wasn't imagining it. Someone named Baneyarl has been watching me, and he knows Carelian. He agreed to teach me, well us. And teach us how they use magic in the planes, not how humans use magic."

They had both paused mid-bite to look at me. Jo choked down the bite and dropped her slice on the plate. "Cori, who exactly is Baneyarl?"

I shrugged. "I think he's a griffin? Maybe a hippogriff? I'm not up on mythical animals."

At this point both of them stared at me as if I'd lost my mind. Maybe I had.

"Are you interested?" I asked a bit desperately. "The offer is there, but you must swear to never tell anyone. I said I wouldn't agree if you two weren't training with me. So?" I knew I was babbling, and I sounded like a lunatic.

"I'm..." Sable trailed off and shrugged, an odd look on her face. "I'm having a hard time believing this. But I'd learn magic from anyone. Especially given what we've found out, it seems knowing this might be better than not."

Jo just ginned at me. "I'm in. Show me the griffin. Anything that helps me learn this shit is good. I wonder if we can put it on our resumes?" Her wink let me know she was teasing, and I stuck my tongue out in response.

~He is Gryphon of High Steppes and is an honor that he assists. He is highly regarded and his magic has been refined over centuries.~ Carelian remarked in our heads making both Jo and Sable start.

"And what does that mean, exactly?" Jo asked as she picked her piece of pizza back up, though she was watching Carelian and me more than paying attention to her food.

"Centuries?" I squeaked. I didn't know why that bothered or surprised me so much. Why should they have the same life span we did?

~That he is not lesser creature. That he left his realm and came here means he was looking for...~ Carelian paused and I looked at him. He stared at the wall fixedly and I wondered if this was what it looked like when he talked to family on the other side. Suddenly all the staring off into space behaviors changed their importance. ~ Call it looking for adventure, and training three queans is high honor. Why else I choose you? Am I some weak creature to not want the most powerful?~ His tone had an odd mix of arrogance and pride that I wasn't sure what to make of.

Questions tumbled over in my mind, but I took the one that bubbled to the front first. "Wait, you chose all of us?"

He flicked an ear at me, either in amusement or annoyance. ~Are you and Jo ever to be separated?~

"No," we both said together, then we both laughed self-consciously.

~Then I would have needed to take both, no?~

I wanted to respond, but I just looked at Jo and shrugged helplessly, and she grinned. "Hey, he knew we were a package deal. But Sable? Where does she fit in?" As she spoke her hand drifted out to touch Sable who grabbed it back.

Will they make it? Are we meant to be together always? Do I want to share Jo?

The mental questions surprised me, and I frowned. I wanted her to be happy, didn't I? Carelian's comment pulled me out before I could go down that path too far, but it still lodged in the back of my mind, wiggling.

~If you make it formal, then I get three. Not a bad deal for a kittar.~ His smug tone caused the two of them to giggle and I smiled a bit, still trying to ignore the thoughts in the back of my mind.

"Okay fine, I'm down with being taught? But where? You're followed about every minute of the day, and I can't really see a griffin being able to fit in here, much less do it without anyone seeing. I mean I'm down, but really how is that going to work?" Jo asked the questions as she looked around the apartment, but she didn't let go of Sable's hand, their skin evocative of mocha and caramel.

~Cori? I ask him show how this works?~ Since I didn't see Sable or Jo react, I got the feeling this was private. I just nodded, still not positive how much of my mind he could read or not.

He twitched an ear in my direction and jumped off the back of the futon where he'd been perching. He walked over to the wall facing out at the courtyard. With his tail twitching he sat and stared, and my nerves jangled. The desire to change my mind and just hide hit me. I took three deep breaths and on the third, the familiar flash spike of pain slammed into my head then disappeared before I had time to wince.

A ripple opened in the air, vertical unlike all the others I'd seen. They'd always been horizontal slashes across reality. Here it unfurled like a zipper, neat and clean. It opened back like how a dress would fall away when unzipped but rather than chaos or colors or things that sucked you in it revealed a clearing with, of all things, a table and tea set.

~He is waiting.~

We all turned to stare at the cat then back at the opening. "He's inviting us over for tea?" Sable whispered, her voice an odd hushed tone.

Carelian flicked both ears towards us, then stood. ~Essentially.~ With that he walked through the rip. I didn't quite panic, though my heart spasmed as he stepped through. But I could see him on the other side, his red tail waving and pink butthole glaring back at us, making it clear he was laughing at our cowardice.

"He's laughing at us, isn't he?" Jo said, looking in on the scene before us.

"Yes," I replied and stood. "Fine, let's go see if we die in horrible ways."

"My father will kill all of us if we do," Sable warned, but she rose and headed towards the tear in reality.

"Ah, but we will already be dead, so we'll be safe." I grinned at her and she snickered.

"That might be true. We probably should never mention this to anyone. Just like the training. I'm pretty sure all the 'responsible' adults in our lives would have a collective heart attack." Sable grinned a wide, wild grin.

"You're a risk taker," I blurted, looking at her and smiling.

"Caught me. I've been being good cause I didn't want to scare her away, but this looks fun." She titled her head towards Jo who had come up behind her and rested her chin on Sable's shoulder.

"Ha! Jo have you been driving safe with her?"

Jo flushed and didn't meet my eyes. "Maybe."

"You two are made for each other," I said and forced down the twinge of pain that went with that statement. "Let's go to another realm."

We all grinned and headed to the rip. With a deep breath, I stepped through the rip and into the other realm.

From being there previously, I wasn't shocked, but when I had stepped back to our realm it had been more like walking into a smoke-tainted room after being in the crisp outdoors. This time it was more jarring. The sounds changed, the scent went from a musty smell I hadn't noticed, not to mention the pizza, to crisp and clean with a hint of jasmine. The rustle of the leaves created a music I just wanted to close my eyes and lean into, maybe get a bit of peace.

I sighed, knowing we didn't have time for that. With regret I moved forward to the table and the tea. It was low to the ground in a style I associated with Asia. I turned in a slow circle looking at the picture-perfect clearing with tall willowy trees all around us. I wanted to say they were elms, but the odds were they didn't exist on Earth. Movement caught my eye and I froze as Baneyarl walked out of the trees through a gap that should have let nothing his size come through.

Behind me I heard Sable gasp and Jo mutter, "Holy shit, she wasn't kidding." I turned and gave her a dour look and she shrugged, mouthing the word sorry at me, though I really didn't blame her. If she had come to me talking about griffins and whatnot, I probably would have asked her what she'd stolen from her brother, Stinky, this time. Last time it had been pot.

From a distance his coat gleamed like liquid gold, and the wings were spread wide as if landing or getting ready to take off. The purple shimmered and shifted shades as he laid them down against his body. The beak looked brighter and sharper in this clear sunlight.

That grabbed my attention. Above us was a sun, but it was a different color than ours. How I couldn't say, but I knew that the sun I saw through the light pink clouds was not ours.

~Welcome Queans. May I know your names?~ His voice powerful and deep rumbled through our minds and it occurred to me he'd been whispering last time. The level of compassion surprised me, and it made me feel much, much better about this entire situation.

I took a deep breath and did my social duties. "Baneyarl," I stumbled—I really didn't remember his full name.

~ ni Keriseo,~ Carelian prompted me. I shot him a smile as I continued.

"May I introduce Josefa Guzman, known as Jo, and Sable Lancet." As I said their names they bowed, an oddly formal gesture.

~It is an honor to meet you. I am Baneyarl ni Keriseo. Please come join me.~ He gestured to the table then walked over and settled down next to the table looking for all the world like a huge cat/bird, which I guess he was, settling in for an extensive snooze.

I headed over and sank down next to the table and directly across from Baneyarl. Carelian curled up next to him, literally sticking his nose under his paws.

I guess that's his way of saying he's not worried.

Whether it helped or not I didn't know, but the tea lifted into the air and poured into our cups. The scent of jasmine and honeysuckle filled the air, making me smile a bit.

~I am sure you have many questions, and I fear Cori was not in a good place to be able to think things all the way through when she was here earlier. This is what I offer, though you will be under the same restrictions as she, if you choose to learn from me.~

Sable and Jo both nodded, eyes wide as they stared at the griffin.

~I will teach you how magic works and how to impose your will on it. However, you may not tell anyone about my teaching of you without my prior permission. You will promise to not attack me with any means, magical or mundane. And finally, at some point there will be a decision you must make. You must hear me out if I come to discuss that decision with you. I have already agreed that if there is a time component, my discussion will not prevent you from making that decision, as per Cori's request.~ He fell silent, looking at my two roommates.

They in turned looked at me. I shrugged. "I agreed. It seemed a small enough price."

"I'm in," Jo said her eyes alight with excitement.

"Me too," Sable chimed in, her eyes wide and taking in everything. I just leaned back and wondered where the hidden price to all this was.

~Cori, you worry too much. You are mine, I will protect you always,~ Carelian rumbled in my ear. I glanced over to where he was. He lay next to the griffin, looking for all the world like he was sound asleep.

I hope so.

Chapter 35

American Native Indian tribes have an interesting relationship with the OMO. They are the only group of people technically outside OMO authority and do not subject themselves to the governing body. Technically, as they have treaties that proclaim themselves as sovereign nations outside of US control, there is no leverage to bring them under the OMO governance. Since the borders of the five reservations in America are all strictly patrolled and they allow no one in or out without clearance from both sides, their level of magic users remains opaque. ~ Magic Explained

ORDER

It took two hours before we got everything figured out. We would come to his glen every Monday, Wednesday, and Friday from six to eight. Baneyarl promised to open a door for us to his home, we'd learn, and then go home to eat. He did promise while there would be some homework, it would only be similar to what Indira assigned us. More playing with our magic than anything else.

It had taken that long for Jo and Sable to come down off the high and start conversing. But it was late and we all had school on Monday, and they had a ton of laundry to do. Me? I just needed to think.

Carelian was sitting on my bed looking at me when my alarm went off Monday morning. I blinked sleep blurred eyes at him.

"Yes?"

~You shield yourself well. I will stay invisible, though I may show up to speak with Arachena.~

I snorted as he verified he could be invisible if he wanted. "Will Baneyarl be watching me?"

~No,~ Carelian's voice had a sour note to it. ~He believes you know enough to protect yourself. He regards it as an excellent test of your resourcefulness.~

"I really wish people didn't think so highly of me. Help staying alive would be appreciated." I sighed and got ready for my day. Whining wouldn't change anything.

I walked into Sable making coffee and pouring sugar in and that jogged my memory. "Sable!"

She jumped and looked at me wide eyed, even at seven-thirty in the morning looking prettier than me on my best day. "What?"

"Is there a history of diabetes in your family?" I blurted out the question as she looked at me confused, and still not quite awake.

"History? Well, umm..." She paused and closed her eyes, thinking. "I think my grandmother has it and her sister had it. But dad doesn't. Why?" Her eyes reopened as she looked at me, still frowning.

"Carelian said your blood smells sweet, a wrong sweet. The only thing that occurs to me when he says that is diabetes."

She looked at me for a long moment, and I had no clue what thoughts were going through her head. After what seemed like an eternity, she nodded once, sharply. "I'll stop by the urgent care and ask them to take my blood sugar. I'm young and don't have any of the contributing factors, but I'll check."

I heaved a sigh, feeling both better and silly. I grabbed coffee and a bagel and stepped out, Carelian slipping out next to me. To my vague surprise Alixant wasn't there. I'd kinda expected him to be waiting for me, but he wasn't. The feeling of having a target on my back intensified and I slapped up the time bubble, setting it a full minute out of sync with everything, and started walking. I glanced around trying to see where Carelian was or at least where he had been, or was it would be? Either way I didn't see a thing, and that didn't help my nerves at all.

Hefting my bag on my back I headed to class, the bubble tight around me. I weaved around people, all of them moving slowly compared to my out-of-time bubble. It both delighted me and gave me the willies. Just the knowledge of what you could do with this if you tried made me nauseous. I got into the building. Opening doors was always problematic, but it was easier if I waited for someone to push it open and then slip in. Once in, I stepped into a corner and dropped the bubble. I waited for the shudder of time catching up with me. I needed to get better at this.

Carelian appeared at my side and brushed against my legs. I looked down at him and realized he was still getting bigger. In the last month he'd gained another few pounds and now pushed twenty or more. But he had no fat and was all muscle. "Hey, see anything interesting?" I bent over and petted him as I spoke.

~No. No one watching you. Just boring birds. Too easy to catch.~

I snickered and headed into my Monday morning class, Magic 101. The class had lots of interesting things, talking about the various spells. Bernard focused on Entropy today, but again always high level about how it worked and the specific ways it created effects. The more I listened the more I realized that we were being actively brainwashed into thinking this was all you could do. I kept that idea in my head for when I saw Baneyarl. I wanted to see what he'd have to say instead.

Charles waved at me, as did Arachena, though I think she was waving at Carelian. When I stepped out of class, I froze. Olivia Jonas pushed herself up from where she'd been leaning against the wall checking her phone. Her mage tattoos seemed subdued today, which made no sense. I watched her warily, and she smiled, though I didn't think it was completely unforced.

"Morning Cori. Was wondering if I could walk you to your next class?"

I bit my lip. While Indira could wrap two of us walking in a bubble, I didn't trust myself enough. Carrying Carelian was different, he was touching me. I had only practiced casting it around me, not anyone else.

~It is safe enough. I am actively watching.~

That comment made me want to ask him questions but for now I just nodded at her. "Sure. Something up?"

She shrugged as she turned to walk with me. I scanned the area as I pushed open the door and saw Carelian dart out before he disappeared into the brush or went invisible. I guess they were the same thing.

"No. Mostly following up on the attack last week."

Oh yeah. I'd forgotten. Amazing how a griffin can completely distract you. Even from WHY you met a griffin.

I steeled myself to practice my not lying even while I scanned the area. It was amazing what constant attempts to kill you did for your situational awareness.

"Do you have any idea what killed the men attacking you and Agent Alixant?" she asked, her voice oh too casual.

I stumbled and looked at her. "I thought Alixant killed them?" I thought back. They had asked me who killed the attackers, and I told them I had assumed Alixant. But then on Sunday, Indira had asked me if the creature could have caused the wounds on the dead mages. Not the cops. I'd gotten pissed and left. I figured Alixant had answered all the questions after I blacked out, but then I realized he'd been there too when Baneyarl woke me up. I'd been so mad I hadn't thought about it. If the KO got both of us, he couldn't have killed the mages trying to kill me.

Olivia shook her head and I ripped my mind away from my spiraling thoughts to pay attention to what she was saying. "No. He said when he went down both were still alive. But before you reappeared in the time bubble, we found both attackers dead. Do you know how or what killed them?"

I shook my head. "I was unconscious. I didn't see anything." I swallowed, not queasy exactly, I mean how many dead bodies had I seen at this point? But more, how had they been killed? "How were they killed?"

284

Olivia frowned at me but she answered. "One had his neck snapped by what looked like a solid blow to the back of his head. The other had his bio-electrics fried. Similar to a KO, but this was on a level we hadn't seen before. At least not officially."

"Oh," I said, my voice low as I walked towards the next building. "No, I didn't see any of that."

"So, you don't know who killed the two attackers? Alixant said the KO knocked him out before he could attack."

"How would I know? I was already unconscious and didn't see anything. Who called it in? They'd have a better idea."

"A student called it in. Said he just saw the bodies not how they got there, with a bubble in the middle that was 'he thought' a time bubble." Her voice was level. In fact, she sounded just like one of the detectives on *Law & Order Magical Case Unit*. That made me snicker, at least internally.

"That was more than I knew. Sorry."

"Figured I'd ask." She seemed disappointed in my answers, but I didn't look to check her temple again. I needed to get in the habit of remembering magic with faces and names, but right now all I could remember was Entropy Mage. Which didn't tell me enough about her skills, but it meant she didn't have truth sensing.

"Anything else?" I asked as we climbed the steps to my building, my eyes still scanning the area, though I still didn't know what I was looking for. It was unlikely a person in yellow spandex would jump out, point at me, and yell "I am here to kill you!"

"No. Just figured I'd check in on you and see how you were doing. Make sure you didn't have any issues."

"Besides people trying to kill me? Or you trying to make sure I'm not talking about what I did?"

"Does it matter?" She didn't look at me, instead did the same looking around I was doing.

"Just means I know whose side you're on. Have a good day, Detective," I said and moved through the doors towards my next class, Carelian on my heels as I left her behind me. I got through the doors and left her on the other side of them.

I headed in to find Indira lurking at the door, rather than being in her classroom.

I fought back a sigh and looked at her. "Checking to make sure I showed up?"

She shrugged. "Is there anything wrong if I did?"

"Makes me wonder if you think I'll get killed that easily or you know something I don't know." I looked at her, both annoyed and warmed by her waiting for me.

"Just making sure you're okay. Mentor, remember? I have a duty towards you." Her voice was slightly chiding, and I nodded.

"True. But I've got a time bubble for me down. The rest I don't know. But maybe three of them dying will make them think twice," I said as I walked towards the classroom.

"Maybe. I know Joanne has spread out the news about you being in Emrys. So that should help also, but it won't be overnight."

"Obviously," I muttered as I climbed the stairs up to my normal seat, Carelian stopping to sniff noses or legs with Arachena. He bounded up the stairs and settled next to me.

"She say hello?"

~Passed on news about the realms. Nothing interesting at moment.~ He focused on his paws instead of looking at me. Typical cat.

I focused on class, trying to think about what she showed us and what I would ask Baneyarl. Today was about the rarer strengths—Non-organic.

"Most people with this as a strength end up in the physical sciences. Even via the draft you'll find yourself pointed to R&D, Space Research, Military Weapons, or possibly the USGS. This is one of those areas where the more you know the better you are at what you can do, which is why specialization is so important." She walked back and forth as she spoke. "My degree is in quantum physics as I'm strong in Entropy and Time, while my specialization is in planar rips. I'm sure this will or won't surprise you, but the OMO regards the Area 51 planar rips as theirs alone and doesn't normally allow those who work for the government access. What this means is I know the structure of atoms, quarks, particles, and other things very well. It also means that if you asked me the chemical makeup of caffeine or salicylic acid I'd have to go look it up." She reached into the box at her feet and pulled out two objects and placed them on the table.

The class giggled as one of them was a giant piece of chalk, like what a kid might use to draw on the sidewalk. The other was a chunk of geode, cut open to reveal the crystals inside.

"Remember, one of my strengths is Non-organic, which means I can use the following spells: Forge, purify, magnetism, id element, call element, move electron/subatomic observation, and electricity. Now I'm sure, as you can guess, magnetism, forge, and electricity won't do us much good with these two items. And to be frank, forge requires a crucible and heat, and we aren't about to do that in a classroom, though you will get to play with it in your labs as you go through your classes. But what I can do is show you how you can use this with only a small offering because I know exactly what I'm looking for."

She lifted the geode up and put it on an old-fashioned projector machine. It showed the beauty of the rock on the screen behind her. "There are little strands of pyrite going through the quartz in here. If you can't see it now, you'll be able to come down after class and inspect it."

Indira set it back down and took a seat next to the table, putting herself at chest level to the geode. "Call element is of great use to mining companies, the USGS, and for those of an artistic bent to create beautiful jewelry." She paused to smile at all of us. "Remember that. Just because you are a mage, doesn't mean you can't follow art, you just need to think about it more."

That made me pull up my phone and do a quick search for mage artists. The search results exploded with links and some of what I saw were stunning pieces of art and drawings. I filed that away. I had no artistic bent, but it made me feel a bit better that maybe the draft wasn't a slave system like I'd feared.

"I had to look up the structure of pyrite, because it isn't something I was all that familiar with. But if you get into professions that require it, you'll learn multiple molecular strands and chains that will become as easy to recall as your family address." She pointed at one of the larger crystals at the top of the geode. "Now this is not as glamorous as they make it sound in the movies, and I'm also not willing to go bald to impress you." There was a round of laughter at that and she flashed a smile, sultry and familiar. "Watch the line of gold."

She glanced at it and held a small dish of white ceramic under it. The gold-colored substance seemed to ooze out of the crystal and drip down into the dish until the crystal was clear except for a small visible flaw.

"Who can tell me the problem about how I did this?"

A few hands shot up. Mine wasn't one of them because I was still trying to wrap my mind around what she had done.

"You had to melt it and move it to get it out," someone answered. I blinked back into the conversation as I tried to understand what she had done.

"Exactly. That requires more energy, but in most cases that is the only way to make this work. Note that you also have to have an opening for it to come through otherwise you'll need to make one, something usually easier to do with a hammer than your magic.

Again laughter rolled through the classroom and she kept talking. I settled in and thought about it, mostly how to use that idea to protect those I love.

Chapter 36

The feared Rogue hunters used by the US government to find mages who have avoided the draft are nothing but hired killers. Why are you forced into hiding if you don't want to get addicted to the power of magic? Your strength marks you as a threat! Fight against the chains of the OMO. ~ Freedom from Magic

SPIRIT

The rest of the day went the same way. I saw Indira twice, and Alixant three times. They didn't approach me, I just saw them as I went from one class to another. I still didn't know where I fell on the annoyance level—amused or irritated.

The smell of chorizo and salsa hit me as I walked into the apartment and I looked at Jo, surprised. "I thought we were going to eat after." Even as I said that I moved closer to the stove. Rice, peppers, chorizo, my mouth totally disagreed with what my brain was saying.

"I know, but I was starving and couldn't settle down to study, so food. This way we don't go on an empty stomach."

"Not going to argue." I glanced at my phone. "We have about twenty, so gimmee." Jo laughed at me as she dished some into a bowl. "Where's Sable?"

"She said she'd be home in a few." Jo shrugged.

The conversation from that morning went through my mind and I hoped Carelian had been wrong. Food was more important than anything else and I couldn't resist taking a bite.

~Want some,~ Carelian protested.

I gave him a look but shrugged. The cat knew what he could or couldn't eat better than me. I dished some up into a small dish and set it at his place on the table. He sampled it, ears twitching as he thought, then he inhaled it to my amusement. I looked up to see Jo laughing too. That was what Sable walked into; us giggling at my familiar eating Jo's Spanish rice.

"Hey gorgeous. How's your day?" Jo asked as she moved to set a bowl at Sable's place. Sable smiled, but I thought it seemed a bit forced.

"Long. But let's talk about it after Baneyarl. I've been thinking about it all day."

A strange sensation, not a buzz or a purr, just an underlying vibration to her words. I'd been playing with my psychic skills as those were the rarest, but one set of homework said you could train yourself to use them more easily than some of the others since so much of it was passive with almost no offerings required. Truth was one of those. Strong Psychic mages could force you to tell the truth and some merlins could rip it out of your mind. Both sounded horrid to me but knowing when people lied might be useful.

So does that mean she's lying?

I wasn't going to pry, not yet. Besides, I was interested to see what Baneyarl said. We all finished eating with Carelian licking his bowl clean. We got ready and stood in the living room, feeling a bit stupid.

"Now what?" Jo asked looking around.

~I let him know. The door should open shortly,~ Carelian said, working on making sure the fur on his tail was perfect.

"You can talk to him from here?" Sable asked. She'd smoothed out, that was the best way to describe it, but Jo kept glancing at her, so I knew she'd picked up on something too.

Carelian's ear flicked back and forward but he didn't answer, instead sat up into the Egyptian Cat pose and stared at the wall. A flash of pain in my mind as it rippled and grew to about six feet, then widened until it was about three feet across. He rose and strode through as easy as walking out the door. Fighting not to be giddy I followed him. I stepped into the clearing. It looked the same, but this time instead of a table and tea there were three pillows and a bunch of rocks on one end with Baneyarl sprawled in the middle.

~Queans, welcome. Are you ready to start?~ Baneyarl asked as he looked at us, his purple wings sleek against his back.

"Absolutely," Sable said, taking the lead. I was still looking around, curious about the changes, but I followed her.

~Excellent. Take a seat. We will start with Elements as all of you have at least one.~ His hawklike gaze focused on Jo first. ~You are Air, while Sable is Fire and Water. Cori has Earth. I have Water as well as Air, so this will work out well. Having the full quartet provides opportunities that others envy. Between the three of you, you have all the elements. It makes you a very powerful coven.~

"Wait, coven?" I said. Carelian had mentioned something like that.

Baneyarl shot me a look I interpreted as amusement. ~Is that not what you humans call a group of witches?~

I started to protest but couldn't and shrugged. "Point."

~Sable, you have Fire. Tell me how you'd burn this feather.~ One of his feathers floated to where we were sitting, hanging in the air.

Sable nodded and talked about what Indira had told us about molecules and moving them faster until they ignited and reducing the amount of offering that was required.

Baneyarl looked at us. While I didn't know how to read an eagle's face, I was sure his look was somewhere around "are you kidding" and "WTF" but that was just a guess. After a long, very long moment of silence, he finally spoke again. ~While I must admire your creativity at how you manipulate the world around you, it removes the wonder of magic more than a little. Most magic is powered by different forces in the universe, though I am now wondering if I need to go back to your realm and practice more magic.~ He shook his head as if shaking away an idea. ~But be that as it may, the elements are in almost all things. All life, all stone, all beings hold some or all of the elements inside them. While each element is pure within itself, they work together in wondrous ways. Earth is the slowest to respond compared to the other elements but it is still the foundation for us all.~

I watched and listened carefully, because something about this sounded not wrong, but incomplete.

~Within the feather are the elements from which it was created. Its cells still have the spark of Fire, of Water, of Air and Earth in them. They were made from them. All you have to do is call forth the element you wish. Fire is always the easiest as it consumes and feeds itself. Sable, as a mage with Fire and Water, you should be able to sense it. Reach into the feather and call it forward. The offering is not the price you pay for magic, but the offering to the element to feed it as it answers.~

Sable looked at Jo with a dubious look, but she just shrugged. We were here to learn and if we didn't believe a creature that was literally magic didn't know how to use it, then we were wasting everyone's time.

Separating out a few strands of hair, she still needed to focus to make sure she offered what she wanted and not some random strands. She'd mentioned the awareness of her body didn't' come naturally to her. Jo and I were both far ahead of her when it came to choosing what to offer.

Shaking out her shoulders Sable stared at the feather.

I couldn't sense anything, but that didn't matter. Other than planar rips, I'd never really sensed magic, but I watched her, eager and worried about my turn.

"Nothing's happening," Sable said, the frown creating creases between her eyebrows.

~Don't tell it to catch fire, call the fire to you. It exists in that feather, and your cells are your offering. Think of it like bait trying to lure something to you.~

Sable shot him a look, then smiled. "Oh, teasing. That I'm very good at."

"Oh yes you are," Jo said glancing at her sideways.

~Yes. Fire is mischievous and fickle, but it is always hungry. Offer the tasty cells and it will come to eat them, then, as Fire is wont to do, destroy what held it if only lightly.~

Sable winked at Jo and, still holding her three strands, looked at the feather again. "Here Fire, Fire, I have nice organic material for you," she murmured in a singsong voice.

One of the hairs she held curled in a wisp of smoke, then it vaporized. A split second after that, the feather burst into hungry flames, brighter and more powerful than what I'd seen candles do. In a second, it had crumbled to ash.

I was struggling to process what I'd seen even as Sable leaned back, her eyes wide. "Wow, that has never happened before."

~Well done. But there you can see the difference in the techniques. I suspect if you had lit the feather your way it would have burned slowly and in the lower heat ranges. But when you call Fire, it comes with all its potential and explodes onto the scene.~

"That was extremely cool—Air and Earth are so boring." Jo pouted a bit.

I couldn't argue with that, but that was why they often used Fire to demonstrate magic, because it was showy and visible.

~Oh, I don't know about that. I believe you saw the power of Air at the appearance of Tirsane on your plane.~ Baneyarl had both a chiding and an amused tone. ~In many ways air is the easiest to call.~

Jo snapped her attention to him. "Really?"

~You are breathing are you not?~ This time the amusement was obvious.

"Oh. Point." But she said the words slowly, as if that hadn't really occurred to her.

~So while air isn't in the objects, it is always around us.~ He paused and tilted his head. ~Unless you find yourself in space. Then you will be at a significant disadvantage.~ Humor laced his tone and Carelian sniffed, but in amusement or disdain I wasn't sure.

"Wait. I can almost process the elements being how you say and having personalities for lack of a better word. What about the others, though? You have Non-organic, Pattern, and Entropy—those can't be beings or essences or whatever," I protested, now royally confused.

~No, but there is always intent. Master mages often use magic in a way that makes sense to them. For example, an

Avian mage I know thinks of everything like music and that is how she performs her spells—they are all songs constructed to do what she needs. Magic is an entity herself.~

I looked at him blankly. He ruffled his feathers. ~All I can do is ask that you try it my way.~

"Oh, I plan to, it just doesn't make sense to me," I protested, feeling like I was being ungrateful.

~It is magic. Even your science only follows rules as you come to understand them. Do you not change them regularly?~

"Yeah, kinda. But some things don't change." I wanted to argue, but I knew he was right. They used to think the Earth was flat, that a god dragged the sun around the earth, and that diseases were caused by demons.

~True, but your explanation of how and why they work changes often. Now, Cori, see that rock over there, the one with the feather laying on top of it?~ He deftly changed the subject, and I frowned but let him. I needed time to think about this. Adding it to my ponder-over-later list, I turned to look at the rocks. One of the smallest had a purple feather laying on the top of it.

"Yes."

~Earth is slow to respond, but it is always around us, even the Water of the oceans knows it exists at Earth's whim. Reach into the rock and ask Earth to separate.~

I had to parse what he meant but couldn't argue. If the earth split open revealing the molten rock that lay at the heart of our planet, the waters would vaporize, though I'd never thought of it like that. So he wanted me to ask Earth to separate? I hadn't gotten to the specialty stuff, that all started next semester and I'd be doubling up on my magic and science classes, so other than the times I'd used Earth trying to protect myself I had only played with it a little.

If this was a class and Indira had asked me to do this, what would I do? Tell all the individual molecules to break their connections and turn to dust, I guess. I reached out with that idea and the amount required made me flinch. I'd lose half my hair length—not acceptable.

"I don't understand. If I try to break it down to individual molecules, the offering would be a lot." I actually knew down to the molecule, but a lot made more sense.

~Cori, you are overthinking this. Earth is slow, it needs to be sweet-talked. Offer it a reward for doing what you ask.~ If exasperation had a sound, it was the rattling sigh he made even as the words were in my mind.

Fine, fine. I'll offer.

I felt ridiculous, but I reached out, looking for Earth or something that felt like Earth.

Want some nice hair cells? If you just break into pieces, it's all yours.

Something stirred in the rock, or maybe it was the rock. A questing brush, then acceptance, that familiar tug, but this time there were emotions attached. The hair I'd visualized crumbled into nothingness as the rock did the same.

"Merlin's Balls!"

Chapter 37

The uptick in wizards and archmages in the United States Southeast is concerning. While normally 80% of those tested are mages, we have historically seen, and continue to see in other regions, a breakdown of 35% hedge, 20% magician, 25% wizard, 19% archmage, and 1% merlin. In the last month only for the American Southeast we are seeing 95% positive rates, with 10% hedge, 30% magician, 35% wizard, 23% archmage, and 2% merlin. ~ OMO internal report.

CHAOS

By the time we left Baneyarl, we were exhausted, but also brimming with excitement. Part of me really wanted to get back to Earth, our Earth, and see if magic behaved the same way. We'd gone over all the elements and they all could be bribed or courted depending on your point of view. He had promised to start teaching us shields Wednesday, which excited and worried me. I just wanted to crawl into my bed. I was past exhausted.

We stumbled back into the living room, or at least I did. Apparently, it helped to pick your feet up and step over the edge of planar rips. I shook my head trying to clear the fuzziness, very glad we'd eaten before we left. Otherwise I'd be going to bed hungry. Even eating sounded like too much effort. I turned to tell them good night.

"Okay Sable. What is going on? Why were you late and what has you upset? Did something happen?" Jo looked at Sable with an expression I recognized, worry, concern, and stubbornness. A pang shot through me and I pushed it away, worry spiking right behind it. I'd forgotten. How could I have forgotten?

I sank down on the couch and Carelian sprang up next to me. But he didn't purr, just pressed against me, his ears flicked forward towards the two of them.

"I-," Sable broke off and sighed. "I really need a drink, but that isn't on the table. Let me get a glass of water and I'll explain. Promise." She turned and headed into the kitchen before Jo could respond.

Biting her lip, Jo sank down into her chair, elbows braced on her knees watching Sable take much longer than necessary to get water and come back. I petted Carelian, trying not to think or guess. My guesses were always worse than reality, so I'd just wait. Even if I wanted to jump up and shake her until she told us.

Sable came back and sank into her chair. We all had our own desk chairs, crowding the living room when you included the club chair and the futon couch. But we made it work and having your own place to do homework helped us turn on and off homework mode. She took a sip of the water then looked at Jo.

"So, Cori mentioned something to me this morning."

"What?" Jo looked stricken and glanced at me, worry in her face.

"Jo, stop it. Nothing bad. Not like that," Sable interjected and I could see Jo relax. That surprised me. She was worried about me not liking Sable? The thought had never occurred to me. I didn't know how I felt about that. Another thing to figure out. "She told me Carelian thought my blood smelled sweet."

"Smelled sweet?" Jo parroted, looking at me, Carelian, and then back at Sable.

"Jo, chill. Let me tell you." Sable smiled at this point and I watched her relax. "Sweet. So I said I'd stop by the clinic after class. It turns out it's a good thing I did. I have diabetes. Type 1. They said they've been seeing more people develop it in their twenties. It's called LADA or Latent Autoimmune Diabetes, though that is just one name. Basically, I have juvenile diabetes even though I didn't have it as a kid. I need to go in for a bunch more tests, but they say I'm just developing it so

I'm eligible for some new drug trials. Either way, it is manageable. I just need to get the tests done and see what we can do. But that means monitoring my food and my blood sugar for the next few weeks." She shrugged, but even I could tell she wasn't happy. "No big deal. I needed to lose weight anyhow." That lie screamed to me, but I didn't say anything.

Jo stood, and I saw the indecision in her body. She wanted to hug Sable and scream at the same time. I took the choice out of her hand. With a grunt of effort—I needed to get back to the gym—I stood and went over and hugged Sable. "I'm glad I told you. Maybe they can find a cure or something. This is a good thing, right?"

"It is, actually. They almost never get anyone coming in this early. Usually they only come in when there are issues and I'm coming in now. So yeah, this is a good thing."

"Move Cori. I wanna hug my girlfriend," Jo said behind me, her voice tight with emotion. I released Sable, and she fell into Jo's arms. I took the time to clean up the kitchen. When Sable excused herself to use the bathroom, Jo stomped into the kitchen and slumped against the counter.

"This sucks. What good is magic? So I can blow a feather around or pull metal from the Earth. It can't cure a disease or stop a heart attack," she ranted, though her arms were wrapped tightly around her, jaw clenched.

"A mage saved Stinky's legs," I pointed out, and she sighed.

"I know, but he fixed something broken. How do you fix a broken pancreas or immune system? How do you make someone not be sick?"

"I don't know. But isn't that why Baneyarl is teaching us? So we can figure out these things? Maybe they can use magic to fix stuff. It would be nice. I want to know how to stop people from dying." My voice broke a bit. I so rarely talked about Stevie. "I want to know why people die. How I can stop them from dying? No one should hold someone they love as they die. It's a horrible thing."

"Oh, I don't know. I always thought if I had to die that would be the way to go," Sable said, coming from the hall into the kitchen. "I mean, it seems like that is the best way out of this life, in the arms of the person you love."

I shrugged. "Maybe, if you're old and gray, like sixty, and have lived your life. Then maybe. But young? No one should lose their child. No one should hold their brother as they die." I said this a bit too forcefully as I set a mug down and it shattered as it hit the bottom of the sink.

"You have Murphy up again," Jo said as she grabbed a paper towel to pick up the pieces.

"Dang it. Maybe there is an easy way to repair. I know a Pattern mage can rebuild it, but you'd still need hours and lots of glue." I looked mournfully at the blue-green bits of ceramic. I'd gotten that for winning the vocabulary bee in eighth grade. That had been the prize. One more aspect of my past in pieces.

"Sorry, Cori," Jo said as she threw the towel with broken pieces away. I pulled down the Murphy surrounding me and forced a smile.

"I don't know about you two, but I'm wiped. I still have classes tomorrow and need to read up for a quiz." At least with most of my papers done I didn't need to panic too much. "I wanted to remind you what Alixant mentioned. We already know we can't tell anyone about this but be careful that anything you do can be explained away as one of the set spells. I suspect we'll learn stuff that we won't be able to cover, but that means not doing it in public. We have to be very careful until we are well done with our draft."

"And you have your own private compound for us to retreat to?" Jo teased me, but I saw the seriousness on her face.

"Pretty much. Starting to think that is why some merlins have compounds. Not to hide, but to keep the government and the OMO out of their business." I sighed. "I want to learn this stuff, but I'd like us not to get killed because we aren't people they can control. Control seems extremely important to them."

"Yeah. Even my dad is worried about that with you. You are a magnet, Cori, for good or bad you seem to be in the center of things you can't control," Sable said, leaning against Jo a bit. She looked as exhausted as I felt, her normal perky smile flat and worn.

"Tell me about it. It is ridiculous, but what can I do with my luck?" I said finishing cleaning up. "We ready for bed?"

"Oh! I forgot to tell you. Mami called me today. She said she'd be down this weekend." I flinched as I knew she would want to go out and I couldn't risk her. I wasn't good enough to shield multiple people—yet. "Stop it, Cori," Jo chided, reaching out to slap my arm lightly. "*Mami* knows what's going on. While she's annoyed at everyone about this, she'll tell you what she's been doing. She would never risk your life or put our family in danger."

I sighed and nodded my head, recognizing something I couldn't change.

"Good. She has her heart dead set on a Saturday brunch with the three of us, so about ten expect her here loaded with everything you could ever want for a brunch. I swear she'll spend Friday night cooking."

"Oh," I said and felt a silly smiled cross my face. I missed her. The entire Guzman family really, but Marisol specifically.

"She misses you and was very bummed you didn't come up with us. But she gets it. The rest I'll let her tell you." A huge yawn cracked her jaw as she finished. "Yeah, bed sounds good. I'll use the extra time tomorrow to catch up on my readings."

A few minutes later I was crawling into bed when Carelian jumped up. Lately he'd decided he preferred to be under my bed on a pillow he'd pilfered, claiming it was the most comfortable option in the house. I gave him a look that I figured he could see. He saw better than I could in the dim light.

"Do I want to know?"

~You did... acceptably today,~ Carelian said, and I shifted as I felt him staring at me.

"Which means what?" I asked, my arms crossed.

~That you will struggle more than I had hoped to balance out the magic and the science. It is magic. For all that your people want to wrap rules and conditions around it, it is still magic.~

"Everything has rules," I protested, frustrated that a cat was being judgy. A magical cat, but still.

~Does it? Do emotions? Do thoughts? Do random synapses have an order in which they fire?~

"Well, no," I muttered. A cat was making fun of me. Either I was really tired or I'd hit the peak of low in my life.

~Cori.~ I stiffened. He rarely used my name. ~You have things to unlearn, but Baneyarl is not displeased, I just—~ he heaved a mental sigh in my brain. It tickled. ~—I wanted my queans to be incredible, not normal.~

"Oh Carelian." This time I sighed and pulled him to me, cuddling him like he was still a tiny kitten and not the growing behemoth he would be. "You are incredible. Give us time. We might surprise you."

~You will never surprise me. I expect you to surprise everyone else.~ He cuddled into my arms purring. I held him tight but deep inside I wondered what he suspected that I had no clue about.

Chapter 38

While most branches have seven spells associated with them, Psychic has only four, and only two of them are actively taught. The other two, Telepathy and KO, are only taught during your draft service. There are some abilities that are regarded as so dangerous or laden with risk that only certain people are authorized to learn them. ~ Magic Explained.

ORDER

There were two more attempts on my life in the next week and I quit being able to think it was just my luck.

The first had been clumsy, and it had to be some idiot from a local gang, as he ran at me with a knife yelling about die and I'll be rich. I took a page from the mage that had tried to kill me in the street and sank him up to his waist in the ground, and just walked away. Carelian peed on him.

The second, oddly enough, involved poison. That Carelian stopped by sniffing my food I'd ordered at the food cart, I'd forgotten to grab a lunch. I used magic to pull out the elements and identified chemical structures, and sure enough someone had tried to use cyanide on me. It would have worked except for his nose. Carelian got extra salmon that night.

It made me jumpy, paranoid, and cranky. The only time I wasn't on edge was either in the apartment, and there I still worried someone might blow it up, or in Baneyarl's realm. Or space. Or whatever his little bubble of existence was called. He made us think of magic differently and while it frustrated me—I liked rules and predictable results—the possibilities were endless.

Friday, knowing the weekend was ahead and the odds were either Alixant or Indira or someone else would be pushing for more information about the incident where Baneyarl had rescued me, we focused on mental and physical shields.

~No matter what you think, there is no difference between mental and physical defenses. They are the same thing, controlling a branch of magic to protect you. What you must do is decide how to use your ability to protect yourself. Cori, I shall leave you for last, as you have a veritable plethora of strong branches to choose from, and start with Jo,~ Baneyarl said, moving his giant head to peer at Jo. She squirmed a bit but stood up and walked to the middle of the clearing.

~Transform is your strength. We will start with physical first. What surrounds you?~

We'd gotten better at his leading questions, but even so she shrugged. "Air, dust, pollen, my clothes."

~Accurate, but not quite enough. Even the air we breathe is filled with tiny organisms, bits of life. If you take those, you are strong enough to make them into a wall around you. Though it is easier with air, which is why you will use Air to augment your Transform ability.~ He kept stumbling over the word Transform and I wondered what he knew it as.

"You can do that?" Sable was leaning forward, very interested. The idea of using magic to augment other skills wasn't addressed much in any of the college classes.

~Of course. That is why merlins are so feared, not because of their power but because they can combine it to do multiple things. Did you not know that?~ He sounded surprised.

We all looked at each other and I shrugged. "Maybe? I mean, I know the best volcanologists are merlins with Fire and Earth, but I figured that just let them do it better, I never really thought about combining it."

"Yeah, she's right," Sable said slowly. "I knew of a merlin with Air and Water, and the weather guys were offering him lots of money as he could sense the changes, but I didn't think about it. They harp that the sections are separate, and you use one or the other at any given time." I could almost hear our minds spinning.

~Humans, always making things fit into boxes when they have no shape,~ Baneyarl muttered. ~You will owe me, Carelian. This is most frustrating.~

~You are enjoying the challenge.~ Carelian seemed unconcerned by Baneyarl and didn't open his eyes from where he lay sprawled under the trees.

Baneyarl flipped his tail once in Carelian's direction and looked at Jo. ~Take your Transform and Air and create a shield. Air doesn't have to be pliable, it has a value all its own. It can even freeze.~

"If I get it that cold, it would be so cold it would kill us all," Jo protested, crossing her arms and glaring.

~You are taking this much too literally. It is magic. Tell the air to hold in place, to be impenetrable, to take the dust and particles and make them rigid, strong enough to block. Remember, Air is bribable—bribe it, ask it to stand still, to protect.~

Jo took a deep breath and stared. The hair at the end of her locks stirred and a tiny bit floated away. The area around her became oddly fuzzy, as if I needed to clean my glasses, except I wasn't wearing any.

A stone flew towards her, hit with a muffled whack and fell down.

"Holy shit, it worked. And it didn't collapse." She poked at it, a funny look on her face. Then she took a step to one side, and it flowed with her. A larger rock flew at her and she flinched, but the odd denseness captured it and it fell to the ground with a thwump, dust flying up from the impact.

~Well done. Not elegant in execution, but with experience you will create it thinner and convince Air to follow you. For the elements, it might be wise to offer them bribes occasionally just because. It makes them more interested in you, which is rarely bad. At least on your plane.~

He went through a similar thing with Sable using Water and Fire. Hers looked more like steam where the moisture caught it and Fire vaporized it. "I don't understand, how can Fire and Water work together?" Sable said as she ran her fingers through her odd wall. "And why aren't I getting burned or trapped or something?"

~It is magic. Do you not think it knew what you wanted, which was a shield to bend and flex with you? And why would it harm that which created it? While Fire can get hungry and burn both, it only happens when it is no longer controlled by you but by its hunger.~

That kinda made sense in my head and explained why Fire mages could throw fire and not get hurt but couldn't put their hands in a flame.

~As to the elements working together, they are not enemies. I have found many of your cultures seem to think Fire and Water are enemies. They are powerful together and can change the other elements. Don't think they can be pitted against each other. You must respect their powers and allow them to work together. Watch.~ His voice dropped off in a way I had come to recognize he was concentrating on something.

A small stream that I had not noticed before—how had I not noticed it?—bubbled, then a spout rose in the air and began to twist and dance. Air lifted my hair causing it to dance around me even as the water took shapes and twisted around in a manner that seemed, for lack of a better word, magical.

"Wow. I've heard of some people that can do that, but I thought it was a pure Water skill," Sable said, her eyes narrowed.

~You can do it with all Water but it requires larger volumes to support the structure. With Air, the requirements are altered.~ He looked at us. ~Now Cori, yours is both the easiest and the hardest. Are you ready?~

"Sure," I lied as I rose. "What do I do?"

From the laughter in his tone I thought he knew I was lying, but I'd still try, ready or not.

~Your physical shield of Earth is the easiest, but I believe you already know how to do that. Demonstrate please,~ Baneyarl said, his wings half mantled as if ready to leap into flight. That added to my stress. Did he think something would go wrong? I swallowed hard and nodded.

The clearing provided much dust, but I decided I'd try the bribe method instead of what I was coming to realize was the brute force method we were taught on Earth. We just wrapped it up in science and made it seem logical, which made me feel better, but I was coming to realize logic had nothing to do with how magic really worked. Visualization was everything.

"Here Earth, I have some blood for you, want to make sure nothing can get to me?" I said it softly, almost singsong for some reason. Dust exploded around me as the drop of blood I'd provided, courtesy of a torn hangnail, vaporized. A rock came flying towards it, but instead of dropping to the ground like with Jo and Sable, it vanished into dust and became part of the shield surrounding me.

"Merlin's balls, Cori. That's incredible," Jo said. I turned to look at her, but it was like looking through a windshield on a car that had just gone off-roading. I could see her figure but no details.

~Excellent. The Earth is active and grabbing any projectile to help protect you. I wonder.~ Something came flying at me and the glint of metal had me ducking, but it hit and crumbled, joining the rest of the material. ~Very well done. That was a small lump of metal and Earth pulled it in just like the rest. Offering blood was an excellent choice. While any offering of yourself is regarded as flattering, offering living blood is the most flattering and effective, well short of organs or other items.~ His voice trailed off and I got the feeling he was listening to something.

"That is pretty cool, but not exactly subtle. Your time bubble is probably easier to deal with," Sable pointed out as I let the Earth go, saying thank you. I felt silly, but it felt wrong to NOT say thank you.

~That is true, but sometimes being out of time is not the best option, ~ said Baneyarl. ~I must say that I am confused. Carelian said you were broken, but you seem capable mages, what about you says that you are broken?~ His head tilted as he scanned us for defects or something like that. I squirmed and saw Jo drawing on the ground with her toe.

"I don't know if it I'm broken, but I apparently have a disease that will follow me the rest of my life." Sable shrugged. "Rather than get into specifics, let's just say my body doesn't deal with food correctly and that can kill me if I'm not careful."

Watching a griffin frown was odd, the ridges of his face pulled down and his glare intensified. It made my skin crawl and I wanted to move away from his gaze.

~That makes no sense. Why is it not being repaired?~

Jo laughed. It was bitter, and I flinched at the sound of it. "We can't fix stuff like that. I guess creatures here are lucky and they don't have issues like that. Me, I have trouble with words and letters. I can read, but they move around and there isn't anything they can do to stop it. So, I'll graduate if I'm lucky, but it will be with a B not an A. No matter how hard I work I can't get things to be perfect and memorizing everything I hear gets exhausting." By the end, she just sounded tired and ready to go home.

~That makes no sense.~ This time his voice sounded thoughtful, and I saw his wing twitch. ~What of you Cori? Are you also broken?~

"Probably. My brother is dead. And I've got all this power. But you'll have to ask Carelian if I am, because I don't know what his definition of broken is. He says we aren't as powerful as we should be. And Jo and Sable aren't broken, just themselves." I had to defend them. My best friend wasn't broken. And diabetes wasn't that big of a deal, only annoying.

~I see.~ He gave us the strangest look, which given he had a beak was saying something. He shook his head, the feathers around his neck flaring up, then settled back down. "Very well. Now for mental shields. Of this, Cori, you will have the easiest time. Then Sable. Jo I will need to work with, so be on your guard.~

The change of subject caused me a bit of mental whiplash as I looked at him. "Okay. What?"

~You have access to the Spirit magic, it calls to you. Those of us with magic in this realm can do things that most do not understand.~

"Wait, you're a merlin?" I didn't know why that just dawned on me, but I looked at him surprised and now looking for his mage tattoos, which he wouldn't have.

His wings shifted a bit. ~It would depend on how that term was applied. Am I a mage that uses magic across the realms, yes. My primary realm is what you call Spirit but I can use Water and a few others as well.~

I shot him a sharp look. I recognized deflection, but I didn't say anything. We all had our secrets.

~Elements are easy to work with, but the Spirit realm can be one of the most powerful. After all, your soul exists in your mind and it is easy to prevent others from touching it.~

"Huh?" What I had managed to read on Spirit magic, and I had barely put a dent in the books Marisol had gifted me, was very explicit about the spells available in Spirit and Soul and how they could be used. This threw me because other than the KO spell, most of them seemed kind of weak and boring. Especially when compared to Fire or Time. In the Psychic branch it had only mentioned four: Telepathy, Truth, KO, and Memory. When I checked with the college curriculum only Telepathy and Truth were taught.

~You cling so hard to your science, you keep forgetting this is magic. Here is what mind reading feels like.~ A whisper of pressure, a feeling of something foreign in my mind and I flinched.

~See. If you are paying attention, it is obvious. Now usually only surface thoughts can be read. In your mind I saw an image of books and spells and what looked like a list of classes.~ Baneyarl made it sound like that happened all the time.

I choked down vague nausea and I nodded. "But isn't that telepathy? They lump it together. So, can I talk to Carelian without sound?" It should have occurred to me sooner, but I didn't even have classes in Spirit spells until my last semester.

~You don't already?~ Baneyarl's feathers flared and he glanced at Carelian.

~She needs to use her magic more before I can teach her. She is too jumbled and blasts everything.~ It sounded like a complaint, and I glared at Carelian.

~Ah. True. They come into it so late and they do not speak this way as most of us do. But all your queans should learn, and soon. It is a great advantage among humans that depend on sound.~

~How?~ Carelian asked as I thought the same thing. Jo and Sable both leaned forward looking just as interested.

"Yes, I thought only Spirit mages could learn telepathy," Sable said frowning.

~No. All mages can speak mind to mind if they wish to learn. It is part of having connections to magic, and as you all have connections to Carelian, it should be easy enough. You may need to learn to meditate and focus on clear thoughts. That should help.~ He shifted his gaze back to me. ~For now, if you feel that pressure, think of a wall of noise between you and the pressure. Try it.~

He spent the next twenty minutes helping me create what he called a rudimentary shield.

~That will do. But we must get you all trained.~ He heaved a sigh. ~Go. I will see you on Monday. I have much to consider.~

Some have argued that Call Lightning, an Air spell, and Electricity, a Non-Organic spell, show that there is cross-over between the branches. There are a few that seem similar at first glance. Call Element and Call Mineral, Non-Organic and Earth respectively, have factors in common. But the way you find and create them is greatly different. All branches have their own aspects and just because of surface similarities you should not think they are the same. ~ Magic Explained.

SPIRIT

Saturday morning we got up and cleaned the house like mad women. While it was cramped with the three of us, we made it work, but it meant we needed it clean by the time Marisol got there. Her look of disappointment hurt too much not to. The counters were ready for dishes and we even got some flowers to put on the table in two hours.

Carelian wisely stayed out of our way until we heard the knock on the door. Jo pulled it open to reveal a smiling Marisol standing there. "Josefa, excellent, here are the keys. Go get supplies," Marisol ordered her.

"*Si, mami*." Jo hugged her tightly and headed out to where her mom had parked.

"Cori, Sable, oh it is so good to see you," she said walking in and dropping her purse off to the side.

Sable walked over and gave her a gentle hug. "You just saw me a week ago."

"And? That means I cannot miss you?" Marisol turned to me and smiled. "Well, come here *mi hija*, you I have missed." I went over gladly and the hug Marisol gave me did wonders to ease some of the pangs in my soul. "Oh, my child, the messes that keep falling on you. The stars must have blessed you with excitement when you were born," she murmured, pulling back and looking at me. "Are you losing weight again?"

I flushed and went to help arrange the bags and bags Jo was bringing in. With everything going on and the stress of attackers and well, everything, I'd been forgetting to eat lunch and breakfast. Another thing to remember to do. At least Jo made sure I usually ate dinner.

"I brought everything I could think of so we can have a wonderful brunch and mi hijas can tell me everything that is going on. Tell me about your classes. And I'll tell you what we've been doing about the Cori issue." Marisol stopped and looked at the bags with a huff of annoyance. "Silly woman, you forget to get the most important part." She went to her purse and handed her keys and credit card to Jo. "I forgot champagne. I brought the orange juice and forgot the stuff to make the mimosas. Please?"

Jo laughed and started to wave it off, but Sable lit up. "Oh please? I love mimosas and it's been a while. It would be nice to have something fun before next week." The look she gave Jo made any attempt at puppy dog eyes I'd ever tried look like amateur week. Jo crumbled in an instant.

"Okay. To the store it is. Need anything else, Mami?"

"No. At least not that I can see. Go, we will be fine. I'll have Cori help me set everything up."

Jo looked at me. "Pull on Lady Luck, you'll need it." With a grin and a wink, she and Sable headed out the door.

"That isn't such a bad idea." I pulled it on with a whisper of a thought. Those two spells cost me almost nothing and I didn't have to concentrate, they were just there.

Intent of magic indeed.

Marisol put me to work combining, plating, and being useful. Carelian watched us from the club chair, content as he knew she'd brought stuff specifically for him. The brunch was for all of us, after all.

The thoughts that had been bugging me, though I'd been scared to put them into words burst out of my mouth. "Am I going to lose Jo to Sable? What happens to Jo if they kill me? What am I going to do? I owe them a decade of service even if I don't get my doctorate." To my horror, I started crying and couldn't stop. I couldn't remember the last time I cried and now the tears wouldn't stop as everything in me broke.

Marisol's arms wrapped around me, holding me so tight that I sagged in her arms. "Come here, mi hija. Sit." She led me over to the couch and sank down with me as I fought to get the tears under control.

Carelian appeared at my side, tail lashing. ~Cori, what is wrong? Why are you crying?~ He sounded confused and up-set and I tried even harder to get myself under control.

Stop it. Stop it! Crying is stupid!

My mental castigation got through and I swallowed the gluey lump in my throat and reached for the tissues at the end of the futon. Georgia allergies required them. I sniffled and blew my nose. Marisol only let me go long enough to do that, then she pulled me back into her arms.

"Feel better?"

"No. Now my eyes are swollen. I don't know why I started crying." Just saying the words made me want to start crying again, but I forced it down.

There was a low, sad chuckle from Marisol. I didn't think I'd ever heard that sound from her before. "Cori, I'm sur-prised you hadn't broken down already and honored that you trusted me enough to break down now."

I looked at her, confused and not sure what she meant. Marisol petted my hair, a long stroking motion, similar to what I was doing to Carelian who curled up next to me alter-nating between purring and growling.

"Give me a minute, *mi hija.*" Marisol pulled her phone out of her pocket, texted for a minute, then set it down. "There. Cori, take a deep breath." I did as she told me, held it, and re-leased slowly. "Again." One more time and I could feel myself calming down. She smiled and squeezed, but then pushed me back a bit so she could look at me.

"Cori—you have people trying to kill you, you emerged and immediately went into a life and death situation, you work all the time, the government is taking way too much interest in your life, you're taking an insane course load to meet terms set before you even knew you were a mage, your best friend is head over heels in love, and you have a new person in your life. Child, I am amazed you haven't cracked before this."

I stared at her blankly. "New person?"

She nodded at Carelian, running a finger over his forehead. "Don't tell me he isn't every bit as important to you as any partner would be, and probably more intimately involved in your life."

"Oh." I sniffed hard and swallowed again, forcing that mucus down.

"So, what part of all this and the many other things like teachers, students, and general life that I don't know about is really bugging you?"

"As stupid as it sounds people trying to kill me pisses me off and scares me, but..." My voice trailed off and Marisol squeezed my hand.

"It's okay, you can tell me." Her voice stayed soft and soothing and I sighed.

"I don't want to lose Jo. I mean, I like Sable, I do, but I'm putting both of them at risk. She only has a four or five-year draft, I have ten. Sable is a junior she'll be out and done before any of us. I'm going to lose Jo as she'll follow Sable. Then where will I be?" Tears started leaking down my face again and I wiped them away with brusque movements, frustrated at my inability to control my own emotions.

Marisol hugged me close and kissed the top of my head. "Cori, of all the things you have to worry about, and yes people trying to kill you should be very high on that list, losing Jo is not one of them."

I craned my head back to look at her. "How can you be so sure? A decade is a long time. They'll move us around and we can't control anything."

Marisol's lips twitched. "When was the last time you tried to convince Josefa not to do something she had decided to do?"

I frowned, trying to think "Probably that escape room over Thanksgiving."

"Did it work?"

"No. She's like a bulldog with a bone when she decides on something," I admitted.

"Cori, my daughter decided you were hers the day after your first playdate. I believe you two went roller skating then spent money at the arcade."

I nodded. I remembered that. I'd had to beg my mom to take me and she'd finally dropped me off but told me to walk home after giving me twenty dollars. That was about six months after Stevie died, still in their numb phase. I hadn't minded, walking three miles wasn't that big a deal when I got to spend a day without memories surrounding me. Stevie and I had never gone to this place, so it was new. At that time, any place without memories was a good place.

"Henri picked her up that day and I remember he said she was oddly quiet all the way home, but she dragged him into the house where I was. I believe I was folding laundry. She made him sit, and remember she was twelve," Marisol said with a laugh. "She looked at both of us and said, 'I found my sister. She's mine and I'm keeping her.' Then headed upstairs to her room. Back then I rolled my eyes and just figured BFF's for a while. When she realized she preferred girls I thought for sure you two would become a couple, but again she told me 'Cori's my sister, not my date.'" Marisol looked at me. "Do you really think anyone, even Sable, is going to change her mind now?"

I sniffed and swallowed again. Listening to Marisol talk made me feel both silly and relieved. "No, probably not. She is stubborn sometimes."

"Sometimes? Cori, I love my daughter with all my heart. But she can out stubborn an elephant on anything that matters to her. What else is bothering you?"

Just hearing her absolute faith soothed. We talked about classes, and all the law enforcement people constantly checking up on me. "I feel like a kid that the adults have said can walk to school by herself but every ten minutes one of them is driving by 'just in case'." I grabbed a tissue and blew my nose. "I don't want to die, but at this point either I avoid the people trying to kill me or I die. I can't see that law enforcement can protect me any better that I can myself. I'm just exhausted and frustrated because I don't understand."

"Hmm, well I might be able to help with that, but Jo and Sable should be here for this part. You feel better?" I nodded, rubbing my face. "And Cori? I think Sable is the one. She and Jo click, but Jo will never be whole without you in her life. So work on finding how you and Sable click. Together the three of you could be incredibly strong." Marisol kissed the top of my head again.

With those words of wisdom, Marisol texted Jo and Sable it was safe to come back, while I washed my face. Carelian followed me into the bathroom.

~She is correct. Triad would be helpful.~ Carelian's voice in my mind didn't surprise me. Nor did his words.

"I'm not in love with either of them," I pointed out, frustrated. "And I have no desire to be intimate with either of them." Even as I said it, I double checked my own feelings. But there wasn't anything there. No desire for anything outside of hugs and friendship. Just love, but not in love, at least for Jo. Sable I liked, but didn't desire, at least I didn't think so.

~Humans. Family and love does not always include sex. Packs don't have sex with all the members. You find packs that work. You would be a good triad. Men distract.~ Carelian laughed softly. ~At least so my malkin would say.~

The unfamiliar word caught my attention. "Malkin?"

~Similar to your mother. She bore me, raised me, and let me go to you.~ He jumped down and headed for the door. ~They are almost back. There is food waiting. Hurry.~ With a flick of his tail he headed out of the bathroom and I heard the click of the front door.

I sighed and dried my face off, still feeling raw and not a hundred percent sure why it all bubbled up. Well, besides the obvious.

"You know you're stuck with me, right?"

I jerked my eyes open to see Jo leaning against the door jamb watching me in the mirror.

"I am, huh?"

"Yep. You're mine. I love you, Corisande Munroe. Always have, always will. Don't know why, don't care, but I promise you, we'll grow old together. With luck Sable will be there and maybe she'll have kids for us to spoil. But either way, I'll be there."

I found tears rising again and forced them down. I'd done enough crying for this year. "Works for me. Now someone mentioned mimosas?"

"Mmmm, yes. And Mami said there was something she and Henri had been doing about your minor assassin problem."

I laughed and followed her out of the bathroom. Sable was sitting at the table, a champagne glass filled with pale orange liquid in her hands.

She looked at me, brows furrowed slightly. "You okay?"

"Yeah. Just a minor meltdown. All good."

"Well, finally." I looked at her surprised and Sable quirked up one side of her mouth. "You needed it. We've been worried about you. You're not superhuman."

That made me feel better and I laughed. "No, just a double merlin—doesn't that count?"

"Nope. Still human, sorry," Sable said with a grin as she passed me a flute full of mimosa. Marisol and Jo sat down with their own.

"A toast," Marisol said, smiling at all of us. "To three powerful and intelligent women who will change the world."

We clinked glasses, and I heard in my head Carelian murmur, ~My queans.~ He was drinking bubbly water. He said he liked the tickle, but alcohol tasted bad to him.

"Okay, Mami, we're all here. Tell us what you've been doing about Cori," Jo prompted, leaning towards her mother.

"Yeah, I mean I don't want you two risking yourselves for me," I said, now worried. I hadn't processed that she and Henri were doing things to help me.

"What do you mean?"

"I don't want you two to risk anything for me."

"Nothing that drastic. We both are long-standing members of our societies and we let it be known that you were the daughter of our heart. We sent a few emails to the heads of our chapters pointing out that enough mages die, why are any of the societies sanctioning the killing of one who is just now starting her education? I don't know it if will help, but it can't hurt. Having a few of the more powerful mages getting annoyed about this would help. Now come on, we have food to eat."

I swallowed my fears and concentrated on enjoying the day. In the back of my mind worry festered that this was opening them up to danger, but I couldn't put a finger on why.

Chapter 40

Interrelations between world governments are affected in subtle ways by magic. While the United States
has deemed no mage may hold office, the United Kingdom
mandates the ruler be an archmage or higher, China's
ruler is always a merlin, and Japan's royal family has no
magic users at all, but a horde of mages in their service.
The majority of Ambassadors are mages, as even a
hedgemage with Spirit can be a boon in negotiations. ~
History of Magic.

CHAOS

The weekend left all of us extra peppy, and even the habit
of throwing on a bubble as I went between classes seemed
less of a grind. Monday I only ran into Indira, but she just
watched, her eyes distant, and I didn't feel like pushing it too
much. Classes with her were rapidly getting boring as working
with Baneyarl in the brief time we had expanded my
knowledge tenfold. Tonight, he would get all of us to nail
down our mental shields.

Dinner was leftovers from the brunch, which meant lots
to eat. I threw some tamales in and gave Carelian the chicken
steak mixture Marisol had developed for him. We were attacking the food when Jo and Sable got back.

"Good news! I qualify for the new drug. They think it may
help stabilize my body so I won't need insulin for up to a decade." Sable's grin was contagious.

"Excellent!" I rose, looking at them. "What do you want
me to prepare? We need to get over there in a few minutes."

"Just anything fast. I'm starving." Jo tossed her comment
back as she set up her books on her computer. With us losing
three evenings a week with Baneyarl, we were doubling

down between classes to get the reading and research done, but it was worth it.

I made them quick bowls of meat, rice, and beans and threw them in the microwave. I grabbed myself a coke, draining it while they ate. The caffeine and sugar would help me stay energetic and maybe I wouldn't crash when we got back, though I didn't bet on it.

The rip in reality opened on time and I stepped into the clearing and froze. Jo and Sable collided with me, sending me stumbling forward a few feet.

"Cori, what the—" Jo froze and I knew she'd seen the same thing I had. A huge cat, the size of a Saint Bernard, with emerald green fur that matched Carelian's eyes lounged on the boulders, while Baneyarl sat in the typical Egyptian cat pose next to it.

~Malkin!~ Carelian's shout made me wince as he bounded past us and onto the rocks where the cat lay. His nuzzles and purrs, clearly audible in the quiet glade, reassured me. But I still couldn't take my eyes off of the magnificent cat.

The fur was a rich green that seemed longer than Carelian's and the tail lay draped like a whip across the rocks. The large head with ears that had longer tufts on them raised from greeting Carelian and she looked at me. The sharp bright blue eyes seemed to pierce through my soul, locking me in place. I sensed Jo and Sable moving around me, but I couldn't take my eyes away from that gaze.

~So you are the one my son left me for,~ purred a cool arch voice in my head.

"Yes?" The word came out a bit squeaky, and I had much more sympathy for Jo meeting Sable's dad.

~Malkin, be nice. Cori, this is my mother or mami, Esmere. Malkin, this is Cori, my quean.~ Carelian's chiding but amused voice came as a relief and I found I could move. ~And my other queans Jo and Sable.~ Oddly I could feel him mentally touch each of them as he said their names.

With shaky legs I made it over to the pillows and sank down, but still couldn't take my eyes off the huge cat. She had the regalness of every cat I'd ever seen, but her coat and eyes just ramped it up. I almost felt like I should kneel before her and offer her treats.

~Mmm, now that is an idea I like. What treats would you offer?~ she purred in my head and I shivered. That answered if she could read my mind.

~Malkin, stop it. She is a powerful quean and I gained two others. Look at my pride.~ Carelian's voice broke the spell and I sank back feeling like I'd been released from an overly firm hug.

~That is yet another form of psychic ability. While Carelian is from the Chaos realm, Esmere is a merlin equivalent in Chaos and Spirit and is powerful in Psychic.~ Baneyarl informed us and I could see the tail lash of annoyance from Esmere—she'd been enjoying toying with me.

The catlike behavior relaxed me. Cats I could handle, even if they were powerful and scary big.

Carelian rubbed his face one more time across hers, then leapt off the boulders to come flop in front of me, close enough that I had no excuse not to pet him.

~So why is my malkin here? Not that I minded an excuse to see her,~ Carelian asked as he leaned into my strokes.

~Concerns about your broken queans. And the fact the Jeorgaz hasn't found her yet.~

I stiffened. I saw Jo and Sable, who'd been watching all this intently, flinch back.

"Wait, why does that name sound familiar?" I searched my memory and it sounded like I should know it.

~It isn't time. Back to the concerns?~ asked Carelian, seeming not at all upset.

"Wait, why is your mom here to look at us? And who is Jeorgaz?" Jo said. I think she'd meant it to come out as strong and stubborn, but Esmere didn't look like she put up with protests.

~He is something we shall not deal with now. While I am what your society would consider a healer, though I have never worked on humans.~ She rose slowly and my impressions were solidified, a large St. Bernard, then she leaped into the air and my heart stopped at the sight of an apex predator coming at me. She landed with a soft thump not a foot away from Jo, who gasped a bit. Esmere's paw could kill with one swipe. ~Peace, young quean. May I look inside your mind? Baneyarl indicated you have issues with words and letters moving, which creates difficulties in your world.~

I watched Jo lean back and square her shoulders. "Sure, I'm all for anything that makes this go away."

I wanted to hug her as I watched the daredevil side take over. It usually came out when she was terrified. A persona she pulled on when faced with anything that scared her. Then she moved and acted as if it didn't.

Esmere's whiskers twitched as her tail curled and uncurled. ~Faith young quean, this will not hurt.~

The clearing fell quiet. Even the leaves seemed to fall still, and we waited. I held my breath, scared I might distract her.

Just when I had to breathe, or pass out, she spoke.

~You, Sable, you do not have this issue with words and letters?~ Her voice imperious.

"No. I don't have any issues like that." Sable glanced at me as if for reassurance and I shrugged. I had no idea about any of this.

~May I examine you? As a comparison.~

"Umm, sure." She had to scoot closer, but I squeezed her hand, smiling at her. Trying to pretend like I knew it would be okay. It had to be okay, I mean, worst case nothing changed. Right?

~Interesting. While I can see definite differences in the brain activity levels, I don't know which area relates to those issues. Most beings here don't rely on reading to learn. There are some like Baneyarl that do read, but most of us learn through doing or stories. Your magic is so structured you've taken the art out of it. But this.~ She sighed and the sound in my mind brought tears to my eyes. ~I fear that even with me practicing my art to the highest degree, the cost might be worse than the disease. I cannot help you, young quean.~

Jo forced a smile but I could see the corner of her mouth trembling as she did. "No worries. Isn't like I can't read. I'm getting by and I'll get better."

~I believe you will. At some point ask Carelian to call me and I will teach you the stories of our peoples. I believe they would be at home in you.~

A smile brightened Jo. "I'd like that. I don't read stories often, but I love movies."

~I thought so. Now for the sick quean.~ Her gaze locked onto Sable whose hand squeezed mine tighter as she met Esmere's gaze. ~You are a bit more straightforward. Your body is not producing the right chemicals to create a healthy balance for a human. I have been reviewing human biology since Baneyarl contacted me. While I think I understand how that organ works, it is slightly different from how it works in my body versus yours. However,~ she paused staring at Sable, ~I believe I understand what cells in your pancreas are damaged. So far it is a small amount. I believe that together we can offer up those cells even as we convince the healthy ones to grow.~

Sable blinked. "They said they thought that was why I was just now developing it, was that my pancreas was failing but they didn't know why. They didn't see a tumor or cancer."

~Machines? Can't your healers smell and sense the wrongness in your body?~ Her outrage came through like shards of glass.

"No. We only have machines that can see if there is something foreign in the body," I said, Sable's nails digging into my hand.

~Humans. No wonder so many of you end up here when you seek too much power. Give me a month to prepare. Then come to me, and I am sure we can heal your ailing organ.~

Sable swallowed and stiffened her back a bit. "How about after my school is done? I'll have a full week after finals before I go home for the summer."

I watched Jo pale at that and realized they hadn't thought that part through. For me, I'd just be staying in the apartment, but I think Jo was planning on spending the summer working in the garage and getting her hands dirty. They would work it out. I hoped.

Esmere inclined her head. ~That will be optimal. You may need to stay here a day or so. But this I have little doubt of. ~ She looked around at all of us. ~You chose well, Carelian. I shall see you later.~ There was a bit of command in that, but Carelian only twitched his tail as I petted him.

~Baneyarl,~ Esmere said with an odd bow, then a ripple appeared in the air about three feet off the ground. She leapt up and sailed into it. A moment later it sealed behind her.

We sat there silent for a moment. "Your mom's kinda scary," Sable said, her voice a bit shaky.

~Yes, she is.~ The pride in his voice made me giggle, and Jo and Sable joined me.

~If we are done, I believe we have more work to do. Your ability to protect your minds is still woefully inadequate.~ His voice cut in as our giggles were dying. We moved back to the art of magic, leaving the science of it behind. I promised myself to figure out why Jeorgaz sounded like a name I should know.

Chapter 41

Major agricultural companies routinely hire Transform mages to work on modifying plants. Magically Modified Organisms yield more protein, complex nutrients, are bug resistant, and grow faster with poorer soil. Regardless of what various groups say, MMO foods are usually healthier for you than traditional. It is suspected that farmers with mage abilities have been doing this for years without anyone knowing. At this point, the odds are all foods are MMO even if they are not labeled as such. ~ Magic Explained Online

ORDER

That evening we all learned to shield our minds and our bodies. I felt much better as Jo learned to keep a subtle shield of Air around her, while Sable turned her perspiration, easy with the spring humidity, into a barrier. That shield also had the added effect of keeping bugs off. A win-win in all our books.

Alixant and Indira were keeping their distance. I didn't know how I felt about that. Mentors were supposed to be there for me, but it felt like they were there for others. I just pushed it away and tried to focus on classes. I'd convinced two teachers to let me just take the finals for their classes as they directly related to what I'd passed with the EMT certification tests. If I passed, I'd get credit for the classes and that would make it much easier for me to get the degree I needed. Which meant when I wasn't in class, either here or in the Spirit realm, I was studying.

Wednesday, Jo was up to something. Her grins and attitude let me know something was up, but I let her keep the secret for now. She'd break eventually.

Shoving the last bites of food into my mouth, I stepped through the portal to gray cloudiness. I halted a few steps in.

"Baneyarl?" I called out, looking around. The muffled sounds behind me told me that Jo and Sable had come in, and the strange feeling was the portal closing.

"Happy birthday!" Sable and Jo called out behind me, the fog disappearing to reveal a clearing full of flowers with Baneyarl and a gorgon. My eyes locked on Tirsane—I knew it was her and not some other gorgon, and my entire body locked up.

"Okay, wasn't expecting her," Jo murmured.

I nodded my head in a rapid bobble movement. Then the rest of it clicked. "Wait, my birthday?"

Jo laughed and pulled me into a rough hug. "Yes. You didn't even realize, did you?" I shook my head and thought back. It was tax day. With everything going on, I'd lost track of the calendar. As of today, I was twenty-two. "Well, we remembered and asked Baneyarl if we could give you a surprise birthday party." She dropped her voice lower. "Though I wasn't expecting that much of a surprise."

The bite on my wrist throbbed as if sensing its maker nearby.

~Happy birthing day, Corisande,~ Baneyarl said in an oddly formal voice. ~We are glad you have shared your life with us.~

The phrasing had the tone of a saying, and it made me smile. It was an odd way to say it, but it felt good. Nice to know people or beings were glad I was in their lives.

"Thank you for this." Able to pull my gaze away from Tirsane, I realized there was a low table with beverages and a cake on it. I took that in but then looked back at the gorgon.

"She's like very intimidating up close," Jo murmured in my ear.

"You've seen her before?" Sable's voice was a harsh whisper of incredulity.

"Stadium," Jo said back.

~Tirsane, you are scaring the poor queans.~ Esmere's voice brought our whispers to a halt, and she strolled out of the trees, a bag held in her mouth. ~Say hello and quit acting the imperious deity.~

I clamped both hands over my mouth to stop myself from falling into hysterical giggles. The old saying about cats having no respect for kings, or apparently gods, sprang into my mind.

~Very well Esmere, it was getting tiring posing. Do you think they would mind if I became less me and more them?~ Tirsane's voice sent musical healing across my brain and I sighed in pleasure.

~I don't know about them, but I would prefer you being less you. It sets my fur on end,~ Esmere said back as she set the bag down on the table near the cake.

~As always you are less than respectful,~ Tirsane said, but she didn't sound upset, simply amused. With that she changed. Whereas before I had the impression of her being a full head taller than Baneyarl and so radiating power you almost couldn't look at her, now with a shimmy of her shoulders she became normal. Well, as normal a woman whose lower body was a snake and wore nothing covering her torso could be. But now the snakes seemed like fancy hair and her breasts were so impressive they seemed more an adornment than actual body parts.

I heard Carelian groan behind me and just like that the tension snapped. Instead of a deity, a mythical creature, and a cat that could stare down most bears, I saw three beings, all different and just as flawed as I was.

Sable and Jo heaved sighs of relief. "Mami sent the cake. And we got you something," Jo chimed behind me nudging me forward with a bump of her hip.

~Indeed, young mageling. I felt your presence in my realm and thought I would come when I heard there would be a party. Your focus was kind enough to invite me.~ Tirsane flowed forward to the table. ~And I have never had birthday cake.~ The word was pronounced slowly as if it wasn't a word she had used before.~

I shot a looked at Carelian, my eyes wide. He flicked his tail and went over to his mother, brushing against her as he stuck his nose in a saucer of red tinted liquid.

~My son has no shame. As is only right. A Cath has neither shame nor regret. We are Cath after all.~ Her voice purred with approval and I shrugged.

"Thank you for this, all of you. And Tirsane," I stumbled a bit feeling rude for saying her name, but I didn't know what else to call her. "I am honored by your presence."

~No one invites me to parties anymore. This should be fun, and I am interested in seeing some day what you have learned and how it compares to your way of doing magic.~

~First cake and presents,~ Carelian demanded.

"I'm with him. You know Mami's cakes are awesome. Stinky drove down this morning and delivered it. I'll serve." Jo said that as she walked over to the cake and picked up the plates waiting there. She knew I hated the happy birthday song and candles, but cakes were never to be turned down. Especially Marisol's. As soon as Jo cut into it, I knew I was right. Cinnamon Mexican chocolate. Something Marisol had created just for me. Rich chocolate batter with cinnamon and raspberry liqueur to give it a kick, and a frosting with white chocolate and the fresh raspberries.

Everyone waited quietly as Jo handed out the plates. Part of me wondered at all of them having opposable thumbs, but it was interesting watching them eat. Carelian and Esmere tore it apart delicately into pieces, popping them into their mouths. Baneyarl ate in a similar manner, tasting each bite thoughtfully, but he put the plate down after a few bites.

~It has an interesting, even attractive flavor, but the lack of protein makes it something to savor in very small amounts.~ Baneyarl didn't apologize, but his regret was clear.

"You know, I bet he'd love the Chinese Five Spice mix. It has the cinnamon and on meat it's pretty good," Sable said giving him a long look. "I get the feeling spices aren't something they play with much here."

~Many of us do not cook often, so I am not sure how that would work,~ Baneyarl said watching us.

"I'll think of something. Mami would hate to think you didn't know about spices."

~Your chorizo is excellent. We should bring some of that next time,~ Carelian interjected. He'd finished his piece of cake and was busy cleaning his face.

~I admit this differs from anything I have eaten prior.~ Tirsane looked at the three of us with a considering look. ~Of the many things I had thought about for trade with Earth, food had not been one of them. But this is a treat.~ She licked the last bit of frosting off the fork and lay her dish down on the table. ~Thank you for the invite.~ She turned her slitted eyes towards me and the cake stuck in my throat. ~I believe it is customary to give a gift on the day of your birth?~

I choked down the piece of cake and licked my lips. "Yes, but only from close friends and family. You are not obligated to give me anything." I babbled out the words, panicking.

~Ah. Either way I find this amusing. I shall give you a gift.~ *Oh crapola.*

I couldn't even say anything as I stared at her, caught in the horror that was my life.

She reached down and pulled at a scale on her hip. It snapped off with a slick sound that reminded me of a joint popping out of place. With a smile that showed off her fangs, she slithered forward and handed it to me ~Not elegant or prettily wrapped as the others, but useful I think.~

I took it from her. The scale was iridescent close up, changing colors in the light from green to purple to pink. "Thanks," I croaked while my mind raced trying to figure out what to do with it.

Her laugh was like bells in my head, and I flinched at the sharp pureness of each tone. ~Do not look so dubious, young mageling. It is a token. If you ever need me, break it. I will know. Use it wisely.~ She turned and bowed to Baneyarl. ~I thank you for your hospitality. I would like to come view your lessons sometime?~

~I would be honored, Tirsane,~ Baneyarl said with a slight bow.

~Excellent. Until we meet again.~

With that she was gone. I didn't know if she could move though rips that seamlessly or if she turned invisible or what. My surprise must have shown on my face.

~Have you never seen someone sidestep? I believe you call it teleporting,~ Esmere asked, sitting back from the table, legs tucked under her in loaf pose, but her tail drifting back and forth as she spoke.

I shook my head, looking at where Tirsane had been. "No. I mean, I know it is a spell, but only a few archmages and merlins can do it. It's advised not to as people disappear."

Almost in unison, Esmere and Baneyarl snorted. ~You don't disappear—you might get lost, however that is only a permanent effect if you choose it to be.~ Esmere's tone dripped contempt. I had the sudden urge to introduce her to Indira and Alixant.

"I have no idea what you are talking about," said Sable. "But Cori still has two other presents to open." She nudged Jo with her elbow. "Go."

My attention snapped to Jo as she stepped forward and pulled a small box out of her pants pocket. Her cargo pants were her favorite during the school year, so the box had not been noticeable as it was not that large.

"Here, for your birthday," she said handing it to me.

I opened it and felt my heart swell a bit. Jo's birthday was the first of October, after all the mess in the stadium. I'd spent some of the money the FBI had paid me and gotten her very high-end headphones to help with all the audio she needed to listen to. Practical and appreciated, but not per-sonal.

This, this was incredible. With hands that shook no matter how hard I tried to make them be steady, I pulled out the necklace. The Spirit symbol shone in gold with inlaid blood red in the Relativity section, a luminous blue in the Psychic, and glowing opalescent in the Soul area.

"Jo, it's gorgeous," I managed to say, choking up. I'd been so emotional lately, but things kept happening and I couldn't stop it.

Her smile was blinding. "We had it created for you, *Mami* and *Papi* contributed. The red is garnet, the blue sapphire, and the white is opal. We wanted you to have something special. You deserve it." Jo stepped forward and put it around my neck. It hit about two inches above my cleavage. It felt right hanging there.

I pulled her into a fierce hug, holding it until I needed to release her to hug Sable. "Thank you," I whispered in her ear.

"You're family. I get that. I'm honored to be part of your family," she whispered back.

Tears stung my eyes as we pulled apart.

~This custom I find ridiculous, yet entertaining. I begin to understand why Carelian demanded I assist him with this.~ Esmere's comment contained amusement and an acerbic dryness. It tasting like sweet vinegar in my mind. We all snickered and turned to see her tail pointedly tapping the bag she'd carried in.

I moved over to table. "This is from you, Carelian?" I asked glancing at him.

~I mentioned to Malkin. She agreed it would be a good gift for you. I trust you will find it useful.~ His voice had an odd tone, and it occurred to me he might be nervous.

I knelt and ran a hand down his back, smoothing the fur. "Thank you."

~Humans. Open the present, this is wasting time.~ I couldn't help but laugh at Esmere's tart remark, matched with her rapidly tapping tail. I reached for the bag, a simple brown one with basic raffia handles. I put my hand in and pulled out a smooth oddly shaped object. I held it up, inspecting it. A sea green translucent lumpy shape, roughly the size of a deck of cards. Oddly pretty, with an almost glowing faint light coming from it, but I had no idea what it was.

"It's pretty, what is it?" I asked, looking at the two Cath.

~The way we Cath view what you call Soul magic is different. For us it is a way to pass memories and knowledge. So this is a learning stone, where our elders explain how they use magic and show you by immersing you in the memory, in the actions. It should work for you, though it may be a bit disconcerting as we think differently from you. Carelian can show you how to use it and over time you will unlock more lessons as you master the first.~ Esmere looked at me with inscrutable blue eyes. ~Please understand there are lifetimes of lessons here, not just a session or two. You will find this something to learn from for your entire life.~

I stared at the object in stunned surprise. "Thank you so much, both of you. This is an unbelievable gift. Thank you." Petting Esmere in thanks didn't seem smart, so I bowed. I did pet Carelian, scratching behind his ears as a thank you.

~Now, if the celebrations are over, I believe we have lessons to do?~ Baneyarl asked, looking at all of us.

With laugher we cleaned up, and Esmere left after talking to Sable in the corner of the clearing for a few minutes.

We dove back into lessons and before we left we all could create mental shields that would protect casual mind reading. An archmage or merlin could force their way past our shields, but we would get better with practice.

High with the presents we stepped back in, tired but smiling more than I had in a while. I hadn't realized how much I enjoyed the time when no one was trying to kill me. Even though it was considered off limits to attack someone when at home, I still stayed hyper aware and nervous.

Jo's phone went off with a rapid beeping as we stepped into the living room. She pulled it out and looked at it. "Huh, Mami sent me a bunch of text messages." Her fingers flipped open the messages and I watched her pale.

"Jo? What's wrong?" Sable asked as I felt like someone was clenching my heart in my chest.

"My parents, they're being sued. For millions, and the person suing them is some company they've never heard of." She lifted her head and looked at me. "They'll lose everything."

Chapter 42

All magic is science, and science is technology. The more you learn, the better you can use this skill set. Don't squander your abilities due to lack of knowledge. ~ OMO encouragement for more education

SPIRIT

It took us until Friday to get all the details. The Guzmans were being sued about a car that had broken down after they worked on it three years ago. They'd even helped with the paperwork to prove the car had been a lemon, but now they were being taken to court for pain and suffering. The law firm was one of the best in the state and they had lots of mages as clients.

I shot all the information over to Alixant and asked, nicely, if he could see what he could find out. Otherwise I doubled down and tried to learn everything. I kept the gift from Carelian by my nightstand. I understood that now wasn't the time to use it. I needed to get my degree first, then I could look and see what the other realms could teach me, but for now I did everything I could to get my degree.

Baneyarl told us that Monday only I needed to come as neither Sable nor Jo could learn what he felt it was time to teach me. Which meant I felt rushed as I hurried back from Law Monday evening. The lesson that afternoon had shed a bit of light onto why our apartment was safe. There were crazy restrictions and consequences for anyone who hurt family members in an assassination and about what disputes the government ignored between mages. Though I couldn't figure out why hitting Jo at the market didn't count.

Jo and Sable were there. The lines of worry on Jo's face didn't help my stress. "Anything?"

"No. Did Alixant get back to you?"

I shook my head and she sighed. "Finals are in two weeks. Then I can go see what I can do. The one thing I don't understand is how fast this is moving. From everyone I've talked to civil lawsuits can take years. They want to go to court next week."

I couldn't stop the bitterness that coated my words. "Because they are using your parents to get to me. If they cause enough disruption, I'll fail a class or miss a final and that is enough to ensure I won't graduate in time to meet the terms of the will."

"Ah." Jo sat silent for a long time then looked up at me. "Cori, I say with love"—she stopped and cleared her throat and I felt my heart stutter stop as I waited. If she wanted me to walk away, avoid the draft, to give it up, I would—"graduate and kick their fucking asses."

"Hooyah," Sable said quietly as she looked at me.

The mix of emotions that went through me left me standing straighter and feeling even more weight resting on my shoulders. "You go it."

Jo gave one sharp nod and jerked herself up from the chair. "I made you a burrito. Eat and go. Baneyarl was insistent you learn this and that means it must be important."

I just took the food she handed me and wolfed it down, while Carelian did the same with the meat she set down for him. Five minutes later, with a bottle of water in my hand, I stepped through the door to his realm. It didn't even bug me anymore, just felt normal to cross from my realm into his.

Huh, is this his realm? I never thought about it. I assumed I was in the spirit realm. Am I?

That thought reminded me I really needed to learn telepathy also. So many things I needed to catch up on. Baneyarl had promised to keep teaching me over the summer so as soon as I had a few spare moments I'd make a list of all the things I wanted to learn.

~Good eve, Cori. Are you ready? This is one of the more difficult things I need you to learn, but it will help protect you.~

I was more than willing to learn anything that would keep me safe but keeping the others safe was even more important. "Then why shouldn't Jo and Sable learn it? I need to keep them safe too."

~Unfortunately, this ability can only be learned by those with strong Relativity skills. While I believe they are strong enough, they do not have access to this affinity.~ He'd used that word before. Where we called them classes and branches, for him they were affinities and spells. I still hadn't decided which one I liked better.

"Okay, so what are we doing?" Carelian headed over to his favorite spot to watch us.

~You saw Tirsane use this ability at your birthday party. We call it sidestepping, but Carelian tells me you refer to it as teleporting.~

I blinked at him, surprised. Teleporting was something you saw in the movies occasionally. The hero would use it, always a merlin, to get to someplace just as the bomb was counting down, but the price was always so high that he had almost nothing left to fight the bad guy or save the victim, depending on the story.

"So, this is like for last ditch I'll die otherwise sort of thing?"

Baneyarl tilted his head at me. ~No. It is an easy mode of transportation, and in your situation will prevent you from being exposed to those wishing to harm you.~

"Easy mode?" That didn't mesh with what I knew, but then movies were pretty much the only things that mentioned Teleportation. Even the Spirit book hadn't said much more than "the ability to move between places at great cost, but also almost instantaneous speed."

~Yes. Most use it to travel between households, markets, or other known places. Traveling to your plane requires us to open a portal. Movement within the same realm never requires that if you have the strength. Granted, ripping the realm walls is more direct, but in the long scope of life, much more risky.~

That went against everything I knew, but that happened regularly with Baneyarl. "Sounds good to me," I managed, and it did, if not scary as all get-out.

~It is easier to go to a place you've been before, but there are other options. For now, let's try going from one side of the clearing to the other.~

I rolled my eyes. "How? Since I have never done this, and other than Tirsane, I've never seen it done. She did it so fast I didn't even register what she did."

Baneyarl clicked his beak together in what I could only regard as a thoughtful manner. ~Close your eyes and picture the other side of the clearing in your mind.~

That was so much easier said than done, it was all trees. But after opening and closing my eyes multiple times, I had an image in my head of a bark pattern that reminded me of the statue of Abraham Lincoln in the capitol. He'd been responsible for ensuring mages in the United States couldn't be made slaves. It had been part of the Emancipation Proclamation. A few people had realized a mage as a slave would kill anyone to get free and magic didn't seem to care about the color of your skin at all. Racism died quickly as you never knew who was a mage or who wasn't until the OMO took over in the 1900s.

"I have it."

~Excellent,~ he said, though I tasted a bit of impatience in his tone. ~Now tell your magic you want to be over there and step to it.~

I opened my eyes to glare at him. "Just tell it I want to be over there?"

~How else would it know where you wanted to be?~ His voice oh so reasonable, to my annoyance.

I hate fuzzy wuzzy stuff.

Only the fact that he'd been right every time we'd listened kept me from sighing audibly. Still didn't mean I had the slightest idea of what I needed to do. The image of the tree on the other side of the clearing, the bark pattern of Lincoln with his hands on the arms of his chair hung in my mind. I closed my eyes to keep the image clear and I asked.

I'd like to be there.

My thought was clear and direct and I stepped to the side. I thought for a second that I felt something. A wisp, an agreement, but it was so fast I couldn't specify what was asked or what was agreed to. A memory about when the cost is so small you don't notice the asking came to mind as I opened my eyes.

On the other side of clearing.

"Huh?" I looked around. The idea that it would work had never really crossed my mind.

~Now back.~

I looked at him, still trying to get my brain wrapped around what had just happened. I stepped and then was across the clearing. The offering—what offering had I made? I thought furiously to recall that tiny ask of an offering, and my instant acceptance.

"I did that on less than a thousand molecules? Why didn't it wait for me to agree?"

Baneyarl arched a brow at me. ~You did, by the very asking. Magic usually only asks if you are very new or the cost is very great. This was so little the request was assumed to be the agreement. Now step again,~ he ordered, his tone unforgiving.

I wanted to stand there and think for at least an hour, but I looked at the other side of the clearing, the patch of grass that still had my footprints on it, and I asked and stepped. This time with my eyes open I saw reality swirl around me, but it was so fast that by the time I recognized colors it had stopped and trees hung in front of me.

"No way. It can't be that easy. It just can't. It takes merlins huge offerings to move from place to place. Why is that so easy? Is it like that for everyone or am I just special?" My hands on my hips, I glared at him, confusion and hope riffling through my brain.

~As I have never witnessed one of your mages teleport, I cannot provide insight, but I can make a supposition.~

I gave him look and I swear Carelian laughed at me, but I ignored him.

Baneyarl ruffled his feathers and I swear he was laughing too. Why did everyone seem to find me so hilarious?

~I suspect they try to make a tunnel between two points. Rather than stepping through magic to reach it, they force a hole in magic, in reality itself. That price is much higher than asking magic to help. Now, I will say magic has been known to say no, but in my experience there is always a reason and it is better to accept than to force.~

"Huh," I said processing. "What about going somewhere I haven't seen. I mean, if I can only go to places I've been it is pretty limited."

~Yes and no. You have the ability to mind read, though you haven't learned to utilize it yet. Otherwise you would rarely speak out loud to me.~

I ignored that. There were only so many hours in the day and as it was, I felt like I was falling further and further behind with what I needed to know. I'd figured out why they wanted you for four years, it gave you time to learn all the magic at a pace that didn't threaten to burn you out.

"I'll learn it for Carelian if nothing else, but so far everything else has been far more important, and since Jo and Sable can't talk back to me it isn't as much use right now."

~Agreed. But when you learn it, you can reach in and take images out of peoples' minds. Places. It needs to either be someplace very familiar, like home or work, or a place that made a great impact on them. That impact depends on the person. For now, I will send you an image.~ My mind filled with the sight of a small pool in the middle of a glade, the crystal blue of the water like a photoshopped picture of the Caribbean. A waterfall splashed into the pool creating rainbows, while green trees surrounded it. It all but gleamed with life and peace.

"You want me to go there?"

~You have the image. Carelian will be waiting for you.~

I turned to glance at the cat, no Cath, but he wasn't there. "Can he sidestep too?" For some reason I felt outraged at that idea, though I'm not sure why.

~No. But all Cath can open doors between the realms and places. It is not as elegant as sidestepping, and much more noticeable, though Cath manage to do it almost unnoticed. It is their nature.~

I thought about it. There had been a slight twinge as the image filled my mind, but I'd spent so much of my life ignoring them that those small sharp spikes of pain were barely noticeable. And I had seen bigger rips, like the doorway we walked through to this clearing, were sharper than the little ones that Indira made. So Carelian making them small enough and fast enough that I didn't notice came as no surprise.

I took a deep breath. "The image again, please?" It filled my head and I locked on it, trying to make it as real as I could. I whispered my ask. "Take me there, please?" and I sidestepped.

The sound of water splashing, the calls of birds, the rustle of leaves hit me before I even opened my eyes. The wet smell and the taste of what I could only describe as jungle air swamped my senses. I took in the area, it was even more vibrant than in the memory, the colors different, but it still ranked as one of the most beautiful places I'd ever been.

"I did it." My voice hushed in the beauty of this place.

~Of course you did. My quean would not be anything less than spectacular.~

I turned to see Carelian batting at something in the water. "What are you doing?"

~Fishing. It has been a while since I had the chance to try and catch my own.~

That sent a wave of guilt through me, but before I could dwell on it too much, I felt a strange implosion of air next to me and turned to see Baneyarl walking towards me.

~Indeed. Carelian does seem to choose his queans wisely. You will find as you travel to more places this will let you move with great freedom. Please test it carefully in your realm though.~ He paused to look at me. ~I have never sidestepped on Earth and the way magic works might be different. So be careful with your practice.~

Those comments dampened my joy, and I sighed. With my luck, something would go very wrong and I'd end up on top of a building or underwater or something.

I shook my head as he had me practice getting an image from him and stepping there. While the excitement of side-stepping had faded, the information was important and each time I reached into his mind, or Carelian provided an image, I learned. Magic always required a price, but when you spoke to it and asked, the price was never as high as when you demanded or forced.

I think that was the biggest and most important lesson he was trying to teach me.

Chapter 43

Contrary to popular opinion, Chaos mages do not make up the majority of mages put to death for crimes. From statistics, the breakdown of mages convicted and executed for crimes matches a standard distribution of mages within the population. In other words, there is no evidence for Chaos mages to be any more likely to commit crimes than any other mage group. ~ OMO Website

CHAOS

Finals were next week, and our stress levels were ramped. I had to get my paper done for a class I was challenging. The professor, tired of arguing with me, said if I did a thirty-page research paper he'd pass me with whatever grade I got, as long as it was a C or higher. I had no issue doing a thirty-page paper on Evolutionary Biology and why we have the functionality we do. Just watching Carelian with his opposable thumbs gave me enough to start. I figured I'd also point out some of the negative aspects of evolution, such as narrow pelvic regions, and constantly being fertile. I knew I could pass, we'd talked about this enough in my biology classes at the community college. Besides, I enjoyed researching.

With the time bubble up, I was heading to the library when an explosion knocked me forward. I lay on the ground, stunned, but held the bubble. I usually only did my bubbles for about thirty seconds, but I hadn't been paying much attention this morning and took a minute bubble. That meant I was sixty seconds out of sync with reality. Which was the only reason the explosion didn't kill me. I looked at the other students that were hurt and dropped the bubble, instead creating a layer of Earth around me as I rushed to help.

"Carelian, where is he or they?" I yelled out. I really needed to step up when I learned telepathy as I dove for the first student. Luckily, it looked like they had expected me to still be at thirty seconds, which chilled me to the bone. They had timed me, thinking I'd be at that spot thirty seconds from where they saw me, but I was past it when it blew. The kids behind me weren't.

~Teleported, but I have their scent. It is familiar.~

I didn't respond to that but focused on the three students. No one died or was seriously hurt, but I growled with frustration at still not being able to seal wounds. By the time campus security showed up, so had administration, the police, and Indira.

"You okay, Cori?" She knelt next to me as I looked at the kids being patched up. Broken arm, cuts and bruises, and at least one possible concussion. And all of that was only because most people kept away from me. My reputation preceded me.

"No. This can't continue. Someone's going to get killed," I said, my voice bleak as I looked at students hurt because of me. Guilt weighed down on me. Maybe I should just quit and walk away. Could I run to the Spirit realm?

"That is our opinion," a voice I didn't know said from above me. I jerked my head up to look at the woman standing over me. Her arms were crossed as she glared at me. The Fire mage tattoo all but sparked in this light, the gemstones in it creating their own glow. I was sure she'd burn a hole through me with her eyes if she could. The tattoo and her long thin white dreads against brown tanned skin told me this was archmage Melinda Kilten, president of GA MageTech.

"Melinda." Indira stood to look at her. "We talked about this. You cannot hold her responsible for things she did not do."

What? They'd been talking about me? Oh, this wasn't good.

Making sure the thin earthen shield was diamond hard, literally, I rose and looked at the woman. "Ms. Kilten. You've been talking about me?"

She waved her hand dismissively as she looked at the damage. "Your mentors have been holding up their side of the contract. Otherwise I would have expelled you the day Josefa Guzman was shot."

That surprised me, but maybe it shouldn't have. They did try to protect me—the issue was what they thought was a valid means of protection and what I did differed greatly.

"I see." I nodded at Indira. "Thanks. But why didn't you tell me?"

She shrugged. "If we could make the problem go away without any fanfare everyone was happy. You, the government, others."

I could read the unspoken words that their handlers were happier too. It served as a reminder to try very hard not to serve multiple masters. I didn't need the stress.

"You do realize there is little I can do about this," I offered to the president of the college. Melinda Kilten wasn't known for being an easy woman, or a pushover.

"I know there is little that has been done about this. But I am telling you now. One more incident, just one, and you're expelled. The government, the societies, and anyone else that has an issue with it can kiss my ass. Fix this. I don't care who does, but if anything else happens I'll go with the nuclear resort and get rid of all of you. Josefa Guzman, Sable Lancet, Indira Humbert—all of you will be gone from my campus." She scanned both of us with light gray eyes and I had to fight not to shiver at the glacial anger there. With a sharp nod she pivoted and headed towards sthe ecurity personnel who as a group paled and stood up straighter with her approach.

Indira sighed and I looked at her. She had circles under her eyes, and her clothes were wrinkled. I didn't think I'd ever seen her looking anything other than elegant. "Japan is very adamant that you are not the inheritor of the estate and it has become a point of honor for them. The government is just as firm saying you are and that research will stay with the US. If something doesn't break soon, we may end up at war."

Whatever bravado I had felt vaporized at that. "What? War? Between the US and Japan over me?"

Indira nodded, looking like she'd been fighting monsters. "There is no give on either side. The fact that you've figured out how to protect yourself is making people on all sides both desperate and arrogant. I'm worried they might break the rules."

"What rules?" My voice squeaked and I could feel my body tightening up in anticipation of a blow, emotional though it might be.

"The ones that preclude attacking dwellings. The consequences are death for you and your family if you destroy a building in an effort to get to a target. But there are more than enough people who have no living family and the price is getting high enough that some might not care if their parents or siblings are killed. It's why you've been safe in classes and at home. But if Japan lifts that stricture..." She trailed off and shrugged again. There was nothing sensual in it, just exhaustion.

I just looked at her, shocked. No idea how to respond to this. It answered my one question, but the thought they might break this rule made my blood run cold and I started flipping through options in my mind.

I could live in the Spirit realm. Only come out for classes, but if they were willing to kill any classmates?

My thoughts broke off. It didn't matter. I was done. There was no way I could let people die for me.

"I'll quit," I blurted, ready to just run. Even becoming a Ronin didn't sound as bad anymore.

"Not yet. Give us over the summer. It should quiet down. If we can't get it done by the Fourth of July holiday, Alixant and I will support whatever you want to do. Up to and including going Ronin."

The amount of defeat in her voice surprised me.

"Okay." I looked around at the devastation and fought the desire to run. "I'm headed to the library. You have my number if you need me."

She just nodded at me and walked towards the police. I wasn't really involved since there was no proof the bomb had been left for me. Though I was curious about what it had been. "Bomb" was what I called it because it exploded, but I had no real idea how they had tried to kill me.

Feeling like the worst sort of selfish person, I dragged myself to the library, the time shield up for a full five minutes this time. Once there I found a back table and dropped the shield. I needed to focus.

The beep-beep of my phone told me I had a text message. Worried, I pulled it up and saw a message form Alixant. Hope, sweet and deadly, rushed through me as I read the message.

Have the information. Is through a dozen shell companies and is backed by Japan. They are trying to pressure you out via Jo's family. Talking to government now. They will represent the Guzmans but there isn't much else to be done now. Will share if find out more.

I sat there looking at my phone fighting not to start bawling or just give it all up and run away. Carelian was on the table butting my hand, but he didn't speak. What could he say?

"Cori? You okay?"

I sniffed trying to keep back tears and saw Charles standing there looking at me, a frown on his face. Arachena jumped off his shoulder and skittered over to Carelian then, in an oddly hesitant motion, one of her twelve legs patted the back of my hand.

That teeny act of kindness from a creature that most people would have run from screaming broke my walls, and for the second time in a month I started to cry. This time it wasn't as much sorrow and fear, more frustration and rage and the knowledge there wasn't anything I could do about any of it.

A handkerchief appeared in front of me. "Here. Use this. It's clean, I promise," Charles said.

Gratefully I took it and tried to mop up my tears and my nose. "Handkerchief?" I asked as I managed get my rage under control.

"Granddad was a stickler about it. And have to admit it's been nice during allergy season. Also, it can go through the wash unlike tissues. Getting pieces of white paper everywhere is a pain."

That brought an unexpected laugh. "Thanks."

"What's wrong? You don't look like the type to be crying because someone is picking on you." He set his books down and looked at me. He seemed curious and more like trying to solve a puzzle than filled with empathy.

"Long story," I said still mopping at my eyes and trying to control my shaking.

"I've got time. Might help to talk it out to someone not involved in your life." He settled into his chair while Arachena stroked my hand and Carelian's paw at the same time. He'd curled up on the table, his head resting on my arm, looking up at me. I took the hand he wasn't trapping and petted him.

"Your loss." I told him everything, the double merlin, the inheritance, the various people trying to kill or control me, it all just came spilling out. The only thing I kept secret was Baneyarl and Carelian's machinations. By the time I was done I was panting with anger and frustration.

Charles leaned back and looked at me. I realized he had light brown eyes, almost amber, and in the funky library light they almost glowed. "Basically, you're fucked or everyone you love is fucked. Nothing in between."

I grimaced a bit but nodded. "Pretty much. Sad when the idea of going Ronin is sounding attractive."

He snorted out a laugh. "There's where we are different."

I looked at him skeptically. "Then what about Daniela?"

"She's a bitch and if she causes me too much trouble, I'll deal with her at that point. So far, she is a pain in my side. She isn't directly impacting me," he replied, his voice level.

But I heard the unspoken "yet" there. Part of me wondered if that should be a warning to me, but given the trouble Daniela had given me, I figured she'd earned anything that happened. Charles smirked at me and I gave him another long look. Pattern mage. Somehow, I knew he was a powerful archmage, close to a merlin.

"So where are we different?" I asked, now curious. If nothing else, talking to him had distracted me enough to get the tears and frustration under control. I still simmered with anger.

"I plan on dealing with my issue. Bullies are all the same. Until you hit them very hard where it hurts, they keep thinking they can intimidate you. Once you hit them hard enough and make it clear that if they do it again, you'll come back five times harder, they back off."

Everything snapped into focus. "You're giving Daniela enough rope to hang herself, but you plan on dealing with her one way or another."

He didn't answer, just smirked. "The real question is, how do you deal with the entities causing you grief? You sure it is Japan?"

"Everyone seems to think so. I don't have any actual proof." I stopped as Arachena triple tapped my hand and I looked at her. "Yes?"

She chittered and looked at Carelian and then Charles. "Huh. She says the patterns align and all the factors lead back to Japan."

"Why didn't she just tell me that?"

~Those of Order follow the proprieties very closely. I am Cath, I choose what is proper.~ Carelian licked the back of my hand and gave a superior gaze at Arachena.

"He just spoke to me," Charles muttered, staring at Carelian. He didn't seem surprised, more as if another bit of information had been added.

"Yeah. Apparently that note about familiars only talking to their mages had never met a Cath."

Charles flinched and closed his eyes. "And Arachena is ripping him a new one. Okay. So, she is almost never wrong. We match on Pattern. It's my strength. It will make me an excellent programmer. With Earth and Air as minor, I'll stay with my computers. I like them better than most people." He shook his head. "But what it means is yes, Japan is the source of your issues, probably their Maiyutsu-shi."

I sighed. "Yeah, that sounds like the guy who would get the stuff if I fail."

"There you have it. Now your choice is continue to work under the radar or shove it in their face and make them stop."

"HOW?" I almost shouted the question and a few people stared at me. I hunched my head between my shoulders. "How by Merlin do I do that?"

"Not a clue. But I've never found a bully that goes away by ignoring them. Sorry."

I sighed and we both fell to our homework and papers, but his words kept swirling in my head.

Chapter 44

Are you a Non-Organic mage? Looking for a career in industrial engineering? Apply now with your degree and gain access to one of the fastest growing careers in developing new transportation options. Your ability to work with elements will make you a star in many industries. ~ *Mage Headhunter* posting

ORDER

The weekend disappeared, and we'd let Baneyarl know we'd be busy with our finals all week, so we were taking this week off from lessons. Next week, Esmere would try to heal Sable's pancreas, and Jo planned on going back to work at the garage all summer, assuming it still existed. The lawsuit was still being pursued and there wasn't anything we could do but worry.

Our first final was bright and early Monday morning. I'd been practicing, so I included Jo in my time bubble. To my delight it worked, though I couldn't get it less than five minutes out of time. The shudder zipped through me as we resynced.

"That felt super odd," Jo said as her body paid the price.

"Yeah, but it makes for safe travel. Easy price to pay."

We watched others go into the classroom, including two people I didn't know, both older than any of the students, in their thirties at least.

"Huh. Wonder who those two are?" Jo said as we headed in.

"No clue, but I'm sure we'll find out. Come on. She said she's doing this in alphabetical order which means you're closer to the beginning and I'm smack in the middle." I grabbed my bag and Carelian streaked in to race up to our preferred seats. Indira said we could leave when we were done, but not being there when your name was called would drop you a full grade on your final. Besides, I wanted to see what other students' final projects were. Lots of companies would ask how comfortable you were using your pales as well as your strong, so for those who wanted to get into some competitive fields this was great practice.

Our final was to research a spell from a list of about twenty and figure out how to do it with the minimal amount of molecules and then use science to explain how you did it and why. Personally, I was betting on many of them repeating the fire and water example, but I had hoped for more interesting examples.

We settled down at as Indira stepped forward and started to speak.

"Welcome to finals day. I hope you are prepared to wow and impress me. But you also better know your basic science. If you can't prove you have a good grasp of the scientific concepts behind your actions, it will hurt your grade." She huffed a sigh and glared at the two men next to her. " The administration has insisted that I have two assistants to help me this year as the last few years this process has taken the full day. They have assured me they are both highly qualified." She rolled her eyes and the entire class snickered and I admired the way she both made clear she wasn't impressed and lowered their standings at the same time. Everyone would want her as their tester now.

I fought back a wave of paranoia as the two men stepped forward and bowed slightly, never taking their eyes off the students in the room. I could see they were mages, but from here I couldn't tell what class. I glanced at Indira gaging, but she just seemed annoyed not worried. Still two strangers? I frowned a bit as Carelian twitched. He usually slept during this class, finding Indira's too pedantic for his tastes.

"Something wrong?" I whispered. Jo glanced at me, her brows drawing together.

~No? Maybe? Am twitchy. But I there is no reason~ He heaved a mental sigh and sank his head down, but his eyes didn't close and his tail kept twitching.

"Then let's start. Amy Abelson," Indira said, and they did. Each of them taking one student and doing three at a time.

I had my experiment ready. I wasn't about to show how easy Fire was even though I should have been null in that. I stuck with something a bit more explainable. Non-Organic was my only pale in Spirit, and it was also one of the few tangible branches, which made any experiment easier. While I'd been tempted to do the Extract Mineral that Indira had done, that seemed too much like the easy way out for me, so I'd decided to work with electricity. It was fun and I had almost gotten good enough to have electricity bounce back and forth between my hands. Though if I didn't concentrate, I'd burn myself. It had the advantage of being very showy. In theory, I should be able to stun people or even make it look like I was calling lighting, though from terrestrial based sources, not the sky.

We were sitting there quietly watching everyone when Jo's name was called by one of the men. She left her stuff, except for the prop she needed. Air was one of her weaker areas, but we'd been working with Baneyarl about that. In theory anyone not strong shouldn't be able to actually use Fly. We'd thought about doing a lightning strike but being indoors killed that idea.

I leaned forward to watch her demonstration. She'd taken all her books down with her and set them on the floor between her and the examiner. I knew what she was doing was asking Air to wiggle underneath the books and push them up, then drop them. Much easier than trying to hold them in the air, at least for this part. Air thought this was great fun. Jo and Sable had practiced in a park one evening and she said that Air acted like a kid playing with them. Only little offerings were required. Flying took more, but Air apparently thought having hair flying around was great. It made me wonder if Air would enjoy capes even more.

What Jo was telling the examiners, however, was how she identified the oxygen, nitrogen, and carbon molecules under and to the side of the books and pulled them under the books, then used the laws of attraction to pull more and more in until the books rose up. She phrased everything in such a way, including what she was offering, that it was the truth. Lying was too risky as you never knew who was paying attention and might start asking questions.

Amazing how "I thought if I" and "Theory is" could mislead almost anyone. The final did make you think of how things worked and how magic worked with them and if you were creative you could see many things you could do outside the prescribed spells. But I'd also seen more than a few students who'd gotten hurt because they were so specific in what they were trying to do, they did it wrong. Personally, I suspected half of the reason for the class was for people to get hurt doing things and back off, to only do exactly what the text and resource books listed.

I grinned as she stopped speaking, took a deep breath, and floated up a few inches. Even knowing what she'd explained, I loved the look of surprise on the inspectors' faces. Indira's double take, causing her to miss her own student's action, both amused me and told me she was paying very close attention to Jo and by extension me.

Jo had an enormous grin as she bounded up the stairs and slouched in the chair. "He asked if I was a merlin or actually strong in Air." Her grin so big I expected her face to be sore. "Showed him my tat and headed back up. Pretty sure I aced it."

"No questions about the 'how'?"

"Nope. Heck, pretty sure they didn't care. They kept glancing around and at each other. Was almost insulting except for the look on his face at the end. And I only had to offer about a quarter inch from a few strands. Now I totally want to go flying."

"And get shot by scared people? I don't think so. Let's plan a vacation someday. The four of us, remote island, and you can fly over the water. Sable can make sure you don't break anything when you fall and hit it."

"Ooh, that sounds fun. Wonder if I get good enough I could take you and Sable flying?"

I gave her a considering look. "That might be fun...over water."

~Water, ick. Takes forever to get your fur back to proper shape.~ Carelian's mutter had us both giggling a bit. The class got smaller and I was actually sad I wouldn't get to see Charles do his as with the last name of Wainscot he was one of the last people.

A commotion outside pulled my attention to the door and I saw Charles glaring at Daniela as she sneered at him. She made a gesture that was anything but polite and stomped away. If I remember correctly, not that I paid that much attention to her, she had a class in the room next to us.

Scowling, he moved up the stairs, away from his normal seat. "That woman is going to regret her choices someday. And I can't wait for the day."

Jo laughed. "Sable will join you. She's a piece of work."

Charles growled and threw himself into one of the seats in the row below us. Arachena scuttled down his arm, patting mine as she went by, then jumped on Carelian. I could hear low chittering as her legs worked up and down his body. He groaned a bit and stretched out further.

"Is it just me or does that look a bit indecent?" Jo asked, watching the two familiars.

"Yes," Charles and I replied at the same time.

He continued with a soft smile. "But I'm also kinda jealous. Looks like it feels good, but she isn't strong enough to do that to me." His voice had a touch of wistfulness to it.

"Don't bet on it. Ask her. What I've been finding out about our familiars is we shouldn't assume they have the same limitations and abilities as their mundane counterparts." I watched them for a minute more then shifted my attention back to the front.

Some of the students' presentations went haywire badly. One of them had Indira shouting for assistance out the door, when his fire experiment, instead of setting the paper on fire, exploded the sealed can of coke he'd had in his cargo shorts pocket. From his screams and Indira's annoyance I figured either the liquid had been scalding or aluminum fragments had embedded in flesh. An EMT came running in with a partner and I crossed my legs and didn't move. This wasn't something I needed to get involved with. I couldn't afford it right now. Besides, he was hurt, not dying. Me sitting this one out wouldn't have any consequences either way. Instead I watched them treat him. From what I could see, second-degree burns and some minor cuts. Not anything worth the level of screaming he'd done.

This delayed us for a bit and I was starting to wish I'd brought a lunch. My stomach agreed with that. They were at the K's so hopefully I'd be called shortly.

I watched a girl do a variation of what I had planned on doing, but where I could get actual visible electricity between my hands, she barely had a spark created and lost a good two inches of hair. Jo's phone pinged, a sound that told me it was Stinky. It sounded like a long loud fart. A few people glanced at us and I snickered as Jo pulled out her phone.

Her body language changed as I watched, growing tense and tight. That made me still and focus on her. "I need to call him. I'll be right back." She was already halfway down the stairs as she said the last words.

My own fear grew and my imagination ran wild. Assassins had killed them. Marisol hurt. The lawyers got them.

Each situation was worse and I felt myself starting to generate a Murphy's Curse. I tamped it down and focused on breathing. Jo burst into the classroom and bounded up the stairs. Various people shouted at her, but she focused on me. "I have to go. Someone blew up the garage. It's in flames. Mom is on the way there. So far it doesn't look like anyone was hurt."

My heart spasmed as I jumped to my feet, grabbing my stuff. "I'm coming too."

She didn't say anything as we sprinted down the stairs. "Indira, I have to go. I'll make it up or dock me. I don't care."

"Cori? What in the world?" I heard her yell as I reached bottom of the stairs. By this time the entire room had paused and was looking at us. Jo hit the doors and held them open.

"Emergency. Have to go. Explain later." When I turned to race through the doors, a gust of wind slammed into me and knocked me away from the door and to the floor. I saw Jo get flung backwards into the hall and the door slammed shut, cutting us off.

"You aren't going anywhere, Cori Munroe. Your death has been paid for," someone said with an accent that sounded Asian. I looked up, my back against the classroom wall and my ass on the floor as one of the 'guest' instructors stalked towards me and the other held off Indira.

"Die now."

Ah crap.

Chapter 45

The United States is considered a very safe country. Crime is low and mages are well treated. Other countries are not as lucky. While no country is stupid enough to treat mages as second-class citizens, different governments enact strict controls but always with a carrot attached. ~ History of Magic

SPIRIT

On instinct I pulled Lady Luck over me and grabbed for an earth shield, but there wasn't enough floating dust and random dirt. They had a very good janitorial staff, to my detriment. I felt his magic reach towards me, which was freaky as all get out. I glanced at the tattoos of the first mage—Air, Pattern, and Transform pale. The second was a merlin—Water and Psychic. That wasn't good. Baneyarl had been teaching us to defend ourselves against attacks, but Water was one of the deadlier ones, and hard to defend against.

Line of sight, remember most mages can only attack line of sight.

Taking a risk, I focused on the other side of the classroom behind Indira and sent a plea to magic. I rolled and ended up rolling into the wall on the other side of the classroom. I jumped to my feet and looked around, trying to think. On most other occasions people had tried to kill me, I'd hidden from them and people had come running. I shied away from remembering the shooter and Jo. This time people were simply trying to run out the door but were blocked by the two mages.

Before I could orient myself, a chair came flying at me and I ducked with a half scream. The chair slammed against the wall behind me, shattering, bits hitting my back.

~Shield!~ Carelian ordered in my head. His worry and franticness hit me hard. I started to panic as I tried to figure out what to use to shield. I'd had time to think when Jo was shot. I needed time to figure out what to do.

A bolt of fire came flying at me and I had to dive away, scrambling. Everyone was screaming and I could barely think. I saw Indira out of the corner of my eye, fire in her hands. In the second I saw her it looked like she was throwing a soap bubble at the attacker nearest her, but I had to scramble away before I could figure out what she was doing.

~Cori!~ Carelian called again, but other students were throwing their abilities around and using fire and chairs as shields. The room filled with the sounds of things breaking and people yelling. I turned, trying to locate Carelian. In the chaos I couldn't focus on anything. Every flash of red caught my attention, but it was never him. I breathed in fast short pants as I kept moving. One mage still fought with Indira, but the other headed in my direction.

Where is he? Where is Jo? Are they okay?

The doors flew open and students rushed out. I strained to see Jo, but all I could catch were glimpses of heads and figures. A flash of blue and white grabbed my attention, and I caught a glimpse of Arachena racing up Charles' shirt. He looked as pale and freaked out as I felt. But he had his bag and was headed towards the door.

Delay. I need to let them get out. But then what?

I had no answer to that. Before I could dwell on it, a ball of fire came spinning towards me, huge and white hot. With a whispered plea, I stepped to my seat at the top of the room. I wasn't fast enough, and the flames seared the side of my left arm.

A scream ripped out of me and I stumbled. Pain lashed through my body and brought me to my knees. Tears filled my eyes as I tried to see. I needed to know where they were.

~Cori!~

Carelian so near, but with all the jumble and the blurriness, the only thing I could see were the flames coming towards me, the white, yellow, and orange promising my death.

I ran my hand up my arm, sobbing in renewed pain. I lifted up my hand, blood and ichor coating it. "Protect," I begged, reaching for Earth pulling.

I just wanted to be safe. But I also wanted those two to pay for what they had done. I wanted Jo safe. I wanted Carelian safe. I even wanted all the other students and Indira to be safe. I wanted this to be done. I wanted to make them pay.

All of those thoughts, that need, were shoved into that one word and the offering of blood, skin, and ichor.

The "yes", the vaporization of what I offered, and the building collapsing all happened in the same second. Noise surrounded me with a physical power. I fell back, hitting the wall. A new scream of pain slipped past my lips. As if called by my cry of pain a spear of Earth, mostly concrete and tile, burst up from the floor less than an inch from me, blocking the incoming fireball.

The flames dispersed across it, not even singeing my hair. The walls of the building crumpled down in perfect unison and created an arena around us. Within the remains of the classroom stood Carelian and me, the two mages, and the slumped form of Indira. Dust filled the air and a strange silence settled as I took in the new area. Brick, concrete, and wood created walls around us. The doors were blocked, and the ceiling looked precarious.

The building hadn't been huge, two stories holding four classrooms on each floor. Now it felt like a giant had stepped on it, crushing it down. The second story had crumbled, and I could see through gaps in the ceiling to the next floor. No one looked back at me and I counted that as a minor miracle. I didn't want to think about how many people I'd hurt, or even killed by my actions.

"Why are you doing this?" I cried out. I pivoted, looking around, but realized no one else was in here and the other mage was a merlin. I couldn't see what exactly, too far away, but Indira's body suggested Psychic.

"Money. Kill one little girl and we receive a lot of money. Seemed like a straightforward job, but you've proved challenging. Thank you," the merlin replied, his voice calm, amused almost. "I must say I'm impressed that anyone as uneducated as you could pull this off." He waved his hand around the arena we found ourselves in.

I swallowed hard. "All this? Just for money?"

"No, for a lot of money. And a favor from the emperor of Japan and his pet mage. How could we turn that down?" He started walking towards me and I grabbed the earth under his feet and pulled. Not asking, just pulling. It slid and he fell backwards. "Cute trick, but my bother has a solution to that."

Japan? The emperor? The Majyutsu-shi is involved in this?

Before I could follow that path any further, he waved at the man to his right and a moment later floated up into the air about a foot off the ground. The man, his brother, grunted and I felt a gust of air head my direction. The merlin floated with the breeze, coming right at me, though slowly.

Well crap.

I spun through the stuff we'd learned, trying to think. It had been basic stuff, Elements, which I barely had, how to talk to magic, working with my Psychic skills to pull out memories, read the truth from people, and time. Moving outside of time did no good. It just let them kill everyone without me stopping them and I didn't think putting us in a time bubble would do anything. Even if I stopped time, I had to restart it at some point, so nothing would change. All this magic and power and I didn't know how to do anything. Granted I never really thought I'd be in a fight for my life either. Stupid in hindsight.

My experiment.

I pulled on the electricity I'd planned on playing with, gladly offering a full inch of hair, and I threw a lightning bolt at him. The bright white, snapping and cracking bolt ripped from my hands and zig-zagged through the air, leaving the sharp smell of ozone behind. It streaked in his direction, then jerked to one side and slammed into the Earth spear that had saved my life earlier.

"Impressive, but it takes years to learn how to control lightning. And you don't have years."

I tried again and again, being reckless with the blood still oozing down my arm. But the lightning never went to the target I was aiming at, and he just laughed, moving up the stadium seating towards me.

"Carelian, go. Get out of here. Go home," I urged as my eyes locked on the man approaching. I had no clue how to protect myself from a water attack. I knew our bodies were mostly water, and obviously he didn't care about killing with magic.

~Never. My quean!~ Carelian bristled with fierceness as he said that, and my heart threatened to snap what little control I had. I needed to do something. He crouched on crushed desks about six feet away, his tail lashing, ears laid back so close to his head that he looked like a snake about to strike.

The movement of the earth and the building collapsing around us had created dust everywhere. I pulled it into a shield as the merlin attacked. I felt him try to pull the water from my body and I put the shield between us. It hit my earthen shield, dry and dusty, and bounced back, refusing to cross what I had created. That surprised me, but I sure wasn't complaining.

"Interesting. No worries. If I touch you, you can't stop me from killing you. But meanwhile. Tanaka, kill the woman. We don't need witnesses." He didn't look away from me as he spoke in a loud voice, just moved closer. He was only ten feet away.

"No," I ground out and created a wall around Indira. The blood seeping from my burns a constant offering. I struggled to stay standing as the pain lashed at me. Every offering exacerbated the burn, and burns hurt, but if I gave in, I'd be dead.

"You are full of surprises. But not an issue." He lifted his chin in an odd jerking manner. "Pull out all the air in that enclosure. That will eliminate any problem."

I swallowed as his brother nodded and concentrated. A puff of dust blew out of the area created and I had no doubt she was now choking, trying to breathe on nothing.

"Now for the cat. Can't have any witnesses, after all, and we know how intelligent familiars are." A ball of flame went whistling towards Carelian.

"NO!" I screamed out the words and lunged, instinct taking over, trying to block the deadly fireball with my body. A rip opened before the ball and it disappeared into it. I fell to my knees, gouging them on the torn stone, more blood on the outside of my body.

~My quean, I am not that easy to kill.~

My knees were screaming but all I could do was shake in relief and anger at the voice in my head. Charles' words of just a few hours ago rumbled through my head. Could I? Did I dare?

Better question, do I have anything to lose? If I don't, I'm dead anyhow.

My legs shook as I stood. "This needs to end." My voice quavered as I said it, staring at the man sneering at me not three feet away.

"Yes, it does. You were worthy prey," he said, condescension in his voice. "It won't hurt much." His arm reached towards me.

"No, it won't." I grabbed his arm and shoved my mind into his, looking for the image of the orders, the place that he would return to when I was dead. He shrieked as I was ruthless. I didn't care if it hurt, I didn't care if it killed him. He had just tried to kill my familiar and my mentor, and because of him I might have killed my best friend. I grabbed the image.

Take me there.

It is a truism that magic costs, and more than one mage has squandered their life reaching for things outside of their grasp. Be smart, learn well, and never reach for things outside your knowledge. It might cost you everything. ~ OMO reminder.

CHAOS

The thought rippled out into magic, I paid the too small price, and stepped to the side. Reality shivered, I spent ten seconds or eternity in between, then I stood in a large room, the man still attached to me. I felt a portal open then Carelian was at my feet sitting regally, his ruby fur brilliant in the subtle hues.

I slammed my electricity into the assassin as he fought me and he convulsed, then slumped, unconscious. I dropped him to the floor and looked around. The room had a few people in it, all Asian, Japanese I assumed. People were screaming, staring at me and pointing. I pulled down more electricity and created a halo around myself, trying to appear impressive.

Fake it till you make it. I have nothing to lose.

I channeled Jo at her fiercest—when she appeared like she didn't give a damn and no one could stop her. I needed that right now. With a grunt, I pushed the unconscious merlin at my feet away from me and stood up straighter. I moved my eyes over the room, inspecting every detail. I hadn't taken the time to inspect the memory of the location, and for a place the emperor was supposed to be, it seemed almost plain. It had a bamboo floor, white walls with paintings of cherry trees on them. At the end of the room sat an elegant, gigantic desk. It had to be at least eight feet long and gleamed a beautiful golden red. Bookshelves lined the wall behind the desk which had a huge computer monitor sitting on it.

But where my eyes rested at the end of the room there were two men, both dressed suits that fit them perfectly. One had touches of silver at his temples while the other looked like a warrior about to attack me.

A stream of Japanese came at me and I had no idea what it meant. From the corner of my eye I saw the other people in the room streaming out an opening where they had moved the wall. And I saw more people running towards us. People with guns, and more than one had a mage tattoo on his face.

"I want the emperor Tomohito Takamado and the Majyutsu-shi Hishatio Yamato," I said, projecting my voice as loud as I could. I knew I mangled the pronunciation, but from the way the two men stiffened I figured they understood me. People were getting closer—I didn't have time for this crap.

Time!

Reaching, I created the biggest bubble I'd ever managed and the longest. The bubble encased me, the merlin at my feet, and the two men at the other end of the room. It stretched out like a soap bubble between me and the men. I set it for an hour, so we were out of sync with time for a huge amount. Coming back in would suck, but better that than allowing the onrushing guards to get to me first.

I was tired of fighting, I wanted this over.

Still channeling Jo, I stalked forward, aware of the blood soaking the knees of my jeans, running down my arm, and dripping on the pristine golden floor. Carelian paced beside me, his tail lashing back and forth.

Another string of angry Japanese as I got close enough to get a good look at both of them. The merlin stood to the side, the three tattoos visible on his face. The other man was rigid with effrontery if I had to guess. Both were in their mid-thirties to early fifties—I didn't know enough to guess better. The merlin had a sharper nose and fuller lips than the emperor, but the big difference was his long black hair compared to the trim cut the other man had.

"I want you to stop this. Or I'll stop it now."

Japanese and glaring.

"Enough. I know damn well you understand English. Talk to me or I'll bring this place down around our heads."

They both crossed their arms and sneered at me. Fine. If they wanted to play it that way. I offered up more blood to Earth and pulled. The ground rocked. The bookcases caught in my bubble fell with a crash of fine china, snapping of wood, and the clatter of metal. I knew in an hour the rest of the palace would shake like a 5.0 earthquake had hit it.

"I can do this until your palace is in rubble. I'll level it to the ground."

The merlin sneered and looked at me. I could tell he was about to attack, so I hit first. I used the same trick I had with the shooter and reached out, grabbing his soul and pulling it out of his body. But this time I could sense the tether and before it snapped, I released it and felt him slam back into his body. Nausea bubbled in the back of my throat, but I pushed it down.

The merlin, Hishatio Yamato, slammed back against the wall, pale and gasping, hand clawing at his heart. For the first time, there was a look of fear and maybe respect in his gaze. He pushed himself away from the wall, a trickle of blood tracing from his left nostril.

"Are we done playing? I have nothing left to lose and if I have to destroy this building and you, I will." I kept my voice hard and hoped neither of them could see how my knees were trembling. Carelian snarled at my side and I glanced down to see his red fur fluffed and tail bristling.

"Are you threatening the ruler of Japan?" Tomohito Takamado said, staring at me, his body stiff, his English stilted but understandable.

"Are you speaking of yourself in the third person? Yes, I am. After all, you've been trying to kill me for three months. Some of your idiots just crossed the line by blowing up the business of the closest thing I have to a family, then they tried to kill me. I'm done. End this now. Or I will." I had no clue how to do that other than what I had threatened, and that made me sick to my stomach.

A string of Japanese and a sly look from the royal merlin.

~They are planning on killing you now. I have an idea. Do you trust me? It will take a minute or two,~ Carelian's voice whispered in my mind.

"Always," I said aloud, then looked at the two of them. "Trying to kill me, even succeeding, won't solve your problem. I can promise neither of you will live to see that inheritance. Or we can work together and maybe come to a comprise." I was bluffing. I had no idea how to fight, and while I could pull the building down around us, it didn't mean they'd die or that Jo and her family would be safe.

A sharp pain pierced my mind, familiar and almost welcome.

"I did not think you understood Japanese," Yamato said.

"I don't. Some things are obvious. Choose. Work with me or die trying to kill me."

"I'll just kill you. I have no need to work with anyone and I want the research James had." He sneered at me and I braced myself for a magical attack.

To my surprise, the emperor reached into his desk and pulled out a gun, pointing it at me. Carelian snarled. I just felt my anger increase.

"A gun. Really? Did your pet mage not tell you who I was? What I am?" I'd been using my chemistry classes to help identify elements, but gunpowder was easy to sense and I knew where it was. With a whisper of a thought I called Fire to the rounds in the chamber.

"*Stäp!*" Yamato yelled, the word sharp and explosive. I didn't bother to listen but made the offering to the gunpowder in the cartridges.

At least I tried to limit it to that. The gun exploded in his hand. Shrapnel went flying out in a radius. They stopped midair, only a few pieces embedded in his hand. The merlin glared at me as they fell to the ground.

Oops. I guess killing the ruler of Japan might be a bad idea.

I watched blood drip from his hand to the pristine desk and I didn't care.

"You useless waste of magic, you will pay for that. No one spills his blood." The words translated in my mind and I bared my teeth at him.

"My blood coats your floors, I see his as less valuable than my own. If you want to kill me, go for it." I took all the blood, skin, the tears leaking down my face from pain and offered it to magic. I felt the acceptance and the question, but I didn't know what to ask for, so I waited for them to make the next move.

There was a long look between the two men and, wrapping his bleeding hand with a pure white handkerchief, the emperor nodded at the merlin. I braced myself for the attack.

I love you, Jo. I'm so sorry, this is all my fault.

The merlin lifted his hands and snarled at me and I tried to figure out the attack, how to block or defend. A spike of pain slashed through my mind. Hard and brutal. I stumbled back, wondering if this was how I would die.

~I think not.~ The voice of someone I didn't remember ever hearing before spoke in my mind, and I saw the two men flinch. A bird appeared out of nowhere and flew up to sit on the top of the computer monitor, his claws piercing it. Glass crunched and fell to the desk as sparks crackled between his talons.

~Hisahito Yamato, James would be ashamed of you. Did you think he would approve of this?~

I stared at the bird unable to process what I saw. About the size of a large falcon, its feathers were white, blue, and green with a tail that fell in loose curly feathers to the floor, a rainbow of blues and purples. It shimmered as I looked at it, and I didn't know if that was my exhaustion or heat.

Astonished Japanese burst from the merlin as he stared at the bird. Carelian translated seamlessly into my mind so I could understand.

"Jeorgaz. You died. I saw you die. James mourned you." He had wide eyes and I could see a trail of sweat appear along his hairline.

~Of course you did and of course he did. He knew my nature. As he also knew he would die before I regenerated. Did you not remember what I am?~ Amused contempt filled the voice.

"Those don't exist. They aren't real!" I heard the denial even through the language barrier, though Carelian did a fair job of making sure I got intonation as he translated.

~And the dragon that keeps the Child of Heaven safe is a mirage?~

The merlin spluttered then stiffened. "It is still my inheritance..." He broke off as the bird slashed its wings at him.

~It is not. It is hers and you know it. I warned James that you were too greedy to allow anything to prevent you. But he still remembered the boys you had been and refused to see the man you were. He was a great man, but he had his flaws. One of them was remembering people as they had been, not as they were. So listen to me now.~ Something changed in the timbre of the voice and it rippled through my heart and mind as he spoke. ~Corisande Munroe is the mage I felt emerge with James Wells before my burning. The inheritance is hers. I avow it as the focus from the Spirit Realm.~

Yamato growled, and Jeorgaz raised his wings exposing the colors of light blue darkening to purple.

~Hear me now Hisahito, if she is killed or dies and it is in any way related to you, I will take you back to my realm and you will be my toy until my next rebirth, which should take centuries. Cease this nonsense and provide reparation for what you have done.~

It was implacable and I felt a tremor of panic at the idea of that voice being turned towards me.

Yamato sighed and his shoulders dropped. "I hear. My lord, do you accept?" He had turned to the emperor at this last part. I had no idea what their rulers name was and really didn't care.

The man looked at his merlin, then the bird, then me. After a long moment he spoke. "Am I to assume if I did not agree, the same consequences would affect me?"

Jeorgaz settled his wings back down. ~That would be a wise assumption.~

A brief look of anger flittered across his face, but then he gave a short sharp bow, eyes never leaving the bird's. "Very well. The emperor of Japan will cease the attempts to direct the inheritance. Japan will not interfere with Corisande Munroe after this point. She is considered anathema to this court and word will be spread that she is neither to be attacked nor helped."

There was a layer of spite to his comments that made me blink, but I'd take what I could get. The odds of me ever needing to work with the emperor of Japan were fleeting.

~Tomohito Takamado your vindictiveness knows no bounds. So be it.~ Jeorgaz turned to me. ~Are you satisfied, young mageling?~

I swallowed past the lump in my throat and straightened my shoulders. "They need to pay for the damage done to my friends' business and what damage I caused protecting myself at Georgia MageTech."

A stiff nod from both men.

~Excellent. I will be following up on this,~ Jeorgaz warned.

"Japan keeps her word," the emperor replied icily.

~I would expect nothing less. Cori, are you ready to leave?~

I looked around at the time bubble. "Don't I need to collapse it?"

~It will collapse as soon as you step into my realm. I wish to speak with you.~

And if that didn't sound ominous.

The best mage is fat, happy, and with all their needs taken care of. Unhappy mages are deadly. ~ Qin Proverb

ORDER

A spike of pain and an entrance to another plane opened. ~Enter Cori. A healer is waiting for you. Step through.~

I glanced at Carelian and he rose and walked towards the gap. With a sigh I let the magic go with an apology. A burst of humor washed around me and then was gone. As I stepped into the other side a rush hit me. It felt like I'd slammed twenty ounces of Stinky's Mexican coffee. And that thought made we worry about Jo and the Guzmans all over. How could I have forgotten?

"What was that? And I need to get back, people were hurt. And the Guzmans," I protested, turning to look at the bird.

~Your friend is fine. You have been gone approximately 15 minutes. The time you spend here will not be noticed. Now allow Esmere to see to your wounds,~ Jeorgaz said. His voice remained friendly but at the same time I recognized arguing with him would be like arguing with the wind.

I turned to see Esmere padding towards me. I expected Carelian to go running to her, but he just sat next to me purring.

~You seem to have damaged yourself. Remove the leggings.~ She sat in front of me, looking at, or through me. I wasn't sure what she saw.

With a shrug I pulled off my jeans. It wasn't like they even had any concept of nudity, so stressing over that seemed stupid.

~I must apologize for my lateness. It took me a full decade for rebirth. The loss of James struck me hard and it took time. Otherwise, I would have found you sooner.~

"Um? What?" I had no idea what he was talking about.

With a trill of music, he settled his wings as he sat on a branch across two rocks. I found it odd how the landscape always matched their needs. Or maybe because they created it, it always did. That was an interesting idea.

~James and I felt you emerge all those years ago. But it was days before my Ash day, and I couldn't go find you. I knew James was dying, but I didn't think he would go within weeks. Normally going from Ash to Flesh takes a year, maybe two. I felt his loss even in between forms. It hurt. It took me a full eight years to re-hatch, then another year or so to get to a point my memories and my form could be of use. I was always going to come find you, let you know you were his chosen heir, but Magic had other ideas.~ He said Magic like it was a person, not a thing.

"Okay? Thanks? Why?" I had so many questions I didn't even know where to start.

~You were the one to follow him. In normal times you would have had me or Carelian from the day you emerged. Helping you and guiding you. But things didn't go as we planned.~

So many questions burbled in my mind, but I didn't know which to ask first. ~Why? How old is Carelian? And who is we?"

Again, that trill of sheer amusement. ~He is only two weeks older than you think. He was freshly weaned when he went to you. As to why? Because you are a young mage of great power. Magic requires we assist her heralds.~

"Wait, herald? Me? I swear if I'm the chosen one I'm running away NOW!"

That caused all three beings to start hacking and laughing. I watched them all, eyes narrowed. I was about to yell at Carelian when I realized my arm and knees didn't hurt.

"Hey, it doesn't hurt," I said glanced at Esmere who seemed to be laughing too, then focused on my wounds. The burned areas on my arm were pink and didn't ooze, while the scrapes on my knees were mostly gone.

~No. I helped heal. Small offering as you had so much there to use already.~

I didn't know what to make of that, but before I could follow up on it, Jeorgaz spoke.

~I lived with James long enough to understand your reference to a Chosen One. No. You are not. There is no fabled savior or anything else. Herald simply means you are a representative of Magic itself. Most of your merlins are, though few realize it or recognize it. The actions of Japan against you were found to be against the wishes of Magic. Hence her assistance. You and Magic are tightly woven, though you still have yet to explore how much. Someday you will understand.~

I glared at him. Partial information did me no good. "Tell me now. I need to know this."

Jeorgaz tilted his head one way then the other, looking like a painted magpie as he did. ~If I explained to you how to fly, what muscles it would take, the flex of my pinons and tail feathers, would it enable you to understand what flight is like?~

"No. I don't have wings, or tail feathers."

~Exactly. So how can I explain to you things about magic that you have no foundation to understand? I will when you are ready. It is impractical to explain now.~ He shifted his attention to Esmere. ~She is well?~

~Well enough. The damage was mostly superficial, though painful. I accelerated natural healing and soothed the pain receptors. She should be fine in a few days,~ Esmere said, sitting in the Egyptian cat pose.

"Thank you," I said with gratitude in my voice. Those burns had hurt and only fear had kept me moving.

~Then let us return you. I would advise keeping up your lessons with Baneyarl. It is not often one such as he deigns to train a human mage, much less three,~ Jeorgaz said watching me.

I gave him a tired smile. "Carelian chooses good queans. Or so he tells me regularly."

~I can see that,~ Jeorgaz said, and I thought the expression on his face might be a smile. With the beak it was hard to tell.

I looked around the area—it wasn't like the glade of Baneyarl's, instead it reminded me of a jungle, with vines and colors everywhere. Every flower shown like the brightest image I'd ever seen, in colors I hadn't realized could exist in nature. There were no birds, but the area felt alive, it felt safe.

"Thank you. I figured I'd die there. Wasn't sure how to win without killing a lot of people, and I really didn't want to do that. But I would do anything for Jo and her family."

~Yes. Your restraint has been noted. Tirsane spoke highly of you, and what you call cake.~

I grinned. While having Tirsane speaking of me caused fissions of fear to run up and down my spine, the cake aspect was amusing. I took a deep breath, pausing for a second to enjoy the sweet tasting air.

"What do I owe you for the assistance? Nothing is free."

I expected something. I didn't know what.

~Ah. There is truth there, but you owe me nothing. James was well liked and earned many favors over the years. I promised him when I ashed I would find you. It is to my eternal sorrow it was as late as it was.~

"What did you promise him?" I didn't ask the second part about what hold a dead man could still have.

~Just to help guide you on your journey. Magical heralds find life more interesting than they might expect or want. But you have an excellent focus in Carelian. I am sure if my presence or guidance is needed, he will let me know.~ The warning and unsubtle hint was obvious. But Carelian washed his face, ignoring the phoenix sitting not six feet from him. ~Oh, Esmere, he is your son.~

~Yes, I know.~ She purred out the words and her pride was evident in them.

"Everyone, thank you, but I need to get back." I ached to make sure Jo was okay, and Indira, Charles. Heck all of them. And for all I knew the school would expel me. I would. The amount of damage I did to that building alone would be worth suing me into bankruptcy. The desire to hide here for a very long time whispered at the back of my mind, but I pulled myself up and smiled. "Please?"

Jeorgaz looked at me for a long time then waved his left wing. A square ripple, the first I'd seen, opened before me. ~I shall follow your life with interest, Spirit Merlin Corisande Munroe. I expect many things from you.~

I shivered at his words. That didn't sound like a nice quiet life.

~She will be a great quean. You will see.~ Carelian rose and twined around my legs as the door to the university re-solved.

~Of that, I have no doubt. Be well, Corisande.~ Jeorgaz gave a weird parting whistle as I stepped through the door into the dust-filled arena. Indira laying there coughing, the brother assassin was gone, and the walls moved to reveal Jo looking in at me.

I met her eyes and we both smiled. No matter what, I'd be okay.

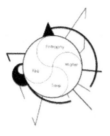

CHAOS

Chaos:

- Entropy
- Fire
- Water
- Time

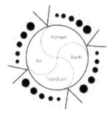

ORDER

Order:

- Pattern
- Air
- Earth
- Transform

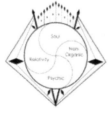

SPIRIT

Spirit:

- Soul
- Relativity
- Non-Organic
- Psychic

Author Notes:

This is book 3 in Twisted Luck, based in the Ternion universe. I have so much more planned that I can't wait to show you.

If you loved this novel, please take the time to leave a review, you will be amazed at the difference it makes.

I swear I'm working on a short story that you'll be able to get via my newsletter, all about Charles Wainscot and Arachena. Sign up to receive it.

If you'd like to stay in touch, you can follow me on social media at the following places:

Website: https://badashpublishing.com/

Facebook: https://www.facebook.com/badashbooks/

Twitter: https://twitter.com/badashbooks

Instagram: https://www.instagram.com/badashbooks/

If you're interested in free books, keeping up with what is going on in my life, as well as sales and launch announcements, you can sign up for my newsletter at my website. You never know what freebies might be in it.

Take care!

Mel Todd

Mel Todd

Mel Todd has over 20 stories out, her urban science fiction Kaylid Chronicles, the Blood War series, and the new Twisted Luck series. Owner of Bad Ash Publishing, she is working to create a place for excellent stories and great authors. With over a million words published, she is aiming for another million in the next two years. Bad Ash Publishing specializes in stories that will grab you and make you hunger for more. With one co-author and more books in the works, her stories can be found on Amazon and other retailers.